INSTRUMENT OF ECSTASY

"I would have you love me while you can," Alyson breathed. "Will you love me?"

"Ay, lass, I'll love ye," Rory said. " 'Tis the only love I may ever know, but I give it to ye willingly."

There was no further need of words. Caught in his arms, his mouth branding her with wine-flavored flames, Alyson could only surrender. It was as if his body were the bow and hers were the string. He played her sweetly at first, testing the notes, refining the tension, until she quivered beneath his touch. Soon the music grew more frantic, his fingers playing across her skin, stroking, caressing, finding those places that made her shiver and moan and finally sound a cry that echoed through the jungle. . . .

PATRICIA RICE

MOON DREAMS

AN ONYX BOOK

ONYX
Published by the Penguin Group
Penguin Books USA Inc., 375 Hudson Street,
New York, New York 10014, U.S.A.
Penguin Books Ltd, 27 Wrights Lane,
London W8 5TZ, England
Penguin Books Australia Ltd, Ringwood,
Victoria, Australia
Penguin Books Canada Ltd, 2801 John Street,
Markham, Ontario, Canada L3R 1B4
Penguin Books (N.Z.) Ltd, 182–190 Wairau Road,
Auckland 10, New Zealand

Penguin Books Ltd, Registered Offices:
Harmondsworth, Middlesex, England

First published by Onyx, an imprint of New American Library,
a division of Penguin Books USA Inc.

First Printing, January, 1991
10 9 8 7 6 5 4 3 2 1

 REGISTERED TRADEMARK—MARCA REGISTRADA

Printed in the United States of America

BOOKS ARE AVAILABLE AT QUANTITY DISCOUNTS WHEN USED TO PROMOTE
PRODUCTS OR SERVICES. FOR INFORMATION PLEASE WRITE TO PREMIUM
MARKETING DIVISION, PENGUIN BOOKS USA INC., 375 HUDSON STREET,
NEW YORK, NEW YORK 10014.

Author's Note

I apologize to the Maclean family for inventing their family history. Like the Macleans of whom I write, the real Macleans were Jacobites nearly annihilated in the Uprising, their lands and castle demolished and taken from them. The sole heir eventually reclaimed and rebuilt the family home just as in my story. I'm certain his history was every bit as romantic as the one I have created. However, for the purposes of this story, all the characters are fictional with the exception of well-known historical figures such as Samuel Johnson and the Earl of Bute.

MOON DREAMS

Prologue

Scotland, 1741

Lightning shot through black clouds, illuminating the interior of the tower more thoroughly than the brace of candles flickering on the small writing desk. The woman at the desk scarcely heeded the raging storm outside as she methodically scratched the old quill pen across the paper.

Not an unhandsome woman, time—if not the fates—had treated her kindly. The gray threading through her thick dark locks added a distinguished air to a full face wrinkled now with worry. She wrote with a firm, sure hand, but the heartbreak in her gray eyes spoke of the wrenching anguish that had brought her to this point.

Finished, she sanded the wet ink lightly and stared down at the stark words with a kind of horror. All of her pride, what remained of her life, and her overwhelming grief lay there, exposed for a stranger to see. It was not her way to bare her soul, but somewhere out there waited a man who must suffer worse than she. With this letter she offered what very little consolation she could.

My Lord,
   We have never met, but please excuse my boldness in addressing you in your grief, for it is a shared grief. My daughter does not know I write this, but as a mother I can only feel that a father has a right to know.
   My daughter is carrying your son's child. Please read this in the spirit in which it is given. They were very much in love and fully intended to marry in the church when his ship returned and he had obtained your blessing. Other than my daughter's protestations, there is

no proof that proper vows were ever given. Whatever happened between these two, it was done with love— that I know. I only tell you this in hopes of lightening your sorrow. I have tried to persuade her to marry another so the child might have a name, but she refuses. In her heartbreak over your son's death, I fear for her health and will not persuade her elsewise.

The child may not legally bear his father's name, but with your permission, we will teach him his heritage, that your son may have this small legacy.

Again, I apologize if my intrusion is unwarranted, but the child will be your grandchild as well as mine, and I knew I would wish to know of him. Let me close by saying your son was much loved, and my heart extends sympathy for this, our shared grief.

The woman stared at the harsh words a while longer, but they no longer held any meaning. She had made up her mind to do this, and it would be done and no more would be said of it.

Sadly she folded the parchment and began to heat the sealing wax. Thunder rolled in the distance, mixing with the roar of the breakers on the rocks below. It must have been a night and a sea such as this that had sent the hopes of two families down to a watery grave, but the thoughts of the woman at the desk had already turned to the muffled sobs from the room below.

The Right Honorable Earl of Cranville stared at the finely lettered hand with pain that grew into rage. He flung the letter to the floor, walked on it as he rose to jab bitterly at the fire, and hours later snatched the piece of paper from the hands of a servant who bent to pick it up. It rode in his breast pocket for another day, scorching through his fine lawn shirt and silk vest to the tearing pain in his heart.

Unexpectedly encountering a portrait removed for cleaning, he stared at the fair-haired youth in the blue, white-trimmed naval uniform and felt those blue eyes staring back at him. With a vile curse that rattled the rafters of the ancient hall, he ordered his carriage brought around and his trunks packed.

*   *   *

He had only to see the honesty in her clear gray eyes
to feel his rage diminish. Her proud chin tilted defiantly
as she swept him a proper curtsy, and he found himself
staring down at a lace-edged cap over unpowdered waves
of black and silver.

The crumbling tower of ancient rock perched on this
craggy outpost of the heathen Highlands was no fitting
site for such beauty. If the daughter were anywhere near
as lovely as the mother, his son would have had to be a
fool not to be smitten.

Upon meeting the sad-eyed woman already growing
round with the weight of a child, the earl acknowledged
his son was no fool. The purity of innocence still stained
her cheeks, and shadowed eyes lifted to meet his with a
grace and pride that denied her shame.

It was with little surprise that the earl heard himself
saying, "I have come to take you home."

Culloden Moor, April 1746

Sleet blew across the icy rocks, and the frozen gorse
crackled beneath his feet as he scrambled blindly down
the hillside, his tears frozen to his face. Rage and horror
rocketed through him in volcanic tremors he could not
control, and his feet moved without the commands of
thought or reason.

The vast insanity below was nearly ended. The musket
shots now were of the redcoats beating the surrounding
hills to slaughter the injured and dying trying to make
their escape. Occasionally the sound of swords clashing rang
out over the cold wind, but it would only be a desperate
Highlander with a stolen sword making a last attempt to
fight off the murderous intent of his better-armed opponent.
Without weapons—indeed, many even without shoes—the
Highlanders had only their tremendous pride and courage
and ferocity to carry them against the well-equipped and
richly garbed British soldiers. Pride and courage had no
power against the cold, modern weapons of war.

The carnage below had brought the boy to his knees,
and he had emptied his stomach long ago. Only the sight
of a familiar tartan on the edge of the battlefield kept his

feet moving inexorably toward the maelstrom of madness
that men called war.

His numbed fingers shook as they circled a handhold,
and his skinny boy's legs slid down a boulder, bringing
him almost within reach of the rock-strewn ground. Puffs
of smoke and jarring thunder still echoed from other
parts of the field, but this one corner had seen the worst
fighting hours ago. His gaze frantically sought the tartan
again, searching for any sign that life remained in this
world besides his own.

His terror and anguish blinded him to the enemy until it
was almost too late. Catching at the ancient flintlock he had
carried all this way, the boy fell flat among the boulders as
a redcoat stepped from behind an outcropping of rock.

In horror, the boy watched as the soldier deliberately
lifted his bayonet over the fallen body wearing the familiar
tartan. In a reaction as instinctive as it was violent, the
fourteen-year-old lifted his musket and pulled the trigger.

The soldier screamed in pain and crumpled to the
ground. The boy threw aside the discharged weapon and
scrambled hurriedly to the side of the fallen Highlander.
His hand encountered the dried stickiness of blood as he
pulled at the tartan, attempting to lift the broad shoulders now covered with icy rain.

Even before he lifted the dark head so resembling his
own, the boy knew. When he met the blank stare of
unseeing eyes, he lifted his head in a wild keen of grief.
The older brother who had been his champion since birth,
whose steps he had followed daily, would never walk beside him again. In his anguish, he cared not if the entire
British army found him here and cut him into ribbons.

Only the curse from the injured soldier beside him
shook his black torment.

"Damn you, Maclean, I'll get you for this!"

The boy looked up in surprise at the sound of his name,
to find the white face of the British soldier glaring at him
as he struggled to his knees. In horror, he recognized his
Drummond cousin, and the bile rose up in his throat.

Before he could shame himself again, the boy Maclean
leapt to his feet and began scrambling up the hill as
swiftly as any mountain goat. Confusion now warred with
horror and anguish in his soul. His brother was dead. His
cousin was a redcoat. And he had just shot him.

1

Cornwall, Fall 1759

Alyson Hampton clung dreamily to the strong hand holding hers and let the wind off the water blow her black cloud of hair over her shoulders. Her eyes reflected the silver gleam of the overcast skies, but only happiness shone behind those dark lashes. A vague smile pulled at the corner of naturally curving lips as she gazed over the choppy sea.

Her companion felt a more-than-familiar tug of admiration as he gazed down into her upturned face. The child had become more than a beautiful woman, and the desire for her that had caught them both by surprise a few months ago blossomed into a strong urge that was difficult to fight. She had not turned away his caresses with coy protests, and his heart hammered a little faster as he considered the possibilities.

Alyson turned questioningly to look up into Alan's handsome face. She delighted in the simple cowlick that inevitably sent a cascade of golden hair upon his noble brow, and she wished he had not bothered with the formality of his powdered wig for her sake. She had not yet developed the temerity to mention her distaste for his wig, however, so she merely smiled as he drew his hand through her hair.

"You are so lovely, you shame the skies for not smiling upon you," he murmured huskily, seeing his own reflection in the mirror of her eyes.

Her lips parted slightly at this nonsensical statement, and she turned her attention back again to the choppy sea. Watching her long-legged spaniel puppy dancing after some creature at the cliff's edge, she suddenly frowned, the expression sweeping across her delicate features with the swiftness of an approaching storm.

"Peabody! Heel!" She spoke sharply, urgently, so unlike her usual musical undertones that both man and beast turned to stare in astonishment.

The puppy bounded happily toward her, and Alyson once again relaxed into her normal, dreamy self, scratching the dog's head absently before straightening to allow herself to be led away by the man at her side.

The sound of a growing cascade of pebbles caused Alan to glance back to the ridge where the puppy had been standing. The soggy mud slowly began to slide after the falling pebbles, and a moment later the tuft of grass where the dog had been standing disappeared in a rumble of mud and stone to the sea below.

Alan caught his breath, then glanced down at Alyson's serene expression as she sought a late wildflower in the rubble beneath their feet. He expelled his breath and grinned at his foolishness.

"Is that an example of that Scots second sight the servants claim you possess?"

Alyson looked at him with surprise; then, noting his mocking grin, she laughed. Picking up the skirts of her apron and gown, she raced him down the hill to the sanctuary of a rolling valley where they were hidden from all sight of the house.

Alan caught up with her in a few long strides, pulling her round, laughing loveliness into his arms as soon as the shadow of the hill hid them. His lips found hers, and in a few brief seconds their laughter melted into whispered sighs.

Remembering that day with a flush upon her cheeks, Alyson leaned over the upstairs balustrade to anxiously scan the hall below. Boughs of evergreen and ropes of holly looped and spiraled down the polished wood of the old staircase and throughout the hall. Tantalizing smells wafted up from the kitchen, and whispered conversations and giggles echoed from the far corners of the house. Excitement raced through her veins as she saw the footman reaching to open the door.

He was here! Heart pumping wildly, she stepped back into the shadows of the upper hall. She knew Alan's formidable parents would precede him, and they would not approve of her forwardness in racing to greet their son. She curled up on the backless sofa at the top of the stairs and listened to the deep male voices carrying up to her. That one was Alan's, and she smiled softly to herself as she imagined him swinging off his heavy greatcoat and handing it to the footman. He would be wearing his formal wig, a short, dignified one unlike his father's old-fashioned full-bottomed one. He would have on his new green frock coat with the buff cuffs turned back and held with gold buttons. She couldn't decide what vest he would wear, but it would look dashing against the starched lace of his shirt and the gold chain of his watch. When she tried to imagine the rest of his attire, her cheeks grew warm.

She was eighteen years old and had never been out of Cornwall in her life, and Alan Tremaine was the only young gentleman she knew. She had no business knowing about a man's smallclothes and what was under them, but she had heard enough from hushed conversations in the kitchen to know there was some marvelous secret to it, and she felt every confidence that Alan would be the one to teach her. Perhaps this very night he would seek her out. It had been so long since she had seen him. She had never known time could go so slowly until he went to London.

Her grandfather's greeting rose from the drafty magnificence of the hall, and Alyson swiftly leapt to her feet to find occupation in the second-floor salon. The earl would be accompanying his guests up the stairs shortly. He would not like to find her hovering here in the dark like a common maidservant.

Although Lady Tremaine certainly thought the earl's bastard granddaughter was no better than a servant, Alyson sniffed as she spread her blue brocade skirts over the armless settee and waited for their guests to arrive. She was well aware her father had never married her mother in the church, but the romantic tragedy of their lives overshadowed the whispered labels people applied behind her back. Besides that, her father's father had married her mother's mother, and it seemed to her that made everything perfectly legitimate, particularly since she had never known her parents. Her father had died at sea and her mother had died of consumption within a year of her birth. Her grandparents were the only parents she had ever known.

Sadness flitted briefly across her pale features as she watched her grandfather enter the salon. Since her grandmother's death two years ago, he had grown old. He moved slowly, and the tired lines in his aristocratic face grew deeper with each passing day. But he carried his tall, lanky frame proudly erect, and his smile of pride upon seeing his grandchild warmed her all the way to the bone.

Alyson rose and curtsied prettily to their guests, blithely ignoring Lady Tremaine's frown as her laughing gaze came up to meet Alan's. He looked somewhat harassed as his mother launched into a monologue of the trials and tribulations of their sojourn into the city, and his father headed directly for the brandy decanter. Alyson drifted back to the settee and dreamed of Alan's kisses while she waited for him to find an excuse to leave the room with her. Surely he must be as eager as she to renew those sweet exchanges.

Accustomed to allowing the conversation to flow unheeded around her, it took some time before she grasped the subject under discussion. She caught it then only because Alan suddenly looked very guilty and turned to pour a drink from the decanter for himself. Frowning thoughtfully, Alyson tried to follow the pattern of Lady Tremaine's chatter.

"It should be an excellent match. She has impeccable breeding even if she is only the younger daughter. Her dowry is every bit as significant as her older sister's. They seem very well-suited. Alan scarcely left her side during the entire visit. They've not decided on a wedding date yet. Of course, they'll reside here most of the year, where dear Alan will help his father in the management . . ."

Alyson didn't hear the rest. A hammer seemed to be battering at her heart, chipping it into little pieces. Surely she had not heard aright. Her grandfather was always accusing her of not hearing one word in two, and he was quite likely right. She had misheard Lady Tremaine's lengthy chatter. Alan could not be marrying another. His kisses had promised her.

With great dignity Alyson rose from the settee, murmured some vague excuse to the company, and drifted from the salon. The malicious look in Lady Tremaine's eyes followed her, but she seldom took notice of the thoughts of small minds. Only Alan mattered, and she held that thought close as she tried to pull all the shattered pieces together until Alan could come explain to her. She had half-hoped it would be this night that he would pledge his vows to her. That was the only Christmas gift she craved. He would come and make everything right.

Skirts lifted by side hoops, she swept down the darkened corridor lined with portraits of her English ancestors. She knew the name and history of every one of them, but she would never belong here. Her illegitimacy barred her from the family tree. This thought had never truly bothered her until tonight, but waiting for Alan raised the specters of all the uncertainties of her life.

As long as she had Alan at her side, she had not cared that she couldn't be introduced to London society. She enjoyed the vast loneliness of her grandfather's Cornish estate. She kept her own company very well, and although she occasionally wished for friends or companions with whom to share secrets, she never missed what she had never had. And since Alan had come down from school, she had not worried about never marrying. Not that she was inclined to worry about such things, but Alan had just made it so very easy for her.

She heard footsteps hurrying down the echoing hallway, and stepped into the moonlight of one arched window, where he could see her silhouette. She had known he would follow. Now he would explain, and everything would be right again.

Alan's arms slid around her waist, and Alyson raised her mouth willingly to the ecstasy of his hard kiss. Her heart beat frantically against the cage of whalebone as he pulled her close. Her hands rested against the smooth satin covering his chest, and as his kisses began to drift across her cheek and down her throat, she sighed. Everything would be all right.

"Tell me about London," she murmured, turning slightly from his embrace when his caresses became too bold. "Who is this heiress your mother has found?"

Alan took a deep breath and held it briefly while he

tried to formulate an answer. Alyson didn't sound angry, but then, he had never seen her angry. She lived in a dream world all her own, where only the most pleasant thoughts intruded. Perhaps it came of living in this isolated spot with only her elderly grandparents for company. Whatever the cause, she had the sweetest disposition and most accommodating charms he had ever known, and he had no desire to lose her.

"You need not worry about heiresses, my love. Lucinda prefers London, whatever my mother might think. I'll ensure the family name and fortune by wedding her, but you're the one I will come home to. It will work, I promise you. Come, give me a kiss, and I will show you what I brought for you."

She could see the outline of his neat bagwig in the moonlight, but in his eyes she could see only shadows. Alan's head descended to find her lips, but Alyson twisted in his grasp. Perhaps she did not know a great deal about the world, but the effects of marriage, or lack of it, she had learned at an early age.

"I don't understand, Alan. I thought you loved me. How can you wed another? Please explain," she asked patiently, waiting for the understanding that sometimes came so slowly to her. She knew she was not stupid, but she had insufficient knowledge of people to always understand what they tried to tell her behind their words.

Alan pressed a kiss to her unpowdered hair and drank in the fresh scent of her light cologne. Daringly his hand slid to the full curve of her breast. She responded so readily to his kisses, he knew he could seduce her into anything if given half a chance. He heard her sharp intake of breath as he stroked the edge of her bodice, and he smiled.

"You know I love you, little turtle. And I've made plans for us. We'll be together as often as we want. I'll provide for you. You need never worry about that. Did you think my love so shallow as to forget how you feel in my arms, how your kisses torment my soul? Look, see what I've brought for you."

He released her breast to reach into the deep pocket of his coat to produce a small box, which he opened with a flick of his thumb. He held it up to the moonbeam from the window, and the magnificent garnet winked against the intricate gold of its setting.

Alyson stared at the lovely ring with incredulity. This was what she had planned and dreamed and hoped, a sign for all the world to know that he claimed her as his. The words of love and kisses were there too, just as she had imagined them. So why, then, was everything so wrong? Perhaps she still misunderstood, and she turned wide light eyes up to scan the handsome curve of his jaw.

"It is very lovely, Alan, but only a wife can accept such extravagant gifts. Forgive me if I am too overwrought to understand. Did you not say you were to wed this Lucinda?"

Alan slid the ring from the box and attempted to place it on her finger, but she had curled her hands into tight, frightened balls against his chest, and he could not pry them loose. He kissed her nose.

"I have no choice, Alyson. The title requires legitimate heirs. Everyone accepts that's the way things must be. But what is legality to love such as ours? You will be my wife in all but name. Wear the ring, my love, for me."

Perhaps she really was very stupid. Others understood their place in the way of things. Why couldn't she? Her mother had borne her out of wedlock, and thenceforth, so must all her own children be the same. It seemed a singular feat of logic that she had not quite grasped before. She grasped it now, however, like twisting her fingers around a fiery brand until the pain seared with white-hot heat through her center, leaving only ashes behind.

"Your generosity overwhelms me, Tremaine. I must go now." Dropping her hands from his chest, Alyson turned and stalked down the hall, not caring if he followed or not. Pain lit her path and pain carried her feet and pain held her head high. She would walk away and never look back. Never. It had taken a long time to grow up, but her eyes were open now.

Six weeks later, that night was no more than a half-remembered nightmare too unreal to recall clearly. The reality was the cold gray mist soaking her woolen cloak and clinging to her lashes and mixing with the torrent of tears that she could not seem to control as the polished coffin slid into its stone tomb and out of her sight forever.

Alyson choked on a sob as the vicar hastily concluded the service before the rain worsened. She didn't hear words of comfort or love in his voice; she had to turn inside herself for that. Grandfather had loved her, and she wanted him to be happy. He couldn't be happy lying ill in bed calling for her grandmother. He was much happier now, up in heaven watching over her. She shouldn't mourn his passing, but be glad for him.

Still, the tears rolled down her cheeks. The earl's death left her with no one except this stranger the solicitor had introduced as the new heir. She knew it was the grossest self-pity she indulged in, but she could not imagine rising in the morning to a day with no grandfather in it.

He had always been there when she needed him. He could be entertaining important guests in silks and velvets and still offer her comfort when she ran to him with a bruised knee or elbow. He had brought her books from every journey he took, helped her learn to read them, discussed them with her in long twilight evenings after her grandmother had died. He was a lonely man, but he had loved her.

She couldn't hold back the sob anymore. Shoving her gloved fist in her mouth, Alyson turned and raced back toward the house, ignoring the black-clad company who had so studiously avoided her. Only the servants dared offer her any comfort, and they had to maintain a respectful distance from their betters during the service. Several peeled off from the crowd to hurry after her, but Alyson was no more aware of them than of the other guests.

Behind her, Alan Tremaine started to break away after her, but his mother caught his arm with an angry hiss and held him back. The new heir to the earldom, Alexander Hampton, watched this exchange with bored disinterest. He had already noted that the old man's bastard granddaughter had a pleasing figure. This young buck had probably already sampled it, but that didn't detract from the allure of a new face and body to play with. A little consolation went a long way, and Alex supposed he'd be trapped in this miserable hole for a while until the estate was settled. She would relieve some of the tedium. Perhaps if she were good enough he'd allow her to stay on to keep his bed warm on those very few nights he would be forced to return to this remote backwater on business.

Later that afternoon, unaware of her cousin's plans for her, Alyson tried to rub the red from her eyes with cold water before going down to meet with the solicitor. Hettie clucked and fussed behind her, shaking out Alyson's soaked clothing, bringing a warm shawl to wrap over her mourning gown, brushing back straying curls into her thick chignon. Unlike most of the company at the funeral today, Alyson had spent very little time over her toilette this morning, and the rustic simplicity of her unpowdered hair and face and drab gown showed her lack of care.

The salon would be full of mourners gossiping over the trays of meats and beverages spread out for their delectation. Many had traveled all the way from London and would spend the night here. The earl had had many friends in government and society, but Alyson scarcely knew any of them. She had been introduced to them whenever they appeared, but none had ever sought to know her better, and she had returned that favor. She had never needed more than her grandfather.

That was a lie, but she consoled herself with it anyway as she patted her hair and arranged her shawl and prepared to meet the gentlemanly old man who had requested her appearance in the study. In typical fashion, she had never wondered what would happen to her should anything happen to her grandfather, but a niggling doubt raised its ugly head now. She knew she had no legal right to the home she had called her own for nearly nineteen years, but beyond that she did not understand. She would have to go down and find out.

Besides the bespectacled solicitor, the only other occupant of the study was her hitherto unknown cousin. Alyson sent him an anxious look as she settled her skirts in the chair. He was very big and cold and distant as he sat there in his extravagant *habit à la française*, the full skirt of his coat flaring out over his velvet breeches, silk stockings, and lace. She had never seen a cadogan wig before, and she tried to keep from staring to see how the satin tie of the wig somehow wrapped around his collar and wound up in front. She had heard her grandfather call these new fashionables "macaronis" with scorn, and she somehow fancied he had thought of this man in that manner.

The elderly gentleman at the desk coughed lightly, and Alyson blushed and primly set her hands in her lap. She had been daydreaming again. She had been warned time enough and again that she shouldn't let her mind wander, but it was so much easier to go off on distant journeys inside her head than to do whatever boring task she was supposed to do, that she had never broken the habit. She tried to concentrate on the formidable legal terms the solicitor began to recite, but she couldn't keep her attention on words she didn't know.

Instead, she watched the way the solicitor rubbed at his temple from time to time, occasionally shot her a glance to see if she were listening, and otherwise indicated his increasing nervousness. A sound at her side made her throw a surreptitious glance to her cousin, and the sight of such fury on those disdainful features held her rapt attention. He seemed ready to choke on some particularly unpleasant morsel of food. She feared in a moment he would turn purple, and she wondered idly if she ought to pat him on the back. The explosion, when it came, did not surprise her. One would feel inclined to expel such unpleasantness violently.

"He was mad! Criminally insane! I'll protest it in the highest court! Bigawd, I'll have you in Newgate for perpetrating this fraud! Don't think I'm some yearling who can be flummoxed like this. Nobody in his right mind could expect me to run this rattling old castle without a cent to spit on."

The solicitor adjusted his spectacles imperturbably. "The land surrounding the estate has always produced adequate income for the maintenance of the property—with proper management, of course, my lord. As a matter of fact, your great-uncle's fortune began with such humble beginnings. He managed his money wisely, invested it carefully, and watched it grow. You have every opportunity to do the same."

"But I'm the heir! The money should be mine, not some half-witted bastard female's." He threw Alyson a furious look that caused her to draw back in surprise. "How do we even know she's a blood relative? There are no marriage lines to prove her mother wasn't just some doxy out for what she could get."

The solicitor's lips thinned into a tight line. "There has never been a question of Miss Alyson's parentage. His lordship documented the facts most thoroughly. And even if there were, he was quite free to bring beggars off the street and endow them with his wealth. Only the title and the estate were entailed, my lord."

Alyson heard the hint of scorn behind the title and lifted her eyebrows. Never had anyone spoken to the Earl of Cranville in such a manner. Her grandfather would not be pleased.

As if suspecting her thoughts, the solicitor turned a gentle gaze on her. "I apologize for losing my temper, Miss Alyson. Your grandfather was a close friend of mine, and I mourn his passing deeply. It has been a long, tiring day, and I will have to return to London immediately. Is there anything I can do for you? Do you need me to go over any of the facts again?"

Facts? What facts? What were they arguing about? Why did that cold stranger stare at her with such fury? She twisted her fingers in her lap and wished she had listened more carefully. She hated that the term "half-witted" appeared justified. She wasn't half-witted. It was just that half her mind was usually elsewhere.

She sighed and sent a pleading look to the kindly man behind the desk. "Mr. Farnley, I'm sorry, but if you could explain some of it in . . . less formal terms, perhaps. I don't quite grasp what is being said."

Her cousin gave a sniff of self-righteous disdain, but the solicitor smiled and began to polish his glasses, watching her with great satisfaction as he spoke.

"Your grandfather regretted that he could not name you his heir for the purposes of entitlement, but he has left you all else. You have a town house in London, tenements and terraces throughout the city, a commercial block in Bath, and a number of other very substantial investments. In other words, Miss Alyson, you are an extremely wealthy young lady."

She felt her mouth fall open with a gasp, remembered to close it, but then could think of nothing to say as she stared at the smiling solicitor. A town house in London? And what on earth was a commercial block in Bath? She had never been out of Cornwall in her life. Odd's fish, how was she supposed to know what to do with these exotic acquisitions?

Flushed, she stared at Farnley with honesty. "I'd much rather have my grandfather back. What do I do with all those things? Why didn't he explain things to me before?"

Farnley ignored Cranville's snort of disgust. The exceedingly winsome young woman in the chair before him had been the apple of the old earl's eye since her birth. Perhaps it was good she wasn't a boy, with all the legal wrangle that would entail, but it certainly didn't help to have a girl of eighteen in charge of all these riches. He turned his palms up in helplessness.

"I suspect he had hoped to live to see you happily married to some fine young man who would know how to take care of these properties. He kept mentioning it was time to bring you out in society, but first you were too young, then your grandmother died, and then, selfishly, he preferred to keep you to himself when you expressed no desire to do so. Do not worry yourself too much about these things just yet. Money has a way of taking care of itself, and I will be more than happy to deal with any problems that arise until you are prepared to make some decisions."

"I'm sure you will, you old humbug," Cranville scoffed, "but as head of the family, I'll see that Miss Alyson's affairs are managed properly. The first thing I will do is have my own solicitors examine your books."

Her cousin had a way of holding Alyson's attention that few others did, but not pleasantly so. She gaped at him in startlement when he spoke. Then, when he sent her that triumphant look which seemed to mark her as part of his entailment, she recovered some of her senses.

Rising, she held out her hand to the solicitor. "Mr. Farnley, if I understand you rightly, the inheritance is mine to do with as I wish. I wish you to continue to look after it, and if it is advisable for me to have someone else go over the books, I will have the courtesy to send you a personal letter with the name of the man I have selected. Will that suit, sir?"

Farnley rose and accepted her hand with a quick, admiring shake and a familial pat. "That will suit excellently. I'd recommend you visit London whenever you are prepared to travel. I will be delighted to introduce you to your city home."

Alyson ignored the rude noise of the man beside her and allowed herself the comfort of knowing she had one friend in the world. Only too shortly, he would be gone and she would be left with the despicable fiend who had inherited her home.

2

It didn't take long to discover that old familiar routines were irrefutably gone. Alyson begged off from her duties that first day, not wishing to acknowledge all the staring faces of strangers. It wouldn't be long before they all knew she was a considerable heiress. The servants had already come to her with whispered questions of rumors overheard from her cousin's drunken complaints. The whole world would know of it soon enough. She didn't wish to contemplate what changes that would make.

When the guests were all gone the next day, she tried to find comfort in familiar duties again, but they all felt coldly hollow as she performed them. What point was there in planning menus when there was no grandfather there to appreciate or compliment her on them, or to sit and share the meals with her? And when she took Peabody out for a walk, she could have no expectation of running into the earl as he argued with one of his tenants or rode his fields. She had no one to share her books with, no one to appreciate the first crocus blooming, no one to talk to at all.

Cranville finally showed up at dinner looking much the worse for what must have been a long bout of drinking. Alyson gazed at his disheveled, uncovered hair with dismay, then quickly turned her attention to consuming the food in front of her as rapidly as was possible. Her grandfather had never joined her at dinner unshaven and unwigged. It did not bode well for the future.

Nervously she felt his gaze follow her as she left the room, but he didn't speak. For the first time in her life, she contemplated the security of the bolt on her chamber door. There was no honor in this man, she knew instinctively.

She wasn't certain she welcomed the arrival of Alan the next day as she walked along the cliff ridge. She wanted to be alone, to feel her grandfather's presence in the strong wind off the sea, to discover what it was best for her to do. Seeing Alan for the first time since Christmas was not conducive to deep thought.

He didn't seem to notice Alyson's aloofness as he dismounted and came forward, extending his hand with every expectation of her taking it as she always had. When she just stood there, the wind whipping at the mantilla wrapped around her hair, he stopped in front of her and gazed down at her with a small frown.

"I have worried about you, my love. You looked so pale and drawn the other day, but the servants would not let me in to see you. I know you have suffered a terrible loss. I wish I could offer you some comfort."

Alyson held herself stiffly, although she trembled inside. She had grown up that night when he had made it clear her illegitimacy destined her only for the life of a courtesan. That didn't mean her heart stopped beating like a caged bird when he was near. She clutched the folds of her cloak and stared back at him.

"I am fine, thank you, Alan. It's chilly out here, and I was just returning to the house. Will you excuse me?"

She turned away from the pain in his handsome face, but he wouldn't let her escape. His hand closed over her shoulder, pulling her back into the circle of his devastating proximity.

"Don't, Alyson. Don't throw it all away just like that." Pain racked his voice as he turned her toward him and lifted his gloved hand to her pale cheek. "I made a mistake. I'm not afraid to admit it. I was a fool. But don't you see? You cannot go on as you have been. Soon the neighbors will be carrying tales about your living with a man not your husband, and the scandal will be enormous. For once in your life, Alyson, you must make some decisions quickly instead of turning your back on problems. Or if you would, let me make them for you. You know I have only your best interests at heart."

The warmth of his hand was so tempting, the solace of his voice such a boost to her spirits, that Alyson almost succumbed. She wanted to be enfolded in his embrace again. She wanted it to be last summer, when all she need do was take his hand and his kisses rained down on her like heaven. She had lived in bliss then and thought it would go on forever. Only he had taught her what lay outside her dreams.

She allowed Alan to wrap his arms around her, and she rested her head against the strength of his chest as she had so longed to do. She needed this small piece of comfort to do what she must. It would have been so easy to accept his apology and forget there had ever been a rift between them; only, once open, her eyes could not be blind again. She understood the significance of his last words.

"You had only my best interests at heart when you offered for Lucinda?" It was so easy to speak as she had always done, without a hint of the pain she had suffered.

Alan looked down sharply at her bent head, but she was not even looking at him. She was cuddled against his chest as before, her delightful roundness filling his arms and his heart, her soft voice dreamily offering him the future. He smiled and brushed the scarf back from her forehead so he could kiss her there.

"No, that was my mistake, love. I thought to be sensible, when there is naught sensible about love. Forgive me, Alyson, then come home with me and tell my family you have agreed to be my wife. You will be safer under my family's protection than with that rake who inhabits your home now."

Just the thought of that daunting old battleax Alan called mother gave Alyson courage. She ripped her heart out of her chest and walked on it in the process, but she still clung to some fragment of pride. Pushing away from his hold, she turned cold eyes up to his.

"My wealth makes up for my lack of name now, so that your family will welcome me with open arms? Is that what you are saying? I'll not ever forgive you for not standing up to them for me, Alan. Never. You took every shred of happiness I ever hoped to possess and ground it beneath your heel like dirt. I'll go to hell with my cousin before I ever run to the likes of you again."

It hurt. By all that was holy, it hurt. She should feel proud and vengeful and triumphant as she turned and stumbled away from that stunned look on his face, but she could only feel wave after wave of pain washing over her. She loved him so. It wasn't fair. Nothing in this world was fair.

Alan made no attempt to follow her. She almost wished he would. If he could only explain, convince her that she was wrong, that she was just having another one of her foggy notions that meant nothing, but he did not. Because he could not. He had been in the wrong of it, and so had destroyed both their lives.

She almost didn't go down to supper that night, but she refused to hide in her room like some lamb terrified of slaughter. If she were going to have to make it on her own in this world, she would have to start now. Only she knew how she quailed inside when she entered the family parlor to find her cousin waiting there.

He had shaved and cleaned himself up to an almost respectable figure. His powdered hair had been pulled back in a neat bagwig, and even though his fingers trembled slightly as he lifted his glass in greeting, he did not appear quite so dissolute as previously. In Alyson's opinion, his face was more striking than handsome, and he still had not learned to smile, but she no longer found him repulsive.

"Cousin Alyson, what a pleasant surprise. The way you've been sneaking around corners made me think you did not want to see me. Help yourself to the fare the kitchen has thrown up for our amusement, and have a seat."

Alyson helped herself to small portions of the informal buffet on the sideboard the Scots cook had prepared to suit her tastes. Apparently haggis and bannocks were not to her cousin's appetite. His plate had not been emptied, but he was already pouring another glass of wine. She found a chair beside the fire and pulled the tea tray in front of her to set her plate on.

"If the food is not satisfactory, I have only to notify the cook. You have some preferences? I'm certain the staff will be more than happy to cater to them." She helped herself to a bannock while she awaited his reply.

"The cursed creatures are accustomed to having you order them about, aren't they? I daresay that will not be too infamous a thing when we are married, not like breaking in a new wife, I suppose. There are many advantages to such an arrangement that I'm beginning to see."

His insolent stare swept over the concealing folds of her woolen mourning gown, stripping away the layers until Alyson felt her skin burn. She kept her hand on her fork and did not raise it protectively to her bosom as he obviously expected her to do. Two arrogant male assumptions in one day were more than her strained nerves could deal with sensibly. She acted on instinct alone.

"We are getting married?" she inquired innocently, without a hint of emotion. In truth, she had no emotion left.

"Of course, you silly chit. It is the only solution left to us. You have the money, I have the name and the house. It took me a while to see what the old man intended, and it was a bloody unfair way of manipulating me, but I'll give him credit for this battle. I'll make arrangements for the special license in the morning. Then we can get on with our lives."

Alyson toyed with that idea as she toyed with her food. Had her grandfather really meant for her to marry his heir? Was this his way of making certain she had a home? She thought it more likely a matter of giving her a choice, but she took care not to mention that to Cranville. She had no thoughts, no plans, no future, just this aching void where her heart should be.

"I'll think about it," was all she replied.

The new earl scowled. Why on earth he had thought he'd get more reaction than that from the bloodless leech, he couldn't say, but her docility irritated him as much as a good fight. Well, he would give her something to think about.

Standing, he pulled her from the chair and toppled back in the nearest sofa with her upon his lap. Just like a plump pigeon, she fluttered her wings frantically, and he chuckled to himself as he pulled at the laces of her gown, exposing the chemise covering her heaving breasts. He'd have pigeon for supper. That was always good sport. And in the morning she would be ruined in the eyes of the world, possibly already breeding his heir, and she would have nothing left to think about.

Alyson squealed with outrage as he tore at her laces and chemise. She tried to slap at his shadowed jaw, but even though she lay on top of him, he exerted full control over her with just one powerful arm. His chuckle infuriated her, and she struggled to find her feet. Instead, he leaned back against the sofa's arm, pulling her flat against him. One muscular leg crossed over hers, and she found her hips trapped intimately against his. That sensation produced only fear, and she began to scream.

Cranville cursed and tossed her over, covering her mouth with his hand, but she'd found all the weapon she needed. Perhaps his pockets paid the servants now, but they had decades of loyalty to the old earl and his granddaughter. The parlor door drew open and the staid butler stalked through, his nose proudly in the air as he contemplated the ceiling.

"You called, miss?"

Alyson bit hard on the villain's fingers, and he yelped. With a shove at his chest, she pushed him to the floor. A footman had come in behind the butler and was seemingly engaged in clearing plates, but she understood the significance of the action. She had only to say the word and they would risk their livelihoods to come to her aid.

Cranville scowled as she rose from the sofa, pulling her bodice together as best as she was able. He stood up and caught her arm, then glanced warningly at the servants.

"Miss Alyson and I are having a discussion. We do not need your interference any longer this evening. The next man who walks through that door is dismissed."

The butler stiffened, but Alyson didn't give him time to respond. Muttering "Like bloody hell," she picked up the teapot keeping warm at the fire and poured a boiling hot stream of tea down Cranville's stockinged leg. He released her arm with a string of oaths that should have blistered the walls.

Haughtily she picked up her skirts and swept from the room, followed closely by the two servants. She seriously suspected they were fighting back smug grins, but she wasn't in a humor to join in. Stomping with most unladylike grace up the stairs, she entered her chambers and slammed the door with a resounding crash. Let the new lord lick his own wounds tonight. She had bags to pack.

Hettie joined her sometime late. Wordlessly taking in the mounds of clothing scattered across the room, she sent orders for a trunk and valise to be brought down from the attic, and promptly set about making order of the situation.

"Now, miss, you'll be traveling by public coach, and a right rowdy lot they'll be. It won't do to let them think you're quality. Mind me, now, you say nothing to nobody until you can get to a respectable posting house and hire a chaise."

Having utterly no idea how one went about traveling by coach or chaise, Alyson listened carefully as her fingers quickly sought and folded those items she most needed for travel. Obviously her riding habit would not suit, nor any of her expensive gowns or sacques. Consulting with Hettie, she sent for one of the younger maids and gave her a choice of her wardrobe in exchange for a servant's dress suitable for her disguise. The girl gaped in astonishment but hastily agreed.

By the time she was garbed in a threadbare cotton dress and cloaked in an old wool that still smelled of the stable, the hour had crept past midnight. The butler reported his lordship had drunk himself to sleep, but they still crept quietly out the back way. A cart had been prepared to carry her trunk to the coach station, and Alyson hastily gave everyone a hug before climbing in.

Alan had wanted her to make a decision. Well, she had. She would go to London and see the world. That her cousin had left her very little choice had nothing to do with it.

The groom made the ticket purchase and stayed with her until the trunk was loaded on top of the rickety wooden coach. Without a single look backward, Alyson waved farewell and climbed into the crowded interior.

She left nothing behind. All the love that once had been hers was gone. Material possessions meant little without the people she loved to share them. The house that had been her home all her life was just a house again—a house inhabited by some gross insect she did not care to combat. Her grandparents didn't live there anymore. They lived in her heart, and she could carry them anywhere she went.

And she was going to London.

3

Rory Maclean cursed and scratched surreptitiously at a suspicious itch beneath his arm. Beneath the coarse wool of his decrepit coat, his stained leather jerkin and threadbare homespun shirt stank from hard use and no washing. Why the devil he had decided to make this trip was far beyond his capacity to comprehend anymore. The country that had branded him an outlaw for all these years would scarcely welcome him with open arms now—even less so if they knew he was more of a criminal now than he had ever been before. But his family had worked hard to obtain that pardon, and it seemed only fair that he should thank them personally.

He stared out over the desolate landscape of a Cornish mining town. The gray colors of day were fading to the various shades of twilight, and he yawned. He could have chosen to arrive in a little more grandeur than his usual disguise, but he preferred to keep the connection between himself and the ship undetected. The men had their orders and would carry them out well enough without him for a while. And they would be ready when he was. This courtesy visit should not last too long.

Sometime after midnight the coach rattled to a halt to change horses and take on passengers, but by this time he was sound asleep.

When he woke again, Rory found the opposite seat occupied by two daunting women who stared at him as if he intended rape at knife point at any moment. One was so obese as to make the act physically improbable. The other wore the prim attire and thin-lipped glare of a spinster. Maliciously Rory gave her a wink and watched her shiver in horror before he returned to staring at the passing landscape.

Gradually the barely perceptible evergreen scent of

heather in springtime assaulted his senses, and Rory began to wonder if one of those damn fleas had given him the fever. Springtime would not have reached the Highlands yet, and he was a long way from those lovely hills now.

The soft rustle of a page turning jerked his attention back to the other occupant of his seat. Since she was not in his direct field of vision, he had not bothered to see what pox-faced servant cringed there.

Adjusting his position so his long legs nearly touched the skirts of the wide-eyed spinster, Rory glanced with curiosity at the woman beside him. A glance didn't tell him very much. The cloak she wore was as disreputable as his own, but it totally enveloped her. The cloak might smell of the stables, but the scent of heather had to be coming from somewhere. He heartily wished he could remove it to see what waited beneath.

What held his fascinated attention was the smooth white hands turning the pages of the book. The hands and the book revealed she was as much a fraud as he—more so, he suspected. But the fact that she was a fraud wasn't what fascinated him. It was the hands. He hadn't been this close to hands like that in years. The women he knew lived harsh lives, and the toil showed in the brown filth and calluses of their hands and nails. These hands didn't appear to have ever lifted anything heavier than roses or touched anything dirtier than crystal. They were small hands, slim and soft. He wondered how they would feel against his skin, but remembering the unshaven bristles of his jaw and the work-hardened coarseness of his own palms, he turned to stare back out the window again.

A woman who read in a public coach was undoubtedly a little daft anyway. Women might read the Bible or each other's letters, but the kind who traveled by coach could scarcely be expected to read at all. He supposed she could be some impoverished governess and those two Medusas across from him could be her maiden aunts accompanying her to her post, but the heather and the hands made that explanation implausible. He didn't know why the problem should puzzle him. She had only to catch sight of a blackguard such as himself staring at her, and she would scream the coach to a halt. To hell with women.

By evening Rory was cursing himself for three sorts of a fool for not just sailing up the Thames and disembarking in London for all the world to see. He was unaccustomed to sitting still this length of time. He contemplated buying a horse to complete the journey rather than continuing to suffer this torture. The fact that he hadn't seen one he would give a wooden penny for didn't change the vehemence of his mental curses for not having done so. If he had to sit idle with these three silent women any longer, he would go mad.

The fat one had snored through most of the day, waking only when they stopped to eat. The skinny one had managed to spend the entire time looking disapproving and pulling her skirts away from his boots. The third one . . . Rory leaned his head back against the hard box seat and contemplated the third one with pleasure.

She had declined to join the others in their meals, but stayed in the coach and evidently lunched out of the basket sitting at her feet. But he had stationed himself where he could see her when she descended to visit the necessary, and he had finally caught sight of the vision beneath that musty wool.

The glimpse had been brief but revealing. Light eyes the gray-blue of a misty Scottish morn stared from a round-cheeked face of palest snow, with just a hint of the rose to her cheeks. A beauteous cloud of ebony hair swirled about her brow and throat despite some attempt to control it with combs and ribbons. He still could not see her figure, but the way she moved across the yard told him all he needed to know. She was an angel down from heaven, and as such, far from the reaches of a devil such as himself.

Lapsing into drowsy cynicism, Rory ignored the temptation to get himself scorned and tried to sleep on the rough wooden bench of this public conveyance. Before he reached that happy goal, the frantic cry of the driver and the sudden unexpected jerk of the coach threw him forward, nearly landing him in mounds of flesh that flailed helplessly at being thus rudely jolted. A faint wailing sound came from the direction of the folds of fat at the woman's throat as Rory righted himself by using her knee as a brace.

The coach came to a complete halt, and the spinster

shrieked in terror at some sight in the road below. The
angel finally surrendered her book to the gray light and
looked outside idly as if to discern the status of the
elements. Rory pushed her back against the seat and
leaned across her to find the cause for this unscheduled
stop.

From this angle he could see a mounted man holding
the bridle of the lead coach horse. Another horseman
held a blunderbuss pointed at the driver, while a third
had dismounted, pistol in hand, and approached the coach.
That didn't require much problem-solving.

Rory unlatched the coach door and jumped down,
seriously disturbing the spinster's equilibrium by bumping against her skirts as he climbed over her legs. His seat
mate only made her delicate frame more compact to
allow him to pass.

The highwayman pulled his tricorne further down over
his brow as he gestured at Rory with his pistol. "Get the
women down." Beneath the kerchief that masked his
jaw, his voice was muffled and unidentifiable.

The spinster promptly screamed again at this command, but she obeyed Rory's whispered reassurances and
took his hand to climb down. The fat one huffed and
complained and rolled out after her. The third one lingered hesitantly, and Rory had to climb up on the step to
urge her to hurry.

"They're likely half-bosky and ready to show their
prowess at the slightest disobedience, ma'am. Giving them
our coins is better than surrendering our lives."

Reluctantly Alyson took his rough hand and climbed
down to the ground. In the darkening twilight she could
see only an expanse of bare trees behind the highwaymen, and she shivered. They had found a barren, isolated spot for this outrage.

" 'And over the val'bles, ladies. And gent," the highwayman added as an afterthought. He swept off his hat
for them to deposit their coins in, revealing a swarthy
face and filthy hair.

"You bloomin' hidget! We ain't arfter the gold. Just
get the female and lets get outter 'ere." The mounted
horseman added a few succinct curses as his companion
began pocketing the coin purses he had taken.

"Which uv the wenches you meanin' to take?" the

bold thief demanded irritably. "They don't look none uv 'em like quality to me."

Rory felt the slim shoulder beside him stiffen, and he rested a reassuring hand there while the highwaymen bickered among themselves over the identity of the mysterious female they had been sent to abduct. Things were beginning to make a little more sense now, and it might be advantageous to take matters in his own hands.

Shoving his slovenly hat back from his brow, Rory spat at the ground and laconically contemplated the gunman. "Don' know who ye be lookin' for or why, but just to get rid of 'er wicked tongue and bony knees, I'd give you this 'un, exceptin' that's my bun she's got in the oven, and I reckon I'll keep what's mine." He felt the girl's angry twitch beneath his hand, and aggravatingly he wrapped his arm around her shoulder and gave her a hug. Be deviled if she didn't feel good squeezed against his side.

"That leaves 'em two." Rory nodded helpfully toward his other traveling companions. "If I was ye, I'd cast my lot on the young 'un. She's got a fine eye to 'er and a lady's ways. She'll be bringin' you the best billet, I reckon."

The spinster didn't know whether to scream in outrage or preen at this description, and Rory smothered a chuckle as the would-be kidnapper grabbed her skinny elbow. The girl beside him tried to jerk away from his hold, but he kept a firm grip on her hood so no one could see her face. One look at that face and even a man without a brain would know she was the one they wanted.

"Come on, miss, we ain't got all day. We ain't gonna 'urt you none, just take you back where you belong. That's all, miss."

Those words coupled with the spinster's screams caused the girl to step back against Rory, and he wrapped a protective arm around her waist. He felt her shudder, but whether it was he himself or fear that caused it, he didn't take time to debate.

With much ado and wails and shrieks of protest, the spinster was carried off in the arms of the highwayman for the first and only adventure of her dismal life. With the gunmen gone, the remaining passengers returned to the coach to the tune of the driver's curses.

The fat woman stared at Rory suspiciously from beneath narrowed folds of flesh. Muttering under her breath

something vaguely resembling "What's this world comin'
to?" she removed a hunk of cheese from among her
voluminous clothes and began to munch.

Alyson sat on the edge of the seat, nervously clasping
and unclasping her hands, deliberately not looking at the
man beside her. "What's to become of her?" she whispered, almost to herself.

Rory smiled at the sound of that musical lilt. Each piece
of this puzzle revealed was better than the last. It almost
made the journey worth it. "That's something I suspect
you would know better than I."

Alyson jumped nervously at this murmur so near her
ear. She gave a hasty glance at the woman across from
them, but after wolfing down her cheese, she had leaned
back and begun to snore again. Guiltily Alyson looked at
the empty place across from her. Apparently the spinster
had been traveling alone.

"I don't know." This rather odious man had saved her.
Alyson realized that, but what she ought to do about it
did not come immediately to mind. The fact that he had
guessed she was the one they were after and that she
knew more about it than he did not puzzle her. She had
long ago accepted that other people knew things that she
didn't, while she knew things that made them look at her
strangely. That was the way the world was. "He'll be
furious, but I shouldn't think he would harm a stranger,"
she said more to herself than to her listener.

Rory crossed his arms over his chest and tugged a little
more on the unraveling strings of the puzzle. "Who will
be furious? Who wanted you abducted?"

Alyson sighed and slid back against the seat. There
was little enough she could do now. The coach rattled
and jerked at a rapid speed to make up lost time, and her
words came out in the same halting gait. "My . . . cousin.
He meant . . . for us . . . to be married." The last word
came out almost doubtfully.

That presented all kinds of possibilities to Rory's imagination, but if she wouldn't even look at him, he was not
likely to ever get to the bottom of this. A warning rumble
from his stomach stirred other ideas. "I don't suppose
you would have a bite or two of something edible left in
that basket, would ye, lass? It looks as if we'll not be
makin' the inn for supper."

Startled from her reverie, Alyson finally glanced at the
stranger who had rescued her, however ungallantly. In
this dusk she could discern very little about him, but her
sight was enhanced by the impressions she had received
throughout the day. He was taller than she, but not
frighteningly so, not so tall as Alan or her cousin. He
seemed very sturdily built somehow, certainly not the
skinny scarecrow one would expect beneath those rags.
Remembering the muscular strength of the arm that had
restrained her, she stirred uneasily in her seat. He was
not so big as Cranville, perhaps, but he was certainly as
strong, and not so soft. That arm had been sheer iron.

His face was something of a problem. Covered in a
week's growth of beard, it appeared formidable, as square
and sturdily made as the rest of him. His hair was tied in
a queue, but since he kept it covered with a hat, she
could tell little more. She suspected she should be afraid
of him, but she had felt him as a congenial presence from
the very first, more so than the ladies, and despite his
familiarities, she trusted her instincts.

Her glance at him now did not contradict her earlier
observations, and she reached for the basket. "You certainly have many voices, don't you? Are you an actor?"
The change from his ignorant accent with the highwaymen to a hint of a Scots burr had not escaped her notice.

" 'All the world's a stage, and men and women merely
players . . .' " he quoted mockingly. "I fancy you're not
quite what you seem either, milady." He threw out the
title on purpose and watched it fly right by her pretty
head as she rummaged in the basket. It didn't make her
suspicious or surprise her or make her laugh. What an
odd duck was this angel.

"Do you enjoy Shakespeare, Mr. . . ." She glanced up
in surprise as she realized she was conversing with a man
whose name she didn't know.

"Rory Douglas Maclean, at your service, milady." He
swept off his hat and made the half-bow the coach's
limited interior allowed him. "Might I have the honor of
yours, milady?"

The soft, lilting roll of his R's enchanted her, and
Alyson smiled happily. "You sound just like my grandmother. I didn't realize how much I'd missed that accent
until now." She produced a linen napkin with a variety of

selections from the cook's generous basket. "I hope some of these will suit your appetite."

Rory accepted the offering without looking at it, wondering if he'd finally found the flaw in all this perfection. What a shame it would be to have a witless angel. Their conversation seemed to be carried on two levels: he would ask questions and she would talk about Shakespeare and accents and grandmothers, which would be fine if that was what he had asked her. But how many witless ladies could even read Shakespeare, let alone recognize the quote? He didna ken, but he would.

Rory opened the napkin, and the scent of pickled salmon hit him strongly. With wonder he sampled the rest of the fare, each discovery bringing another enraptured cry. "Bannocks! Ach, my bonny lassie, do ye not know what I would give for fresh bannocks? And speldings! It's been years . . ." His ecstasy disappeared in the mouthful of bread and fish he deposited between his lips.

Alyson giggled at this reaction. Alan had always turned up his nose at the exotic fare her grandmother's Scots cook produced. Her grandfather had learned to accept it, but even he'd turned his nose up at speldings. The cook had learned to make the earl's favorite dishes and thus kept her position, but she couldn't always resist the spell of the Highlands. Alyson had grown up loving whatever she produced.

"I should have known the Maclean would like this fare. My name is Alyson Hampton. Pleased to meet you."

Rory nearly choked on this charmingly ingenuous recognition of his Scots title. He hadn't introduced himself as laird, nor did he show any outward sign of it. He wasn't even certain why he had given his proper name after all these years of hiding it. Maybe she wasn't the one who was witless, but he.

She offered him a jug of cool, sweet water, and he took a gulp, wishing it were something stronger. Angels and half-wits and kidnappers all in a night strained credulity. Handing back the jug, he glanced in curiosity at her bent head as she nibbled daintily on a scone. The hood had fallen back and he could see the white sheen of her bare nape in the moonlight, delicately adorned with black curls. She showed no apparent fear of him and seemed to have forgotten the highwaymen entirely. Definitely mad.

"I'm pleased to meet you, Miss Hampton. Should I recognize your name, since you so obviously know mine?"

Alyson let the last tender morsel of scone melt on her tongue as she contemplated the evening's events thoughtfully. Cranville must really want her back to go to such drastic measures. Or perhaps it hadn't been Cranville. Perhaps the highwaymen had heard of her inheritance and meant to hold her for ransom. Or perhaps they weren't after her in particular at all. But she knew they had been.

Frowning, she trusted the question to the man beside her. "Do you think p'raps I ought to go incognito?"

Rory gulped and swallowed his last bite practically whole. All that blessed loveliness turned tauntingly to him, and every bit as mad as a Bedlamite. "Incognito?" he questioned stupidly, not at all certain how else to reply.

She didn't appear to notice the inanity of his reply, but began to repack her basket. "If my cousin is so very desperate to have my money, he must try again, mustn't he? I thought I'd hidden myself very well, but p'raps that's not enough. P'raps I should change my name. What name do you think I should use?"

As long as he didn't distract her with questions, she was beginning to make some small amount of sense. Rory wiped his fingers on the damask napkin she had given him and gave the matter some thought. How in hell was he going to make sense of her predicament if he could not ask her questions?

"Perhaps you should tell me the whole story first," he suggested gently, leaning back in his seat and following her silhouette with his eyes.

Sleepy now, Alyson curled up under her cloak and closed her eyes and let her thoughts drift back to the beginning of this tale. Without self-consciousness she told of her mother and father and their ill-fated romance that had left the earl without legitimate issue, and how she had come to inherit a fortune.

Rory could not believe his ears. As the musical voice drifted on, unraveling the whole story for his amazement, he had the urge to warn her not to talk to strangers. She had no business telling him all this. He was absolutely the worst possible person for her to confide in—couldn't she see that?

But, of course, she could not. Angels knew nothing of the guilty thoughts and suspicious minds of lesser beings. When she finally fell asleep and her head naturally gravitated toward his shoulder, Rory wrapped his arm around her and settled her comfortably against his side. Here he was, bankrupt, dispossessed, and a hardened criminal, holding probably one of the wealthiest, most innocent women in the kingdom in his arms. God might as well have parted the clouds and dropped the kingdom of heaven on him. He couldn't be any more dazed.

The feel of her gentle breathing against his chest stirred other emotions, however, and not all of them were base. Perhaps, just once in his life, he would do the right thing.

4

London, February 1760

They switched transport somewhere during the night, the Maclean driving some poor man out of his bed and insisting they could not wait until morning in this pestilential hellhole they called an inn. Alyson smiled to herself at the authority with which her new companion had hired the chaise and driver and ordered food and hot water for washing for themselves. She would never had been able to do all that. On her own, she would still be sitting in that unsprung coach across from the snoring fat woman, wondering if they would ever get to London.

And now they were nearly there. The country lanes had turned to mud flats and the dismal hovels of squatters and scavengers on the outskirts of the city. The sooty fog of thousands of chimneys hung in the distance, and Alyson began to twist the strings of her reticule in nervousness.

"I'll need to tell the driver your direction shortly," Rory prompted her.

Alyson returned her attention to the rough-hewn features of the man who had befriended her. He had washed and shaved at the inn and looked considerably more presentable than earlier, if one could consider an ostler more presentable than a chimney sweep. Now that it was clean, his hair had taken on a definite auburn hue she found quite attractive, particularly with those deep, brandy-colored eyes of his. But in the bright light of day there was no denying he was more rogue than gentleman.

"I will need to go to my solicitor's office. I have the address here somewhere." She rummaged through her bag until she found the card Mr. Farnley had given her.

Rory glanced at the address and handed it back to her. He was developing a talent for dealing with her vagaries, and he gave her what he hoped was a brotherly smile.

"Lass, should you appear at Mr. Farnley's in that gear and in the company of the likes of me, he would have a failure of the heart. Why don't I have the driver take you to your grandfather's house, where you can deck yourself out in finery and purloin a maid and a groom to accompany you?"

He seemed to know a great deal about everything, but little enough about her. Alyson shrugged blithely. "I have no other address than that. Mr. Farnley will help me."

Rory rolled his eyes skyward. "You have come all the way across country with no other address than the solicitor's? What if you had arrived by night? Did you expect him to be there then? Have you no relatives, no friends you can call on? Are you really quite as mad as you seem, Miss Hampton?"

"It isn't night, so there's no need to worry, is there?" she replied practically. "I'm certain Mr. Farnley will understand when I explain. There is still the matter of my cousin, though. I really do think I should change my name."

There simply wasn't any use in arguing with her. For her own sake, he could only hope she fell under the protection of some powerful noble who would have her cousin's head chopped off if he bothered her again. Her description of the night she had left still had his blood simmering. She had dismissed her cousin's assault as an infuriating incident, only because she was too innocent to know what the man had intended. London would rob her of that innocence soon enough.

"Miss Hampton, let me give you the address of my aunt. You will need a companion who knows her way around, and I believe my aunt might be helpful. If you will allow me . . ." He took her card and with a stub of lead scrawled the direction under the solicitor's. If he stayed around the silly wench much longer, he would be talking just like her, and neither of them would get any answers.

Alyson accepted the card with a smile. The Maclean was looking at her as if he couldn't decide whether to eat her or strangle her, but she felt confident he would do neither. He really was a nice man for all that he tried to be an irascible curmudgeon.

She gazed with wonder at the vendors weaving their carts through the street, hawking their wares while ragged urchins dodged in and out between their feet. Watching a maid in an upper-story window empty a slop jar into the street below, she wondered how all this mass of humanity came together in these narrow streets without killing each other. She had never seen so many people in her entire life, and she wasn't at all certain she wished to encounter them all at once.

As Alyson sent a dubious gaze after a sedan chair being carried by two liveried servants and bearing a corpulent and overly dressed gentleman in the last stages of dissolution, Rory smothered a grin. It would be amusing to see London through the eyes of an innocent again. He only wished he had time in which to do it.

When the chaise finally arrived in front of the impressive facade of the law offices of Farnley and Farnley, Rory felt a momentary pang of regret at parting from the one and only angel heaven would ever send to him. In thirty-six hours of her company he had become as daft as she, to let a lovely heiress out of his arms just like that. Perhaps he was building up credit in heaven against whatever fate held for the future. He must be out of his mind, but he leapt down from the carriage and assisted her to step out.

Instead of releasing his hand when she stood beside

him, Alyson continued to hold it, smiling up into the Maclean's face. He certainly wasn't handsome like Alan, but she liked the strength of his square jaw and broad cheekbones. She wondered what it would be like to be kissed by lips as hard and . . . Her mind sought the word that described the slight fullness of his lower lip. Sensual? She felt a shiver of pleasure at the thought, and her smile widened.

"I shall never forget your kindness, Maclean."

Stunned almost to a state of shock by the full brunt of that devastating smile, Rory scarcely absorbed the sense of her words. Recovering only partially, he shook his head, and still holding her hand, asked, "Will you tell me how you knew I am laird?"

Alyson removed her hand from his grip and righted her cloak. "You told me, of course."

At least she had answered, even if not sensibly. Rory tried one last time. "I gave you my name, lassie, not my title. It is not a thing I throw about, under the circumstances."

Hearing only the pain behind his words, Alyson frowned in sympathy and touched a gentle finger to his rough jaw. " 'Tis time now that you begin. The Maclean is a proud name and title. You wear it well."

Then, as if she had said nothing any more astonishing than farewell, she swept up the polished marble steps to the solicitor's office.

The man behind the desk was no less startled than the one in the street when the shabby maidservant drifting into his chambers turned out to be the lovely Cornish heiress he'd left behind just days ago. He kept removing his spectacles and rubbing his eyes, but the vision didn't go away.

When he fully understood her story, he surmised she had just been suffering maidenly hysterics in describing the new earl's actions, but he was willing to indulge her whims. He polished his spectacles again and gave her a kindly smile.

"Well, you certainly have every right to set up your own household, Miss Hampton, every right indeed. Of course, a young unmarried lady will need a suitable companion. I am certain you must have other cousins we can consult . . ."

Alyson drew out the card the Maclean had scribbled on and handed it to the solicitor. "This lady was recommended to me. Do you know her?"

Farnley looked from the card to the earl's granddaughter and back to the card again. "Lady Campbell? Yes, of course, but . . ." All the objections that immediately leapt to mind would have no impact on the lovely young woman before him. That the lady in question had been a suspected Jacobite in her youth, who had escaped the full process of law only because of her Tory husband, would be meaningless to Alyson. That she was related to Jacobite traitors and since her widowhood had lived on the thin edges of poverty would only stir the girl's defenses. There was no questioning the lady's good breeding, however, and in a day when morality was something to be discussed philosophically but never practiced, Lady Campbell had a faultless reputation. Farnley gave up the fight without a battle.

Standing, he picked up his hat and offered his arm. "Come, we will visit the lady and see what she recommends."

The Campbell house was in one of the older residential districts, its narrow facade squeezed in between a palatial limestone mansion and a small church. The windows appeared to lack paint and to be in dire need of cleaning, but the front step was well-scrubbed, and the maid who answered the door equally scrubbed and cheerful. She bobbed a quick curtsy, led the visitors into a small parlor, and carried Mr. Farnley's card away on a silver salver.

The next person to enter the room was almost tiny. Garbed in a relatively simple lutestring sacque of dove gray adorned only with a handful of pink silk roses, her brown hair pinned close to her head and covered in a lace cap, she appeared almost doll-like until she smiled and entered the room like a royal duchess.

Mr. Farnley immediately made a leg and bowed deeply. After the first few courtesies were made, he turned and brought Alyson forward. The lady's magnificent blue eyes went from the perfect angelic features to the indescribable clothes without comment.

"Lady Campbell, I would like to present to you Miss

Alyson Hampton, granddaughter of the late Earl of Cranville."

Lady Campbell could have challenged Mr. Farnley's obviously improper introduction. An earl's granddaughter would most likely be Lady Alyson, or at the very least an Honorable, but she politely held her tongue in check as the solicitor continued.

"Miss Hampton has only recently come up from Cornwall, since her grandfather's death. She has few acquaintances here, and it has been recommended that she be put under the tutelage of a suitable companion. Your name being mentioned, Miss Hampton asked that we discuss the issue with you first."

If her blue eyes looked vaguely startled, Lady Campbell's voice showed none of it as she offered seats to her guests and perched herself on the edge of a striped brocade settee. "Might I inquire as to who recommended me?"

A certain lift of her eyebrow directed at Alyson suggested she might have some hint already. Alyson met her steady gaze with ease. "Your nephew, my lady. He was most courteous in my behalf, and I respect his opinion. I trust I have not been too forward in responding to his suggestion."

Lady Campbell gave a delighted, tinkling laugh, her dancing gaze sweeping to the staid solicitor and back to Alyson. Exchanging conspiratorial glances with that young lady, she said only, "Of course, he mentioned some such to me, but I paid no mind to it. He is quite right, though, child. We shall suit. I can see that now. Mr. Farnley, I am certain you and my solicitor can work out whatever arrangements are necessary, but I should think Miss Hampton ought to come directly to me, immediately. The poor child needs a tub and a maid and a good sleep."

In a flurry of maternal flutterings, she pried Alyson from her bodyguard and charmed Farnley into saving all the messy material details to another date so as not to offend the delicate sensibilities of the heiress with talk of financial matters. In a matter of minutes Alyson became a permanent fixture in the shabby but genteel Campbell household.

Within a fortnight both the Campbell residence and Alyson had taken on a new glitter and polish. Alyson gazed in her full-size gilt-framed mirror and stared at her London self with amazement mixed with a judicious amount of amusement. While the house had acquired new carpets and draperies and a discreet servant or two, she had acquired a powdered coiffure with lovely fat sausage curls and any number of extravagant gowns, of which this one tonight was the most extravagant.

The Maclean had certainly known what he was doing by sending her to his aunt, Alyson mused, gazing at the yards of white satin brocade embroidered in gold threads that made up her coming-out gown. Whatever arrangement Farnley had made with Lady Campbell to recompense her for her troubles had made a decided improvement in that lady's financial standing. Alyson had no objection at all to the lady profiting from this arrangement, since she herself had done so well by it. She would never have dared to order a gown like this on her own.

The elbow-length sleeves dripped with fine lace, and gold bows accented the shoulders and were repeated again in the long train of the *robe à la française* held up by wire side hoops at her waist. Her gold stomacher accented her tiny waistline, and the corset pushed her breasts to a fullness that matched that of the grandest of ladies she had seen in the park. Staring at the image in the mirror, Alyson decided she had found a more effective disguise than she could ever have created. No one would recognize this elegant young lady as the earl's bastard granddaughter.

She wrinkled her nose at the daring hair dressing. It was the height of French fashion, the hairdresser had assured her. None of the other ladies had tried it yet, but it was perfect for *mademoiselle*, whose own hair was so full and luxuriant. Why hide behind the tight curls of old ladies? Alyson lifted a fat curl and decided it added to the disguise. Besides, it made her feel very sophisticated.

She needed the courage of sophistication to meet the evening ahead. Lady Campbell had decided Alyson was ready to meet society *en masse* tonight and had devised a small party just for her introduction. Of course, over these last few weeks Alyson had met many new people, but she still wasn't quite prepared for what lay ahead. What could Lady Campbell say that would coerce all society into accepting a female marked with the bar sinister?

Not inclined to worry over matters over which she had no control, Alyson lifted her skirts and followed the maid who summoned her. The ballroom was on the third floor, but Lady Campbell waited for her in the newly refurbished salon in the family quarters. What the house lacked in width it made up for in depth and height, and Alyson had time to feel excitement begin to race through her veins before she reached the designated salon.

She heard voices behind the panel, but there was no time to hesitate. The maid rapped on the door, then flung it open for her, leaving Alyson revealed to all within.

The man filling the room's center clenched his glass so hard it nearly shattered as he stared at the vision floating into the room. Deirdre had prepared him for the change, but nothing could prepare him for this. The tousled angel who had slept in his arms had become a much more worldly angel in satin and bows, but to Rory she still appeared to have wings and a halo. Where before she had been all heather and mist, now she was the sparkling, crystalline drifts of Ben Nevis in winter. My God, he was taking leave of his senses, and she had not yet said a word!

Alyson's smile of delight at seeing the Maclean again faltered when he said nothing, but continued to stare. She threw an uncertain glance at Lady Campbell, who merely smiled and shook her head silently. Turning her gaze back to the elegantly garbed laird, Alyson returned his gaze with interest.

His clothes had certainly improved his appearance. He was wearing one of the new elegant coats with the narrower skirt, and the shorter vest emphasized his narrow hips and flat belly. The dark blue velvet of the coat contrasted nicely with the paler blue of the vest and breeches, and the freshly starched lawn jabot and lace at his cuffs accented the dark coloring of his face and hands. He looked every inch the Maclean tonight, and that included the silver hilt of the sword at his side.

The soft smile forming on her lips as she returned his rude stare nearly turned Rory's tongue to mush. There had not been time for gentlewomen in his life. If he faced it squarely, there had been little time for any women at all. Seaports were the most he had seen of land; the type of women to be found in them were at best exotic. The scent of some fashionable French perfume wafted toward him as she stepped closer, and he felt a fleeting moment's panic before remembering his manners.

Grateful for the first time in his life for the polite rituals of etiquette learned at his mother's knee so long ago, Rory took the angel's hand in his own and bowed over it. Small fingers curled trustingly around his rough ones, and when he straightened, he could see the misty moors in her eyes again. Homesickness welled up in him, but he had learned to deal with that emotion long ago. Bracing himself, he smiled coolly.

"Miss Hampton, I can scarcely credit it. Are you certain you are the same person who shared bannocks and speldings with me in a public coach?"

Alyson lifted her fan thoughtfully to her chin and appraised him lightly. "No, sir, that was some other man, I do believe. Should I know you?"

Lady Campbell laughed and came forward. "Lady Alyson Hampton, may I make known to you my roguish nephew, Lord Rory Douglas Maclean, who has consented to come out of hiding to escort you tonight."

The laird raised a skeptical eyebrow at the title bestowed upon the lady, but he wasn't so indiscreet as to mention it aloud. Instead, Alyson did it for him, amazingly reading his mind when she could seldom answer an openly phrased question.

"Mr. Farnley said I was legally adopted, and Lady Campbell insists on the formality. I think the theory is that if I wear a cloak of respectability, then I must be · respectable. Would you agree?"

So she was not simpleminded at all. That was a relief. He had difficulty making light conversation as it was. To do it with a simpleton was beyond his capabilities.

"My lady, if it is respectability you strive for, you have found the wrong escort. Shall I make my bows now and leave you to more suitable admirers?"

Alyson made a wry face. "I fear we are in every way suited, my lord, both of us hiding behind false fronts. Bow out only if Deirdre has coerced you into this against your better judgment."

Rory took her hand and slid it through the crook of his elbow. "If you think I'm going to let you out of my sight, you must think me a lunatic. Shall we go, ladies?"

He offered his other arm to his aunt, who accepted it benevolently, swaying like thistledown at his side as they left the salon. The wide hoops of the women's skirts made it impossible for him to stay at their side, but Rory managed the maneuver without disgracing himself.

All in all, both young people comported themselves with surprising success, Deirdre decided with satisfaction some while later. The Maclean's notoriety ensured that Alyson would be flooded with curiosity-seekers asking whispered questions, and Alyson's rumored wealth brought endless inquiries to the man who had escorted her. London society was quite willing to embrace any new curiosities, for the moment.

Finally disengaging himself from a trio of town gallants who had gone beyond asking Alyson's antecedents, to impertinent questions concerning her present situation, Rory pushed his way through his aunt's overcrowded ballroom with irritation. Spying Alyson momentarily alone while waiting for her last dance partner to return with lemonade, he placed himself at her elbow and whispered, "Have you chosen your husband yet?"

Far from being surprised either at his sudden appearance after neglecting her all evening or at the tone of his odd question, Alyson merely flipped open her fan and inquired, "Who asks?"

"That trio over there. They wish to know why you have never been introduced to society before, if we are by any chance engaged, and if your wealth is as fabulous as they have heard."

Alyson heard the annoyance in the low rumble of the laird's voice as she leaned closer to his shoulder so no other could hear their words. "And what did you tell them?"

She was laughing, and that served only to annoy him more. That, and the heady fragrance of her perfume as she came close enough to wrap in his arms, was enough to drive any man to irascibility. "I told them your grandfather thought you too ugly to be presented, that I have compromised you quite beyond repair, and that your wealth consists of a derelict tin mine on an island covered with water half the day."

Alyson's laughter rang out loud, causing heads to turn and brows to wrinkle at such boisterousness. The pleased look on the face of the dark man at her side brought a flutter of concern to those mothers there who had already decided the lady might do quite well indeed for their impoverished younger sons. Neither of the couple concerned took notice of these reactions.

"Since I am now so thoroughly ruined, would you mind leading me someplace where I might breathe? I have only lately come from the country, and I fear there is something in this mixture of perfumes that does not quite agree with me as well as fresh air."

Rory offered his arm with alacrity and escorted her toward the hallway. "I suspect it is not the perfumes so much as the stench of a hundred unwashed and over-heated bodies melting in the brilliance of a thousand candles. I'd rather smell sweating sailors any day."

"Ugh." Alyson turned up her nose at that thought as he steered her into the semidarkness of the library. A small fire burned in the grate, and candles on the table illuminated the brandy decanter for any gentleman tempted to escape the crush. "I cannot think the salt air would quite eradicate that smell."

Rory threw open the casement windows and seated her on the settee below it. The ballroom might be packed with malodorous bodies, but hers wasn't one of them. She still smelled as fresh and sweet as when she first came down. The urge to touch her was almost uncontrollable, but he was a strong man, and he had already made up his mind about this one. He would not be the one to corrupt her innocence. He had every intention of leaving the country as soon as his ship returned.

"That is no topic for conversation in any case." Rory propped his elbow against the mantel a polite distance from her. "Tell me, have you chosen among all the eligible suitors my aunt has presented to you tonight?"

Alyson turned away from his inquiring stare to look out over the steeple of the church next door. "Will I disappoint Deirdre greatly if I do not make a grand marriage?"

"What? Would the heiress settle for less than a marquess?" Fascinated despite himself, Rory pulled up a chair and straddled it, crossing his arms over the back as he stared at the winsome wench in the window. Firelight flickered across the soft flesh rising above her bodice, and he fought back a stirring in his groin. He'd found a willing whore as soon as he reached London, but obviously she wasn't enough. He wriggled into a more comfortable position as he awaited her reply.

"I see no purpose in marrying. Why would any woman voluntarily hand over her freedom to some man to do with as he wishes? Why should I take a husband so he might make himself free with what is mine while giving me only what pittance he chooses out of the charity of his heart? I can see no reason to do such a mad thing."

Rory smiled at this innocence. "That is spoken like a woman who knows nothing of love."

To his surprise, Alyson snapped her fan and turned back to face him vehemently.

"Don't be patronizing. I know of love. That's why I know women are fools to believe in it. We love with our hearts, while men love with their heads. Well, I've learned my lesson, and I won't forget it. I can see no advantage in marriage."

He had apparently hit a chord that roused the drowsy miss to battle. Rory's dark eyebrows rose but his voice remained implacable. "Tell me who the cad was and I'll slit his throat."

Alyson had to smile at this gallant nonsense. Not daring to touch him as he sat there all stern and frowning like a protective gargoyle, she ran her fan down the bridge of his nose and tapped it lightly against the strong lips she had admired earlier.

"Oh, he is quite willing to marry me now that I am an heiress, but I will not have him. So you see, love does not matter either. I shall choose to be single."

Some nagging pain in Rory's gut refused to let him quit the subject. How far had the other man gone with her innocence? What kind of bloody parasite would hurt a priceless angel like this one? If he had his hands around the cad's neck right now, he'd strangle him. "What of passion?" he ground out between clenched teeth. "Did your lover teach you that too? If so, you must be a coldhearted wench to abjure it for all time."

Alyson stared at him in astonishment. No one had ever spoken to her like that before, and she was not at all certain she liked it. Gathering her skirts around her, she tried to stand and get around the obstacle of his chair. Rory's hand reached out to grab her wrist, and he rose, towering over her as he waited for his reply.

"Let go of me, Maclean."

"Tell me his name, Alyson."

"It is no business of yours." She tugged at his hold, but it was relentless.

"Tell me it is only your heart he has touched."

Wide-eyed, she glanced up at this frightening tone. "What difference can it make? Do I ask you how many women you have kissed? It is naught to me."

She had him there. He was making a complete fool of himself. Taking a deep breath, Rory released her arm, but touched her shoulder gently to keep her from running away. "I am that sorry, lass. Forgive me. But I feel responsible for you somehow, and before I sail, I would like to know that you are happy. It is not so very easy to stop loving as you try to pretend."

Alyson turned her head from his penetrating stare. How right he was. She had asked Lady Campbell to put Alan's name on the guest list, but he had not even bothered to reply. It hurt more than she would ever admit to anyone.

"You are sailing soon?"

Rory wanted to crush her shoulders between his fingers in frustration. "That tactic works only once, lass. You will answer my question before I answer yours. If the man has taken you in lust, he must be made to accept the responsibility. I think old Farnley would be clever enough to tie up your wealth so he cannot squander it."

Such an idea had never occurred to Alyson, and she considered it, but the first part of his question bothered her. It sounded very much as if Alan could be forced to marry her, but what was the difference between lust and love?

"I do not understand you, my lord. What responsibility is involved in exchanging a few kisses and vows of love? Alan promised to love me. He said nothing of marriage. That was only my foolish daydreaming."

Rory wanted to hug her. He wanted to pick her up by that tiny waist and smother her in kisses in his relief. He wanted to find this Alan and tell him what a bloody fool he was. He did none of these things. Alyson looked ridiculously sophisticated in that costume Deirdre had disguised her in, but she was still the untouched country lass beneath. He didn't know why he should be so relieved to discover it, but he was.

He grazed her cheek with his knuckle and gave her room to pass. "Perhaps I better have Deirdre explain these things to you. Just do not let another gentleman touch those ruby lips of yours without a promise of marriage. Agreed?"

"No kissing?" Alyson stared at him in wonder. Kissing was so very pleasant. Why should anyone be denied it? She very much wanted to know how the laird's kisses would feel, actually. But finding out wasn't worth the penalty of marriage.

"Not until you are betrothed," Rory answered firmly, putting his hand to her back and guiding her toward the safety of the ballroom.

"You are no fun at all. I shall be glad when you sail." Like some spoiled child, she picked up her skirts and swept away from him, leaving him standing in the hallway chuckling.

Only when he spied Deirdre watching him quizzically did Rory narrow his eyes and bear down on her purposefully.

"Did Alyson ask you to invite anyone in particular to this little crush of yours tonight?"

Deirdre touched the patch at the corner of her mouth with her forefinger and tilted her head as she gazed at her frowning nephew. She had not missed the fact that Rory had not singled out any woman but the little heiress, and she considered that a good sign. His question was even more interesting.

"I believe she asked that some of her Cornish neighbors be invited. Why?"

"Their names?" Rory refused to indulge his aunt's curiosity.

"Tremaine, I believe. Sir Thomas and Lady Tremaine. And their son, I think. Now, let me think, what was his name?" She wrinkled up her delicate brow in deep thought, bouncing her fan off Rory's chest as she considered.

Impatiently he caught the fan. "Would it be Alan, by any chance?"

Her face brightened with delight. "Alan, of course. Do

you know him? How could I have forgotten? They just arrived a few minutes ago, something about a broken carriage wheel delaying them. Shall I take you to them?"

Rory whirled and stalked into the ballroom without answering. It took only one quick glance to find the white gown and the lovely frame of curls in the room full of gaudy colors and closely pinned caps. His fists knotted as he saw her smile politely at the older couple in front of her. He could tell just by the look on the lass's face that she wasn't listening to a word they said, and the tall young man at her side was the reason.

Damn and blast, but she had made a pudding of his brain! He would talk to Farnley tomorrow, make certain the money could be tied up in some manner, then he would get the hell out of here as he had meant to do earlier. A man in his line of work had no business loitering so long near civilization.

5

Farnley stared at his visitor with ill-disguised irritation. The new Earl of Cranville was a physically imposing young man who treated his inferiors in stature as well as status with impatience. He swept around the room now, pounding his great fist against the desk in a show of strength.

"I want her direction now, old man. As head of this family I am responsible for the chit. I'll not have her hiding behind the skirts of strangers."

Technically, the man was quite correct. The girl belonged with her family, and Farnley would have upheld that position to his dying day, had the family been any other than this spoiled dandy. Besides that, the earl had not solicited his services, but Miss Hampton had. He knew where his loyalty belonged.

"I understand she is staying with friends of her mother's family." That was what he told himself. He had no other idea how the heiress had come to know the Campbells. "I'm certain she's being well-treated. I'll let her know that you have inquired after her. There really is no more I can do for you, my lord. She knows how to find you if she wishes to consult with you."

"Bigawd, man! Do you think I will let you get away with this? I'll have your head on the block before this week's out!"

The earl stormed from the room with a flutter of the many capes of his greatcoat. His booted feet could be heard all the way out of the building. Not until he reached the street below and signaled his carriage did the building's occupants breathe a collective sigh of relief.

The earl's thoughts weren't quite so serene. He realized he had made a botch of it from beginning to end. He had underestimated his adversary and lost the advantage of surprise. Any new tactics would have to be carefully planned. If rape and abduction didn't work, what in hell was left?

It only took a few inquiries at his club for Cranville to locate the missing heiress. He growled in black humor as his companions wagered among themselves over who had the best chance to win the lady. It was only a moment's work to warn the fools that any suitor would have to go through him to claim her hand, but any rake with a brain in his head would see through that bluff soon enough. He would have to act fast.

He caught Alyson by surprise, appearing in Lady Campbell's drawing room, where they entertained a bevy of callers come to compliment them on the previous evening's entertainment. Alyson's cup rattled against her saucer as the earl's familiar towering figure appeared in the doorway, and she felt the malevolence in his black eyes. Everyone else saw only the handsome new lord come to call on his ward. She saw a hulking monster come to devour her soul.

Lady Campbell did what she could to keep the man away from her protégée. Knowing Alyson's story and seeing the fear in the girl's eyes, she surmised this was the wretch who had sent her fleeing from her home, but there was little enough she could do. She was in no position to have the earl thrown from her drawing room.

And when he finally grew impatient with her delaying tactics and asked in front of all these people that he be allowed to speak with his cousin alone, she could not deny him. All she could do was send the servants after her and pray.

Unaware of the butler stationing himself outside the door and a footman racing down the street with a message, Alyson felt the parlor door close behind them as she would a prison door. Trapped without protection in the same room as the man who had hired highwaymen to abduct her, she could only feel all hope lost.

"I have my man of business working at obtaining a special license now. We can be married in the morning. I'll have the town house opened up. We can reside there for the time being. For the sake of the entitlement and so there can be no question about the inheritance, you'll have to bear my heir first before we can go our own ways. After that, you will be free to do as you wish. A married woman has much greater freedom than an unmarried one."

Cranville considered the speech very prettily said. Enough women had set their caps for him that he knew himself to be a veritable catch. It had been a long time since he had courted a virgin, and he realized he had moved much too swiftly with this one, but he felt certain his assertiveness would overcome that obstacle with this docile child. He had only to calm her with his good intentions, speak to her of children, give her a few lingering kisses, and nature would take care of the rest. He waited to see the effect of his speech before moving in on his prey.

"What happened to the lady you kidnapped?"

That hadn't been the answer he was prepared for. Cranville stared at the pale nape of Alyson's neck that she had presented to him upon entering the room. It was a very fragile neck, topped by a thick cloud of ebony tresses. It wouldn't take any effort at all to snap it, but he felt certain a murderer could not inherit the victim's wealth. It was the money he wanted, after all. After years of expecting his uncle's great wealth, he had accumulated a vast amount of debts. Already the claims collectors had sniffed out the news that he had not come into the funds expected. He could not even return to his lodgings without some guarantee of a good deal of blunt for their pockets. They were camped on every doorstep. Without her wealth, he would have to flee the country or rot in debtors' prison.

"She wasn't a lady, and I sent her away well paid for her inconvenience. I didn't find your little trick amusing. I have told you I will marry you. You will be the Countess of Cranville. A bastard can scarcely ask for a better title than that. Surely you aren't simpleton enough to hold out for love? Your birth and your wealth will only attract the worst sort of rake. I at least can offer you your home and a decent name."

"I can make my own home, and I have a feeling your name will not be decent much longer. No, thank you, my lord. I cannot accept your offer." Alyson kept her back toward him. She could be more courageous when she didn't have to see his eyes. She would be able to read her fate in those eyes, and she had no desire to know her future.

He moved up closer behind her, his large hand reaching to cover her shoulder. "You have no choice, cousin. You will marry me in the morning, and we will get along suitably well. Or you can refuse and find your friend's home in flames, her person set upon by thieves and rogues, and yourself bound and gagged on the way to a whorehouse in France. I have friends in a great many interesting places. You would be much better off joining me than fighting me."

With satisfaction Cranville felt the shudder sliding through her. He had already marked her for one of those frail, cowardly females who would run at the first sight of a real man but cower at his feet forevermore after he bedded her. He preferred a more spirited wench himself, but he didn't have time for fireworks. It was all to the good that she was weak and dared not call his bluff. He had no intention of carrying out any of his threats, but anyone foolish enough to believe them needed a man's protection. He would be doing her a favor to wed her innocence to his experience.

His hand slid up her throat to cup her chin and turn it to face him. She had odd eyes. He had never paid much heed to a woman's eyes, but hers were impossible to escape. They were all he saw when he forced her chin up.

He had thought them a washed-out blue at first, but as he held her, they turned an icy gray that would have frozen a lesser man. Behind that heavy fringe of black they were a witch's eyes, but he was not the superstitious sort. He lowered his head to claim the luscious lips that would be his alone until he tired of her.

Aroused by the spell of the woman in his hands, the earl failed to hear the click of the door as it opened. Not until the bitch sank her teeth into his lower lip and he yelped in pain did he hear a laugh behind him and know his humiliation had been witnessed. Cursing, Cranville shoved Alyson from his hold and grabbed for his sword.

The man leaning against the doorframe had not the earl's claim to height, but the nonchalant manner in which the intruder crossed his muscular arms across his chest warned there was strength behind the sword dangling at his fingertips. Cranville's eyes narrowed as he took in his opponent's insouciant air. Here was no anxious lover, but a soldier looking for a brawl.

"No introductions are necessary, lass. I can assume this is Cranville. I go by Maclean. Now that the amenities are accomplished, where shall I send my seconds?" Rory ignored Alyson's gasp. He scarcely cared if it were astonishment or fear that made her raise her lovely hands in protest. His rage was such that it would spill out and scald all within sight until he had this monster's head on a skewer. Alyson might choose to throw herself away on a fool, but no one was going to force himself on her while Rory Douglas Maclean had a breath in his lungs. He could do that much to protect the only good thing he knew in his life.

The earl was no fool. He didn't know who this arrogant stranger was, but he could see death in his eyes. He had learned swordsmanship for amusement and to keep his more persistent creditors at bay. He had never raised a weapon against a trained killer before, and he would not now.

He lifted his big shoulders in what he hoped was a casual shrug, then drew out his card with his direction. Maclean watched him with suspicion, but stepped aside to let the earl pass. Cranville turned for one last look at his errant cousin.

"Remember what I have told you, Alyson. After I

have disposed of your lover here, I will be coming back for you. I expect you to be waiting."

Rory's fist clenched around his sword hilt, his desire to run the blade through this vermin so strong that it almost felt like an outside force. He restrained himself, however, and when he glanced back into the room at Alyson, his thoughts flew in another direction.

The vibrant beauty who had so daringly defied a man twice her size moments before had dwindled into a dazed waif who neither met his eyes nor replied to his call. When he stepped into the room and held out his hand to offer her comfort, she did not even seem to know him. More terrified than he had ever been in battle, Rory rebuckled his sword, then caught her shoulders in his hands, reassuring himself that she was alive and well somewhere behind those glassy eyes.

"Alyson! Say something. What is wrong? What did that bastard say to you? Alyson, dammit, wake up and tell me what happened!"

Rory's tortured cry brought Alyson out of her trance, but she scarcely comprehended his words. The fear and horror were still in her, and there was nothing anyone could do about it. She looked at him blankly, seeing the anxiety in those gentle brown eyes of his, and a soft smile formed on her lips.

"My lord, how can anyone fear a man with eyes as beautiful as yours? I can see right into your soul." With that, she rested her hands on his chest and stood on her toes and kissed him lightly on the lips.

The sensation was more than pleasing, the shock of it thrilling through her until she was full awake, and aware of what she was doing. Fortunately, the Maclean was a gentleman, and he released her as soon as she pulled away, although the shock in his eyes was almost as great as her own.

"Do not worry. I will not let anything happen to you or your aunt," she murmured before drifting right past him as if he were not there, to disappear somewhere in the rooms beyond.

Rory ran his hand through his loosely bound hair and stared after her, no longer the picture of an arrogant man in full control of his life but a man whose soul had just been plunged into torment.

Deirdre found him there shortly after, but she could get no more sense from him than Rory had been able to get from Alyson. He suggested that she and Alyson spend the night with friends, then calmly walked out on her before she could question him. She stared after him in perplexity, then went searching for her guest.

Alyson was already packing her trunk. She had laid out the shabby maid's costume she had arrived in and was now sorting through her new wardrobe for the simpler gowns and petticoats. At sight of Deirdre, she smiled vaguely and continued packing.

"I do wish someone would explain what is happening," Deirdre complained, taking a seat at the vanity and poking around the bottles and brushes while keeping an eye on the younger girl in the mirror.

"I told him I should travel incognito." Alyson firmly folded a flaring petticoat and shoved it to the bottom of the trunk.

That wasn't very helpful, but Deirdre let it pass in pursuit of further enlightenment. "Rory says we are to leave the house and spend the night elsewhere. Is your cousin that dangerous?"

"I thank you very much for your hospitality, Deirdre, but I cannot impose on you any longer. I will write and tell you how I fare. Thank Rory for me. Besides my grandfather, he is the only true gentleman I have ever known. I regret that he had to become involved in this."

In the last few weeks Deirdre had grown accustomed to Alyson's vague mode of conversation. She seized upon the remark that most interested her. "You are talking nonsense, child! Anyone who calls Rory a gentleman is all about in the head. Have no illusions about my nephew, Alyson. He is well able to take care of himself, has done so since he was a child. You needn't be protecting him by running away. I'll just send a servant over to Lady Hamilton's, and we'll pass the night comfortably until Rory and your cousin have put an end to their differences."

For the first time, Alyson looked up to her companion, and with a sad smile shook her head at the ignorance of people who ought to know better. Why couldn't others see what she did? There wasn't time to explain. She had to change and get to the bank before it closed.

"Rory has nothing to fear from my cousin. You do. Go

to your friend's house tonight. I will be fine." This last was a lie. The vision had been filled with terror, but she could not pin a name or place or face to it. She had known nameless terror before. Just before her grandfather died she had felt it. It was a cold sensation that surrounded her heart and stopped it from beating and filled her thoughts with wispy vapors of fear, but the source was never clear. She just knew this time that it was directed at herself, and she could surmise Cranville was the source of it. She knew other things too, vague things that were not always clear until the moment came. That was the frightening part, waiting for it to happen, wondering how and where it would strike. But action, any action at all, was better than sitting still. By separating herself from her friends, she assured herself that they would not inadvertently be struck by whatever befell her.

Alyson said nothing else, but continued methodically gathering her belongings, until Deirdre gave up and left to scribble a message to Lady Hamilton. On second thought, she scribbled one to Rory too. She didn't know what had happened between these two, but she was woman enough to know that Rory would be distraught if the girl disappeared without a trace. That was the only sense she could make out of the scene upstairs.

A fog was beginning to roll in from the water when Alyson finally completed her packing and changed to her unobtrusive maid's costume. As she left the house with her reticule wrapped snugly around her wrist and hidden beneath the old woolen cloak, she glanced warily around the nearly empty streets. The unusual warm weather had turned suddenly bitingly cold for March, and the damp fog made it more pleasant to stay inside. There were few passersby to observe her direction.

She hurried to the corner on Piccadilly where she knew she would find a hack to take her the distance to Cheapside. It had not been easy getting out without a footman or a groom or a maid tagging along, but she had no desire for any of the servants to get in trouble for what she meant to do. Surely no one would blame an entire household if she just disappeared quietly on her own.

The mist settled on her cloak, dampening it quickly, until an empty carriage rattled along. She felt it would almost be faster if she walked, but she didn't like the looks of the empty streets and the shadows darting in and out of the fog. The hackney gave some measure of security.

By the time she finally arrived on Cheapside, the bank was preparing to close. It, too, was nearly empty, and the clerk was impatient when interrupted by a female of dubious importance. The account she drew upon, however, was a healthy one, and after some fussing, he provided her with the funds requested.

With enough coins to travel anywhere she so desired, Alyson set out to locate a post chaise. She had learned a good deal about getting around in these last few weeks, but not so much as she would like. It would be better if she had a definite destination, with someone in it that she knew, but Cranville would only make life a misery for any friends of hers. Better to just disappear and reappear somewhere else as someone new. She owned property in Bath. That gave her a direction, at least.

Her mind cluttered with these thoughts, she scarcely noticed that the nearly empty street now contained a few more shadows than earlier. London was a dangerous place for a woman alone, but Alyson had not been there long enough to be impressed by that fact. Accustomed to coming and going at will in her grandfather's protected estates, she felt little fear of traversing these wide city streets, with help just a scream away.

She couldn't have known the desperate lengths that desperate men will resort to. As she turned from the wide street of the financial district into a short alley that would take her to the hiring inn, the men who had been following her since she first left the house felt safe in acting at last. They moved in with a rapidity that left no chance of escape.

When Alyson first saw the man coming down the alley toward her, she felt only a slight nervousness. Garbed as a servant, she could have nothing that would interest a thief. But as she hurried on, she heard two more pairs of footsteps behind her. That was when she knew she had been a fool to think Cranville would wait until morning.

She began to run, but she had no hope of outdistancing three strong men while running in clogs and long skirts. She had hoped the man in front of her might be friend and not foe, but that hope died as he reached to grab her before she could pass. She kicked and struck him with her reticule, and almost succeeded in shoving his arm away, when the two behind her caught up. No amount of struggle could free her from three pairs of sturdy arms. Her screams brought no reply. A heavy, sweet-smelling rag covered her face as her arms were jerked behind her, and then she fell, a deadweight, into their arms.

The man holding her waist chuckled and slid one hand beneath her concealing cloak, finding a pleasant fullness to tempt further explorations. The girl only moaned and moved restlessly as he tested first one ripe breast and then the other. His sharp face developed a predatory hunger as he glanced to his companions, who were busily tying her wrists and ankles and recovering the heavy purse she had used to strike at them.

" 'E didn' give no time we're to bring 'er, did 'e?"

Opening the reticule and ignoring this question, his stocky companion whistled. "We're rich, yer bastids! Rich! Blimey, just look at this!"

Hauling their burden into a doorway, they quickly emptied the coins into their own pockets, arguing spitefully among themselves as to who should get the greater share. But even with this wealth to worship, the sharp man still felt a more primitive hunger calling, and he knew he needed the cooperation of the other two to satisfy it. With this uppermost in his mind, he quickly placated the argument and gestured toward their sleeping burden.

"We've got more bloody gold 'ere than 'e offered us to fetch 'er. What if 'e finds out? She's got a mouth on 'er. She'll tell."

That brought a sudden silence. The man who had hired them had an unpleasant temper at best. He had only warned them not to let her get away. He hadn't said anything about taking what they could get. Knowing the gent, he would want the gold for himself. The silence grew more solemn.

The thin, sharp-faced one spoke up. "She's a prime piece. Molly would let us live like gents for a week if we brung 'er somethin' the likes of this. Maybe even let us break 'er in to the trade, if you gets my meanin'."

The sturdier man looked interested. "Yeah, then arter we gots what we could, we could tip off the gent that we knows where to find 'er, and maybe 'e'd pay to 'ave 'er back. 'E wouldn't 'ave to know we was the ones to roll 'er."

The third and oldest man shook his head dubiously. " 'E'll kill us fer not bringin' 'er directly back. 'E'll know she's gone. It won't do."

The argument continued until someone appeared at the alley entrance to see what the noise was about, and they hastily decided to make their decision in a safer place.

Untying her, they carried Alyson with her arms wrapped about their necks like a drunken doxy. Arguing and singing, they made their way back to their favorite inn in a shabby waterfront district near London Bridge, just off Bishopsgate, easily within walking distance of their posh surroundings.

6

Rory Douglas Maclean stood on the wharf staring out over the jungle of rigging and masts that filled this point of the Thames. His ship was anchored out there on the edge of the current, ready for sailing at a moment's notice. More than ready. He scowled and contemplated the fog rising and filling the rigging with clouds of insubstantial sails. The fools hadn't completed their run, and the casks filling the false bottom would make the ship lie low in the water, a certain signal for the customs officers.

He cursed silently to himself. The fog would hide the ship for now, but it would also prevent its sailing. His entire livelihood rested in that ship. He had to get it out of here. The seaman who had brought the message said the revenue cutters had been waiting for them. That meant they were out there now searching for the *Sea Witch*. It had been a bold maneuver to sail straight up the Thames—bold but foolish. The cutters would figure it out soon enough and come looking for them if the customs officers didn't find them first.

There was no time left. That villain Cranville hadn't been at his lodgings when Rory's seconds went around to call on him. There had been creditors enough on the doorstep willing to report his comings and goings, but they hadn't seen him in days. The coward evidently had no intention of returning there until he had his hand on Alyson's money. He couldn't leave the girl with a predator like that hovering over her. What in hell had he gotten himself into?

Well, Alyson and Deirdre should be safely installed at Lady Hamilton's by now. He wouldn't have to worry about Cranville immediately. Pulling out his watch, Rory considered the hour and decided there had been time enough for Dougall to get back to the inn. They could map out a plan to get the brandy out of here, and he could meet them later, after disposing of the obnoxious earl.

Tugging his tricorne down over his brow and pulling the caped greatcoat closer to his body, he stepped over the sprawling lines and set out for Bishopsgate.

When he entered the tavern of the inn, Rory halted in the doorway, surveying the inhabitants. A man in his occupation learned to be careful. Besides every variety of illegal goods, information could be bought and sold in these waterfront taverns. The man sitting there at the bar could be a customs officer looking for the owner of the *Sea Witch*, or just another retired navy man reliving his youth. The secret was to know which was which, and after fifteen years on the run, Rory Maclean had a pretty clear idea of which men wanted his scalp.

He also had an exceedingly low opinion of British revenue officers. Not one of them had the imagination to come in here looking for him. That old tar at the bar was just that. Rory relaxed and swung his shoulders, searching for some sight of Dougall in the dim recesses of the low-ceilinged, lantern-lit room.

The sight that greeted him instead turned his stomach in horror, nearly making him white-haired in the space of a moment. He thought at first he was having some hallucination, that somehow the afternoon's events had haunted his fevered mind to produce an angelic apparition where actually there was none. But seeing the filthy vermin laughing as she groggily tried to hold up her head with a wrist tied to the table, he quickly disabused himself of all fanciful notions.

Ignoring his first urge to pull his sword and decapitate every man in his path, Rory stepped back into the shadows, removed his gold-braided hat, untied his queue, loosened his jabot, and grabbed a mug of ale from an astonished barmaid. Then, disheveled and rolling drunkenly, he made his way across the room to the table where his particular angel awaited.

Pulling up a chair, Rory sat down without ceremony, splashing ale from his mug as he slapped it against the worn planks. "Looks like you gents got a morsel of trouble on your hands."

The small, sharp-faced man poked his prisoner further into the darkened corner between bench and wall. Rory gritted his teeth as Alyson moaned unconsciously. The bastards had drugged her, and from the torn state of her bodice, that wasn't all they had done. Pain washed through him, not a crippling pain, but a vengeful, murderous one. He came from a breed of warriors with tempers fiercer than the winter snows of his home. He would slit their throats slowly, giving them time to swallow their tongues in fear. Then he would go after Cranville. Planning what he would do to that unlucky earl kept him calm as his new companions objected to his intrusion.

"Move on, mate. We ain't lookin' fer trouble. We're just havin' this 'ere friendly discussion." The sturdier one stood unsteadily to block the newcomer's view of their troublesome prize.

Rory modified his accent to match theirs. "If I were you gents, I'd get 'er off me 'ands just as soon as I could. The word's out for 'er. Daughter of a bleedin' earl or some such. They'll probably draw and quarter the blokes unlucky enough to be found with 'er. Plannin' on shippin' 'er out to France, are ye now?"

The older man blanched and pulled his companion back down in the seat beside him. Neither of them looked at the skinny fellow guarding his prize with a possessive grip.

"We talked uv that, but we ain't found a likely prospect to pay us what she's worth. We figured Molly would 'ave 'er, but if word's out, Molly ain't goin' to pay 'arf what we ought to get. I'm for takin' 'er back to 'er bleedin' old man what's offered to pay for 'er already."

Rory felt the rage roiling in his stomach, but he kept a steady hand on the table. The other rested on the hilt of his sword beneath the greatcoat. "Figured 'at's what yer were about when I saw 'er. You're in luck, gents. I'm about to set sail for foreign shores this night, if you get what I'm sayin'. I can always use another item to trade. Where I'm goin', they don't even speak the King's English, and she can squeal all she likes, but they won't be able to nail yer. How's 'at sound?"

"Fergit it. This 'ere piece is mine and I ain't givin' 'er up till I've 'ad a part of 'er. I ain't ever 'ad nothin' like this before, and ain't likely nothin' like it ever come my way ag'in. Yer can all go yer own way and quitcher worryin' 'bout it. I'll take care uv 'er."

"Hell, Tommy, with the gold we got tonight, yer can buy the fanciest piece on the market." The older man turned to Rory. " 'Ow much you offerin' for 'er?"

Judging from the way the skinny one was holding on to his victim, he wasn't going to come away from this without a fight anyway. Rory named a sum that would have bankrupted him had he any intention of paying, then rose abruptly from the table.

"The tide's turning, mates. I got to be gettin' back to my ship. Bring 'er along and we'll talk terms on the way down to the docks."

The other two men scrambled eagerly to their feet after him, but the younger remained seated, blocking access to Alyson. A knife appeared in his hand, and it glittered evilly in the flickering light from the overhead lantern.

"I'll give yer what I got in me pockets, Rob. Then the two of yer can take off with this nosin' bloke here and leave me to me pleasures."

"Tommy, she'll 'peech on us when she comes round. I don't wanter 'ang. You knows what they do when they draws and quarters yer? Your guts 'ang out right before yer very eyes, yer bleedin' idgit. Now, let's take the man's money and get."

Rory read the stubbornness in the younger man's eye as it turned on him, and he didn't wait for the knife to come arcing out of the night. With a well-placed kick, he overturned the table. In the same movement he drew his sword and pointed it at the youngster's neck.

"Get up slowly, Tommy, my boy, or you'll not enjoy another piece of tail anywhere in this world again. Start contemplating what kind of females they have in hell, son."

Instead of dropping the knife, the crazed thief slashed upward with it, intending to throw off the weapon cutting into his windpipe. He didn't count on Rory's rage, however. The sword never wavered, but neatly severed his jugular. As blood spurted from the wound and the man slumped, Rory shoved the body aside, slashed at the rope tying Alyson to the table, and threw her over his shoulder, all before his stunned watchers could act.

He was moving toward the doorway before anyone else in the room had any idea of what had happened. From the corner of his eye Rory caught sight of Dougall's worried face, and with a jerk of his head he indicated that he follow in the trail of the protesting men following him out. Like the jackals they were, they were demanding payment for their ill-gotten goods.

A roar rose up in the tavern behind them as a barmaid screamed over the discovery of the dead body in the corner, but Rory was outside on the street now. The dead-fish-and-sewage-scented fog curled around them, masking their escape. Bow Street wouldn't have time to arrive before they disappeared into the maze of alleyways between the warehouses and the wharves.

Rory waited until they reached the entrance to a dark street away from the long slabs of yellow light of the inn. Turning abruptly, sword in hand, he inquired with a cold sneer, "Have you any weapons on you, gents?"

The two thieves stepped backward at this sudden change in demeanor, only to find another sturdily built seaman behind them, dagger in hand. They grabbed for their meager weapons, but Rory's sword moved faster than they, disarming them with almost invisible slashes of the sharp blade.

"Too bad, lads, I really would have enjoyed skewering you like your friend back there, but unlike you, I don't pick on the defenseless. Go back to your employer and tell him the devil is on his trail. Maybe he'll pay you well to guard his back, but you'd better be well-armed the next time you cross my path. I intend to have the bastard for breakfast."

Lowering the sword threateningly to a vital point on the older man's anatomy, Rory sent the two thieves scurrying into the night. When next he looked up, Dougall was staring at him strangely. Without comment, he started down the alleyway, this time gently carrying his precious burden in his arms.

"Captain!" Dougall hurried through the thick fog after him. Not daring to make any mention of the woman struggling feebly in his employer's arms, he imparted the news that had made him late. "Customs officers are askin' after the *Witch*. Word is, they're settin' out at daybreak."

Rory cursed a string of curses that carried them through the alley and down the street to the wharf, where a variety of small craft bobbed up and down. Using every foul epithet at his command, he located one that seemed seaworthy, lowered his burden into the puddle at the bottom, and stepped aboard. Dougall hurried to follow, slashing the keel line with his knife as his captain reached for an oar. Their own boat was farther down the river, but the noises drifting from up the street warned that the two thieves had decided to raise their cronies in pursuit. The Runners would be down to see what the hue and cry was about in no time now. The water was the safest place to be.

They rowed swiftly and silently into the ebbing current. The tide was on its way out. Their dark shapes disappeared into the fog, making them invisible from shore. Only the slap-slap-slap of the waves against the boat and the occasional splash of the oar slicing the water could be heard anywhere about. Rory set his jaw with grim determination as they neared the *Sea Witch*.

The girl was alive, but he didn't know how badly she had been hurt. He couldn't take her back within reach of that villain Cranville until he'd had time to dispose of him. And he couldn't go after Cranville until he had shaken the cursed customs officers. He was not a man to dally over decision-making, even when all the choices were unpleasant.

As the rowboat slowed and hovered in the shadow of the larger sloop, Rory whistled for the watch.

In minutes they were raising Alyson to the deck.

Not until the ship hit the Channel and maneuvered sharply into the choppy waters, throwing Alyson from the bunk, did she wake again. Icy air blew across the floor, returning consciousness, and, shivering, she struggled to sit up. Blackness surrounded her still, but it was a more substantial blackness. She could feel the shapes of objects around her, and her thoughts were more coherent.

She sensed no one in the room, and felt around, finding the bunk she had been thrown from. Easing herself up, she touched a heavy blanket and drew it around her hurriedly, trying to keep her teeth from chattering. Another wave lifted and carried the ship, sending it lurching to starboard, and Alyson tumbled to the side.

The violent heaving of the ship didn't aid the queasiness in her stomach. She didn't know where she was or how she had got there, but she knew she had to get out. This, then, was what her premonitions had warned of.

As her eyes grew accustomed to the darkness, she gradually made out shapes. Pulling the blanket tighter, she tried standing, bracing herself against the wall. She needed a door. That much made sense.

Her fingers trailed along the wall slowly, grabbing whatever came to hand when the ship lurched, then moving again when she steadied herself. From the howl of the wind and the shouts above, they were sailing into a storm, but she couldn't piece that together with her need for escape. Snatches of conversations came back to her, raising black fears in her mind, and she knew she had to get away.

She succeeded in finding a break in the paneling, and her hands rapidly slid over the door, searching for a latch. With a sigh of relief, she found what she needed and turned it. Nothing happened. Frowning, she turned it the other way. Nothing. She jiggled it back and forth, then pushed and pulled and twisted and lifted, growing more frantic with each motion. The latch wouldn't open.

She gave a cry of frustration, and a tear trickled down her cheek as she dragged the blanket more securely around her. She was a prisoner, and if her cousin were her captor, she was most likely on the way to that French brothel he had threatened her with. She'd heard the gossip about those places. The rumors were all over London. They said Frenchmen would pay high prices for young English girls, and it wasn't just London's prostitutes who found their way over there. Some came back to tell their tales, the rumors said, but Alyson didn't think she would be one of them. She would die of shame first.

Nauseated from the effects of the ship's rocking and the lingering fumes of ether, damp and cold and terrified, she continued her search of her prison cell to find just what she expected. Nothing. No escape. No weapons.

Her mind had finally grasped the fact that even could she get out of this prison, she had nowhere to go but overboard, but it couldn't grasp the fact that she would soon be sold to a house of prostitution. That was too far beyond her ability to imagine. She wasn't even certain what went on in those places that made people lower their voices to a whisper when they were mentioned.

Wearily she crawled back into the bunk to face the wall. Perhaps she would die of misery before they reached land.

Drenched to the skin, his feet shriveled to frozen bone in the puddles that his boots had become, Rory staggered down the companionway to his cabin and dry clothes. No sighting had been made in the last hour of the navy cutters that had been chasing them, and he felt safe in taking some respite before the storm worsened. For it would worsen, his long years at sea had taught him. At least they were out of the Channel now and in the long stretch across the sea. He felt safer than he had in weeks.

Not bothering to light the lantern, he peeled off his soaked garments, sitting at his desk chair to wearily pry off his boots. He could use a pot of coffee, but fires couldn't be lit on a night like this. A sip of good Scots malt would have to do, and he lifted a flask from his desk and took a long drink.

The fiery liquid warmed his insides as he toweled himself dry. Then, before the heat had time to wear off, he fell down on the bunk and reached for his blanket.

His welcome bed erupted in a crescendo of shrieks and

flailing limbs, nearly unmanning him before he had time to register the presence of a visitor. Vulnerable in his nakedness, Rory hung on to the blanket. A clog caught his shin, and, cursing, he grabbed with his free hand at an arm aimed at ripping his eyes out. As another kick found its mark, he flung his leg over the dangerous weapons of her feet. Alyson! How had he forgotten Alyson?

Because he'd wanted to. Because he knew he had exceeded all bounds of propriety by taking her into his protection, and that there would be hell to pay when everyone came to his senses. It looked like the lass had already come to hers. Rory caught her wrists behind her back and pulled her up against his chest, slowing her struggles.

"Hush, lass, it's just me. I forgot ye were here. Calm down and I'll find some dry clothes."

The reassuring lilt of those rolling R's brought Alyson's heart back down from her throat, and fighting hysteria, she nodded silently against him. The iron bands of his hands released her wrists, and she brought her arms around to rub the circulation back. Rory moved slowly, his hand hovering over her as if wishing to alight somewhere, and she almost wished it would. She was freezing.

But reluctantly he rose from the bed and rummaged in his trunk until he found a dry pair of breeches. He had few enough clothes and hated to rumple a good shirt for sleeping, but with a grumble he pulled one on. He had gotten himself into this; he would have to learn to live with it.

The problem of sleeping arrangements remained. Sitting down on the edge of the bed, he reached out to touch the pale shadow of her face in the darkness. "I'm sorry to have frightened you, lass, but it is that weary I am that I canna think. How are you feeling?"

Numbly Alyson shook her head and gathered the blanket tighter. She was half-frozen and completely confused. She didn't even know where to begin.

"Are you taking me home?" She finally managed to get these words out between chattering teeth. Rory wouldn't be taking her to France. She trusted Rory.

"And where might that be, lass?" He felt her shivers and ran his hand down her blanket-covered arm, wishing he could warm her. "We'll talk in the morning. I need a few hours' sleep first. If you'll spare me the pillow, I'll sleep on the floor this night."

Where *would* home be? That was a good question, one Alyson's numb mind could not hold on to. What she did finally comprehend was that she was lying in Rory's bed, and she had no great desire to leave it. She struggled up on one elbow and untangled the blanket to give him a length.

"If you won't be uncomfortable, there's room for two. The floor's awfully cold."

He started to protest. Every gentlemanly bone in his body rebelled. But the cold and the disgust and the rage of the past night had brought out the worst in him. He didn't know whether or not she knew what she was asking, but he was too tired to be asked twice.

Without another word, Rory sprawled his long length out beside her, accepted the offered cover, and promptly fell asleep with his fingers tangled in ebony curls and the scent of heather in his dreams.

Alyson did not sleep so soundly as the Maclean. Her thoughts skittered like mice between the walls of her mind, never settling in one place for long, but rattling madly all about. The heat of the man beside her warmed her skin, but a chill lingered around her heart. Somehow, he had come to her rescue again, but she wasn't at all certain that this time he didn't serve his own purposes. She only knew that this night in his bed compromised her beyond recovery. What tale would he tell when he returned her to the city?

That thought brought a whole series of questions she had not the strength of mind to confront. Gradually she allowed the sound of Rory's heavy breathing to lull her, and when his strong arm fell across her waist, she obligingly moved closer to his heat and fell asleep.

When Rory woke to the cold gray light of dawn, he sensed something was wrong. Starting to push himself up, his hand encountered a soft curve that shouldn't be there, and his eyes flew open.

How had he ever thought those eyes of hers to be misty like the summer hills? Behind that dark fringe they were icily clear, and he gulped, his gaze traveling downward to where his hand had inadvertently found the torn bodice of her dress. It felt so right resting there that he couldn't resist cupping the full weight of her chemise-covered breast in his palm before reluctantly sliding to the relative safety of her fully clothed waist.

A teasing smile twitched at his lips as his glance leisurely traveled over the woman pinned between his arms. That fool last night had been right. He had never had a woman like this in his life, and he was not likely ever to have one again. Full, sweet curves beckoned a man's touch, milk-warm skin begged to be tasted, and if he let his thoughts stray to her eyes and mouth, he would not be able to stand up straight, as her tension told him he would have to do shortly.

"Good mornin', lass. Did ye sleep well?" Pulling the blanket around him to cover his lap, Rory sat up.

Released from the trap of his arms, Alyson hurried to right herself, tugging at the torn laces of her bodice and wrapping her arms over the rent as she sat up in the corner farthest from him. She'd had plenty of time to study Rory in the cold gray light, and the conclusions she had drawn did not waver with his gentle greeting. With his auburn hair cascading into his eyes and his broad jaw sporting a day's worth of stubble, he looked every inch the part of buccaneer. Her gaze faltered when it reached the strong column of his throat emerging from his unfastened shirt, and she quickly slid her eyes away before she could take full note of the dark shadowed mat beneath the thin muslin.

"Rory, tell me truly, what happened last night?" With the morning's dawn, her thoughts had gained clarity, and she had pondered this question long and hard in the minutes before he woke.

Rory frowned and stood up, unable to face the shocked innocence of those lovely eyes. "That I don't know, lass. I found you in a place where you shouldn't be with men you shouldn't be with. From what they said, I think they hadn't had you long. Your clothes were like they are now. Only you can say whether they had time to harm you."

His voice was cold and distant, and Alyson shivered and reached for the blanket that he had abandoned. She could not answer the question in his voice. She did not feel any different. If she had been violated, it certainly hadn't changed her in any world-shattering way. She only felt cold and hungry.

"How did you find me?"

Rory closed his eyes and gave a prayer to a God he had long abandoned, then turned to meet her wide, questioning gaze. "By accident, I assure you. I thought you safely at Lady Hamilton's with Deirdre. Why weren't you?"

Alyson ignored the question. "Where are we now?"

Rory made a gesture of futility and surrendered to her method of conversing. "On my ship, the *Sea Witch*."

She smiled at that, a soft smile like the coming of dawn that nearly knocked Rory to his knees. He caught an overhead beam and stared down at her. "That pleases you?"

"I have always wanted to sail on a ship. Can I go up and see the sails?"

He sighed and ran his fingers through his hair, shoving it back from his forehead. "Not now. The water's still choppy and the wind is picking up. This is just a lull in the storm. I'll have to be on deck shortly. Is there anything I can do for you before I go?"

"Where are we going?" She pulled the blanket around her and slid to the edge of the bunk, heedless of the heated intensity of his stare.

Here it was. He had hoped that in her wandering way she would not stumble across the thorn in the rose just yet, but it had to come sometime. "Charleston."

Alyson's head snapped back to meet Rory's eyes, throwing her loosened curls into a tumble about her shoulders. "Charleston? In the colonies? How can that be?"

"That's a long story, lass. We'll talk it over later, when I have more time."

Alyson leapt to her feet, standing boldly up to his greater height, her eyes blazing. "You cannot take me to Charleston. That is kidnapping. Leave me anywhere on the coast. Leave me in Ireland if you must. Do not do this to me, Maclean."

With a tired sadness he touched her cheek. "I canna do that, Alyson. We are gone past any coast you know, and I canna be turnin' back without riskin' myself and my men. It's too late, lass. You'll be going with us."

Before she could react, he dropped his hand and strode across the room, walking out without another word.

Alyson felt all the breath leave her, and her shoulders slumped. Rory didn't slip into his Scots lilt unless he was deeply stirred by something, she had learned. She didn't know what had forced him to this criminal act, but it had to be a matter of great import. She would wait for his explanations before acting.

She had much longer to wait than she had anticipated. A shy cabin boy brought her a cold breakfast and fresh water but resisted answering questions. As the gale winds increased, the cabin grew darker, until she could scarcely see her hand in front of her face. Knowing nothing of the cabin, she could not locate lantern, wick, or flint with which to light it. In any case, the ship began to toss so erratically that she could not keep her feet to look for them. The hours grew long and stretched from day to night as she huddled in the corner of the bunk.

The noisy sound of several pairs of feet approaching startled her from a dozing sleep some hours later, and Alyson sat up quickly. Voices grumbled outside the door, a latch slipped free, and the door burst open. She leapt from the bed in fright, dragging the blanket with her as two rough seamen entered.

In the light of the lantern they brought with them, her gaze traveled to the long burden sagging between them, and her stomach lurched uneasily.

With a grunt, they swung Rory's unconscious body into the bunk. The younger man turned to Alyson, and tugging his forelock, said respectfully, "He was knocked against the mast by a broken spar, ma'am. Will'm here will run fetch for you. We got to get back on deck."

They left, leaving Alyson standing, staring down into Rory's pale and bleeding face while the small cabin boy waited helplessly for her orders.

7

Alyson knew nothing of tending wounds, but now was not the time to mention it. Thrown from her books and the comforts of home into a cold world she did not understand, she had only this man to shield her, and he could be dead.

Curtly she ordered the boy to find bandages and lint and water. Warm water would have been nice, but she had already learned the limitations of her surroundings. She would be lucky to get fresh water.

After the cabin boy returned, Alyson knelt beside the bed and began to sponge the blood from the wound on Rory's forehead. His stillness nearly paralyzed her with fear. What would happen to her if he died?

"You can't die, Rory Maclean," she informed him angrily as she uncovered the ugly gash opening his forehead from hairline to eyebrow. "Where would I be out here in the middle of the ocean with a ship full of strangers? You got me into this, Rory Maclean, and I'll not let you rest until you get me out. So help me, if you die, I'll follow you to the gates of hell to drag you back."

"Lass, if you dinna be careful, you'll be following me sooner than you think."

Brown eyes opened warily, and Alyson ceased her scrubbing to stare at him in astonishment. She had never seen anything so lovely in her life as the beginning of a twinkle in that cursed dark face, but she resisted the urge to kiss him for his contrariness.

"Don't think I won't, Maclean," she warned, but she could not hide her relief. His answering grin showed her voice had betrayed her.

"I believe you'd try, dear heart, but not just now. I think I've cracked my ribs, and I'll be needing you to bind them. Can you do that?"

Despite his words and his attempts to relieve her anxiety, Alyson could tell he was in pain. She glanced down at the great length of him and frowned. "Can you sit up? I don't know how else to get a bandage around you."

"Patch the hole in my head first, lass, then have William over there help you. The storm's almost done, and I've got a little rest coming to me anyway."

His jest at his inability to stay awake did not go over well with the pale-faced girl working feverishly to stop the flow of blood. Rory struggled to maintain some semblance of consciousness so he could tell her what to do, but his strength was fading fast. He did not like the idea of being a burden on her fair hands, and when William tried to lift him, jarring him awake, he realized he had passed out again, and he swore irritably.

Alyson's lips tightened at the curse, but awkwardly she helped the boy to prop his captain against the head of the bunk. Removing his shirt caused some consternation, until Rory groaned to them to just leave the damned thing on and get on with it.

Following his instructions, Alyson tore a sheet into wide strips, and with the help of William, wound it as tightly as she could manage around the Maclean's brawny chest. Terror kept her from concentrating too long on the strength and breadth of the masculine planes of his chest beneath her fingers. Instead, she feared for Rory's breathing, so tightly did they wrap the binding, but he nodded approval when they were done.

"That's good. Now let me back down and bring me the whisky flask from the desk there."

But by the time they had him lying flat and ran to look for the flask, Rory had passed out again. Alyson gazed down at him with dismay coiling in her stomach. Already the blood was seeping through the clean white bandage she had so carefully applied to his head.

The cabin boy stoically restoppered the flask and offered his first words. "Cap'n will come round. I'll get summat for ye to eat."

With that terse statement he handed Alyson the flask and left the cabin. Staring at the silver bottle as if it were a serpent, she contemplated tasting the contents herself. A drunken stupor might be the only way to survive this storm.

As if hearing her thoughts, Rory lifted one heavy eyelid. "It'll make you braw sick, lass. Gie it here."

Watching him drink with difficulty from that position, Alyson caught herself wondering if perhaps in some manner or form Rory Douglas Maclean might not be gifted with the Sight himself. He had certainly developed some extra sense for reading her.

The storm died later that night, and the first mate returned to the captain's cabin for orders, only to go away empty-handed. The small exhausted female who answered the door looked at him with great gray eyes that seemed to see beyond him to the future, and showed him to the fevered man in the bunk. The captain was well beyond giving orders anytime soon. The seaman tugged his forelock and bowed his way out.

Alyson closed her eyes and swayed with weariness. Her grandfather had never pampered her with luxuries, but she had never known want either. She had always been warm and well-fed, but she had never appreciated her good fortune until now. Was this the kind of life Rory had lived all his years? Was it possible to survive like this day after day? The books she had read had never led her to imagine such harshness. Even now, she wasn't certain any of this was real.

After choking down the bread and hard cheese that served as supper, Alyson washed hastily in the cold water William brought to her. Then, looking down at the sad gown she had not had time to repair, she closed her eyes and moaned in shame. She did not even wish to know what Rory's men thought of her looking like this.

Deciding if she were to be left with only one gown for untold days and nights, she had best treat it with care, she finished unlacing the rest of the bodice and skirt and stepped out of them. Surely now that the storm had stopped the crew would all be resting and she would not be disturbed.

With the help of the lantern William had lit for her, Alyson searched the cabin until she found a small sewing kit in the captain's trunk. A practical man like the Maclean would know how to mend simple things, and she had felt confident she would at least find needle and thread. The kit with scissors and thimble and choice of dark and light thread was better than she expected.

The gown needed a good washing, but then, so did everything else she wore. She was grateful she had chosen to wear one of her sturdiest quilted petticoats beneath the maid's rough gown. At least it kept her legs relatively warm while she worked. She could not say as much for the thin muslin of the chemise under it. Although the wide sleeves went down to her elbow, the gauzy material provided no warmth and little in the way of modesty. Alyson prayed Rory would not wake just yet.

With the rent in the gown repaired, she had another problem to tackle. She desperately needed sleep, and the only bed in the room was already occupied by Rory. She had slept beside him fully clothed last night, but the thought of spending another uncomfortable night in the stiff gown and stays did not appeal. She wished wholeheartedly to rid herself of garters and stockings too. These she could wash out in the basin and leave to dry overnight if she thought Rory would sleep and not notice her immodesty.

Remembering the large linen shirts in Rory's trunk, she brightened. Those shirts were long enough to make a robe of sorts. She would leave on her chemise and pull the shirt over it, and while she wouldn't be fashionable, she would be modestly covered and comfortable. The quilted petticoat was much too large to fit beside the injured man in any case.

With that happy decision she at least wore something clean and dry, and she felt almost human again. Washing out her stockings in the basin, then carefully folding her small store of clothing over the captain's chair, she contemplated the problem of sleeping arrangements.

Last time, Rory had politely slept on the very edge of the bunk so as to give her a respectful space to sleep in. Tonight he lay unconscious in the center of the bed, with only two narrow sides to choose from. Neither choice looked comfortable, and there was certainly nothing decent about the position she would be in, but the only alternative was the floor, and she already knew how cold and hard that was.

With a sigh of resignation, Alyson felt Rory's brow, bathed it gently in cold water, and when he did not stir,

climbed in beside him. If she lay between him and the
wall, she was less likely to be thrown out in the night.
She would just have to pray her bedmate would not
roll over and crush her.

She adjusted the blanket over both of them. The heat
of his fevered body engulfed her, and she felt comfortably warm for the first time in . . . What? Days? How
long had she been gone from home and propriety? Two
scandalous nights at least. She was truly ruined, but that
was the least of her worries now. For her own safety, the
well-being of the man beside her had to come first.

Drowsily she curled into a tighter ball, and her bottom
brushed his hip. She had never shared a bed with anyone
before. The sensation made her nervous. But after a
while the sound of Rory's gentle breathing and the warmth
of his closeness relaxed her, and she slept.

Whether from the light filtering through the porthole
or a change in her patient's breathing, Alyson woke with
a start. Sometime during the night she had rolled over,
and she found herself lying close to Rory's side, her hand
resting on his chest. The position seemed an oddly natural one to be in, and she found herself relaxing to the
even beat of his heart beneath her fingers. Only when
her brain belatedly remembered her predicament did she
hastily withdraw her hand. Cautiously she lifted herself
to observe the captain's countenance. He seemed to be
sleeping, and she breathed a sigh of relief.

The fresh bandage she had applied to his head was still
clean, so the bleeding had finally stopped. He felt fever-
ish, but not dangerously so, she judged. When he woke,
he would need better nourishment than had thus far been
provided. Surely, now that the storm had abated, they
could prepare some hot broth.

Preparing to climb over his unconscious body to see
about breakfast, Alyson felt a sudden change in her
patient's breathing, and glanced downward to find Rory's
eyes wide open and focused on the open neckline of her
impromptu nightshirt. Between the ungainly and unfastened shirt and the loose, low-cut chemise, an immodest
amount of bosom was revealed, and Alyson gasped as she
looked down at herself. Hastily she pulled the edges of the
shirt neck together and tried to complete her maneuver,
but Rory's hand caught her waist and held her there.

His gaze slowly drank in the disheveled beauty of black tresses tumbled in thick curls about her breasts and shoulders, the sleepy look of those dreamy light eyes, and the puffy pout of full lips begging to be kissed, and his fingers tightened on her waist as he gave an involuntary groan.

"What devil's trick has cursed me with angels in my bed?" He closed his eyes again, and without the strength to hold her, let his hand fall back upon the bed.

Hurriedly scrambling to the floor, Alyson gazed back at him dubiously. Rory's dark face seemed a shade paler than usual, and there were lines of pain about his beard-stubbled lips. She didn't know whether to scold him or worry that he was delirious.

"Perhaps a drink from your flask will help?"

Rory heard the uncertainty in her voice and saw clearly in his mind's eye the wanton beauty she had just revealed to him, and his body stiffened with the raging conflict between desire and propriety. He was in no humor for being proper, but neither had he the strength to satisfy his desire. He had definitely dug himself a hole to hell and fallen into it. It would take a saint to dig him out again, and he certainly wasn't any saint, as the irritation in his reply showed.

"Get out of here, Alyson. Fetch William."

She stared at him in disbelief at these monstrous orders. "You would have me run about your ship in little or nothing? Fie on you, sir! I'll go when I'm ready, and not before."

Rory held his eyes closed against any further onslaught to his already beleaguered senses. "If you think I'm going to lie here and watch you dress yourself, you're madder than I thought. Get out, Alyson, now. Or get back in this bed with me."

That seemed a very odd choice to make. She almost contemplated climbing back in bed with him, since she felt much safer there than roaming a ship of strange men in her chemise, but something in Rory's tone warned that that would not be a wise choice. Grabbing up her gown and praying, she ran out of the cabin.

Luckily, the small common space where the captain normally shared his meals with his officers was empty. Although she wore no stays or stockings, she struggled

into her gown and laced it as best she could, then set off
to explore the ship.

She refused to return to the captain's cabin. She had
taken all the humiliation one person should have to suffer. Easily finding William scrubbing pots in the galley,
she sent him to tend to the wretched Maclean. She, on
the other hand, set about making friends with the garru-
lous old man who served as cook. She might know nothing about sailing, but she was at least familiar with the
activities of a kitchen.

Sometime later William returned to inform her that the
captain wished her to return to the cabin. Alyson looked
up from the dough she was kneading with a smile that
made the young boy's knees turn to jelly. Her reply,
however, gave him good cause to worry about the state
of his health if he had to carry the news back to the
captain.

"Angelo says I can hang a hammock in here. That way
I can get up in the mornings and have fresh biscuits
cooking, while the flour lasts." She added the last hastily
at a raised eyebrow from the cook.

Since she hadn't directly said no, William held out
some hope that he just hadn't made himself clear. The
thought of fresh biscuits every morning was very pleasant, but they held no comfort against the captain's wrath.

"Ma'am, my lady . . ." He wasn't at all certain where
she stood in the rank of things. She wasn't like any other
he had ever known in his short life, but he had caught
glimpses of ladies on the streets of London, and she came
closer to matching their mystique than any other he knew.
"The captain wants to see you now."

"Hell hasn't frozen over yet," Alyson replied cheerfully.

William threw an anguished look to Angelo, but the
cook was struggling to maintain his usually stern demean-
or and wouldn't meet his eye. Perhaps the lady was like
the simpleton that used to live in the village, and she
really didn't know what she was saying. That thought
gave him courage, and he hurried to report to the captain.

He wasn't so certain a few minutes later when the
captain raised himself up on his elbows and stared at
William as if he had just removed his head and put it
under his arm.

"She said what?" Rory glared at the terrified boy,

began a string of curses; then, realizing he was taking out his temper on a go-between, he sank back against the pillow and contemplated what he should do now. Hell hasn't frozen over, indeed. He didn't want to know where she had learned that particular phrase. Working in the galley would undoubtedly teach her a good many more. It would be much easier if she did stay in the galley, but this was a smuggling ship, and some of his crew he wouldn't trust in a dark alley, and certainly not with a woman like Alyson.

His gaze fell on the stack of neatly folded undergarments that had taunted his imagination all morning. She was out there roaming the ship with practically nothing on. It didn't take a great deal of thought to discover what had caused her anger. Or he assumed it was anger. The boy had said she seemed quite cheerful. With Alyson, who the hell could tell the difference?

Angelo would look after her for a while, but she was his responsibility. He would have to learn to deal with it. Staring at the ceiling, Rory ordered more calmly. "Tell her she cannot go about barefoot, and that if she does not get in here and put on her shoes and stockings, I shall personally get up and come after her."

"Aye, aye, sir." The boy leapt to do his bidding once more.

Alyson contemplated this new message with more interest. The weather had turned warm again, and the kitchen fire provided quite a nice heat, but she was not accustomed to going barefoot. She would dearly like to have her shoes and lovely petticoat back, but she had no privacy in which to don them. That was the whole problem with this ship. She had no place in it.

She puckered her bottom lip in a frown. It wouldn't do to have Rory coming after her. He should be resting. If anything happened to him, she could be in serious trouble. With a sigh, she threw the bread dough back in the bowl, covered it, then wiped her hands on the apron Angelo had given her. She would have to confront Captain Rory Douglas Maclean and find out his intentions.

Not realizing she was marching off to war, William smiled in relief as the lady proceeded toward the captain's cabin as ordered. For anyone to defy the captain seriously disrupted the orderliness of this world as he knew it.

Rory's eyes were closed when she entered the cabin, and Alyson hesitated, letting her gaze sweep over him anxiously. Someone had helped him to shave, and he had obviously felt well enough to sit up and allow someone to change his bandages. He now wore no shirt at all, just the binding around his chest. With fascination she noted his shoulders were as sun-browned as his face, and she felt her cheeks pinken slightly at this unseemly thought.

She was still hesitating, daydreaming, when he opened his eyes and stared back at her. The look on his face was almost tender, but he covered it quickly, pointing at her clothing. "I will not have you go about catching your death of cold. Put those on."

Alyson did nothing so simple as picking up the offending articles and donning them. Instead, she drifted to the side of the bed and touched cool fingers to the portion of his brow not covered by bandages.

"You're still warm. I think you're supposed to be drinking lots of liquid. Can you sit up?" She calmly proceeded to sit down on the edge of the bed beside him, like the lamb beside the lion.

Rory closed his eyes and groaned inwardly as his body suddenly leapt in response to her unexpected proximity. Without her stays, her gown would not close tightly, and she was practically spilling out of her bodice. It was so much easier to play the part of gentleman when everybody concerned was wrapped in several dozen layers of clothing and surrounded by people. This forced intimacy with such unassuming innocence was harsh retribution for past sins.

He would have to keep reminding himself that she was an innocent, that it was his fault she found herself in this situation, and that she was now his responsibility. She thought of him as an uncle or older brother. That would have to be the attitude to take.

"I am fine, lass. I'll keep my eyes closed. You go put on yer stockings and things. It's not so warm that ye can be cavortin' about in yer bare toes."

The soft burr of his R's indicated he was not entirely in control of himself, and Alyson gave him a puzzled look. Perhaps his head hurt, and he did not wish to admit it. Obediently she rose, and turning her back to him, pulled the heavy petticoat up under her skirts. Then she sat down and began to work on her stockings.

She heard a soft moan from the bed and turned to glance over her shoulder, but Rory was lying with his arm over his eyes. She adjusted her garters, slipped on her large-heeled shoes, and returned to the bed.

"Rory?" she questioned softly.

That was the first time he had ever heard her use his name, and Rory slid his arm away to look up into the full loveliness of her face. Was it God or the devil taunting him for his sins? She was so lovely standing there, that black cloud of hair tumbling about her shoulders, those wide gray eyes watching him with all that trusting innocence. She was everything he had ever imagined a woman could be, and he had no right to be in the same room with the likes of her, even if she were but a poor orphan. The fact that she was the granddaughter of an earl and as rich as Croesus put her beyond the pale for him. Fate was almighty cruel.

"Pull up a chair, lass, and don't look at me as if I'm dying. I've survived worse than this." While she actually went to do as told, Rory struggled to pull himself upright. His ribs felt as if all the demons in hell were ripping at his insides while the devil pounded at his head, but he had to make things straight with the girl.

Alyson brought the chair but poured a glass of water from the pitcher and handed it to him before she would sit down. Rory grimaced at the stale taste, but drank it as she settled gracefully into her chair.

"Lass, we'll have to learn to live together these next weeks. I'm that sorry about it, but I couldna do aught else at the time. I could save you or the ship, but not both, without taking you with me. Do you understand what I'm telling you?"

Alyson knit her hands together and studied the craggy planes of the Maclean's dark face. Fierce brows pulled down over a nose that had almost the look of a hawk's beak, but there was a tenderness about his lips when he spoke to her, and it was to that she responded. She never had been very good at her lessons. Instead of listening to the teachers' words, she had studied their faces. In the same manner, she heard Rory's explanations.

"I don't know anything about Charleston." That problem had dwelled on her mind ever since he had mentioned it. "I've never met savages before, and I don't think I'd like living in log cabins very much. Do we have to go to the colonies?"

Rory grinned at the odd tack her mind took. Here he was worried about their sharing sleeping quarters, and all she wanted to know about was red Indians. Maybe he ought to let her lead the conversation, just to see what fascinating byways they found themselves on.

"Charleston is a lovely little town, lass. I think you'll like it. I have friends there who come from a fine old family in England. They have a daughter who must be about your age by now. It's the best place for you while I finish my trading."

Alyson's eyes widened. "You will be leaving me there? You can't do that. What will they say? What will they think? I have no clothes. I have no money. Why would strangers wish to take me in?"

Rory could see she was suddenly near tears, and the tremble of her bottom lip created all sorts of manic urges. He wanted to take her in his arms and hold her and tell her everything would be all right. He wanted to say, "marry me and I'll take care of you forever." He wanted . . . Lord, but he wanted. And couldn't have.

Steeling himself, Rory tried to talk sensibly, knowing that applying logic to Alyson was a futile quest at best. "I will tell them you are my ward, that your maid died on the voyage, your luggage was washed overboard—anything you like, lass. They will take you in because they are my friends and will want to be yours. I'll buy you some new clothes and you can go to parties and teas and whatever else young ladies do with their time."

"But I don't know if I can repay you! I'll have disappeared off the face of the earth, and Mr. Farnley will think I'm dead! I'll be penniless and homeless, and all because of you, Rory Maclean! You can't do this to me. You've got to take me home."

He was rapidly losing patience. "Alyson, I can do any damn thing I want! I don't know why in hell you were wandering the streets of London looking like a char girl when I told you to go with Deirdre to Lady Hamilton's, but you did, and you're bloody lucky I found you before you ended up in some French brothel. You haven't got the sense God gave a goose, and if I were to send you back to London, Cranville would have you for dinner, and that could be a lot worse than being stuck on a ship to the colonies. So for now consider yourself penniless and homeless and let me take care of things."

He couldn't have hurt worse if he had slapped her. She had thought that, out of all the greedy, mean people in the world, Rory Maclean was her one true friend, but he just considered her a foolish nuisance who had got in his way one too many times. She had spent too many years hiding from the snide, cutting comments of the outside world to allow him to see her hurt, however. Gathering her ruffled feathers around her, Alyson rose and walked toward the door.

"Thank you for saving my life. I shall do my best not to disturb you for the duration of the trip."

"Alyson, wait!"

His cry came too late. The door closed softly behind her.

8

Rory did not allow her to get away with it, of course. Whatever he might have become in these last years of exile, he had been brought up to treat ladies with respect and courtesy. True, he had encountered very few ladies since leaving home at the age of fifteen, but that did not mean he didn't know what was proper.

Alyson glared at him mutinously when he sent two of his more trusted men to fetch her from the galley at day's end. He had given her time to cool off, given himself time too, although anger wasn't exactly the worst of Rory's problems where Alyson was concerned. He tried to meet her appearance with composure, but as he well knew after staring at them all afternoon, she had not trusted him enough to take off her gown to don her stays. Her ripe figure taunted him with every move she made.

"You summoned me, my lord?" The sarcasm was laced with sugar as she stood between the two huge sailors and defiantly met the gaze of the man in the bed. He had put a clean shirt on over his bandages, and tied his auburn hair back in a queue, but she knew a pirate when she saw one.

"Jake, Dougall, you can go now." He dismissed his officers with a nod and they obeyed immediately, although he detected the wry lift of a brow from Dougall. He owed the man explanations, but he was damned if he knew how to give them.

He turned his gaze back to Alyson. "There is good reason for the superstition that a woman on board is bad luck. Men who have been without women for long periods of time tend to go a little crazy. I'll not have knife fights and brawls among my men over your tender little body. From now on, Dougall or I will escort you to the galley and back when you wish to go. Only William and Angelo will be allowed in the galley when you are there. If any other man enters, William has orders to come directly to me. At all other times, you are to stay in here or with me. Do you understand?"

She didn't, actually, but something in his tone told her he had not the patience to explain any better, so she disregarded the question as rhetorical. She jammed her hands in her pockets and let her gaze wander to the curtain of sheets and ropes that had been constructed during her absence. The bunk and a small table and the cabin door were on this side of the curtain. She knew his desk and trunk were on the other side. What could the purpose be other than to make an already cramped room a little narrower?

"I should think it would be easier to dry your linens in fresh air," she observed, finally concluding this could be the only purpose of the ropes and sheets dividing the room.

Rory closed his eyes and prayed for divine guidance. He had spent the entire afternoon composing that impressive sermon, and it had drifted right past her like the wings of a dove. What did he have to do to connect with the intelligence he knew existed behind all that innocence? Remembering a night when they had discussed men and marriage, he tried to appeal to that lucidity.

"Unless you wish us to live as man and wife, I thought to offer you some privacy. I have no strong objection to making a lass such as you my wife, but I thought you stated your dissatisfaction with that happy state."

That brought her back to reality, Rory noted dryly. She stared at him as if he had grown horns and tail. With some effort he raised himself from the bed and, standing, poured a swallow of Scotch from his flask to a tumbler on the table. He would be a drunkard by the time this journey ended.

Alyson watched his movements with a hint of suspicion, but when he made no move toward her, she returned to contemplating his staggering words. In his very odd way, the Maclean had said he would marry her. Of course, given the circumstances, any gentleman would be forced to say that. She had learned that much during her short stay in London. The odd thing was that she didn't think it was propriety that made him say it.

She flashed him a puzzled look, but Rory was drinking his whisky with every appearance of unconcern. She spoke without thinking. "I have considered what you said about Mr. Farnley putting my inheritance in a trust so a husband could not touch it, only I doubt that Alan could be made to take me now. But if Mr. Farnley thinks me dead and gives away my funds according to my instructions, I will have no choice but to marry you."

Rory gulped the whisky down the wrong way, spluttered, coughed, and grabbed for the flask to take another drink. She would drive him mad before she killed him. Marriage! He had introduced the topic as so patently ridiculous that she would have to wake up and realize her position. Never had it entered his head that she would in any way entertain the idea. He would have to disillusion her quickly. He knew he couldn't have what he wanted, but Alyson still lived in a fantasy world.

"I daresay Mr. Farnley will not be too amenable to giving away all that money without a fight. Does Cranville get it then?" he calmed himself and tried to think his way out of this one.

Alyson took the chair he offered and settled her homespun skirts as if they were silks and satins. "I expect he thinks so, but he will be rudely disappointed. When Mr. Farnley suggested that I needed to have a will, I told him

I wanted it all to go to homes for mothers and children
who have no family to care for them. I think he started
drawing up something he called a trusteeship that will
build a home and operate it. I do not understand the
details, but I do know Cranville won't get a farthing of
it."

Rory chuckled. He could just imagine Cranville's black
face when presented that instrument. He would take it to
court, undoubtedly. The solicitors would eat it up for
years. Alyson might be naive, but she was no simpleton.

"I don't think you have to worry about your inheritance, then. By the time I return you to London, Cranville
will be in debtor's prison and you will be free to choose a
more suitable husband. If Alan is so foolish as not to
want you, there will be a hundred more better than he.
You might even meet a better man in Charleston."

Alyson accepted the glass of wine he poured for her,
and watched as he settled himself with some degree of
pain into his chair. He had already dismissed the idea of
marrying her. If Rory didn't want to marry her, then she
didn't think any man would, but she held her tongue. If
her inheritance was safe, she need not marry at all.

"How long do we have to live like this?"

"Depending on the winds, six weeks, more or less. I'll
try to make it as easy for you as I can, lass. We've not
had an auspicious beginning, I know . . ." Rory gestured
helplessly. He would never understand what went on
behind those inscrutable light eyes.

"Perhaps it is just the blow to your head. You have not
quite been yourself," Alyson decided, biting her finger
thoughtfully. That would explain many things. If he didn't
want to marry her and only considered her a nuisance, he
really shouldn't look at her as he did sometimes. Perhaps
he didn't even know he was doing it.

Rory gave a sigh and took another gulp of whisky as
William carried in their meal. Maybe another blow to the
head was what he needed to bring him to his senses. He
was almost beginning to agree with her.

Later, when he lay in the hammock hung on the far
side of the curtain, listening to Alyson undress and wash,
he again contemplated a good solid blow on the head to
put him out of his misery. He could hear the rustle of her
petticoats as she slipped them off, and could almost see

her standing there in that billowy sheer chemise he had glimpsed behind her bodice. She would take that off too, so she might wash. He greatly suspected she wore nothing else beneath that, and he tried not to groan as he imagined all those soft round curves uncovered. Why couldn't she be one of those skinny gangly women who needed all the hoops and stuffing to make them round? Or even one of those stout females who needed extra stays to cinch them in, and even then looked as broad as they were tall? Why did she have to be so confounded perfect that he could find no fault or flaw?

"Shall I turn the lantern out, Maclean?"

He felt her voice whispering in his ear even though he knew she had not gone beyond the curtain. He couldn't bring himself to answer. It took all the strength he possessed just to stay where he was and not get up to see what she wore to bed.

Assuming he was already asleep, Alyson contemplated checking on him to be certain the fever had not returned. Some second sense warned her that might not be wise, and she turned down the lantern instead and climbed into the empty bunk. It would feel very strange to sleep there alone. She almost wished Rory would join her. She had liked knowing he was beside her. He made her feel strangely warm all over, almost as if he were kissing her. Did that have something to do with why men and women married?

Curling up inside the blanket, she tried to imagine what it would be like to be married to Rory. It wasn't easy. He had never even really kissed her. She was certain that marriage and kissing went together. She was also quite certain that kissing Rory would be a very pleasant experience. That one brief touch had been more exciting than anything Alan had done. She tingled down to her toes just thinking about it.

The day had been a wearing one, and these thoughts gently carried her off to sleep.

The vision came to her sometime during the night, so Alyson could not tell what was real and what was not. She only knew it was dark, and that she was someplace strange, and that she was afraid. She opened her eyes to find a man hovering over her, pressing against her, pinning her down. His masculine nakedness filled her vision, and terror shivered down her spine as she realized she was naked too. Whimpering softly, she lifted her gaze to the man's face, but she did not need the sight of his wild eyes to tell her it was Rory. When she felt something piercingly hard pressing between her thighs, she started to scream, but he smothered her with his kisses. His hands were hot as they ran down her cold flesh, and she felt herself struggling oddly, rising against him as if to push him off. His kisses fed on her mouth, and his hands held her imprisoned. Only when she felt the final pain of his possession did she scream. And scream.

Rory fell from his hammock and cursed the pain shooting through him as he stumbled toward the curtain. The whimpers had woken him, but it had taken her scream to jar him into action. Surely no man of his would dare enter this cabin while he was in it. What in hell could be wrong?

Alyson thrashed against the blankets, her eyes open but staring blankly into the low light of the lantern. Puzzled, Rory sat down upon the bed and tried to take her hands, but she fought him off. Could a person dream with her eyes open? She didn't seem to be conscious that he was there.

Gently he lifted her struggling figure into his arms. She wore only the loose chemise, but his mind was not on that now as he tried to calm her hysteria. She fought him until he had her pulled firmly into his lap and his arms closed around her. Then she collapsed, weeping, against his shoulder. Awkwardly Rory caressed her back, holding her tight. Thank God he had worn his breeches to bed, or she would have something to scream about. She was so soft and light in his arms . . . He kissed the top of her head and tried to murmur sensibly reassuring words.

"Hush, lassie, it was naught but a dream. I won't let anything hurt ye. I promise I won't. Shhh, my little one, do not greet so."

He was holding her, reassuring her as if she were a child. And she could feel the rough fabric of the bandage around his chest and the buttons of his breeches against her hip. He wasn't naked as in her dream. And neither was she. It must have been a dream, a terrible nightmare. Alyson cowered in the strong hold of his arms, seeking comfort from his greater strength. Rory would protect her, wouldn't he?

But looking up into his face, she saw the face of the strange Rory—the one whose brandy eyes were not gentle but burned with a strange fire she did not understand. His hold on her tightened, and she knew he meant to kiss her, just as the Rory in her dream had. Terrified, she tore away.

Rory let her go. He did nothing to stop her. Surprised, Alyson sat in the middle of the bed and pulled the blanket around her, feeling the sudden chill at the loss of his embrace. He was watching her with curiosity, but he made no move that she could consider threatening.

"Will you tell me, Alys?"

The soft burr of his voice and the familiar pet name brought tears to her eyes. It was all so strange, so new. She had nothing of her past, her home, anymore. She was all alone, and there was only this man to remind her she had once been loved. Her grandmother had talked with an accent like his, and she had called her by that name too.

"It was a dream. A terrible dream. I'm sorry. I did not mean to wake you."

Rory heard the tears in her voice and his hand instinctively lifted to brush at the moisture on her cheek. She flinched from his touch, and he pulled away in puzzlement. Not until now had he realized Alyson had always come to him trustingly, allowing him a familiarity that no other would have. Not until she withdrew it did he have the sense to recognize it or know how precious it was to him. What had happened to suddenly take away that trust?

"Sometimes it helps if you talk about it, lass. Do you have these kinds of dreams often?"

It hadn't felt like a dream. She had seen him, just as she had seen other things at other times that made no sense. But she couldn't explain that to him. Only her grandmother had understood what she meant.

"I used to dream about my father. It's odd, but I never dreamed about my mother, just my father. Sometimes I would see him walking down the path to the beach, or sitting in the library, staring at the fire. Other times, he was in strange places I didn't recognize, but I always knew he was my father. Is that odd, or do you ever have dreams like that too?"

She seemed calmer now, and Rory relaxed. He didn't think he could get to sleep anytime soon after that, and he rather enjoyed talking to her and watching her with her hair all tumbled about her lovely face. He contemplated this choice of topics she had chosen.

"My father died when I was sixteen. I remember him very well, but I can't say that I ever dreamed of him. I thought your father died before you were born. How could you know him in your dreams?"

Because they weren't dreams, but Alyson did not bother to explain that. It would be like saying she saw ghosts, which she apparently did. "There was a portrait of him in the hall. I would recognize him anywhere. He was in the navy, and he wore his uniform and had a big white-trimmed hat under his arm. In the portrait, he wore one of those fat old-fashioned wigs, but in my dreams his hair was golden. I once asked my grandfather about it, and he said yes, that would be the color of his hair. So I know it's him."

An officer in His Majesty's Navy. Gad, but it was a good thing her father wasn't alive now to see his daughter on one of the free traders that plagued the British frigates in colonial waters. That was all he needed, someone in the navy with a personal vendetta against him. They had been after his neck for fifteen long years. It made his throat itch just to think about it.

Idly, just to keep the conversation going, Rory inquired, "Do you know how he died, lass?"

The commonplaceness of the question and the lilting reassurance of Rory's warm voice made it easy to forget her fears. Alyson drew her knees up under her chin and recited the explanations she had been given long ago.

"He was in the navy, as my grandfather had been in the navy before him. It was a family tradition. Of course, since he was the only son, it was expected that he would not stay, but he liked it, until he met my mother. Before she died, my mother said he had promised that he would resign his position, but he had to complete this one tour of duty. She went out and visited the ship and met his captain and everything. Or at least that's what my grandmother said."

Alyson lowered her voice as if speaking only to herself, imagining what it must have been like for those two lovers, met by chance and separated by fate. What chance would they have had if fate had not intervened? The earl's son and the poor daughter of a Highland widow. But it had worked between her grandmother and grandfather. Anything was possible.

"My mother claimed they were wedded on board, that the captain wrote it down in his book for all to see, but they knew it wasn't in the church and proper and legal like it should be. It was his last night onshore, and they just pretended that it was real. Then he sailed away to the West Indies and never came home again."

The story, or perhaps the way she told it, was haunting, an eerie echo of love lost. Rory could see it now, could easily see how it had happened, and looking at the bent head of the result of that union, he was glad it had. He touched a finger to her chin and lifted it until he could see the misty gray of her eyes.

"Your mother was Scots, was she not?" Alyson nodded. "So they met in Scotland?" Alyson nodded again, her gaze finally fastening on him with curiosity. "Then if your mother's words are true and they said their vows in front of witnesses in Scottish waters, under Scots law, they were well and truly married. They didna need the kirk to make them man and wife."

Alyson's eyes widened into two miniature beacons of light. "Then I really would be Lady Alyson and have just as much right to my father's house as Cranville."

Rory grinned and tapped her nose lightly. "Unfortunately, lassie, you have the same problem as before. Without the captain, the log, or the witnesses, you canna prove a thing. Remember that if you should ever feel foolish enough to do the same. Churches don't go down in the sea."

Alyson made a wry face. "It would serve my cousin right if I could find that log. Or a survivor." She brightened. "There may have been survivors. The ship went down in a storm off the coast of one of the islands. Some of the men could have escaped, couldn't they?" And maybe her father was one of them. Maybe that was why he wasn't dead in her visions.

Rory didn't smile at her sudden eagerness. "Do not

start dreaming fancy dreams, Alys. A storm in the islands is no laughing matter. Unless there was someone there to pull them ashore, they would most likely be battered on the rocks or coral or swept back to sea. The currents are wicked, and in a storm . . . The chance is slight. And even if one man survived, how would you find him? I'm sorry, lass, but you had best be happy knowing they loved each other."

She smiled sleepily. She had known they loved each other, but now she knew a little bit more. They had been married, and there still lingered some chance she could prove it, if only to vindicate her mother's good name. She yawned, and Rory patted her hand and rose from the bed.

"You can sleep now?"

She nodded, and reluctantly Rory left her to return to his side of the curtain. Maybe, just maybe, he was doing the wrong thing by saving her for some elegant nobleman with name and title and little more. Why should he let her go for the likes of an Alan Tremaine or Earl of Cranville?

And then he remembered the brandy in his hold and the false letters of marque in his desk and the man he meant to kill back in Scotland. They were just the beginning of any number of reasons why he couldn't marry now. Even Cranville looked good compared to the likes of him.

9

Charleston, Spring 1760

Their first sight of land came at the beginning of May. Fair winds and calm seas had courted them all the way, and Alyson's pale face had taken on a honey hue from the hours she spent watching the crew climbing through the rigging.

That was what she was doing now, Rory observed as the first cries of "Land ho!" echoed from above. Instead of searching for the shoreline, Alyson was sitting on the lid of a water barrel watching the brisk flapping of the sails in the wind. She had made a cap of sorts out of an old piece of linen, but the bit of scrap and ribbon could not hold that mass of ebony curls in place. They frothed about her face like a wild sea, and Rory wondered for the millionth time what it would be like to have those raven tresses spread out on a pillow beneath him. He could almost feel what it would be like pressed into her welcoming softness, teaching her the wild ecstasy hiding behind those delicate features.

It was no use contemplating it, however. She seemed more comfortable in Dougall's company than his. The easy camaraderie that had sprung up between them had disappeared the night of her dream, never to come back quite the same. She regarded him warily and took care that she no longer came close to him, a pattern of behavior that did not seem natural to the free spirit Rory had seen in her. But it had made the strain of these weeks easier. If she had not learned to restrain her carefree behavior, he would have bedded her by now. The need was so great as to bring him anguish every time he looked on her.

Unaware of the thoughts of the man at the tiller, Alyson finally brought her gaze down from the sails to the green haze of land in the distance. She would soon be in another country, an alien place where she knew no one and no one knew her. She had wanted a new identity. What better way than this?

If only she didn't have to worry about relying on the Maclean. If she had the coins the thieves had stolen from her, she could disembark and walk off and never have to see him again, and then the vision couldn't possibly come true.

It had taken these weeks and snatches of conversations and glimpses of male habits to knit together some meaning to the vision. Most of the understanding came from what she felt inside when Rory came near her. Her insides grew shaky and uncertain and she waited anxiously for his every touch. She had no genuine knowledge of what happened between a man and a woman, but she knew now her complete vulnerability. The thought terrified her, but more than that, the hollow ache inside her when Rory touched her hand or just gave her that tender smile—that terrified her even more. She *wanted* what he would do to her. That thought alone was enough to make her contemplate escape. Rory had no mind for marriage, and she had no mind to bring a child into the world without it.

Alyson frowned at the horizon, contemplating a plan that had begun to form nebulously in her mind since discovering the hoard of gold in Rory's trunk. She could not escape without the coins to keep her until Mr. Farnley could send her a bank draft. That would be months and months. But if she could just borrow some of Rory's money, she could repay him easily when her funds arrived. The only objection was that Rory would never lend it to her without knowing all the whys and wherefores, and that was what she hoped to avoid.

If the thought of leaving Rory caused some pang of regret, she ignored it as she had learned to ignore all the other hurts in her life. She had lived without friends all these years and not felt their lack to any extent. She could very well go on living without them.

They did not reach Charleston or attempt the river until the tide turned at dawn the next day. Rory allowed Alyson up on deck as he maneuvered the ship up the narrow channel, and he pointed out various buildings and called their names out as they sailed by.

To Alyson's amazement, the town appeared to be built entirely of sturdy brick structures, some of them quite substantial. Up the bank from the river she caught glimpses of several lovely residences. After the streets of London, these streets seemed clean and orderly, and even the market opening up near the waterfront appeared fresh and new. The air was hot and clean, without the incessant belching of smoke from thousands of chimneys. Charleston was definitely the nicest place she had ever seen.

Thrilled with this discovery, Alyson almost forgot her plans, until Rory came down to collect her and lead her back to the cabin. His words as they returned inside sent her heart anxiously to her throat.

"I need to leave the ship briefly to arrange for the unloading of my cargo, lass. Stay here and tidy yourself up, and when I come back, we'll go into town."

He was already pulling on his coat and reaching for his hat as he spoke. She noticed he was careful to tie his jabot and shake out his cuffs and put on his best vest also, but he didn't bother with the formality of a wig. She would have to learn the manners of this new society, but judging from Rory's appearance, it could not be so very different from London.

He accepted her silence as agreement and strode off rapidly, caught up in the business at hand and not noticing Alyson's withdrawal. When he was gone, she set her plan into motion.

She carefully counted out the number of coins from Rory's hoard that she expected to need. Perhaps if they weren't enough, she could supplement her income somehow. She wouldn't make a very good teacher, but she could be a lady's companion, and she sewed a fair hand. Rory would scarcely notice the amount she took, but she would not betray his friendship by taking more than she needed. Carefully she penned out a note with supplies from his desk, stating her name and the amount she owed, and promised to repay one Rory Douglas Maclean upon demand. She had learned the words from the markers Jack and Dougall used when they played cards. They sounded quite legal enough, so Rory need not worry about being reimbursed.

This time she was not so careless about storing her coins. Quickly she opened up holes in the quilting of her petticoat and stored a coin in each little pocket, resewing them as neatly as she was able. She kept a few small ones in her pockets for immediate use.

By the time she was done, she was terrified Rory would have returned, but the men seemed to be going about their chores as usual, if Dougall's shouts from above were to be believed. Now came the hard part. She used Rory's brush and shaving mirror to straighten out her hair and tidy her fichu. The gown was well worn after so many washings in seawater, but she could not wear the sailor's breeches she had occasionally used when her own clothing was being cleaned. She must strive to somehow look like a lady, if a poor one. Then she had to contrive some way to get off the ship without being seen.

That was an impossibility, of course. The ship had docked at a wharf, and a gangplank had been thrown out

so Rory could reach land, and men swarmed all around
it. The sailors were busy checking lines and sails and
scrubbing the decks. She might possibly skirt them. But a
small crowd of people was gathering at the wharf, specu-
lating on the contents of the ship, and she dreaded the
thought of walking off alone.

Dougall spotted her small figure hovering in the shadow
of the bulkhead, and he hurried forward to greet her.
The captain's orders had been very specific concerning
the lady. They didn't include allowing her to wander
unaccompanied on the deck with the men.

"Miss Hampton, is there something I can do for you?"
He swept off his hat and made a hasty bow.

Dougall was some years older than Rory but had not
Rory's hard appearance of a man who looks into the
future and sees his own destruction. Bushy red-gold eyebrows made his pitted face remarkable, and the kindness
in the faded blue of his eyes made it clear why he and the
captain had managed to get along for so many years.

"Rory asked me to mend his good linen shirt, but I
have used up the last of the thread on my petticoat. I
know he wishes to wear it today, but I hated to bother
anybody. Everyone else has his own chores. There ought
to be some way I can do this one small thing myself.
Surely there is a booth where I can buy notions in that
market somewhere?"

Dougall knew what she left unspoken. She was afraid
Rory would be angry for wasting the thread on some
frivolity, leaving him without a decent shirt to wear. He
had been a recipient of Rory's tempers often enough,
and the captain's mood had been uncertain at best throughout this trip. He might very well raise a ruckus over such
a simple thing. The decision didn't take a minute to
make.

"I'll send William out to look for some thread. He will
have it to you in plenty of time, I promise. The captain
had quite a few errands to run before he'll be back."

"Thank goodness." Alyson managed to look relieved
instead of frustrated. She tried another tack. "It's been
so long since I've been on land, might I go over with
him?" She looked embarrassed, and glanced away. "There
are some other things I really would like to buy."

A confirmed bachelor, Dougall wasn't about to speculate on what kind of personal items a lady would like to buy alone, but he was certain there were all sorts. Still, the captain's orders were quite clear, and he wasn't about to start breaking them now.

"If it were up to me, I'd say yes, Miss Hampton, but the captain gave strict orders that you weren't to go about without me or him. It's for your own protection, you know."

Alyson sighed and continued to look out over the wharf. Small boats, canoes, and pirogues maneuvered in between the larger ships, unloading the fresh produce and fish for the day. People were starting to accumulate among the fish and vegetable stalls to inspect the merchandise as it arrived. Soon the wharf would be quite crowded. If she could just get across that plank . . .

"I'm sure it is, Dougall, but it does make it very difficult for me to show my gratitude for his care. How can I surprise him when he is always with me? His best coat needs new buttons, and . . . well, I ruined his blotter when I emptied most of his inkwell on it. I thought it might please him if I replaced it."

There was such soft longing in her voice that Dougall felt his lonely heart crushed between her tender hands. It was obvious that the lass had fallen in love with the captain. It wasn't the smartest thing in the world to do, but she was young and impressionable, and the captain had his good points. He would do better to take a wife like this and settle down than to continue his current wayward path. Perhaps the lass had the right of it after all.

"All right, Miss Hampton. Wait here a minute while I tell Jake where we're going, and I'll escort you personally. The captain can't object to that, once he understands how you feel."

Alyson breathed a sigh of relief as Dougall strode off to relay his message. She had never done anything so difficult in her life, but she had a feeling it would get worse instead of better. Now she would have to lose poor Dougall in the crowded streets of Charleston.

That part went quite well. She lingered so long over the selection of buttons in a storefront just off the wharf that the bored man took to watching the pretty girls passing in the street. It was a simple matter to have the shopkeeper show her his warehouse of goods behind the store, and from there to step out the rear entrance into the street above the one Dougall waited on. She was free!

Fat matrons in unpanniered skirts elbowed her aside as Alyson tried to lose herself in the crowd around the market. Black servants perversely blocked her way when she tried to get around them. Small boys in slouch hats and loose homespun shirts dodged in and out around her legs, nearly sending her stumbling into a portly wigged gentleman sniffing at a fruit she did not recognize.

After the routine of six weeks on a ship, this crowd of colors and people, sights and sounds and scents, was exhilarating, but exhausting. Her stomach rumbled at the sight of fresh strawberries and the smell of pastry baking nearby. She wrapped her fingers around the coins in her pocket and wished heartily to indulge in a brief spurt of marketing, but she could not. She had to find somewhere safe before Rory found her gone.

She would have enjoyed sharing the excitement of Charleston with him, she realized with regret. He would have told her what those strange fruits were, explained why the black ladies in their drab clothes wore those colorful kerchiefs around their heads, told her which of those scrumptious-smelling pastries would be the best. Instead, she had to hurry past them all without knowing, wondering if she would ever know, or if she would ever see him again.

The whole purpose of her flight was to never see Rory again, she reminded herself. She was bad for him, her vision told her clearly. She could see no other explanation for that stranger she saw behind his eyes sometimes when he looked at her. She would make him do wicked things, and he would destroy her. She could interpret that much of her vision. She couldn't let that happen.

That thought put a brisk pace in her step, and she traversed the market stalls without further delay. A shop window for a milliner made her hesitate once she reached the main thoroughfare, however. Rory had said she looked no better than a char girl in this gown. It would really be better if she could look more like a Lady Alyson Hampton, but dressmakers took time. A new hat would be quick and easy, but one glance down at her faded skirt declared she would be wasting her money. Someone would think she had stolen it.

She would have to quit her daydreaming, as Rory called it, and get on with it. She had already made up her mind that the first place to go was to a solicitor's. Mr. Farnley had been extremely helpful; surely she could find some gentleman in Charleston who would be the same.

With that thought in mind she passed up the shop windows and began scanning the wooden signs and discreet brass plaques on brick walls to determine which ones might be solicitors. It wasn't quite as easy as she thought it would be. There were taverns aplenty, shoemakers, clothiers, dry-goods merchants, and blacksmiths, but she trudged up and down dusty streets in a sun that grew rapidly hotter without finding any trace of anything resembling the impressive edifices of Farnley and Farnley.

Carriages bearing ladies in beautiful silks and parasols rolled by. Wagonloads of straw and farm products rattled past from some bountiful source. Rough seamen in baggy breeches and elegant gentlemen in long frock coats and all the levels in between brushed past her or stared after her, but she dared question none of them. She could scarcely tell them whom she was looking for when she didn't know herself.

At last she escaped the crowded street of shops and found herself in a quiet side street of shuttered brick town houses. The shutters were pulled closed on many of the elegant windows on the south side, and Alyson imagined the rooms inside to be dark and cool against the sun. Her throat was parched, her feet ached, and she felt filthy and disheveled from head to toe. Perhaps she ought to just apply for the position of servant at one of these elegant houses and learn more about the city before searching further.

It was then that she saw the sign in the lower window of one of the older structures: "Harold B. Lattimer, Attorney-at-Law." Would that be the same thing as a solicitor? Mr. Farnley knew the law. He could write wills and things. Perhaps this Mr. Lattimer could do the same.

Alyson gazed up at the brick town house with its facade of evenly spaced Georgian windows, matching lintels and pediments. It looked respectable, weathered, and well-cared-for. What better way to judge the occupant?

Having approved of the office, Alyson gave no thought to the occupant's approval of her. She knew who she was and where she was going, and although she was arriving in a slightly bedraggled state, she had very good reason for doing so. With all the confidence of naiveté, she entered the building.

A male clerk standing at a tall desk with an open ledger glanced up at her in surprise. He had seen her in the street earlier but had never thought the little maid would come up the walk. He gaped openly at the unfashionable mop of black curls around a delicate face moistened with the day's heat, and said nothing.

Since there was no one else about that he could be staring at, Alyson self-consciously brushed down her woolen skirt and checked her fichu to make certain nothing had become disarranged, then met the gawping stranger's gaze directly. "I have come to see Mr. Lattimer," she announced calmly but firmly.

The youth closed his mouth and ran ink-stained fingers up under his tilted wig. The accent out of those lovely lips was pure gold and totally unexpected. She looked little more than a waif off the streets that he needed to direct to the back door. No waif he had ever known spoke in those clear, rounded tones, however. Even he didn't speak as well as that.

Prodded by the slight lift of her eyebrow, he stumbled into his usual inquiry. "May I ask who's calling?" Any person of respectability would produce a card, but this one didn't even have a bag to carry one in.

"Lady Alyson Hampton, if you please. It's quite important. Is he in?"

She had to be mad. That could be the only explanation. He knew all the names of the nobility in town, including the guests at the governor's. There was not a Hampton among them. Not that anyone expected an English noblewoman to dress like a scarecrow, either. She was off her head, barmy.

He took the excuse she offered. "No, my lady, he's not in right now. Do you wish to make an appointment?"

"I'm afraid I don't have time for that. I need to see him immediately. Do you know when he will return?" Alyson was growing restless. Rory would know of her escape by now. She did not know for certain, but she

suspected he would be combing the city for her. She
daren't leave the safety of this house until she had some
guarantee of protection.

The youth stuttered over his lie. "Anytime, I suppose,
but he's busy. If you would . . ."

Without listening to whatever senseless suggestion he
might make, Alyson picked up her hopelessly heavy skirt
and advanced toward the door leading into the rest of the
house. She would not be thrown out into the street by a
mere clerk. "Thank you. I will make myself at home
until Mr. Lattimer arrives. If you would, a glass of
water—if you have nothing better—would be refreshing."

These last words were uttered as she pushed open the
door and sailed into the hall. To her right was obviously
a library of sorts. To her left, a gentleman in powdered
wig and old-fashioned full-bottomed frock coat was just
stepping from an office, hat in hand. Alyson heard the
clerk's protesting "Mr. Lattimer!" behind her, and she
frowned. The boy had lied to her.

The gentleman glanced up in surprise at his clerk's
alarmed cry, to meet the imperious frown of a most
remarkable young woman. Hair flying loose like a child's
after a day's romp, patched and faded skirts lifted as if
they were satin, to reveal a petticoat of expensive quality
although equally worn, the girl lifted matchless gray eyes
to his with a grace and hauteur he would have recognized
anywhere. He made a polite bow.

"Is there something I might do for you, Miss . . . ?"
He looked inquiringly over her shoulder to the nervous
lad behind her.

Alyson supplied the name the slow-witted youth did
not. "Lady Alyson Hampton. Mr. Lattimer, I assume?"

"Yes, of course, my lady." With a courtly gesture he
indicated the way into his office, then again threw an
inquiring look at his clerk. The boy shrugged, and Lattimer
scowled, then followed the strange young woman into his
office.

Alyson had already made herself comfortable in a leather
chair by a window overlooking the street. Her small feet
sat primly side by side and her soft hands were crossed in
her lap as if they were clad in expensive mittens. Black-
lashed eyes followed him as he settled into the chair by
his desk.

"Now, my lady, how might I help you?"

"I have been abducted and brought here against my will, Mr. Lattimer. I would like you to send a letter to my solicitor in London at once informing him of my whereabouts and that I am quite well. He will need to draw on my funds and send me a bank draft sufficient for a comfortable return journey when it is safe to make one. If at all possible, I would also have him look into pressing charges against my cousin, the Earl of Cranville, because while he walks the streets, I am not safe."

If it were not for the precise quality of her speech, Lattimer would have been quite convinced she was insane. A man who deals with the public learns to separate the wheat from the chaff quickly, and he set about doing so now.

"Your solicitor's name, Lady Alyson?"

"The senior Farnley, of Farnley and Farnley, Chancery Lane, London."

He knew the firm, and the name Cranville was beginning to ring bells. He jotted down the information while he gathered his thoughts, then took another stab at disconcerting her. "I should think the Earl of Cranville to be a trifle old to be your cousin, Lady Alyson. We belonged to the same club when I was attending Oxford, and he was considerably older than myself."

"You knew my grandfather? That is wonderful. Then you will understand my situation." Alyson sat forward eagerly in her chair. "You will help me, won't you? It is terrifying to be in a strange place where I know no one. And I am so afraid my cousin will try to prove I'm dead and steal my money, and then where would I be? And I cannot return until I know he cannot harm me again."

This wasn't quite as easy as Lattimer had hoped. Cranville ought to be worth a fortune by now. His ships sailed into Charleston on a regular basis. He had owned mines over half of Cornwall when Lattimer had first known him. If this young woman was any connection at all, she was sitting on a fortune.

Wheat from the chaff, he reminded himself. Glancing at her strange costume, he made one more attempt. "You do realize that your request will take a considerable amount of time and money?"

"If you are going to charge me an exorbitant amount,

you will have to collect it from Mr. Farnley, for I am going to have to replenish my wardrobe and find somewhere to stay until I have a reply." Pulling out the gold coin she had placed in her pocket for just this purpose, Alyson set it on the desk before the startled solicitor. "Will this be sufficient to begin the process?"

Genuine coins of the realm were such a rare commodity these days that Lattimer had to overcome the urge to pick it up and test it with his teeth. It sparkled and winked with the sunlight from the window, taunting him. He could try a murder case on the basis of an advance like that. As far as he was concerned, if the coin were genuine, so was the girl's claim.

"Lady Alyson, that is more than sufficient. I shall have that letter out on the next ship, in the packet of a personal friend of mine. You will be assured that a response will be immediately forthcoming. Now, I will need to know more of your story so Mr. Farnley may begin filing charges, but first, why don't I take you to meet my wife and daughter? I think you will be much more comfortable once you have had a chance to rest from your ordeal."

Proud of her accomplishment, Alyson sailed out of the office on the arm of Mr. Howard Lattimer, attorney-at-law. Let Maclean try to find her now.

Maclean was trying to do just that. Returning to his ship loaded down with packages full of all the feminine finery he could acquire at a moment's notice, he found the *Sea Witch* strangely quiet. He had not given any of his men permission to go ashore. There was the small matter of a hold full of illegal brandy that had to be disposed of first. He had paid the necessary bribes, and the wagons would be arriving shortly. Where in hell was his crew?

Stalking through the empty ship, Rory entered his cabin in a fury edged with panic. Dougall waited for him, a sorry Dougall with bloodshot eyes and loosened jabot and an entire bottle of Scotch nearly emptied before him. Rory glanced around, and finding no Alyson hiding behind the curtains, felt his panic grow a little closer. He dropped the packages on the bunk and grabbed his first mate by the collar.

"Where is she, Dougall?"

"I dinna know. It's all my fault. I wrote my resignation. It's right there." He hiccuped and pointed to a sodden note on the table. He didn't even try to free himself from Rory's stranglehold. "She just disappeared. I have no idea . . . The men are searching for her. Maybe she just got lost."

Rory flung his friend back in the chair with disgust. "How, Dougall? How did she just disappear? Did she take wings and fly? Did a hole open up in the deck and swallow her? How? Dammit, man, tell me!"

"She wanted to buy you buttons." Dougall's words slurred only a little bit as he carefully recited his story. "I was right there with her. I dinna think it'd hurt. She's in love with you, you know, and she wanted to make you happy, and she was going to buy you buttons and a blotter." Remembering that odd piece of information, Dougall threw a nervous look to the captain's desk. The blotter looked perfectly intact to him.

"Buttons? Blotter?" Rory stared at him with incredulity. What did love have to do with buttons and a blotter? Was Alyson's madness contagious?

Dougall tried to maintain some semblance of dignity as Rory flung him back in his chair. "That's what she said. So I took her up the street and waited while she picked them out. Only I looked away for a minute, and she was gone. I dinna know how, Maclean, honest, I dinna!"

Rory knew how—the same way she had done it several times before. She just picked up those dainty little feet and walked out, right into a pot of trouble, every time. He was going to wring her neck when he found her this time.

"I'm not accepting your resignation, Dougall. You're under arrest until I have time to hang you. Now, come along and show me where you lost her."

He didn't know what had sent her flying this time, but this was the last time he was going to pull her pretty little neck out of trouble. Damned if he wouldn't have the brat branded and manacled when he caught up with her.

10

Three days later, Rory hadn't found a whisper of Alyson's whereabouts. His men had willingly tracked through every brothel, tavern, and inn in town, and there were plenty. Alyson was too distinctive not to be noticed, but no one had seen her.

That left only alternatives Rory couldn't bring himself to consider. It wasn't possible for Cranville to have followed her here. There was no reason for anyone else to murder her on her first day in town. But unless she were dead and buried, he could think of no other way she could have disappeared totally.

He had even checked and found all the other ships on the river that day. The ones still in dock reported no sign of her. The ones that had sailed were fishing vessels that would soon return. He had to have missed something, somewhere, but for the life of him, he couldn't imagine what.

He didn't know why it was destroying him. He had cursed every minute of every day since she had come into his life. She had caused more consternation and confusion and frustration and downright terror than any one person had ever inflicted upon him, except one, maybe, and that one was his mortal enemy. He ought to be glad she had walked out of his life. Why, then, did he feel the skies were dark and the sun didn't rise, when it was May in Charleston and a cloud never crossed the sky?

It made absolutely no sense. He was almost glad, instead of angry, when he finally stopped to call on Kerry and Katherine, and young Margaret greeted him with her news. She was on the way to tea with a real English lady just over from London, she informed him proudly. It didn't take a long stretch of the imagination to guess who the lady might be, and a great sense of relief swept over

Rory, before anger replaced it. For once, unexpectedly, she had landed on her feet. As Margaret chattered on, he began to relish the thought of Alyson's expression, should he appear. Damn, but he was going to get his revenge for these days of torment.

Learning that Kerry was still at the plantation and Katherine had gone to visit her stepdaughter, Rory invited himself as Margaret's escort. The eighteen-year-old's green eyes turned up to him in adoring wonder, but he had not the conceit to notice. His mind was entirely on a certain pair of mist-colored eyes, and he paid no heed to any other. Offering his arm, he stepped out into the bright heat of a Charleston street with one of that town's most eligible young ladies, but his thoughts were solely on revenge.

Seated in the small but elegant Lattimer parlor, garbed in a white and rose-flowered dimity the mantua-maker had just completed, Alyson listened to her companion's conversation with a half-smile. Jane Lattimer was a year or two older than she, older than the usual marriageable age for this society, she had ascertained from several mother-daughter conversations. But the strong-willed Jane had rejected what few suitors she had acquired, and Alyson was beginning to understand why she had so few. Her opinions on every subject were strident, her scorn of the vast majority of the male populace did not go unvoiced, and although at heart she was a very kindly person, her demeanor gave no such impression.

So it was with great surprise that Alyson observed a softening change in Jane's expression as she gazed out the front window in expectation of Miss Sutherland's arrival. Alyson had looked forward to meeting more of this society now that she was appropriately attired, but she had been of the opinion that today's guest was female. The look on Jane's face was not that of a young woman anticipating the arrival of her best friend. Excitement trembled through the older girl's hands as she dropped the draperies and hurriedly seated herself on the vacant sofa behind the tea tray.

Still, Alyson had no warning when Captain Rory Maclean walked through the parlor door. He was accompanied by the loveliest, daintiest blond she had ever had the misfortune to see, but Alyson's thoughts could focus only on Rory and his rage. Her heart stopped beating and didn't resume again until she looked into Rory's cold gaze; then it began to pound at such a thunderous pace it echoed in her ears.

"Captain Maclean, how good of you to call!" Jane was gushing effusively, leading her guests to their seats, neglecting introductions as she attempted to part Margaret from her escort in order to place the captain on the sofa beside herself.

Since the tea tray indicated their hostess's seat, and there was no other sofa in the room, Margaret reluctantly relinquished her prize to take a chair beside Alyson. Rory, despite Jane's admonitions, remained standing. His gaze scarcely left Alyson as introductions flowed around them. As Jane attempted to introduce him to her guest, he waved her words aside.

"Lady Alyson and I have already met, haven't we, Alys?" The insinuation in his voice and the use of her familiar name was quite plain to the other two women; they looked slightly shocked and extremely curious. Alyson simply looked at him in that vague manner of hers and took a sip of tea before answering.

"Oh, yes, I arrived on the good captain's ship. We are old friends. Rory, do please seat yourself before you give Miss Lattimer a crimp in her neck."

That airy pronouncement quite neatly took the poison out of his words, and Jane and Margaret looked decidedly relieved, if not still a good deal curious.

Alyson looked too damned beautiful to strangle. He should have known better than to try to fluster her. The only times he had ever seen her perturbed were times when she had reason to believe no one would see her. Remembering how she had cursed him and sworn she would follow him to hell if he died, Rory studied her placid countenance with a little more care. He wanted explanations, and he would have them if he had to pull them from her by force, but for now he was content to watch her.

Alyson felt his gaze as a physical presence lingering on her hair, caressing her throat, boldly touching her bosom. She had never been so uncomfortable in her life, and it took all her capacity for control to keep from squirming in her chair. She answered questions politely without knowing what she said. She sipped at tea and nibbled at sandwiches without knowing what passed her lips. If the glances of the other women grew even more curious, she was not aware.

Rory was the one to react first to Jane's increasingly sharp remarks. He was aware that on past visits Jane had smiled upon his appearance, but his thoughts had always been more of the business to be transacted than of the women around him. Alyson had managed to distract him, but there was still business to be done. If Jane's remarks were for his benefit, he would put an end to them. He had no partiality for sharp-tongued females.

Retrieving his hat, Rory bowed courteously to his hostess. "I trust you ladies will forgive me if I depart hastily. To be surrounded by all this loveliness after weeks at sea has left me dazed, and I have forgotten an appointment. My ship will be in port a few days more. Is there any chance I can induce your lovely selves and your parents to join me for a small supper party at the inn where I stay?"

Rory noticed Alyson's wry grimace at this polished invitation, but scarcely took heed of Jane or Margaret's excitement. He had to hide the amusement threatening to turn up his own lips. His little lady did not believe him for an instant, and rightly so. He had no appointment, stayed at no inn, and knew the proud parents of these young ladies would never consent to their visiting a sailors' tavern.

"Oh, Captain Maclean, I am certain my mother would be delighted if you could come to dinner this evening. You may ask my father then about your party." Jane rose and boldly laid her hand upon Rory's coat sleeve to hold his attention.

"How could I resist such a flattering invitation?" Achieving what he sought, knowing by Alyson's angry intake of breath that she had seen through his ploy, Rory bowed himself out.

Alyson fielded the eager questions of Jane and Margaret with feigned disinterest, then pleaded a headache and retired to her room. The Lattimers had graciously extended an invitation to her to stay with them while waiting for some response to her letter, but they would not be so gracious if Rory chose to reveal the details of their journey. She had used the excuse he had provided earlier by saying her maid had died en route, and then added that she had escaped from her abductors with just the clothes on her back, but even that tale put her reputation to question. Rory could decimate it, and then where would she be?

She paced up and down the room in a fury of emotions. Rory had known she was here. He had not been surprised to see her. What did he mean to do? She knew he was angry. He had every right to be angry. But how could she possibly explain why she had run away?

She couldn't. She couldn't possibly look the Maclean in the eye and say, "I have every reason to believe you will violate me." That was not only insulting but also insane. She was mad even to consider it. If she started believing nightmares, she would have to begin believing her father's ghost walked the earth. She saw him just as vividly as she had seen Rory.

She could run away again, but it wouldn't help. If Rory destroyed her reputation, she would have to move out, she supposed, but she could go nowhere until she heard from Mr. Farnley. Charleston wasn't large enough to lose herself in, apparently.

It did no good to worry. She would have to wait to see what happened. Perhaps that exquisite creature he had brought with him would so fill his time that he would forget about her. It certainly seemed that both Jane and Margaret had taken a fancy to the captain. If she didn't know better, she could almost imagine a twinge of pain at the thought. She really was developing a headache.

By evening Alyson wasn't much calmer. The mantua-maker had hurriedly basted in the hem of a sea-green taffeta and a pink-and-white-striped underskirt for Alyson to wear for evening, but that did not help her dismal mood. She glared at the pink cloth roses pinned to her bodice and detested the entire ensemble, but it was too late to protest now. The colors were all the rage in London, as she had told the dressmaker, but that did not make her appreciate them any more. She felt like wearing scarlet tonight. Brilliant, bold scarlet with a bodice that plunged to dizzying depths. Give Rory something to think about while he spent his flattery on Jane.

Such a rage of emotion did not suit her. She had gone

through life cosseted and protected by the cotton batting
of her grandfather's love. She ached for that safety now.
These emotions bubbling through her were too raw and
painful to endure for long. If Rory would just go away,
she could return to normal. Even Alan had never stirred
more than a quiet happiness in her until that day she
came to her senses. She would give anything to return to
her former idyllic peace now.

Deciding she had dallied long enough, Alyson gave the
mirror one last frowning glance. She had no maid to
dress her hair, and powder made her sneeze, so she wore
only her own dark hair pinned closely to her head. Unfortunately, that style did not suit the abundant thickness
of her hair. It escaped in soft tendrils wherever it could,
and where it was supposed to lie flat and prim, it curled
and billowed. Muttering a curse she had learned from
Rory, she stalked out.

Just as she descended the lovely curved rosewood staircase, Rory entered the wide hall below. A maid accepted
his hat and sword, but his gaze never left the image
floating down from above. He caught glimpses of tiny
green heels and the delicate rose embroidery covering
slender limbs as Alyson lifted her skirts. The pleasurable
sight suddenly disappeared in a flutter of petticoats as she
spotted him. His gaze continued upward over the graceful sway of side hoops, to a tiny rose-bedecked waistline,
and lingeringly it slid over the full curve of her bosom.
The maid's gown and fichu she had worn throughout the
voyage had covered her from neck to toe. The décolletage
of this fashionable gown offered him a tantalizing view of
all that had been hidden. Had he been subjected to the
temptation of those milk-white curves earlier, he would
have gone mad for want of touching.

By the time Rory finally lifted his eyes to meet hers,
Alyson was glaring at him, and he couldn't control his
grin. He had begun to realize that to draw any emotional
reaction out of her at all was an accomplishment indeed,
and he delighted in being able to succeed so quickly. He
made a polite bow in her direction.

"Good evening, Lady Alyson. You appear in fine spirits this night. Shall we go in?" He nodded toward the
parlor, where the sound of voices hummed happily.

Alyson took a deep breath, forced herself to a smile

she didn't feel, and descended the remainder of the stairs in a daze. He looked too damned handsome with the white lace of his jabot setting off his rugged features and auburn hair to perfection. No, "handsome" wasn't the word. "Attractive"? "Appealing"? What did you call a man whose features were all wrong but made you want to touch them with lips and fingers? She was going insane. She knew she was. Perhaps the moon was full tonight. She had heard that the full of the moon had strange effects on the mind.

Rory caught her small white hand in his hard brown one. There was just a hint of lace at his wrist, and the smooth texture of the deep blue silk of his coat, reinforced with some stiff backing, accented the white and brown. Cautiously Alyson raised her eyes to the center of his chest. The coat was new, as was the simple white brocade vest. Unlike the more fashionable styles, his had only a modicum of gold thread and gold buttons to set it off. The rest was the deep blue silk that reminded her of the sea. She decided she liked this style much better than the elaborate ones, but she refused to lift her gaze any farther. Just the sight of that wide chest made her lungs constrict painfully.

Without saying a word, and ignoring his proffered arm, Alyson removed her hand from his and picked up her skirts to enter the parlor. Infuriatingly, Rory stayed close behind, his hand coming to rest at the small of her back just as everyone in the room turned to greet them. Not one eye failed to note this familiarity, and eyebrows raised as Rory made a show of seating Alyson on the sofa Jane had again appropriated, then standing behind her with one hand proprietarily on the cushion near Alyson's shoulder as he exchanged pleasantries with the elder Lattimers.

Alyson sat stiffly upright, away from that compromising hand, while Mr. Lattimer inquired into Rory's journey, subtly searching for the reason an English lady would board a ship known in these waters as a smuggler, if not a privateer. Her face stayed taut as Rory glossed over "old family relation," making it seem as if both their families had united in spiriting her away to safety. Mr. Lattimer would have to know that was nonsense, but the

ladies seemed to accept it with awe-filled exclamations
and sympathetic clucking noises.

She could not relax. Every time she tried to sit back,
Rory's rough finger began idly tracing patterns on her
bare shoulder. Even when she sat forward, Alyson felt as
if her corset were cutting into her lungs with each breath
she took. She kept waiting for the ax to fall. Sooner or
later Rory would exact his revenge for her tricking of
Dougall and disappearing without a word. That was understood between them. All she could do now was sit
breathlessly wondering in what manner it would come.

Perhaps he meant to take it out in small torments. He
gallantly led both Alyson and Jane in to dinner. He
seated Alyson first, and she could feel the warmth of his
breath against her ear as he leaned forward to whisper,
"We'll talk later." A shiver went down her spine, but by
that time he was on the other side of the table, seating
Jane and taking his place beside her, across from Alyson.

The meal was a blur. If Jane turned on hidden charms
for the reckless captain, Alyson didn't see it. The only
thing she recognized with any consciousness was the number of times she felt a heated brown gaze watching her,
taking note of her every movement.

By the time the meal ended, Alyson had surrendered
to the inevitable. She could not fight Rory. She didn't
even know where to begin. When he somehow separated
her from the others with murmured excuses, leading her
out into the walled garden behind the house, she didn't
even object. All she wanted to do was get it over.

The warm night encompassed them as their feet found
the brick walk and wandered. The scent of an early
night-blooming nicotiana perfumed the air, and Alyson
felt her senses awakening again. She couldn't avoid noticing the proximity of wide masculine shoulders at her side,
and when his fingers clasped hers, she didn't pull away.
The time had come.

Behind a hedge, out of sight of the house, Rory brought
them to a halt. He pulled Alyson around to face him and
stared down into the ever-changing depths of her eyes.
He saw a hint of blue behind the mist tonight, and
flowers might scent the air, but he smelled only the
heather of the hills of home. She had been here only

three days, but somehow she had acquired that perfume he thought of as so hauntingly hers.

Longingly Rory touched her ebony hair, only to feel her shiver beneath his touch. That woke him sharply from his reverie, and his expression hardened. "Why, Alyson? Why did you leave me to think you drowned or abducted and murdered? Why did you hide?"

The shiver was not one of fear, but of need. She needed Rory to touch her, to put his arms around her, to hold her and promise her everything would be all right, as he had done that night after her dream. She wanted to feel the muscular hardness of his chest, the pounding of his heart beneath her ear, the strength of his arms around her back. She wanted her own destruction.

With a sigh, Alyson disappeared into that vague world that protected her from reality. She could see Rory frowning down on her, waiting for an answer, but she had none to give. A small smile played upon her lips as she noticed the new leaves of the roses climbing a trellis just beyond his shoulder. She had never really paid attention to roses before. These had produced a single full bloom shimmering white in the moonlight, exuding a delicate scent that crept up unexpectedly.

Rory followed her fascinated gaze and cursed inwardly. Plucking a bud, he tucked it behind her ear. He should have known better than to confront Alyson with direct questions. This fey child was beyond his ken; he ought to leave well enough alone and get the hell out of here. Instead, he found himself promising the moon.

"You scared the hell out of me, Alyson, and I didn't like it. For now, I will assume you have your reasons. I would have taken you to Margaret's parents—they're much easier to live with than the stiff-necked Lattimers— but if you're happy here, I'll not quibble."

Alyson's attention drifted back to Rory, and a puzzled frown began to form upon her brow. "You aren't angry with me?"

Well, he'd succeeded in catching her attention, anyway. Rory plucked another bud and handed it to her. "Yes, I am, but what good does it do me? I could lecture you about the dangers of young women wandering strange streets alone until I was too hoarse to talk, and you would do the same thing again. I briefly contemplated strangling you, but that rather defeats the purpose, doesn't it?''

He was talking in terms she could understand, and a tentative smile began to replace the frown. Still, she refrained from standing too close. She was too aware of the hard body beneath the elegant silk breeches and coat. She returned her gaze to his face. "What purpose? What does it matter to you what happens to me?"

A very pertinent question. In her own roundabout way she had a knack for pinpointing the crux of the matter. Now it was Rory's turn to squirm. He shoved his hands in his deep pockets and frowned down at her delicate face illuminated by moonlight. His body gave one answer to her question, his head could think of a dozen more, but none of them had anything to do with what his conscience said was right.

"I feel responsible for you, lass. I brought you out here; I want to get you home. Is that so wrong of me?"

She searched his face and saw the lie there, but still she hesitated. His concern was genuine, and for that she was grateful, but the stranger lurked behind his eyes. She was wary of that stranger, for he stirred in her emotions with which she was not prepared to deal.

"I do not wish to be a burden to you," she replied stiffly. "I owe you for my life. I do not think I can afford to owe you for more."

That might be as close to an explanation as he would ever get, Rory surmised, and it wasn't enough. "Someday I might need friends in influential places. Let us leave it at that, Alyson. I want you to promise me you will stay right here until I get back from the islands. You are safe enough here, and I will not worry if you promise me that."

"How long will you be gone?" She tried to keep the tremor from her voice as she asked.

"A month, six weeks. It depends on the weather and other things. There won't be time for you to hear from Farnley, if that is what worries you. I'll be back well before then to hear what he has to say. If he says it is safe for you to return, I would see that you traveled on a sound ship with a good captain. Will you promise me?"

"I suppose there is no harm in promising what I cannot change. Will I see you again before you leave?"

"Aye, if I can, lass. I thought I might make a few inquiries about your father's ship while I am there, just to satisfy curiosity. Do you mind?"

Hope leapt to Alyson's heart with these words. There was the Rory she knew. She could hear the tenderness in the soft burr of his voice, and see it in his smile, and joy flowed through her veins.

Her smile reflected that joy, sending the blood pounding to Rory's head. He could not resist any longer. He would be gone for weeks, maybe months. He would have some reward now, a promise for the future, some payment for his restraint. His hand lifted to the dark curl at the nape of her neck; then he cupped her head in his palm, tilting her face so he could read the brilliant shine of her eyes.

He thought to seek her permission first, but he didn't want to chance her refusal. Without a word of warning, he bent to sample the full sweetness of her kiss.

The shock of his hard lips actually pressed against hers trembled through Alyson, holding her motionless for the length of time it took for the tremor to run from her head to her toes. Then his hand came up to touch her waist, guiding her closer, while his mouth moved gently, enticingly along hers, teaching her the response he wanted, and she was lost.

Her hands flew to his chest, burrowing into the silkiness of his vest, clinging to the rougher fabric of his shirt, while her head spun beneath the gentle ecstasy of his kiss. She responded eagerly, drinking of all the excitement she knew she would find there.

Her response led him on, and deliriously Rory hugged her closer, tasting of her sweetness, then pressing for more. His tongue teased at her lips while his arms wrapped achingly about her round softness. She filled his arms so perfectly, her breasts pressing into him with a promise that made his loins ache, her hips at just the right height so he need only lift her slightly to meet his own. He could not ask for more perfection.

The touch of Rory's tongue sent another shivering shock through her, but Alyson parted her lips willingly, eager to deepen the experience. Had she known what her body's raging response would be to this heated invasion, she would never have given in to it. As it was, it was all she could do to balance on her toes while their breaths mingled and Rory gently took possession of her mouth, exploring and claiming it as his own. Alyson leaned into his embrace, desiring to know more of these sensations, and Rory's arms tightened instinctively around her.

Finally sensing the completeness of her surrender, Rory retreated, returning Alyson to the ground and brushing her lips with a light kiss that drifted to her cheek and ear before he could bring himself to stop. He was reluctant to let her out of his arms. Although Alyson's petticoats protected her from feeling the extent of his need, there was nothing to protect him. The ache of it brought a cold sweat to his brow as he gently disengaged himself. Before he could apologize, Alyson turned those cursed eyes of hers up to him with perplexity.

"I thought you said I should not kiss a man unless he meant to marry me."

"Aye, and I wish I were the one who will someday have that pleasure, lass. You will make some man happier than he deserves. The moonlight has driven me to madness. I'll not abuse you so again."

Outraged but not quite understanding why, Alyson stared at him in confusion for a minute before replying. She could still feel the imprint of his hands on her back. Her lips burned with a fire he had fed and not quenched. She felt an ache in parts of her that no man had ever seen, and she somehow knew he had the means to ease that ache. And he refused. He set her aside as if she were some pleasant toy with no feelings of her own. She hated this man worse than she had ever hated Alan for his betrayal.

"If the moon is what leads a man to madness, I'll be certain to lead all my suitors down the garden path in its light. Then they shall be as mad as they think I am, and I can choose the one who kisses me best."

With a flounce of her skirts, she fled back toward the house, leaving Rory to contemplate his pain in silence.

11

Summer 1760

Rory called again before he sailed, but Alyson refused to see him. She probably had the right of it, and he should be grateful, but the ache of not seeing her was worse than the pain of seeing and not touching. At least when she was with him he could enjoy the pleasures of her delightful observations, the scent of heather, the sight of those gray-blue eyes turning color at every new wonder presented to them. He had not known how much he would miss all that until this week spent alone in his hollow cabin.

He was not a man easily led astray by women. He had a head for business and he used it to the exclusion of all else. He had a goal which came closer with every profitable voyage across the sea. After unloading the illegal French brandy, he had taken on a shipment of rice, indigo, and tobacco that the British customs officials thought intended for London. The goods would bring a high price in the ports of the British West Indies, an even higher price in the ports of the French colonies, a trade totally illegal under the Navigation Acts. In the Caribbean he would fill his hold with barrels of raw sugar and molasses and return to the colonies, where the rummakers would buy everything he could smuggle to shore. Rebelling against the injustice of forcing freemen to buy and sell only with a country on the other side of the world added a certain satisfaction above and beyond the profits he made. Rory had no great love for the injustices of British Parliament and Farmer George.

But the challenge and the satisfaction failed him this time. He found no joy in adding another bag of gold to his growing hoard with this journey. As the *Sea Witch* sailed down the river under Dougall's direction, Rory stared down at the fortune he had amassed with a restlessness he had not known before. He was not independently wealthy by any means. He had responsibilities that strained his pockets at times, but the amount he had invested back in England and the coins he kept with him for trading had almost reached a level where he could consider returning home, had he a home to return to.

Therein lay the problem. Rory knelt beside the trunk to see how much remained after paying the planters. He frowned as he realized it was a sum less than he had thought. The piece of paper he had shoved aside took on new significance, and he shook it open impatiently. If he were to return to Scotland, he would have to have the sum necessary to offer for the Maclean estate. Any inroads into that sum would delay him from that goal.

He almost laughed at Alyson's oddly phrased voucher. He didn't doubt her ability or willingness to pay the entire sum plus interest. He had fully intended to gift her with enough to replenish her wardrobe while she stayed in Charleston. He almost threw the paper away, but he enjoyed seeing the strongly rounded curves of her words, could almost hear her saying the stilted phrases. He neatly folded the note and placed it in his desk, where he could look at it again when the longing grew too strong.

Not having any idea of the meaning of the restlessness Rory's absence created in her, Alyson set out to assuage it by capturing the city. She began by exploring every nook and cranny of the lovely little town, delighting in each new curiosity to come her way, reluctantly restraining her purchases to those few coins she allotted herself each day. The coins went quickly, particularly when it was necessary to hire a mantua-maker for new gowns for special occasions, but she intended to make them last. The Charleston nights were too enchanting to miss.

Her list of suitors grew in proportion to the number of festivities she attended. No one knew she was only the bastard granddaughter of a dead earl, and no one asked. That no one bothered to inquire into her antecedents amused Alyson greatly, until her own discreet inquiries began to reveal that many of the families who entertained her had a skeleton or two to hide themselves. It seemed that in this fascinating country a butcher and a pirate could rise as high as an English lord. That made her enjoyment of the evenings that much greater, and she amused herself deciding which of these glittering ladies and polished gentlemen descended from pirates or Newgate deportees.

But as the weeks passed and she learned the streets of Charleston as well as the back of her hand and the same faces began to pall, the restlessness grew stronger. Rory had promised to search for news of her father, and she told herself she was impatient to hear if he had found anything. It didn't matter if she never saw the Maclean again, but she had to know of her father. Then she wanted to go home. She wanted to wander the rocky shores of Cornwall again. She wanted to see Deirdre and Mr. Farnley. She wanted something she could not put a name to, but it was not to be found where she was.

Margaret's parents invited her to stay with them for a while, and Alyson gratefully accepted. Jane had grown cool to her after Rory's behavior that night, and she was tired of pretending it didn't matter. The Maclean could have Jane, for all she cared, but she could not imagine his harsh brown face softening into tender lines when he held the likes of Jane in his arms.

Alyson enjoyed the carefree environment of the Sutherland household. It took some while to get all the names and faces straight, with children and grandchildren and various strays running in and out, but she found she liked it. Anna, the eldest daughter, or stepdaughter, was married to a former sailor who now worked as an associate of Lord Kerry. Maureen, the next eldest, arrived for a summer visit with her twins. She lived in New York with her husband, who was apparently making a name for himself as a portrait artist. And then Chad arrived from England, and the noisy household was almost complete.

Only a few years older than herself, but with Oxford and years on his uncle's estates in England for experience, Chad created the perfect foil for Alyson's quiet beauty. While she liked to listen, he loved to talk. When she preferred to watch the dancers, he preferred to propel her onto the dance floor. His open admiration of her charms made her shy, but she thoroughly enjoyed the ease of his generous friendship.

Katherine watched her guest's reactions to her charming son with speculation, but although the two spent as much time together as they did with Margaret, she saw no lasting attachment forming. It seemed a shame, since Alyson's odd manner of drifting off in the midst of conversations and her occasional startlingly astute observations reminded her much of her younger self, and Katherine felt closer to her than to most of her son's admirers. Still, they were young yet. There was time.

When July had nearly passed, the usual family trip to escort Maureen back to New York seemed in doubt, until Alyson understood that their hesitation was due to herself. They begged her to accompany them, but Rory was long past overdue and Mr. Farnley's reply should arrive any day. She couldn't bear waiting even the extra time it would take a message to reach her.

The Lattimers welcomed her again, Mr. Lattimer assuring her a letter should arrive soon. He had word that a British ship, the *Neptune*, would be arriving shortly, and he fully expected the letter to be carried on that worthy vessel. Alyson refrained from asking if he had heard anything of the *Sea Witch*. Rory should have returned a month ago, but she would not give Jane the satisfaction of hearing her inquire.

When word came at the end of July that the *Neptune* had actually entered the Cooper River, Alyson began pacing up and down the parlor floor. There had still been no word from Rory. What if the *Neptune* carried a letter telling her to come home? She had promised Rory to wait, but he had promised to come weeks ago. How could she leave without knowing what had happened to him? How could she not leave at the first opportunity?

Perhaps the *Neptune* would not have a letter. Perhaps she was worrying over naught. 'Twas foolish to worry over things beyond her control. She would have to collect herself and keep occupied until Mr. Lattimer returned at lunch.

The Lattimer household sadly lacked good reading material, so Alyson joined her hostess in the small upstairs parlor, picking up a corner of the embroidered coverlet Mrs. Lattimer was working on. The lady greeted her with a smile but little conversation, and they sewed in silence, Alyson listening for any sound that might indicate a messenger.

The only arrival was her host as he returned for the midday meal. Alyson politely greeted the attorney as she came downstairs, and to her surprise, he gestured for her to join him in his study.

Trying to hide her hopes, she followed him in. He stood with hands behind his back, rocking on his heels, looking pleased with himself. He had news, she knew he had, and she waited impatiently for him to impart it.

"I told you I would get an expeditious response to your problem, Lady Alyson. As I predicted, the *Neptune* carried your reply in today."

Alyson clasped her hands together and settled into the nearest chair. "May I see it, please? What does Mr. Farnley have to say?"

"He did much better than merely sending you a letter. A lady of your consequence shouldn't be so shabbily treated. No, he has sent a personal representative to see to your safety. I have made arrangements for you to meet with him this afternoon."

A personal representative? Alyson's hopes sank and she moved uneasily in her chair. She didn't need someone to hold her hand all the way home. She wanted to leave when she was ready to leave, and not when some man told her it was time to go. She had grown accustomed to doing things her own way these last few months. A "personal representative" sounded very much like some officious aide who would insist on things being done properly.

Clenching her fingers into her palms, Alyson looked up to her host with the question that bothered her the most. "And the *Sea Witch*? Has aught been heard of her? I promised Captain Maclean . . . He was to tell me which ships would be the safest to return on."

Lattimer frowned slightly. "Captain Maclean is a smuggler and quite possibly a privateer, my lady. He cannot be relied upon to keep schedules. He's an excellent young man, but his occupation leads him into dangerous waters. He could be out chasing an unsuspecting frigate or down at the bottom of the ocean. I'm sure you can rely on Mr. Farnley's representative to guide you in your choice of

vessels. The *Neptune* is an excellent example. I should
think that would be the one to choose."

Alyson hid her anguish behind a vague smile. "Of
course, Mr. Lattimer. Does Mr. Farnley send me a letter? I shall need to reimburse you for your trouble."

"That will be discussed this afternoon. Shall we dine
now, my lady?"

Alyson picked nervously at her meal. Why hadn't Mr.
Lattimer brought this obnoxious "representative" with
him? This waiting to see what fate had decreed for her
did not help her state of indecision. She wanted to know
what had happened to Rory. Surely, if his ship had gone
down, news of it would have come to Charleston? Why
couldn't her visions come to her when she needed them?

And then it occurred to her. If the vision she had of
Rory and herself were to come true, he had to be alive!
Perhaps something had happened to the *Sea Witch*, perhaps she would never hear of what had happened to her
father, but what really mattered was that Rory still lived.
She could not go back to Deirdre with that doubt still in
her mind, but she no longer had cause to doubt. Sooner
or later, Rory would come after her.

That should make her even more nervous, but Alyson
felt strangely relieved, and excitement began to build.
She hurried to prepare herself for her meeting with Mr.
Farnley's representative with a much lighter heart than
before.

She entered the office on Mr. Lattimer's arm, and a
gentleman in a rather drab brown coat hastily rose and
scraped a bow. Alyson studied his nearsighted gaze and
the ink-stained calluses of his hand and decided this must
be one of Mr. Farnley's clerks. He would make a dull but
easily manipulated traveling companion. This one wouldn't
send her to her cabin and order her to stay there!

As usual, she paid little heed to the conversation.
Apparently Mr. Farnley had sent this clerk instead of a
letter, but Mr. Lattimer seemed pleased with whatever
arrangements had been made. They obviously thought
her too stupid to deal with the financial details of the
journey and her stay, and she didn't attempt to disillusion them. She was beginning to learn the advantages of
letting men think themselves superior. They were so easy
to fool when it came time for her to behave otherwise.

It became apparent that they were waiting for her to reply to some question she had missed, and Alyson offered a faint smile. "I'm so sorry. My mind wandered. What were you saying?"

The smug look on both their faces brought a bubble of laughter to her lips. Rory wouldn't have put up with it for a minute. She had confused him briefly on a few occasions, but he was quick to learn and much too sharp by far. He had a way of making her listen, or perhaps she just enjoyed listening to him more than these fools. She was going to miss him on this journey home.

"Mr. Clive would like to show you the cabin that has been reserved for you on board the *Neptune* to see if it meets with your approval. The vessel is part of your grandfather's shipping line, and they will make any changes you request, but they are already behind schedule by making this extra stop in Charleston. The captain is understandably in a hurry to be off. If you would go with Mr. Clive, I can send someone to the house to make arrangements for packing your things. You could be off on the evening tide if we act swiftly."

Alarmed by this sudden rush, Alyson instinctively retreated. With a vague gesture, she addressed the attorney. "I must have a maid. And there are several gowns yet to be finished at the mantua-maker's. I cannot possibly leave in so short a time."

Mr. Lattimer spoke with suppressed impatience. "Lady Alyson, far be it from me to give you advice, but it seems as if your best interests would be served if you journeyed on your own ship. And as it is your ship, you should be interested in seeing that it returns to England on schedule, so as to make the best profit. Your gowns can be sent on a later date, and a maid has already been hired. Mr. Farnley is quite efficient."

He was quite right about that. Too damned efficient, if anyone asked her, but she could see they had no desire to hear her opinions. She was getting a little tired of these abrupt removals, but at least she could leave with some decorum this time instead of running off at midnight in a public coach or being thrown over the shoulder of a pirate and fighting the British navy through the Channel.

With a mild look of reproval, she took Mr. Clive's

skinny arm, nodded her head in curt farewell to Mr. Lattimer, and allowed herself to be escorted to the river.

The wharf still fascinated her with its exotic milieu, but Alyson tried not to be distracted as she searched for the ship that would carry her home. It was difficult to miss. The head of Neptune with its streaming locks bulged from the stern in a formidable manner. The merchant itself was nearly as large as a frigate, much larger than Rory's sloop. The towering masts seemed to scrape the sky, and Alyson's gaze strained to see the crow's nest on the mainmast.

Too large to dock at the wharf, the *Neptune* waited in the deeper part of the river channel. A rowboat waited to bring her aboard, and Alyson nervously joined the seamen in the little dinghy. In the reflective heat of the July sun off the water, she felt strangely dizzy, and her head began to ache just behind her eyes. Closing her eyelids, she touched her hand to her forehead, and the brilliant summer's day faded.

The gray mists in her mind parted, and instead of the formidable *Neptune*, she saw Rory standing at the bow of his ship, his hand shading his eyes as he gazed over some distant water. She recognized the eager impatience with which he shoved aside the spyglass someone handed to him. He looked ready to jump from the ship and swim for shore.

The next vision came and went much faster, leaving a sense of horror and bewilderment. Cranville! Her cousin's visage flashed briefly and dimmed. He seemed much changed, worried, somehow, instead of so arrogantly self-confident. But just the sight of him made shivers of fear run through her veins. He didn't appear to be in prison.

Alyson blinked and looked up and found herself already on board the *Neptune*. She could not shake the sense of alarm the vision of Cranville had instilled in her, and she met the captain's greeting with only a vague recognition of the introduction.

The captain's gracious welcome died at this reception, and he threw Alyson's escort a puzzled look. Clive made some gesture behind her back that he seemed to understand, and the captain made a formal bow and walked off. Alyson felt only the cold chill of alarm and looked anxiously toward the railing. The familiar sight of Charleston seemed a million miles out of her reach.

"I want to go back to shore," she announced suddenly.

Clive looked startled, then patted her hand reassuringly. "Of course, my lady. Just let me show you to your cabin. If there are changes that need to be made, we can order them before we go back into town."

That seemed reasonable. At least he wasn't arguing with her. She was still free to leave if she wished. Maybe she would just order the ship to leave without her. She ought to have the authority to do that. The only problem was that Mr. Farnley apparently hadn't sent her a bank draft. She had a few coins left, but not many. She couldn't wait too long for another ship.

The cabin Clive led her to had to be the captain's cabin, if she had acquired any knowledge of the architecture of ships at all. She could see where his personal pictures must once have hung upon the wall, and she wondered what he used for a desk now that the only one was hers. She ran her fingers over the disfigured wood. The captain had a bad habit of slamming hard objects when angry, she surmised from the dents upon the surface. The bunk had no curtains, but the heavy duvet looked comfortable. A braided rug lay between the bunk and a brazier. She would not need Rory to keep her warm in luxury such as this.

That thought depressed her, and she dismissed it by turning to Clive. "I must thank the captain for his sacrifice. You mentioned a maid?"

"Yes, my lady." He made a servile bow. "I will fetch her. Just one moment, my lady."

The minute he left her alone, Alyson left the cabin. Her visions were uncontrollable and usually meaningless when considered logically, but she was not overly given to logic. Instinct told her there was danger ahead, but she did not know if it was for her or for Rory or for both. For all she knew, Cranville could be the one in trouble, but this ship held a clue. It was her proximity to this ship that set off the alarms. She wasn't going anywhere on it until she knew it from stem to stern.

Not that she knew where stem or stern was. She simply wandered wherever her feet took her. Obviously a goodly portion of the crew had been given shore leave until the tide turned. The few men she met stared at her in disbelief when she smiled at them in greeting, and she was gone before they could recover enough to say a word.

She found the galley and the hold, but did not venture below. What she was searching for wouldn't be with the cargo. She hadn't found any sign of Clive or a maid or the captain, she realized. Perhaps she ought to return to her cabin to see if they were there.

This vague uneasiness brought her back to the companionway between the officers' quarters, and it was there that she heard the voices. Her feet halted as one particular voice struck fear in her heart. It couldn't be! Cranville couldn't be here!

Another voice interrupted, and she couldn't be certain she had heard right. How could Cranville be here? Her letter had warned Mr. Farnley of his treachery. Mr. Farnley would never have sent her cousin for her. She must be hearing things. She was overwrought and nervous and dodging at shadows.

"No, I'll surprise the girl when we sail. She's likely to take exception to my presence, actually. She'll blame me for her abduction, I daresay, so I won't be high on her list of people to see. But I'll not rest easy until I see her safe home again. She's a bit lacking in the upper story, but she'll come around eventually, they always do. But you've seen her, Captain. Don't you think she's worth the trouble?"

Cranville's laugh was unmistakable. With flying feet, Alyson raced for the deck above.

12

Rory's weathered visage grew decidedly grimmer as the buildings of Charleston came into view. Dougall sent him a wary look and kept out of his way. If the captain's black temper grew any worse, he would have a mutiny on his hands.

No one in particular could be blamed for the disastrous delays that had decimated the captain's usually calm demeanor. Sudden squalls followed by days of no wind at all had impeded their progress throughout the journey. Any seaman knew to expect that, although they had run into more than their fair share this time. The mix-up at the docks could be blamed on some incompetent clerk somewhere, Dougall supposed, but it wouldn't bring back the days lost while waiting to unload. And they had sailed without their full shipment of molasses because Rory had grown tired of the planters' incessant delays. It hadn't made any difference. They lost even more time avoiding a British frigate guarding the port where they had meant to sell the cargo. Another meeting place had to be arranged, with subsequent delays, although they had managed to unload the molasses faster than Dougall ever thought it could be done. Still, Rory hadn't been satisfied. He had been pacing that deck for days now, his temper growing ever shorter.

True, they should have been back by the end of June and not the end of July. But Dougall had thought they ought to be happy to be back at all. He had expected Rory to be grinning from ear to ear at the prospect of seeing the little lass again. He certainly wouldn't mind seeing that dreamy smile, even if she had played him for a fool. Anything could be forgiven for a smile like that.

Instead, another string of curses rang out from the bridge, and Dougall glanced up to see what had brought these about. He groaned at the sight of the British merchant filling the main channel as it righted itself in preparation for sailing. The tide would be turning shortly. The *Sea Witch* ran with it now, but if they had to wait for the big ship to embark before they could anchor, it would be hours before they could reach shore. Dougall discreetly removed himself to a task on a lower deck, out of range of Rory's fury.

Alyson's frantic race carried her to the rail, but not to safety. There was no convenient gangplank to escape on, no visible method of reaching shore. There had to be a rope ladder somewhere that she could climb down, but the shore looked an impossible distance away. Even if she could figure out how to lower a dinghy, the chances of rowing it to shore by herself were slim.

If she could only attract the attention of one of the small fishing boats . . . But it was a lovely day, and they were all out to sea except those too derelict to sail. Perhaps if she could just find a workman repairing one of the derelicts who could row out, she might slip away, but her screams would more likely attract Cranville than anyone on land.

She could hear footsteps coming up from below, and she quickly dodged behind a water barrel in the shadow of the bulkhead. She couldn't see who it was from here, but he wouldn't see her so readily either.

Perhaps if she could find the captain . . . Surely if she owned this ship the captain would have to obey her. But she suspected the earl had convinced him otherwise. She didn't know what instinct warned that the captain would believe Cranville before her, but she followed it. Only as a last desperate measure would she plead her case to a man who was obviously a part of the earl's plans for her.

She listened as the footsteps turned toward the stern, and she hurried in the opposite direction. It was early yet, but perhaps a fishing boat would be taking advantage of the tide to come in early. Anything was better than cowering in the shadows waiting to be caught.

Alyson cursed her wide petticoats as they caught on splintery barrel staves. Her high kid heels made it difficult to do anything quietly, but if she removed them, she would be walking on her skirts. She cursed her conceit in wearing the fashionable gown. She should have been better prepared.

As she finally caught a glimpse of the incoming river, Alyson's hopes soared. A ship! The sails were being trimmed in preparation for anchoring, but it was coming this way. All she had to do was make them understand she needed rescuing.

Alyson bit back a groan of dismay at this thought. Why would that tiny sloop down there dare defy a British vessel of this massive size? Even if she should make it clear that she needed help, what could they possibly do?

Knowing she would have no escape from Cranville if she allowed this ship to sail without making some attempt to escape, Alyson bit her lip in determination and hurried toward the railing. She would do whatever it took to get off.

Running from the shadows into the brilliant sunlight, she was momentarily blinded, but she could see the big white sails coming closer. She took off her small frill of a cap and waved it excitedly, but could not see a response. She reached down and removed her shoes, hoping to fling them to the deck to catch their attention, but when she stood up, her eyes widened.

The *Sea Witch*! Rory was coming after her! Her vision hadn't lied.

But he wouldn't even know she was here. He had no reason to look for her here. She could see the men climbing into the rigging now, preparing to take down the mainsail. They would be going into shore, and Rory would go to the Lattimers', and by the time he returned, the *Neptune* would have sailed.

Perhaps not. She cast a nervous glance to the *Neptune*'s rigging. The usual activity of a ship preparing to sail didn't seem to be in progress. They must be waiting for the rest of the crew to return. Still, the idea of waiting patiently for Rory to come to her did not appeal. What if he didn't go directly to the Lattimers'?

That thought and the sound of approaching footsteps made her heedless. She screamed. She waved. She flung her shoes as hard as she could across the narrowing gulf between the ships. One hit the water, but the downward draft carried the other so it glanced off the port bow.

A seaman knotting a rope in place looked up, startled. Before Alyson could scream again for help, a shout from behind her warned she had been seen.

Swiftly she lifted her skirt and began ripping at the ties of her petticoats. There would not be time to struggle out of her gown, but if she could unhook the petticoats she had worn instead of hoops . . .

"Alyson! My God, what are you doing? Alyson, stop that!" The shouts came closer, unmistakably Cranville.

The heaviest petticoat came off and she flung it over the side. If the *Sea Witch* didn't see that coming at them, they would all have to be blind drunk.

She threw a glance over her shoulder. Her cousin was almost upon her, and others were running up from below at the sound of his shouts. There wasn't time for thought.

She placed one foot on the railing and pulled herself up to the first rung.

At the first sound of a shout from one of his crew, Rory glanced in the direction of the *Neptune*. By pulling this close, he was effectively blocking the merchant's exit, but he wasn't overly concerned about delaying some pompous ass of a British captain. He expected the shout to be a warning, but the sight of a woman leaning over the railing, waving her petticoat, nearly tumbled him off the deck.

The petticoat sailed off on the wind, but Rory's sharp eyes had already seen the man racing down the other vessel's deck. Beyond a shadow of a doubt he knew who that petite figure climbing the railing was, and who it would be running after her.

Cursing, he shouted orders for the dinghy to be lowered, the mainsail set, and the cannon loaded. Then, throwing off his coat as he ran, Rory dashed down to the rail in his shirtsleeves to expedite the dinghy's progress.

Alyson hesitated as she threw her stockinged leg over the top rail, and Rory looked up with another curse as he saw Cranville bearing down on her.

"Jump, Alys, jump!"

"I can't swim!" she wailed, glancing over her shoulder once more.

The earl threw himself forward to catch her skirts, and closing her eyes, Alyson jumped.

Rory was in the dinghy and rowing toward the place where she had disappeared beneath the muddy waters before the ripples had time to break. He was aware of the shouts from both ships, of new scrambling for ropes and ladders and boats, but he kept his gaze focused on the circle of ripples. His heart beat faster than it ever had before, but he was already jerking off his shoes and preparing to dive in. Damned if he wouldn't do her a favor and follow her into hell to drag her back.

She came to the surface just as he hit the water. Grabbing a handful of soaked black curls, Rory jerked upward, pulling her face from the river. She gasped, then began a spluttering cough he could not rectify now. The *Neptune*'s dinghy was fast approaching.

"I'll have your head for this, lass," he growled, throwing his arm over the side of the boat. Unceremoniously he lifted her with his other arm and flung her half on, half off, while he clambered in without tipping the whole thing over.

Alyson fought to pull herself completely inside, but her skirts dragged at her legs and the coughing drained her energy. Impatiently Rory grabbed her by the waist and jerked her in, then struck out for the *Sea Witch*.

The commotion from the two ships had drawn a crowd to the waterfront. Excited, gesticulating spectators pointed to the other dinghy quickly keeping pace with Rory's. The sounds of Cranville's panic-filled shouts and the British captain's bellowed orders echoed across the narrow strip of river. Grimly Rory reached the *Sea Witch* and the ladder his men held ready.

He wouldn't have time to get Alyson on board before the other dinghy was upon him. With a practiced jerk of his head, he signaled his cannoneers.

Had Alyson had the breath left to scream, she would have screamed at the sound of cannon shells exploding overhead, sending up sprays of water around the dinghies, and filling the air with the stench of their smoke. Instead, she spluttered and gasped and clung unsteadily to Rory as he dragged her up the ladder and onto the *Sea Witch*.

He began shouting as soon as he hit the deck. The lateens swung out and filled with wind as the sloop lurched and slowly came about. Cries of anger from the brigantine were greeted with the whining of cannonballs overhead. The curses of the men aboard the *Neptune* and in the dinghy below grew fainter as the maneuverable sloop set sail and headed back out to sea. The current was against them momentarily, but already the tide was turning. And the brig couldn't follow without its full crew.

The cannon fired a few more warning shots for good measure as Rory took the tiller and aimed for open sea. He was well aware of his shy cabin boy and the taciturn cook bending over Alyson's soaked and gasping figure on the main deck below him, but he didn't have the time to lend his efforts to theirs. He had to get the *Sea Witch* out of here before half the ships in the harbor took sail to strike him down for piracy.

Rory was still cursing their near escape sometime later when he returned to his cabin to find Alyson wrapped in his blankets, her soaked gown spread across his desk chair and dripping upon the floor. She was threading her fingers through her wet hair in a vain attempt to untangle it when he entered. Her frown of concentration fled as soon as she saw him.

"Now that I have the British navy on both sides of the Atlantic after me, would you care to explain what the hell you think you were doing? Or do you just enjoy departing in a blaze of glory?"

Rory's sarcasm drifted right by her as Alyson contemplated the angry crease above his nose. His sun-darkened visage looked quite ferocious when he frowned like that, but he never stayed angry for long. She smiled vaguely as she adjusted the blanket more securely around her shoulders. She had forgotten the intensity of those brandy-colored eyes when they focused on her. The shock of that gaze brought a strange warmth to her middle.

"Why should the navy be after you?"

Her look of innocence nearly worked its spell as usual, until Rory remembered the clever mind behind those wide gray eyes. The treacherous little witch had a penchant for getting into trouble, but sooner or later she always landed right where she wanted to be.

He refused to let her divert the conversation. "The navy tends to frown on people who fire on ships carrying the British flag. Why were you on it, Alyson? You promised to wait for me."

Dismissing what had already happened and could not be changed, Alyson focused on the problem remaining and smiled sunnily as she realized she could solve it. "You need only tell the navy that I ordered the ship fired on. Surely I can shoot at my own ship if I want to, can't I? You didn't hurt anyone, did you?" She asked this last almost hopefully. Cranville had been nearly the only person on deck.

It took a moment for her words to seep through Rory's anger. When they finally did, he reached for the desk chair for support, ignoring the soaking garments flung upon it. "Your own ship?" he asked warily, making certain he understood what he thought he heard. A ship the size of the *Neptune* would have made his fortune twice over. The *Sea Witch* was little more than a fishing boat in comparison. And the claimant of such wealth sat nearly naked in his bunk right now.

Alyson shrugged. "So they say. I certainly can't compliment the officers on their loyalty or obedience, but men do have some difficulty accepting the notion of a woman in command, don't they? I daresay they preferred to believe Cranville the true owner."

If he had not talked to Farnley himself, Rory would have believed her mad and prattling nonsense. No doubt the officers of the *Neptune* did have a difficult time believing her. A woman in command of a ship that size! It strained the borders of credulity.

"You could be riding in comfort aboard the *Neptune* now. Shall I turn around and return you there? A little persuasion might see Cranville removed and you installed in his place."

Rory stood there in his sodden clothes contemplating the enchanting pixie who had just danced into his life one fair morn. He had known she was an heiress, but the vastness of her wealth had not sunk in until he had seen that ship. A man who owned a ship like that could control vast quantities of power if he used it carefully. He was quite certain the late earl had used it carefully.

Alyson looked horrified at his proposal. "They think I'm mad. And the captain was going to allow Cranville to *force* me into marriage while believing I'm mad. Can I have the captain of my ship removed when we return to London?"

Feeling as if he had lost complete control of this entire situation, Rory surrendered. Since he had met his personal angel, he had been held up by highwaymen, challenged an earl to a duel, killed a kidnapper, and fired on a British merchant. He was down to his last three decent shirts and one of those was clinging clammily to his shoulders right now. He was better off when he courted the devil, despite the fact that Alyson looked more delicious in a blanket and dripping ringlets than any other woman he had ever encountered.

Rory forcefully resisted that thought with curtness. "Lass, you may talk to your solicitors about that when you return. Right now I would like to change into some dry clothes. If you'll excuse me, there may be one or two left in my trunk."

Alyson watched with interest as Rory threw open his trunk and rummaged around in the contents. His soaked shirt was plastered to his skin, molding to the broad muscles of his back, and an odd curl of pleasure at the sight warmed her blood. She wanted to touch the hard plane of his shoulders, but she could never be so bold. Instead, she leaned over the bunk to watch as he emptied his trunk in search of a dry shirt. She remembered now that his wardrobe had been in a sorry state the last time she left, but he had dressed with such elegance that night at the Lattimers' she had forgotten about it. Come to think of it, she was now without all her new clothing once again. All she had was the saturated gown over the chair, and not even her good petticoat this time. It was a good thing she didn't spend much time worrying over her appearance. Finding what he sought, Rory sat back on his heels and came face-to-face with Alyson as she bent over the trunk with obvious interest. The shock of finding her so close was startling enough, but if he had kept his eyes on her face, the encounter wouldn't have been quite so shattering. Instead, the devil that had sent him fleeing in the first place now prompted him to follow the firm curve of her chin to the slender throat shadowed beneath. That glimpse told him she wore nothing but a blanket, and it was only a single step further to slide his gaze to the fair expanse of sloping shoulders and breasts revealed by the sagging wool to send him into the first circles of hell.

He gave himself credit for tearing his glance away before his hand could reach out to remove what little covering she wore. Grabbing the first handful of clothes his fingers touched and dropping the trunk lid, Rory stood unsteadily. Without looking back, he stalked out the door.

Alyson stared after him in astonishment. Had there been something terrible in the trunk to send him away so quickly? Surely he wouldn't have left her here with it if so. Perhaps he had forgotten something and had hurried off to take care of it. He hadn't exactly been in the best of moods anyway. Perhaps he would be more cheerful when he returned.

Remembering her own sad state of dress, Alyson knelt beside the trunk to see if she could salvage anything for her own use. Before she could inspect the contents properly, William knocked at the cabin door, and at her call, entered with a pitcher of hot water.

Delighted at the prospect of washing off the muddy river water, Alyson leapt to her feet, tugging to keep the blanket in place.

William turned his shy glance to the wall as he spoke. "Dougall said I was to remind the captain that he stored the lady's things beneath the bunk. Shall I find the captain and tell him?"

"I shall be certain to pass on the message, William, don't you worry about it." Alyson could scarcely wait for the lad to leave so she could search beneath the bunk. Lady's things? What lady? And what things? Oh, please, Lord, let some of them fit her.

In triumph, she found the packages shoved hastily into the large drawer. With William gone, she let the blanket fall free so she could use both hands to tear at strings and parcel paper. The largest bundle revealed a froth of lovely gray-blue satin that spilled over her hands and lap in yards of skirt. Locating the bodice, Alyson shook it out and scrutinized it with a practiced eye. Whomever Rory had intended this for, she was larger than his aunt. Maybe he had other relatives who had requisitioned the garment. The exquisitely embroidered stomacher in white satin with silver and blue threads would probably fit her without much adjustment of the laces.

The other packages revealed matching petticoats, stockings, and even blue satin shoes, Alyson discovered with delight. Silently commending Rory's good taste, she hastily threw aside the blanket and poured the hot water into the basin. Rory might be displeased at her appropriating garments evidently meant as a gift for someone, but she could easily replace it once they reached London. For now, she wished to appear as something a little more than the bedraggled waif he was always fishing out of some trouble broth.

As she scrubbed the river mud from her hair, Alyson tried to contemplate why she should be concerned with Rory's opinion of her, but the effort was too great. Rory was the only friend she had been able to rely on since her grandfather's death. She didn't know why he had been so late in returning to Charleston, but she felt certain he had excellent reasons. Perhaps he considered her something of a nuisance and was occasionally inclined to be short-tempered, but she would be the first to admit that he had every justification in being so. Perhaps that was why it was so important that she impress him favorably now. She would not even attempt to wonder who the paragon of virtue was that the exquisite gown had been designed for.

Having changed into dry breeches and shirt and chastened himself severely for his lack of control, Rory gathered his wits together long enough to remember he had ungallantly left Alyson soaked and without warm garments. Never before had any woman ever sent him into such disarray. He had little contact with the ladies of society. His occupation took care of that, if not his total lack of interest in unobtainable objects. The women he purchased when he felt the need were nameless faces, with the exception of one or two. He had hoped the one he had just left behind would have quenched his physical hungers enough to deal with Alyson on this return trip, but he could already see that was a futile quest. Alyson had not been on board for an hour, and already she had brought him practically to his knees. He would have to come to some solution soon, but for now, he had to find dry clothes for her.

Resolutely he turned his steps in the direction of the great cabin. Dougall was up on the quarterdeck pretending to ignore him, and the rest of the men seemed well-occupied. Perhaps none had noted his hasty retreat to the men's quarters to change clothes. The fact that the shirt he had grabbed was missing its buttons and lay open to the waist would not necessarily be noticed by his men in this warm climate. And he certainly didn't have to excuse himself to one Alyson Hampton, heiress and troublemaker extraordinaire. After all, she had been the one to choose his modest ship over the luxury of her own.

With these rationalizations, Rory stepped down into the cabin to generously offer his passenger the garments he had bought for her those months ago in Charleston.

Alyson looked up with surprise as the door flew open. Rinsing off the last of the soap she had lathered herself with, she wore nothing but the wet cloth in her hand. At the sight of Rory standing there in the doorway, a dazed expression upon his face, she froze. Beads of water rolled down her breasts and dropped to the floor, but she could only return his stare.

Instead of frightening her as before, the heated intensity of Rory's eyes sent piercing waves of excitement slicing through Alyson's insides. She felt a tightening in her midriff that was almost painful, and the memory of their last kiss returned with startling impact. The longing for that touch again was nearly insatiable, and so overwhelming she nearly forgot her state of undress.

In those few frozen seconds Alyson's gaze drifted from the taut, sun-darkened squareness of Rory's features to the wide spread of his shoulders and the dark curls of hair upon his chest beneath the open shirt. Her eyes dilated at this exposure of a man's nakedness, and the resulting realization of her own made her gulp and reach for the blanket on the floor.

Alyson's movement released Rory from his incredulous stupor. For a few brief seconds his vision had been filled with the glory of satin-smooth curves tinted with pink, shadowed delicately in black curls. Closing his eyes, he stumbled out the door and slammed it shut, collapsing in one of the chairs at the table behind him.

He had to be out of his mind. The fierce piercing pain sweeping through him had to be unbridled lust, but he had never succumbed to such temptation before. Why in hell had he opened that door without knocking in the first place? He knew the answer to that one without thought, but his mind refused to acknowledge it. She was an innocent child. He had no business playing adult games with an unprotected child.

But the memory of Alyson's full and glorious curves was emblazoned upon his mind. Those were the ripe curves of a woman full grown and made for love. She had not screamed or run from him in fear, but returned his gaze boldly.

Rory buried his face in his hands at that irresponsible thought. Not boldly. Alyson never did anything boldly. She just drifted in and out of situations as the notion took her. And due to his own inept handling of this particular situation, she now had notions that weren't at all seemly for an unmarried lady.

Well, that suited him just fine. Slamming his hand against the table, Rory rose and stalked out. He had been branded a traitor and an outlaw at an early age. He owed the British aristocracy no favors. If they couldn't take care of their own, why should he?

13

Unaware of the tumult she had created of Rory's emotions, too confused by her own to think clearly, Alyson carefully dressed herself in her new raiment. The gown fit as if it had been made for her, and the shoes were considerably more comfortable than her ruined ones. The only problem lay in the fact that she had no fichu to tuck in her bodice for decency. The square neckline had no lace or modesty piece to disguise the full swell of her breasts, and although she knew it was very much the fashion in London, she could not but feel it a trifle daring aboard a ship full of men.

There was no help for it, however. None of the packages or Rory's trunk revealed any fabric that could be used for scarf or shawl. Her own ruined morning dress had a high neckline and no need of a fichu. Under the circumstances, she had little to fret about. Rory had already seen all of her that there was to see.

So when he pounded on the cabin door and asked, "Are you decent?" she was left in some confusion.

"Decent?" She voiced her curiosity out loud. She wasn't certain the gown was decent, but she didn't think he would be overly concerned about that.

Rory stared at the cabin door in disbelief. Behind him his two officers sat at the table and listened with interest. Did the little devil expect him to ask if she were still naked?

The question became rhetorical as Alyson opened the door and stood there with her thick ebony curls waving over her breasts to her waist, nearly concealing the enticing cleavage revealed by the delicate gown. She blushed as the two men behind Rory hastily jumped to their feet and somehow managed to bow without taking their eyes off her. Rory merely scowled at their antics.

"Isn't one of you supposed to be up on deck?" His glare sent both of them hastening from the cabin before he turned back to Alyson. "I see you found the gown."

Alyson brightened as she realized his anger was not directed at her. Sweeping the long skirts back and forth with delight, she stepped aside to allow him to enter. "It is lovely. I hope you don't mind my wearing it. I will pay you back just as soon as we reach London."

Her cheerful innocence made him feel even more a cad, but his mind was made up. He would be a howling idiot if he tried to take her all the way to London living like brother and sister in this cramped cabin. That left only two choices, and he very much suspected she would object to both of them.

"I meant the gown for ye, lass. Don't fash yerself o'er it. It suits ye well."

At this amazing speech, Alyson stared at her taciturn Scotsman. He seldom slipped into his lilting accent unless he was upset by something, but he did not seem to be angry. In this case, "lass" seemed almost a term of endearment. His tone and the look of appreciation in those dark eyes certainly indicated a small amount of tenderness. Her heart beat faster as Rory lifted a strand of her hair and pushed it back over her shoulder. He stood nearly a head taller than she, and she felt slightly nervous as his gaze traveled lingeringly from her face to the shameless décolletage of the gown. She wasn't certain how much he could see from that vantage point, but she felt an odd heat rising from those places that his gaze touched.

"I thank you, but I don't believe it is proper for me to accept such a generous gift. Please, do sit down. You are making me very nervous."

William had brought in a chair from the other room and set up their supper on a small table. At Rory's command, two place settings had been brought up, and

Alyson had evidently waited for him before dining. Pleased that some organization had been achieved out of the disaster of this day, Rory chose his desk chair and held it out for Alyson to sit in.

She had slept in the same bed with this man, nursed his wounds, berated him for his misdeeds. Why did she now feel like a foolish child about to face her first suitor? She could not remember ever experiencing such sensations, and she was not at all certain that she liked it. Steeling herself, she managed to sit gracefully in the chair offered and reach for her napkin without wondering where Rory's eyes wandered now.

Noting he had actually managed to fluster her for a change, Rory took his seat with some small amount of satisfaction. Considering the delicacy of their situation, he preferred to feel himself in control. He knew all too well how easily she could decimate logic when he was not.

It was difficult to make civilized conversation over this less-than-civilized meal. Alyson pushed the overcooked mush about on her tin plate, watching it with rapt interest rather than meeting Rory's eyes.

"Did you enjoy your stay in Charleston?" Rory asked politely, watching her bent head with more interest than the unpalatable meal.

"Very well, thank you, but I am ready to go home. How long will it take before we are in London?"

"That's a subject we need to discuss a little later. It promises to be a beautiful evening. Perhaps you would care to stroll about the deck for a while after dinner?"

That was totally unlike Rory. On board ship he roared and commanded and stayed busily out of her way. Something was wrong, but Alyson could not quite put her finger on it. She lifted her head to gaze at him thoughtfully.

He met her look without evasion. The lines that wrinkled up about his eyes when he laughed were not noticeable, but neither was the frown that usually puckered the bridge of his nose when he was angry. The rich color of his eyes seemed warm and inviting, and the hint of a smile added a certain sensuality to his lips. She did not need any second sight to know what he was thinking, and she shivered. She had never experienced this kind of awareness with Alan, the one man she had ever loved. Why did Rory strike these odd sensations in her?

She ought to refuse his offer, but she could tell by the way he was looking at her that it would be useless. She nodded uncertainly. "I'd like that, thank you. Will we talk about London then? Do you think my cousin will be there before us?"

"We will talk about London then, and yes, Cranville will undoubtedly be there before us. I apologize for your meal. There wasn't time to lay in supplies at Charleston."

He said it with such an ironic drawl that Alyson had to smile, and the rest of the meal was much easier.

By the time William came to clear the table, Alyson was laughingly reciting the tale of Chad's attempt to take two young ladies to the charity ball without either knowing of the other. When the discovery was finally made, Alyson had interfered in the impending screaming argument with a better plan. The Honorable Charles Edward Sutherland had spent the remainder of that evening as a wallflower for the first time in his charmed life when every lady in the ballroom refused to dance with him.

Knowing the charm and good looks of Lord Kerry's eldest son, Rory watched Alyson with care throughout this recital, but she showed no regret at having left him or anyone else behind. He was uncertain of her feelings for Alan Tremaine, however. She had refused Alan once in anger, but women were notoriously fickle about such matters. Maybe part of her eagerness to return to London was to see if Alan had waited for her.

Rory closed his mind to such thoughts. Alan Tremaine was a spoiled, shallow lad, and he would not concern himself over such as that. He had learned the hard way that the only one who would look out for him was himself, and this he meant to do. Out of respect for Alyson, he would give her a choice, and in all honesty he could not predict which path her bewildering mind would take, but first and foremost he would look after himself.

Alyson noted Rory's confident smile as he helped her to rise, but by now she had recovered some of her equilibrium. She knew now her vision had not been a dream and that sooner or later Rory would teach her what it was like to be a woman. The knowledge had once been frightening, but she was discovering she felt safer in

Rory's company than with anyone else she knew. Rory wouldn't willingly hurt her.

Taking his arm, she offered him a blinding smile of confidence in return, nearly staggering Rory before he recovered sufficiently to open the cabin door. They stepped up onto the main deck into the blissful warmth of a summer evening in silence.

Rory had not bothered to don coat or neckcloth for dinner, and Alyson was pleasantly aware of the hard muscular strength of his arm through the thin linen shirt. She had even grown accustomed to the deep V of his sun-bronzed chest revealed by the unfastened shirt. She tried not to dwell on it too long, however, because the sight evoked the vision much too clearly, and she wasn't quite ready to deal with that much nakedness yet. So she held firmly to his arm and gazed out upon the open sea in the moonlight.

" 'Tis truly beautiful, Rory. Now I can see why you might spend so much of your life out here."

Blocked by the bulwark, the wind lifted her hair in gentle waves, blowing wisps across Rory's shirt as he gazed down on her. In the moonlight her pale face was like translucent porcelain, and the mysterious clouds of her eyes drifted between sunshine and shadow. He had never seen a face quite like hers before, so serene and lovely but disguising moods as fascinating as the sea. Even now, when she looked with obvious pleasure over the silvery waves, he knew her thoughts weren't entirely on the moment.

The high-pitched squeal of a school of dolphins carried over the slapping of the waves against the ship, and Alyson turned moonstruck eyes to him expectantly, waiting for explanations. He located the leaping, cavorting dark shapes in the wide swath of moonlight, and guiding her to the rail, pointed them out to her.

"They're marvelous! Almost as if they could be your pets." In the same breath, without diverting her attention in any way, she added, "I miss Peabody."

That statement caught Rory completely by surprise until he remembered her earlier mention of the spaniel she'd had to leave behind. Since she still clung to his arm, he could not hug her as he would like, but he intended to rectify that situation immediately.

Guiding her back into the lee of the bulwark, where her hair did not swirl in wild gusts about them and where the man at the helm could not see, Rory turned Alyson around to face him. At his touch, her eyes became mirrored, and he could see only his reflection when he gazed down into her face. His hand went out to touch the smoothness of her cheek, testing her reality, and a slow, hauntingly sensual smile appeared on her lips.

"By all that's holy, Alys, do you have any idea what a smile like that does to a man?" The words came out involuntarily, torn from Rory's tongue by a force he could not name. "Don't answer that," he added firmly when the smile widened. Whatever her answer might have been, he felt certain it would destroy his logic, and he needed all the logic he could muster.

"You were to tell me of London," she prompted him. In the moonlight, Rory's teeth gleamed pearly white against his sun-darkened features as she swayed closer to him with the roll of the ship. Legs spread, he stood easily with the motion, but he leaned one hand against the bulwark to provide a shelter for her. This was not the gallant gentleman who had escorted her into his aunt's ballroom, nor the hardworking seaman who had carried her to these strange shores. The Maclean was a man of many facets, she was learning, but she liked the way this one was looking at her.

"London, yes." Rory grazed her cheek with the back of his finger, not wanting to scare her but unable to keep from touching. "London is a long way off. That is my problem."

Alyson shivered slightly as his hand stroked her hair behind her ear, then strayed to her throat. She held her own hands clasped tightly behind her as she leaned back against the cabin. She wanted him to touch her more, she could feel the anticipation rising in her breasts, and for the first time she noticed how they tightened beneath the satin binding of her bodice, as if demanding something she did not yet know of. Whatever he wanted, her body obviously offered no resistance, but thoughts of shame never entered her head.

"There is some problem? You do intend to return to London, don't you? I would not mind sailing with you awhile longer, but I miss England, and I'm worried Mr. Farnley will still think me dead. I'd like to go home."

"So would I, lass, so would I." Rory said this with a heartfelt fervor his words did not entirely explain. He needed the solace of her kiss to balm the wounds that wouldn't heal. Gently, very tenderly, he bent and applied his lips to hers, seeking just a taste of the comfort offered there.

Alyson's surprised gasp at this unexpected touch left her vulnerable to more thorough probing. Her hands flew to his chest as Rory's tongue slid suggestively along hers, and then there was no holding back at all. His flesh burned her palm as his kiss enticed her into a wickedness she had never dared imagine. While her fingers curled longingly in the soft mat of hair across his chest, her lips parted beneath his onslaught, giving him the access that he sought. Her body trembled at the unexpected invasion that followed, but she made no effort to resist. As his tongue captured and conquered this first stronghold, their breaths mingled, and Alyson surrendered totally to his gentle attack, her defenses breeched, her willpower fled.

A brief oblivion ensued while his lips gave her these first glimpses of tenderness and passion. Alyson's hands slid around Rory's neck of their own accord when he caught her waist and drew her against him, so that she could feel the full length of his muscular body pressed into hers, and she strained to know more. The heat of his mouth held her captive, and she drank eagerly of the passion she found there, clinging to the need and desire she felt within him. It was as if their two souls rose up to join as one, without the consent of either of them.

Rory was the first to break this forbidden paradise. Reluctantly releasing the warm softness filling his arms, he brushed a lingering kiss against her cheek and gently set her back so he could stare down into bewildered, misty eyes. "That's my problem, lass," he finally admitted with a trace of sadness. "A man can resist only so much, and then temptation triumphs. Do ye ken, lass?"

The lapse into broad accents cleared some of the mists, and Alyson solemnly stared into warm brandy eyes. Her heart was pounding faster than usual, and she longed only to have Rory's arms tightly around her again, but she realized he was asking her a question she did not fully understand. She concentrated mightily as she asked, "We should not kiss like that again?"

Rory offered up a wry smile at this naiveté. "That is one way of looking at it, dear heart, but you would have to tie me to the mains'l before you could keep me from doing it again. And again. What I'm telling you, lass, is that I canna take you back to London unless you're willing to share my bed. I canna speak it any plainer. I've not survived this long without learning my weaknesses, and you're one of them, lass."

Alyson looked up quickly to scan his face at this admission. She had thought Rory strong, much stronger than herself, and perhaps he was. He, at least, was trying to resist this mysterious attraction between them, while she would gladly surrender to whatever he asked. She tried to listen to his next words, but her heart was pounding so fiercely at the sight of the desire burning in his eyes that she could scarcely hear them. She was his weakness, he had said. Those words she had heard, and they were burned indelibly in her heart.

"I have some unfinished business in the islands, lass. We can find another ship for you there, or if you prefer, we can sail back to Charleston and set straight the *Neptune*'s captain. The choice is yours, Alys. I'll abide by whatever you decide."

Alarm suddenly flooded her features as Alyson comprehended at least part of this choice he offered her. She could not go back to the *Neptune* and Cranville. She knew that without logical thought because she refused even to consider it. The offer of another ship did not ease her fears to any great degree. She had learned more of the world since she had so blithely set out in it so many months ago. She knew ships were full of men, and very few men could be trusted. The prospect of sailing with a ship full of strangers was not only daunting, it seemed foolhardy when the one man she trusted stood before her.

Rory's hand had taken to wandering up and down her side, testing the boning of her bodice and the fullness of her petticoats, and encroaching implacably closer upon the curve of her breast. If he thought to reassure her, he was failing miserably, Alyson thought as she tried to gather her wits about her. It would be so much easier not to think about it, to surrender mindlessly to his caresses, but she had done that with Alan and she would not allow it to happen again. She struggled for comprehension.

The only thing that was infinitely clear in her mind was that if her vision were to come true, Rory would have her, whatever her choice might be. She knew very little about what went on between men and women, but it had something to do with making babies. The circumstances of her own birth told her that a child could result with or without marriage. That made things considerably clearer. She could return to the *Neptune* and Cranville. She could take another ship and return to London and Cranville. Or she could stay in Rory's protection. And whichever route she chose, eventually she would find herself in Rory's bed. Her vision had revealed that much. That left no choice at all.

The vagueness of her smile as she came to this conclusion left Rory uneasy, but he still wasn't prepared for her reply when it came.

"Do they have clergymen on these islands?"

Had he not known her better, he would have thought her mind had drifted off on another of its strange tangents, but Rory followed the drift quickly enough. He stared at her in incredulity, however, not believing even Alyson could be foolish enough to suggest such a thing. What was it about women that always brought to mind marriage, when it never entered a man's head?

"Alyson, dear heart, you cannot know what you are saying. Marriage is for a lifetime, not for a few weeks across the sea. Think, lass, what would you do with a husband like me?"

"You would prefer I marry Cranville?" she asked with more tartness than was her customary manner.

She had him there. He most certainly didn't want her to marry that villain, but for the sake of honesty, she would be better off with the handsome earl than with himself. Rory shook his head in confusion. He had thought he had lined the problem up very neatly. Leave it to Alyson to discover the improbable solution.

Rory caught his hand in her wild mane of hair and held her head tilted where he could read the storm clouds of her eyes. Sweet-natured she might be, but all the passions of a royal hellion welled up in those eyes at times.

He wanted the sweetness of her passion, not the tartness, but he would take both if he could have her.

"Nay, I would not prefer Cranville, but I think you might after a few weeks of my life. I have no home, lass. This is all I have and all I am. Until recently I could not even walk the shores of England without risking my head. Even now I am in danger of being blown out of the water every time I cross the path of the Royal Navy. It's no life for an earl's granddaughter. I will love you and teach you the ways of love, but I would do you a great disservice if I married you."

Alyson's eyes grew troubled as she searched the stern lineaments of Rory's face. She felt the coldness in his soul, had known of it for some time, but the harsh wind of his words revealed more than she had ever known. For a brief moment she saw a cruel snowstorm in his eyes and felt a wrenching pain, but the moment faded, leaving her more confused than before.

Her hand wandered wonderingly to the bare expanse of his chest, reassuring herself of its warmth. She ignored Rory's hasty intake of breath as her fingers traveled the hard ridges of muscle beneath the soft mat of hair. She felt his arms tighten possessively around her, and she swayed closer into his embrace, her mind working frantically to find an answer to this puzzle.

"Stay with me awhile, Alys," he pleaded against her ear, holding her gently in his arms, as if in fear of breaking her in two. "I want you more than anything or anyone else in my life. Just don't let me ruin yours." The anguish in this whisper was all the warning he could give her.

Alyson wasn't at all certain if she heard his words or dreamt them, but they answered a wounded ache in her own heart. Alan and her cousin had offered marriage only when they knew she was an heiress. Rory might not love her, but he wanted her more than her money. That had to count for something. Rory would say that was a most illogical way of looking at things, but when she was in the protection of his arms like this, feeling his heart beating with hers, she had no desire for logic. She wanted to be loved.

She lifted her face to meet his gaze. "I have homes, Rory. You do not need to provide me one. And I'm certain the Royal Navy is in the wrong, and it will be discovered soon. I do not care what you have been in the past. I know what you are now, and I want to stay with you."

Those were the kindest words he had heard in many a year, and Rory smiled affectionately at her assumption that the entire navy was in the wrong. But he could not let her daft logic soften his heart, if only for her own good. He pinched her chin between his thumb and forefinger and met her gaze steadily.

"The Royal Navy is not wrong, lass. I am a smuggler. I have made my fortune breaking the law and do not intend to change my ways. The only reason they have kept a wary distance is that I hold letters of marque from the governor of Barbados, and they cannot be certain whether I'm smuggling British goods or stealing French. That is the kind of man you would give your life and wealth to, lass."

Alyson jerked her head away from his grasp and stared out over the fathomless sea. How could she tell him that words had no meaning to her, that she had seen things he would never believe even if she told him? Perhaps in his own logical way he was right, and she was better off being mistress of a pirate than wed to one, but she had never acted on logic and could not easily start now. Perhaps her one attempt at being careful was wrong too, and she turned back to stare up into his taut face with puzzlement.

"I was born on the wrong side of the blanket, Rory. In society's eyes, I am well-suited to be a smuggler's wife, but I do not want the same shadow to plague my children. Isn't it better that they have a smuggler for a father instead of no father at all?" She handed this question of logic to a man who had more experience in thinking that way.

And he laughed. A wide grin sprawled across Rory's square jaw and broke into a deep laugh as he lifted her into his arms and cuddled her closer. When she tried to shake herself free, he caressed her hair and murmured, "Nay, lass, I'll not let you go now. If that is all that troubles ye, I'll take care that no bairns come of our loving. We'll be free as the wind and there will be none to say us wrong."

Pressing her heated cheeks against his broad shoulder, Alyson tried to contain the anticipation rising inside her.

She loved the way his soft burr murmured against her ear. She loved the way he was holding her with tender strength against his chest. And she loved the way his kisses felt as they burned butterfly touches across her face. Somewhere in the back of her mind she knew this was wrong, but it was not her mind that he was holding.

Alyson eagerly turned her lips up to meet his kiss in unspoken agreement.

14

Rory's contented whistle as he left Alyson to prepare for bed while he checked their course and consulted with Dougall gave fair warning to his crew that something was brewing. Rory seldom whistled unless he had just pocketed a hefty amount of change from a shrewd deal.

Putting down his sextant, Dougall stared at his friend and employer with suspicion, but he offered no comment until Rory spoke first. When the captain made his request, the smaller man's bushy eyebrows shot upward and his eyes narrowed with incredulity.

"No wonder the lass ran away from ye. And here I was thinking ye an honorable man, Maclean. If ye've left her thinking it's all legal and aboveboard, I'll tell her different and help her run away again."

Rory scowled at his first mate. "And if that's the kind of loyalty and obedience I can expect from you, I'll let you go, but the girl stays. She has run away once too many times already. I mean to put an end to it."

Dougall made a rude noise. Older than Rory by only a few years, and by his side for many more years than that, he behaved more as brother than officer. While Jack frowned at his captain's orders and continued to keep his hold on the tiller, Dougall crossed his arms over his chest and glared at his friend.

"I'll not let you do it, Maclean. She's a good girl and deserves better. You've already ruined her reputation, and probably worse. Either marry her proper or put her on the next ship back to London."

Unaware of Alyson's wealth, Dougall had no understanding of Rory's predicament, and Rory had no intention of enlightening him. Still scowling, he began to chart their course to the nearest deserted island off the coast of Georgia.

"She already knows what I intend and has agreed to it. I only mean to give her a little ceremony to mark the occasion. I'll thank ye to keep yer long nose out of what ye canna ken."

When Rory lapsed into his thick Highland brogue, Dougall knew it was time to shut up. Closing his wide mouth in a thin line, he clambered down from the quarterdeck and stalked toward the men's quarters to relay the orders the captain had given them.

As the raucous cheer rose up from below, Rory eyed the silent man at the tiller. Jack was neither a kinsman nor even a Scot, but he had been with him since he first bought the *Witch*, and he valued the older man's opinion on things nautical. Beyond that, neither of them had much experience. He could see the man's frown, but whether it was one of disapproval or thought, he could not discern.

"I'm protecting her the only way I can," Rory growled as he swiftly charted their course.

"Your damned bloody revenge means that much to you?" From Jack, the curse words meant little, but the tone of his voice hinted at disapproval and not curiosity.

"It's not revenge, although I mean to have that too. I can't allow a feeble female to stand in the way of what I've worked for a lifetime to accomplish."

"Seems to me she ain't half so feeble as you make her out to be. She got away from you before, and she'll do it again."

That certainly hit the crux of the matter, but Rory had no wish to pursue that line of thinking. Acquiring a woman in his life had never been one of his goals. Alyson was free to do as she pleased. He only wished she was as easy to forget as the woman he had just left behind.

Unaware of the dissension she had created, Alyson rummaged for one of Rory's last remaining shirts to use as night rail. It seemed very calculating and coldhearted to be left to ungarb herself on the eve of becoming a man's mistress, but Rory's was a practical nature. He had better things to do than untie and unhook dozens of little fastenings, and it would probably be most embarrassing with both of them fumbling about in her petticoats. She had just thought it would be more romantic, that "it" would just happen without her having to think about it, sort of like kissing.

Her fingers began to tremble as she unlaced the bodice and pulled it over her arms. The warm night air caressed her bare shoulders, but it raised goose bumps just the same. Untying and unfastening her full skirts and petticoats, she stepped out of them slowly, reluctant to expose herself to the seductive elements of a southern night and the certain knowledge of what she meant to do.

When she had rid herself of all but the frail finery of chemise and stockings, Alyson glanced down at herself doubtfully. She could not imagine Rory buying these intimate things for her. Had he gone into the dressmaker's and chosen them particularly, or just stood at the counter and told the modiste to wrap up whatever was available? He had to have given the woman some idea of her size, and a hint of amusement played about her lips as she tried to imagine that scene.

She ought to be fearfully embarrassed, but mostly she was curious. She had no mirror to see herself in, but she knew she was not tall or slender or graceful like the women she had admired in London. On the other hand, she needed no padding as so many women did to fill out their fashionable gowns. She had no idea what men preferred, but she would have to assume Rory liked her the way she was. That thought brought a flush of pleasure to her cheeks.

She was going to do what her mother had done, but without even the pretense of a marriage to make it right. True, Rory had murmured words of love, but so had Alan. Men meant nothing by those words; they couldn't. Perhaps even her father had lied to her mother on that night she had been conceived. Else he would have waited until they were well and truly married.

A brief moment of sadness removed the blue from her eyes, but Alyson shook off the elusive premonition causing it. She could take care of herself much better than her mother had. She was wealthy enough to do whatever she liked, and Rory was quite right in denying marriage. If there were ways of loving without producing a child, then she wanted to learn them. It would be very nice to have a child someday, but only after she had found a husband who truly loved her. She trusted Rory to protect her reputation once they returned to London. He might call himself by criminal names, but she knew his gallantry from experience.

When she finally decided that Rory would prefer her in the chemise instead of his long shirt, Alyson returned the neatly folded linen to the trunk and crawled between the covers of Rory's bunk. She shivered as the cool muslin rubbed against her bare skin, but it was as much the memory of sharing this bed as the coolness that caused the tremor. Soon Rory would be here beside her again, and it would be his hands she felt against her skin, and not cold muslin. She had to wrap her arms around herself to keep from trembling all over.

She fell asleep before she could learn that Rory never returned to the cabin.

When she woke, the ship was strangely still except for the shouts and footsteps above her. Rubbing her eyes, she ascertained it was daylight. Then, remembering the night before, she turned and hastily searched the bed, as if Rory would be disguised by the blankets.

She had not had time to pull together her tumultuous emotions at discovering his desertion when a loud knock sounded at the door.

"Up with ye, lass. It's too late to be lying abed!"

Rory's voice. The same Rory who was supposed to share her bed last night. The one she had trusted with her most intimate feelings. And he had not even bothered to avail himself of her offer.

Furious, embarrassed, she grabbed his shaving mug and flung it at the door.

The resounding crash raised Rory's eyebrows, and he rightly surmised he had somehow managed to do something wrong again. Shrugging his square shoulders, he walked off. To let himself in now could be suicidal, judging by his previous encounters with enraged women. Alyson's good nature would prevail eventually.

When he heard that William had successfully delivered

her breakfast and lived to speak of it, Rory returned to the cabin. Deciding the degree of intimacy she was about to grant him made knocking a false modesty, he simply walked in.

He caught her trapped in the entanglement of donning her gown, and he stopped to admire the view of slender ankles and well-turned calves. As she hastily jerked the bodice waist in place, he was given a fine view of scantily clad breasts that sent a hot surge of desire boiling through his blood. But it was not his intention to take her like this, and he gritted his teeth into a sour smile when she pulled the bodice closed and held it there with a death grip.

Rory regarded the elegant satin gown with a practical eye and shook his head. "It will not do. The heat will kill you. Take it off and let us find something more suitable."

Alyson simply glared at him and deliberately began fastening her laces.

Rory stepped forward, grabbed two great handfuls of skirt, and jerked upward. Alyson's dark hair and hands disappeared in a swirl of blue satin, and she shrieked as the unfastened waist caught on her breasts and left all else bare for his perusal. Rory chuckled at the sight of the thin chemise riding up to her hips, leaving only her stockings and garters below. She was a joy to behold, and his gaze lingered on the full curve of hip and rounded thighs before he gave in and pulled the gown the rest of the way off.

He flung the satin over a chair and resolutely headed for his trunk without drinking his fill of the sweet sight she would offer him. If he were to last through this day, he would have to avoid tempting himself beyond the bounds of endurance.

"It is summer and the heat here is more than Charleston. Save the gown for cooler months."

Tight-lipped, Alyson grabbed up her beautiful gown again and held it before her. She had not even the time to brush the snarls from her hair, and now he was in here acting as if he owned her. Surely those few kisses they had shared last night did not give him the right to take over her life.

"Shall I go about in nothing, then? That should be sufficiently cool." In truth, the cabin had grown overly stuffy, but she had hoped the wind on deck would be pleasant. Only now she realized the reason for the ship's odd stillness. They weren't sailing, and she heard no wind.

Rory pulled out the long linen shirt she had intended to use as night rail the night before. Trying not to look too closely at the flimsily covered curves revealed as he again threw her gown aside, Rory pulled the shirt over her disheveled black curls.

"I have no particular desire to share you with my men." With a sardonic twist of his lips, Rory contemplated the impromptu gown. The billowing sleeves hung down below her fingers and the neck closure plunged nearly to her waist. Only the chemise preserved any modesty, and as he looked closer, he could see the erect tips of her breasts pushing temptingly against the thin material. No wonder women wore all those foolish garments. Any less, and men would lie raving in the streets.

Meaning only to lace the neck closure to hide some of her generous proportions, Rory found his hand straying from its assigned goal. Alyson looked up at him with startlement as his hand slid to cup the full curve of one breast and play erotic games with the thinly covered crest. Just this touch created a crescendo of pleasure and excitement pulsing through her veins, but she refused to collapse into his arms again as she had last night. She closed her eyes and held herself taut against the tidal wave of pleasure brought by just this touch.

When she did not flee his hold, Rory reacted with a pleased smile. When her startled look slowly transformed to a more sensual one and she began to sway toward him, he pressed a warning kiss against her lips and reluctantly moved his hand away.

"Don't let's fight, lass. It's much more pleasant to take things as they come. Trust me."

Alyson's eyes flew open again as Rory tied the knot in the lacing, successfully hiding most of her nakedness. She watched warily as he inspected her less-than-elegant garb. The shirt hung to mid-calf, revealing the enticing sight of embroidered stockings and blue satin slippers. The problem of the long sleeves was easily solved by using her old garters as bands to hold the flowing material high enough for comfort, but Rory shook his head at the way the thin material revealed all the full, womanly curves beneath. Men would kill for less than that.

He rummaged in the trunk again until he produced one of his old flare-bottomed vests. The yellow silk was beginning to molder, but the quilted lining had a good deal of strength left. He held it out for her, and Alyson quickly slipped into it. She didn't need the arms, and he sliced those off at the shoulders. Alyson's eyes widened in surprise at this action, but she appropriated the length of material that resulted, looped the two pieces together, and fastened them in a knot around her waist. She looked like a pirate, but all except her legs was covered.

"Aye, you'll do. It's better than William's breeches, leastways." Contemplating the satisfying fact that her impromptu skirts came up much more easily than boy's breeches came down, Rory congratulated himself on his sartorial inspiration. To test his talent, he ran his hand over the curve of her buttock. When she looked up in surprise at this touch, he grinned. His men could not see what the cloth concealed, but he could feel those lovely curves quite well.

"Shall we see what there is to see, my love?" He made a courtly bow, then opened the cabin door to escort her out.

"But I haven't even brushed my hair!" Alyson protested, glancing nervously toward the outer cabin. She sensed Rory's anticipation, but she did not know what to expect of it.

Rory picked up his brush from the shaving stand and offered his arm. "I'll do it for you later. You could never look less than lovely."

That flattery astonished Alyson into silence, and she accepted his offered arm to gingerly step out into the bright light of day in her daring dishabille. On that first trip, when her other garments were being washed and she had been forced to wear William's clothes, she had stayed hidden in the cabin until her skirts were returned to her. She was unprepared for the crew's reaction to this garb.

They cheered. They yelled. They whistled until a bright scarlet flush suffused Alyson's cheeks and Rory scowled with a ferocity that had the men nudging each other and winking.

"If all ye layabouts have naught to do but embarrass a lady, I'll send ye to scraping barnacles," he finally roared into a lull in the commotion.

That sent men scurrying into the rigging, and Alyson breathed a little easier as she glanced around her.

Somewhere during the night they had sailed into the protective cove of what she could only assume to be an island. Sandy beaches ran down to the water, and scrub palmettos seemingly filled the interior. She could hear the ocean's breakers, but they provided little disturbance behind the barrier of the reef.

Rory was watching her questioningly, and she began to have some understanding of what he was offering her, although she did not quite know why. The island provided an escape from the confinement and lack of privacy of a small ship. She could almost smell the freedom of those deserted shores, and she smiled at last.

Relieved, Rory gestured to the men working on a spar above. "There wasn't time in Charleston to make the repairs we needed. I'd prefer to have them done before we sail any closer to the islands."

Having very little knowledge of the economic and power struggles going on in the small Caribbean islands controlled by a diversity of European nations, Alyson accepted this statement without understanding the danger. Her gaze wandered to the rigging, where every day men performed the most miraculous balancing acts. She could not imagine standing so high, but she loved to watch them.

Suddenly her vague smile disappeared and she tugged on Rory's arm. "Make him come down, Rory, please."

She did not raise her voice or convey her urgency in any untoward way, but Rory heard it and frowned as he followed her gaze. He saw nothing and glanced at her questioningly. "Who, lass? What is wrong?"

"William. I want to see William. Have him come down now, please."

Since William had nearly reached his goal high atop the mainmast, this was not a particularly reasonable request, but she stated it in a most reasonable tone. With another woman, Rory would have dismissed it without a second thought. With Alyson, he couldn't help but have second and third thoughts. He signaled to Dougall, who gave the shouted command for William to return to the deck.

William quickly complied, scurrying down the mast with amazing speed, until he reached the deck and promptly presented himself at his captain's feet for orders.

Not having any good reason for calling the lad, Rory lifted a quizzical eyebrow in Alyson's direction.

With a vague smile of apology, she asked, "Have you a hat I could borrow, William? I fear I will become dreadfully sunburnt out here."

Boy and man stared at her in incredulity, but a sudden frightened cry from above turned their gazes upward. The splintered spar the men had been lowering came crashing loose from a frayed rope, swinging in a wide arc along the mast, knocking loose the gaff spanker that had been William's destination not minutes before. Had Alyson not called him down on her ridiculous errand, the boy would have been knocked clear of the rigging and onto the main deck to his death.

William turned white as he realized the nearness of the miss. Some of the other crew who had been in a position to see both William's departure and the accident now turned to each other in relief and called shouts of encouragement to the lucky lad. The remainder went about righting the spar with hefty curses, blessedly unaware of the incident. Rory stared down at the woman beside him through narrowed lids, but Alyson's misty eyes revealed naught but the shadows of the clouds crossing the sun.

He sent William on his errand; then, placing his hands on her shoulders, he turned Alyson to face him. He had seen that look on her face before, and uneasiness pinched at his innards as he gazed into her vague expression now. When he was quite certain he had her attention, he asked tautly, "You have the Sight, don't you? That's why you look at me sometimes as if you're looking through me. What else have you seen, Alyson?"

Her lips turned up with a surprised smile that did not reach her eyes. Without a word to the demanding man who held her, she walked away from his protective hold and drifted over to speak to a shaken Dougall, leaving Rory to stare after her with a mixture of confusion and understanding.

Of course she would not admit to possessing the curse

of Sight. It had labeled women as witches for centuries, or set them so far apart from their peers that they became virtual hermits. He knew of a woman in the village near his home who was reported to have the ability to see things no other could. She had no friends; her family deserted her. The only ones who sought her out were those desperate to know the secrets of their future, young girls in love, old people preparing for death. He did not know the results of their conversations, but he remembered clearly what he had seen with his own eyes. She had appeared in the street one particularly brilliant day, grabbed a toddler playing in the dirt, and shoved the child into the arms of an irate mother. Seconds later, a load of heavy whisky barrels had tilted out of a malter's cart and gone cascading down the hill just where the child had been playing.

He had tried to convince himself that the barrels had fallen first and that the woman had merely rescued the child from the obvious danger. But he had been in a position to see both woman and barrels, and he could not lie so easily to himself, no more than he could lie to himself now.

It would be easy to call it coincidence. Another man might have. That was the beauty of Alyson's deception. For years she had been convincing people of her half-wittedness with her vague habits, when in truth she had just adapted to the behavior expected of her, the one that explained her strangeness to everyone's satisfaction. Believing her half-witted was preferable to believing in the supernatural. The ridiculous reason she had given William for her call had completely fooled the lad because he thought her foolish. He would never know that it had been more than the hand of fate that had saved him. Alyson's quick-wittedness in the moment of danger was astounding, once the veil of deception was removed.

Rory watched her gesture idly with her lovely hands as she soothed Dougall's fears. He had almost believed her foolish innocence himself. Had he not been such a curious bloke, or so infatuated with her confounded hands, had they not been forced into long confinement together for the length of that coach ride, he would have believed her half-crazed. No wonder the old earl had kept her hidden in the country where no one had the opportunity to learn of her true character. Her disguise worked best at a distance or with those too blind to see beyond their own noses. Dougall was neither, and Rory moved in hastily to send his first mate back to his duties.

Alyson looked up questioningly at Rory's abruptness, but William came racing up with a disreputable-looking straw hat and intruded before either could speak. She beamed with delight at his offering, perched it rakishly over her curls, and struck a pose for his approval. The boy grinned with more boldness than was usual, then sprinted off to return to his assigned tasks.

"If you have that boy talking more than two words at a time, they'll call you another kind of witch. Come on, lass, you and I will do some exploring."

When it became obvious Rory meant for her to climb down into the dinghy to be rowed ashore, Alyson hesitated, glancing back at the protection the ship and crew offered. Rory waited patiently for her to come to terms with this next stage of her life. She had been more or less forced from the shelter of her grandfather's home into the world at large. She had been given no choice at all when Rory kidnapped her from London into his public protection. Accepting the intimacy of his private protection would have to be her own decision, something she must live with for the rest of her life.

Alyson looked from the crew to the rugged squareness of Rory's visage, and her lips turned upward in happy decision. Without further hesitation she gripped the rope ladder and swung her unencumbered legs over the side.

Rory scarcely heard the appreciative catcalls behind them as he hurried after her, his heart beating wildly. He hadn't been at all certain that last night wasn't a moon-struck dream and that dawn would return them both to their senses. His imagination ran free now, picturing sun-drenched days and moonlit nights in the arms of the fairest angel he had ever chanced to come upon. They didn't have to hurry back to London. Perhaps he could persuade her to linger in these warm waters until England's harsh winter had ended. Anything was possible. Alyson had proved that beyond questioning.

15

Alyson dug her toes into the hot sand and gazed dreamily overhead into the fascinating pattern of palm fronds above her head. A scarlet vine spilled over the sharp palmettos on either side of the path Rory had made through the undergrowth, and a strange bird crackled and cried somewhere above. They had left the mournful cries of the gulls at the ship sometime earlier, but this miniature jungle had other captivating sounds to catch her ear. Each moment was more diverting than the next, until she had managed to forget all the problems of reality in this fantasy world to which Rory introduced her.

The heat was like a tangible weight upon her skin, and she longed to pull her hair off her neck and cut the sleeves from her shirt. Rory had unfastened his shirt to the waist and rolled up his sleeves as he hacked through the vines with his wicked-looking knife, but he didn't appear much cooler. Alyson lowered her gaze from her study of the sky to the powerful sway of the Maclean's shoulders beneath his sweat-drenched shirt and the bulge of his arms as he cut at the undergrowth.

Just the sight of his shirt plastered wetly against his back sent strange vibrations through her middle. He was not an overly tall man, but she knew the strength of those muscles rippling beneath that thin fabric. His tight breeches revealed even more, accenting the hard lines of his legs and other places she was not bold enough to admit seeing. Her need to know more of the man beneath the clothing would certainly be her undoing. She was harboring dangerous fantasies already.

It was with relief that Alyson finally greeted the object of Rory's exertions—a placid blue lagoon shimmering in the shadows and sunlight of overhanging trees. Crowded undergrowth prevented easy access from three sides, and a ragged cliff of gray rock blocked the fourth. Their privacy would be perfectly protected here.

Rory waited until Alyson was beside him, his Eve in pirate's clothing in the Garden of Eden. He still could not quite believe his good fortune, and instincts warred with upbringing. He had never bedded or dishonored a lady before, had never even thought of doing so until Alyson came along. As a gentleman, he should not even be considering it. As a man, he could do nothing else. He bowed and gestured toward the lovely lagoon.

"Your bath, madam. The water is not deep, and it is all yours." He produced a sliver of soap from his pocket and shrugged. "As a valet, I fear I am sadly lacking. I didn't think to bring a towel."

Alyson looked upward to find the heat of his gaze beneath half-lowered lids, but he made no move or gesture toward her other than producing the soap. She knew he was as hot and sticky as she, yet he offered her the privacy of bathing alone when he did not have to. She blushed as she realized what she had been expecting him to do, and glanced toward the beckoning water.

"You will not go far?" She wanted the reassurance of his proximity, but she longed for the privacy of a decent bath also. She could see already that this degree of intimacy they had embarked upon could cause all kinds of strange dilemmas. Quite possibly her mother had been a woman of easy virtue and she had inherited her ways. She had no objection whatsoever to this outside bath with only a man not her husband in attendance.

"I will be right here should you need me. If you go over by those rocks, I think you can lay your clothes there without being seen." He offered this in the interest of his own sanity. Rory wasn't at all certain he had the willpower to close his eyes while she undressed, and he could almost guarantee that he wouldn't stay in this stifling jungle just watching, once he had her nakedness within his view. He had no propensity for voyeurism. He wanted the real thing, as Alyson would be able to tell from the bulge pressing at his breeches, had she been any less innocent.

Accepting his gentlemanly behavior at face value, Alyson nodded and trotted off in the direction indicated. Per-

haps Rory had changed his mind about her. Perhaps the
incident this morning had given him a dislike of her.
Some of the servants at home had feared her and made
signs of the cross behind her back, but she didn't think
Rory would believe in such superstitious nonsense. Besides, he had not come to her bed last night—before he
had any knowledge of her silly visions. He must have
changed his mind for other reasons.

Curiously, she felt no relief at that. Reaching the protection of the jutting rock formation, she glanced back
over her shoulder. The path where Rory stood was no
longer visible, and she had a sudden terror that he would
disappear and leave her here. Knowing full well that was
childish, she began to untie her improvised belt. She
should be glad he no longer desired her. She was certain
there was no advantage to be gained by surrendering her
virtue so easily. She knew better than to expect love in
return, and he had made it clear he did not intend marriage. Still, she felt a great sense of disappointment.

Fully undressed, she hesitated at the water's edge,
again glancing back to the path they had traversed. This
part of the lagoon was well-hidden from view, and Rory
was an honorable man. The hidden terrors she harbored
could be callously disregarded in Rory's company. She
liked that feeling of security, and with more confidence,
she stepped into the water.

Warm liquid lapped around her soothingly, like bath-
water, just as Rory had promised. Delighted with this
new experience, Alyson immersed herself fully, sitting on
the sandy bottom near the shore and leaning back to
soak her hair and bask in the heat. Everything was warm.
The air was warm. The water was warm. There were no
cold drafts to make her shiver when she sat up, no need
to keep a bucket heating over the fire. What a lovely way
to live!

Rory heard her splashing about and groaned inwardly
at the image leaping full-blown in his mind. Since his
fifteenth year he had been driven by one goal, to restore
his father's name and lands, and in doing so, have revenge against the man who had taken them. With this
single-minded purpose driving him on, there had been no
time for idle daydreams or selfish pursuits. To fall victim
to them now was not at all to his liking, but he could not

set aside the image of Alyson with long hair streaming across full, uptilted breasts. He could see her tiny waist, nearly feel the flare of her hips beneath his hands, and he longed to see the expression in those mist-haunted eyes when he held her beneath him and claimed her as his.

Standing idle only encouraged such thoughts, and, cursing, Rory stripped off his stiff clothing. With one swift stroke he glided into the glassy water, wishing it were a Highland stream in order to cool his overheated ardor. The action of swimming relieved some of the tension, however, and he deliberately stroked in the opposite direction from Alyson.

At the sound of Rory entering the lagoon, Alyson stopped soaping herself and dived beneath the water. Not that the clear lagoon hid very much, she noted with chagrin, but it felt better than nothing. She located his dark head moving away and breathed easier. Of course, he needed to bathe too.

A tiny sliver of his soap still remained, and magnanimously Alyson drifted through the water to lay it atop the pile of his clothing. Then, before he could turn around, she paddled hurriedly back to the protection of the rocks.

Rory lay floating on his back, listening to her progress, judging at what point she would climb out on the rocks to dry off. He pictured her sitting there like a mermaid, combing her long tresses, and the shock of this image nearly paralyzed him. He went down spluttering and came up determined.

He couldn't see her as he swam back toward his clothing. She was somewhere on those rocky ledges, hidden from sight, as he had told her. So much for his good intentions. He found the soap and quickly scrubbed, then climbed dripping from the water to don his breeches.

Using Rory's silk vest to sit on and his shirt as a towel, Alyson was doing just what Rory had pictured, drying herself in the sun and idly attempting to untangle her snarled hair. The sun felt delicious against her skin, and she wantonly basked in its rays. Rory had made her aware of these physical sensations, and she enjoyed exploring them on her own. She felt quite delightfully wicked and free as she tilted her face up to the sky and felt the heat of the sun scorch at her breasts.

Knowing she would burn if she lingered too long,

Alyson turned and lay on her stomach, allowing the breeze to pick up her hair and caress it dry. Something fell and brushed against her bare arm, and she lifted one eyelid sleepily, seeing nothing. She closed her eye, only to feel another petal-soft brush against her buttocks. Worrying about insects, she turned and glanced over her shoulder, but she saw only the brilliant arched bract of a bougainvillea fluttering away. Smiling at the vivid sight, she glanced around, looking for the vine that pelted her with its lovely foliage.

More petals drifted downward, clinging to her hair, gliding along her skin. Like a colorful snowfall, they began to form in drifts in the crevices of the ledge she lay on. A sudden suspicion made her look upward, to discover Rory's tanned figure crouched on the ledge above, shredding an unfortunate vine as he grinned down at her.

"Maclean!" Indignant, Alyson hastily sat up and grabbed for the discarded shirt. How long had he been up there without announcing his presence? Gentleman, indeed!

Rory came down off the rocks in a few strides, swinging his shirt in one hand, wearing only his white breeches. His flesh gleamed golden, and Alyson could scarcely catch her breath at sight of the sheer physical beauty of him. He swept the shirt from her hands and sat down beside her before she could protest.

"You'll get too much sun and not be fit for anything by tonight." He surveyed her shamelessly, finding no flaw in her smooth white skin except a tiny brown freckle nearly hidden beneath the undercurve of her right breast. He held out a finger to touch her there, and felt her sudden intake of breath, but he was too engrossed in his explorations to take immediate advantage.

As he suspected, her waist was as slender and supple as a man could wish, without the need of corsets and lacing. She sat with her legs curled up and twisted half behind her, but he could see the dark thatch of down between. Rory flattened his hand to travel from the tiny freckle to the lovely valley of her waist, down over her flat stomach to gently test the springy curls at the base. Somehow, knowing he could have her whenever he wished made it easier to be generous with his time. He wanted her to come to him willingly and unashamed, when the time was right.

Alyson did not flinch from Rory's touch, but quickly learned to seize this moment to learn more of this man and his strange moods. His proprietary touch left her flesh tingling and brought an odd knot to her stomach, but the sight of Rory's bare flesh caused even stranger sensations. She desperately wanted to explore him as he did her, but the tense twitch of his jaw warned her that his restraint had a price. So she contented herself with gazing fully on sun-tinted shoulders and chest, tracing with her eyes the way the muscles flowed and flexed beneath his hair-roughened skin. The soft curls on his chest were darker than the rich auburn of his hair, and she wondered how they would feel against her palm.

When his fingers found the thatch of curls at the base of her belly, Alyson glanced up with some alarm to meet Rory's eyes. They smoldered with the hidden fire she knew from her dreams, and the knot in her stomach tightened to nearly unbearable proportions, but still she did not move. She held his gaze, mesmerized by the flickering fires she found there. It wasn't quite relief she felt when he slowly drew his hand away, and she did not lower her gaze from his as he slid his palm against the tautened crest of her breast, then withdrew it completely.

"Do you have any understanding at all of what it means to share a bed with a man?" he asked in an odd, taut voice.

"I think I am beginning to learn," she answered carefully. "Will it hurt?"

"They say it does the first time." He said it softly, unable to tear his gaze from the loveliness that was his to behold. The demands of his body began to drown out thought, and reluctantly Rory pulled Alyson's shirt over her head, hiding the twin temptations of rose-pink buds ready to be plucked.

"Why me?" he asked suddenly, the rougher burr of his voice catching Alyson by surprise.

Squirming into the long shirt and wishing it to Hades, Alyson finally conquered the folds of material and lengths of tangled hair enough to meet Rory's gaze again. "Why you?" she questioned uncertainly, searching for some clue to his meaning in his face. He had been so gentle with her, making her feel as if she really had something to offer him that he desired above all else. She had felt

proud when he admired her. His tone of voice now
worried her, taking away some of the pleasure.

"Why me and not Tremaine? Or Cranville? Or any of
the other men who would gladly have you? I can offer you
nothing. Why would you let me be the one to teach you?"

Comprehension came slowly, and as it did, she stared
over his shoulder to a fluffy cloud gliding a distance off
along the horizon. How could she explain the feelings
Rory gave to her? Didn't he have these same feelings?
Perhaps not. The thought was disappointing, but she had
learned to expect that. Alan certainly hadn't returned her
feelings, and Cranville never made any pretense at having any. She had always known she was different; she
had just assumed that Rory was different too.

Shrugging her shoulders, she brushed aside the question. "Why not? You offered me a choice and I chose the
one I found most acceptable. Are you saying you are
regretting giving me a choice?"

He knew the meaning of that misty gray look that had
come into her eyes, and Rory refused to be diverted.
Tangling her ebony hair between his fingers, he drew her
closer, then circled her waist with his arm and pulled her
into his lap. She weighed next to nothing, but his quick
move had pulled her shirt up, and he could feel her bare
buttocks against his thighs. The sensation excited him
more than feeling another woman completely naked. It
took immense concentration to return to their conversation.

"I regret nothing, lass, but I am going into this with my
eyes wide open, and you are not. You are trusting me,
when I am the last man on earth to be trusted. Why?"

Now she understood, and Alyson smiled contentedly,
leaning against his sun-warmed chest and daringly exploring the soft curls spread across it. She liked the way his
large hands held her so competently, and she liked the
feel of his shoulder beneath her head. She liked a number of other things about this position too, but she wasn't
certain how to enumerate them.

"You won't hurt me on purpose," she answered easily.
There was no other way to explain it. She knew he might
one day hurt her, but in the meantime, he would protect
her and be gentle and like her just the way she was.
Other than her grandfather, she had known no other
man like that.

On the face of it, her reply was quite insane. He was deliberately going to take her virtue and then leave her to her own affairs when they reached London. Perhaps she was so naive as to believe that wouldn't hurt, but Rory doubted it. She was innocent but not a fool. If anything, he was the fool.

He cupped her breast in his palm and pressed a kiss to her cheek, enjoying the singing of his blood through his veins as he did so. He couldn't seduce her here on the hard rocks. She deserved better than that, but it was growing damned hard to remember that fact.

"If you're looking into the future for that silliness, the Sight lies, lass. I am more likely to hurt you than any other."

Alyson smiled and shifted her position to run her bare leg down his. He wore no stockings and his breeches were unbuttoned at the knee, allowing her to feel the muscular strength of him. Rory's hold on her waist tightened, and she leaned against his shoulder to gaze up toward the sun.

"Why will you not marry me?" she asked lazily.

"Because I can only bring you hurt." He couldn't be angry with her. He knew in her innocence she did not know the pain she caused him. He just wondered where her thoughts had taken her now.

"Why did you come back for me? If it is only responsibility you feel, you could have arranged for me to take some other ship."

That was a question he preferred not to consider too closely. It was much easier to play the part of older brother acting out of concern, but he was about to put the lie to that act. Abruptly Rory set her down on the next ledge so he could rise. "Because I am a fool, no doubt, and meant to honor my promise. When do you mean to answer my question?"

Alyson gazed up at him with that angelic expression that made his soul groan in protest. "I did, didn't I? If marrying me will cause me pain, and leaving me behind would be unkind, then you are trying not to hurt me. If what I choose to do now will cause me pain later, then that is my choice and not yours. No one else has ever given me that choice."

Rory stared down at her in blind amazement, not

seeing the half-dressed mermaid, but something else, something so long denied that he could not recognize it for what it was. He only knew that she filled him with inexplicable joy instead of shame, that for the first time in years he felt an emotion above and beyond the calculated needs of day-to-day living. He daren't put too fine a face on it, but it could not all be attributed to lust. He wanted her, no doubt, but what she had done to him since that very first day he laid eyes on her had little to do with lust. He was quite probably bewitched.

"You are a naive simpleton, my jo, if ye think I've given ye any choice a'tall, but if it pleasures ye to think that, I'll not be arguin'." Rory stepped down beside her and caught her by the waist. "There's more to see. Do ye wish it?"

Alyson sensed he asked another question, but she was not yet ready to trade anticipation for actuality. She wished to know more of this man she would marry with her body if not by legal vow. She held the bare arm at her waist with hers and leaned back against him. "Tell me your story, Maclean, and I will go with you where you wish."

16

It wasn't much of a story by any standards, and Rory's taciturn monosyllables made it dry as dust, but Alyson heard with her heart and not her head, and she wept inwardly at the cruelty of man and fate.

He had been too young and immersed in his studies to get caught up in the political fervor between Tories and Jacobites. The fat German king in England and the handsome young prince in France had little effect on the self-centered life of fourteen-year-old Rory Douglas, younger son of the head of the Maclean clan. He worshiped his older brother, James, but his brother's political speechifying bewildered more than enlightened, and their separation due to the demands of land and school prevented better understanding.

While Rory studied in Edinburgh and the titular head of the Maclean clan, his father, spent his time and money on research and with his professional colleagues at the university, James was left to actively administer the Maclean estates in the Highlands belonging to his grandmother. There he made his choice to support his fellow Highlanders in the royal cause of Bonnie Prince Charlie against the usurping German king, and it was from there that James led his kinsmen to slaughter by the bloody butcher, the king's son, the Duke of Cumberland.

At learning his heir had actually raised arms and soldiers for the Glorious Cause, Rory's father had rushed to Stagshead to stop him. He did not return. Alarmed by his father's fears, Rory was more alert than usual when rumors of the royal duke's march on Aberdeen circled the capital many months later. If his brother had taken up arms, it would be to Aberdeen that he would go. Without further thought, Rory had left the comfort of Edinburgh for the April snows of the Highlands in search of his brother.

Rory's story grew glum and curt at this point. In the magnificent golden sun of this southern island, with hibiscus and bougainvillea swaying in the balmy breeze around them, the snows of Scottish mountains and distant years seemed unreal. By now he should have learned to live with what had happened, but he could not. Not only had that disastrous day ended life as he knew it, but the repercussions had continued to plague what was left of his existence for years afterward. He could not escape that day. He would never escape it, unless he took matters into his own hands and corrected them.

Rory didn't say that out loud, but Alyson heard the vow in his voice as he spoke of the result of his brother's rash decision. James died that day at Culloden Moor, whether at the hands of his English cousin Drummond or another of the duke's troops could not be known for certain, but Rory was adamant in his belief that Drummond would have killed James had he not already been dead. Later events proved his theory beyond a doubt in his eyes.

Alyson listened without understanding as Rory explained how the English king and Parliament took away his grandmother's lands that rightfully should have gone to his father, then bestowed them on his Drummond cousin. His grandmother had died from the shock of it, and the Maclean himself had been locked away in prison for treason. Rory was forced to take to his heels upon petition by his cousin that he had been among the Jacobite traitors. His father had died in that prison, a proud man brought to his knees by shame. For that loss, Rory would never forgive.

Next to the loss of his family, the loss of his lands and rightful title meant little to him at the time, but they had become a cause worth fighting for since then as he learned of the ill treatment of the crofters who had always depended on the Macleans for their livelihood. Even in winning, his cousin had not learned family pride. He drained the estates to support his London habits.

By the time the story ended, the sun was dipping toward the ocean. The tide lapped about Alyson's feet as she dangled her legs over the side of a fallen tree on the empty beach where they had wandered. Rory had made lunch for her out of turtle and fish, but the pangs in her stomach warned it was near time to eat again. Rory's competent hands finished weaving a hat of palm fronds for her, and he presented it to her without comment.

She knew the icy snow at his center for what it was now, and silently mourned the man he might have been had fate not intervened. The boy Rory had had a gentleness to him that might have turned him into a man of love and laughter had it been nourished carefully. Instead, he had been forced to develop that hard streak of practicality that stood between him and the rest of the world, twisting everything until he found its advantage. Alyson did not doubt that he would someday accomplish his goal, but only at the cost of his better self. It would take a harshness and cruelty he did not yet possess to dispose of his cousin and his pretensions.

"You will need to marry a lady with great influence at court," she murmured, almost to herself. Her toe drew a pattern in the sand, and she watched the tide roll up to wash it away.

Rory shrugged away such an impossible suggestion.

"Even had I title and wealth enough to attract such a creature, I would prefer the kind of fight I understand. The courts and the law only drain a man. Let us see how my cousin fights when it is just the two of us."

"You cannot get your land back by killing your cousin!" Alarmed at his tone, Alyson glanced up to the man leaning against the log beside her. His skin had drawn tight over his cheekbones, and there was a hard look in his eyes that she would not want directed toward her.

"The land, I'll buy back. He's courting bankruptcy even now. I've almost enough for what it's worth, but he'll not sell it to me. That is why, someday, we'll have to meet. Now, lass, it is time to go. Have you changed your mind any about me? Shall we sail on to Barbados and find you another ship?"

Rory lifted her from the log and held her against him so Alyson had to tilt her head backward to see his face. The need to have his arms around her had grown stronger with each passing minute and evolved into a desperate desire to feel his kiss again. As if his needs paralleled hers, Rory had seldom taken his hands from her throughout the day, and now she could see the kiss burning in his eyes as he waited for her reply. He would retreat instantly should she say she had changed her mind, but she would not trade the fires in his eyes for the coldness that would replace them for all the coins in the world.

"I need no other ship but yours, my lord. Will you take me?"

"Aye, I'll take ye." Rory's soft burr spoke of where he would take her, and if she did not understand, there was his kiss to tell her. He bent his head to capture the sweetness of her lips.

Alyson's hands threaded themselves behind his neck as Rory lifted her squarely against him. The heat of his bare chest burned through the thin linen of her shirt, and an odd tingling began between her thighs where he had touched her earlier. Then his mouth was claiming hers, and all of the sensations came together as one, burning through her, melting what she once had been into some new and, as yet, formless creature.

Rory's lips caressed hers, making love to her with their tenderness, stroking and persuading until her passion began to rise to meet his. When Alyson's lips parted in eagerness, his tongue darted and swirled inside, teasing her into further response until she strained against him, wanting whatever it was his kiss promised. His hand traveled from her slender waist to cup her buttocks, pressing her tightly to the hard bulge pulsing against her thigh where he had lifted her. Rory groaned lightly as he released her lips.

"Ach, lass, I'll take ye, will ye, nil ye, if we do not return to the ship now. There is time yet to do this with a little more ceremony."

Knowing nothing of what he meant, Alyson could only regretfully follow his lead as he set her back on the sand. Gathering up their odds and ends of clothing, helping each other to dress and fasten buttons and ties, touching as often as possible, they prepared to return to the company of others. Hand in hand, they walked around the beach to the cove where the ship was anchored.

A well-fueled fire burned on the sand, and the shadows of Rory's crew moved beside it as they approached. Rory's grip on her hand tightened as the men recognized them and a raucous cheer broke the stillness of the sudden twilight.

A retinue of men came out to greet and escort them toward a pallet of palm leaves near the fire. Alyson marveled at the sudden change in the normally unshaven, ill-kempt crew. Beards had been trimmed or shaved. Clean white shirts had been donned, often accented with colorful neckerchiefs. Dirty hair had been trimmed and washed, queued or braided, until they could almost pass as respectable fishermen. Even Dougall and Jack, who normally maintained a decent appearance, had dragged out coats and cleaned their shoe buckles until they sparkled. Dougall had actually donned a cravat.

In comparison, Rory and Alyson were less than elegantly dressed, but no one seemed to notice. They were seated like royalty beside the fire, handed pewter mugs of wine appropriated from the officers' quarters, and entertained with jokes and anecdotes that often left Alyson in bewilderment. Her puzzlement produced even greater laughter as the meal was served and the drinking began in earnest.

Alyson felt Rory's arm resting reassuringly behind her as she sipped cautiously at the strong red wine. He seemed to find nothing odd in his men's behavior, and his laughter at their odd jests about strange fruits and stolen treasures came easily. She enjoyed the sound of his laughter, the way it rumbled up from deep inside him and burst like breakers upon the shore. She liked it even better when he turned those brandy eyes on her with warmth and a deep affection that she could sense even if he did not voice the words. With his fingers, he fed her the more tempting nuggets from the bowl of fruit they had been served last.

Rory grinned when she licked the last drop of juice from his fingers, and he kissed the smear of pulp beside her lips. "I bet your grandmother never taught you table manners like that," he murmured against her ear.

"My grandmother taught me to respect the customs of my hosts," she replied demurely, tasting the juice running down her own fingers.

"That could get you into very serious trouble if you continue to keep bad company, lass." Rory captured her fingers and carried them to his mouth, tasting them one by one, enjoying the way her eyes widened into oceans of blue as he gently sucked them clean.

The tingling she had enjoyed earlier was rapidly growing out of control and into something Alyson did not understand, but she had no intention of fighting it. A kind of heat blossomed in its wake, and she felt warm all over. The tips of her breasts rose into hard aching points against her cumbersome shirt, and she squirmed nervously at the hot moisture forming in her nether parts, but just the touch of Rory's lips or hands held her captivated.

She found her wineglass refilled with something stronger and sweeter as the meal continued. The jests became tales of the sea, of heroes and villains and impossible feats and beautiful women. Rory's hand began to roam, not satisfied with resting behind her. The fire flickered higher as his fingers traced the curve of her breast and lingered at her waist. He sat contentedly cross-legged beside her, and Alyson's glance more than once inadvertently traveled to that part of him that made him male.

As the tales grew bawdier and Alyson's head began to swim with the heady nectar in her cup, Rory's caresses grew bolder. His kisses found the nape of her neck, sending shivers of excitement down her spine. In the shadows, hidden by the unbound length of her hair, his fingers traveled the path of her breast, circling in on the aching tip until she nearly groaned with pleasure when he finally stroked it. The heat had become a raging fire to equal the flames in front of them, and she could no longer raise the cup to her lips to quench it.

Strange music began to play, and Alyson tore her mesmerized thoughts from Rory's hands to the musicians. An odd assortment of instruments had appeared, flutes and whistles and mouth harps, a cracked and worn fiddle, some hollow object covered with leather for a drum. The sounds they produced had very little to do with melody, but the beat pounded through the night air much as her pulse beat through her veins.

Before long, those of the crew not playing began to dance in unsteady jigs about the fire. Alyson smiled as they pantomimed courtly bows and then swung into country reels. Seeing her smile, Dougall came forward and bowed over her hand, glancing to Rory for permission to join the others.

"I think not." Rory refused him with a glance down at Alyson's black curls.

Alyson looked up in surprise, more at the sultry tone of his voice than at his refusal. When Rory stood and held out his hand to her, it was Dougall's turn to register surprise. The dour Scotsman never joined in his crew's revelry.

Pleased at his offer, Alyson leapt up to join him, taking Rory's hand and swinging it joyously as they joined the antics about the fire. The crew made room for them and an impromptu reel ensued, in which Alyson found herself swung from one to the other, with much shouting and laughter and stumbling over toes. Even shy William took his turn, and Dougall was granted the favor of one circle before Rory came to claim his turn again.

Alyson's breath came quicker as the music raced faster and louder and the wine danced crazily in her head. The crackling fire sent off swirls of smoke, mixing with the rich, mossy scents of the heavy undergrowth all around them.

Awareness heightened by the alcohol consumed, Alyson found herself acutely sensitive to the sway of Rory's narrow hips and the press of his muscular thighs as he swung her around in his arms. Giddily, she scarcely felt her feet touching the ground, and she became more conscious of the masculine scent and warmth of his brown chest than of the sights and sounds beyond them.

The men began a chant that had little meaning to Alyson's ears. With all her senses wrapped up in Rory, she scarcely noticed that the others had stopped dancing and formed a circle beside the fire. Rory, however, had known this moment was in the making, and with a grin and a glance to her rounded breasts beneath the thin fabric, he caught her close and led her toward the waiting crew.

"The broom! The broom! Give them the broom!" The laughing chant made no sense to Alyson, and she glanced around for understanding.

The men were sitting and standing around in a rough circle, brandishing their bottles and jugs and mugs and grinning hugely as Rory presented her. One of the crewmen, a giant African, had apparently been selected as spokesman, and he stood blocking their entrance into the circle. For some odd reason, the men behind him were waving a worn-out broom from the ship's galley.

Alyson could not comprehend the low rumble of the African's monotone, but she suspected no one else could either. He had been selected for the sonorous qualities of his voice and perhaps his ceremonial sway as the rhythm of his words caught him in its grasp.

When the speech came to its end, the music jumped to even rowdier levels and the circle closed around behind them, forcing them nearer the broom that was now held across their path, a foot from the ground. The chant of "Jump the broom!" swelled louder, the circle closed tighter, and before Alyson understood, Rory had leapt across the broomstick, carrying her with him.

A cheer rocketed through the night, but the African obviously had not done with them. Brandishing a wicked knife, he halted them before the circle could open again. Rory's hand tightened around Alyson's, and he looked down at her questioningly, as if she had some choice in what happened next, but the African grabbed their joined hands and held them up before she knew how to reply. The pounding in her head and the swirl of her senses

prevented understanding. It was not until the point of the
knife cut into the vein at the base of her thumb that she
felt anything at all.

There was not even time to cry out before the process
had been repeated with the heavy pad of Rory's palm.
With further stertorous intonations, the African rubbed
their bleeding palms together, and Rory's fingers twined
around hers. Their blood mixed and flowed into each
other, and Alyson felt the completeness of this joining as
her legs threatened to give way beneath her.

Her head spun in light-headed circles, and she felt she
had no weight at all as the pain in her hand throbbed
against the bleeding wound in Rory's. His eyes held her
steady, and her heart began to pound somewhere in her
lower regions as he lowered his head to hers. The kiss,
when it came, was applauded with riotous clamor.

Somewhere, somehow, the circle opened and the empty
shadows of forested vegetation engulfed them, but Alyson
had little knowledge of how they came there, nor of how
she came to be in Rory's arms. Tall grasses, twining
vines, and stunted trees closed in upon them, but Rory's
feet were swift and sure as they moved along the path.
Alyson felt his heart beating near her own, and she
buried her face against the loose folds of his unfastened
shirt. The primitive hunger roused by the strange ceremony made explanations unnecessary. In front of man
and God, she belonged to Rory now, and he meant to
take full possession of his claim.

No church or law made legal what they were about to
do, but Alyson had no doubt or indecision about their
right to do so. She wondered if Rory felt the same, if he
had felt the rightness of the ceremony that had joined
them, but she could not yet speak the words. She clung
to his shoulders, felt the strength of the arms holding her,
and waited.

He set her down outside a small thatch-roofed hut, its
walls made of worn mosquito netting scavenged from a
ship's trunk. Alyson turned questioning eyes to Rory, but
he merely swept aside a corner of the thin curtain and
gestured for her to enter.

Inside, the crew had created a pallet of palmetto leaves
and lavished it with all the linens and pillows to be found
in Rory's threadbare coffers. The effect had been fin-

ished off with a swath of white silk apparently hoarded for some special occasion and never used. Alyson lifted and rubbed it between her fingers, enjoying the sensuous touch of such an extravagant bedcover.

The man standing uncertainly behind her said nothing, apparently waiting for her to speak. He filled her senses to such a degree that she could know his closeness, the shape of his body, the placement of his hands, without turning to see him. She wanted him closer, touching until the only scent and sound and sight she knew was of him.

Alyson turned and tentatively lifted her wounded hand to his shoulder, lifting her eyes to find his. "You will show me what to do?"

Her whisper was so faint that Rory would not have heard had his mind not been solely on her. He lifted her bloodstained palm, and finding the bleeding already stopped, he kissed it lightly. "We are joined already, lass. You will know what to do."

The languorous drawl of his words brought a soft smile to Alyson's lips, and she stepped closer into his embrace, feeling Rory's arm closing tighter around her waist. "What promises did we make with this joining? I heard no words I understood. How are we bound?"

One of Rory's hands roamed up and down her spine while the other located her nape and played gentle games there. She felt his hardness pressed against her belly, and she shivered as she felt his words vibrate through her.

"We are bound only by the promises we give each other. For myself, I need no other woman as long as I have you. You are more than I ever dared dream, Alys. What promises would you have me give?"

Thick lashes curled upward as she studied the tension in the strong lines of Rory's dark features, shadowed in this primitive shelter. Her answer came without conscious thought, pulled from the wind and carried on the moonbeams.

"I would have you love me while you can, just for this while. Will you love me?"

She could not mistake the tenderness in his gaze as he lifted both hands to cup her face. His thumbs traced patterns on her skin as he spoke.

"Aye, lass, I'll love ye, make no mistake aboot that,

'Tis the only love I may ever know, but I give it to ye willingly."

His mouth closed on hers then, and there was no further need of words. Caught between his hands, his mouth branding her with wine-flavored flames, his breath filling her lungs, Alyson could only surrender. Her fingers curled against his chest as her lips parted to allow him entrance, and she was swept along by his need as surely as she had been swept from her feet earlier.

Rory's firm hands moved downward, stroking her throat as if memorizing the vulnerable slenderness, sliding beneath the satin vest to push it down over her arms, coming around to cup her full breasts beneath the thin cover of linen while his kisses continued to play havoc with her breathing. Alyson allowed the vest to fall to the ground, then returned her hands to the hard ridges of his chest, flattening her palms against the smooth skin and sliding upward.

She felt his quick intake of breath and knew satisfaction that her touch affected him as his did her. She had never known how far kisses could lead until Rory taught her. Now she wanted to know more.

Rory's kiss grew more demanding as she discovered the hard buds of his nipples and began to play them as he had hers. But when her hands traveled from there to slide beneath his shirt to his waist, Rory released her mouth and buried his face against her curls with a groan.

"Lass, if you do not release me from these damned tight breeches, I'll not be of any use to you this night or any other."

Alyson laughed low in her throat and ran her fingers along the waist of his pants until she found the buttons. He had unfastened her enough times that she felt no shame in returning the favor, but she was quite unprepared for Rory's reaction to this release.

He pulled his shirt from the loosened band and threw it to the ground, then caught her clothing in both hands and drew it all over her head in one forceful stroke. Alyson gasped as the night breeze suddenly had full access to her flesh, but she had little time to dwell on her sudden nudity. Rory lifted her up and carried her to the makeshift pallet, gently laying her across the silk, where he could admire her with his eyes while he finished shedding his breeches. In the moonlight filtering through the netting, Alyson lost all awareness of her own nakedness in the sudden discovery of his.

Her gaze swept wonderingly from the V-shaped mat of curls on his broad chest to the taut flatness at his waist. Fearful of being brazen, she quickly bypassed the proof of his maleness to follow the muscular lines of his legs. She barely had time to finish her inspection before he was beside her.

She felt him more than saw him. Rory's heavy weight collapsed the fragile pallet closer to the ground. One hard, hair-roughened leg slid over hers, pinning her against the silk. His maleness rubbed her hip as he leaned over her, and she knew her vision hadn't lied. That was Alyson's last conscious thought as Rory's tongue tasted her lips and his hand came up to tease her breasts into wanton points.

It was as if his body was the bow and hers was the string. He played her sweetly first, testing the notes, refining the tension until she quivered beneath his touch. When his mouth began to suckle at her breast, Alyson moaned and rose against him, and the music grew more frantic.

The pull of Rory's mouth heightened all her senses, or what was left of them, as the heavy wine seeped through her veins and made her reckless. His fingers played across her skin, stroking, caressing, finding those places that made her shiver and moan and brought her closer to the crescendo he sought.

When his hand slid between her thighs, Alyson tried to protest, but Rory quickly chased away her words with his kiss. The twin invasions of tongue and fingers warned of what was next, and the fear from her vision made her whimper slightly at the pain to come. Still, her hands wound around his shoulders to welcome him.

When Rory moved over her to lie between her legs, he continued making love to her lips and throat and breasts, worshiping at the altar of her beauty, giving her no opportunity to shy from his further advances. Not until Alyson was crying his name and covering his chest and shoulders with her kisses did he dare take the sacrifice she offered.

Alyson's wild cry as Rory entered her echoed through

the nighttime jungle, at one with the call of the other creatures around them. He moved swiftly, stretching her tightness to accept him, carried by the passion that had long burned behind the closed walls of his heart. Alyson could not hope to keep pace with him, but as he filled the yawning emptiness inside her, moving to salve the hunger he had taught her, she surrendered to all his demands and was swept along on the tide of his needs.

The moment came too soon, exploding in a bright heat that warmed Alyson all the way to her belly and caused Rory to groan and gather her closer while his body shook and trembled above hers. Thoroughly dazed by what had happened, Alyson could only stroke his hair and try to memorize the exact quality of his skin against hers, the number of pounds of his weight pressing her into the ground. Mindlessly she registered the scent of wine on his breath, the soft curl of his hair against her tender breasts. Nothing could quite distract her from the place where they still lay joined together. Try as she might, she could not daydream away the man inside her, nor the knowledge that she was now irrevocably his.

Feeling the blood rushing once again to his loins, knowing he would have to have her again soon before he could reach any level of satisfaction, Rory rolled to his side and carried Alyson with him. He pulled the silk into a cocoon around them so as not to cool her heated flesh too quickly. He found a pillow for her head and made her comfortable within the circle of his arms. And he held her close so he did not need to leave the tight sheath of her scarcely tried body.

His kisses rained lightly against her nose and brow, and Alyson lifted her face to their gentleness. His fingers caressed her cheek lightly, pushing away damp curls. He felt her lips part in a soft sigh, and he captured it with his kiss.

"I did not wish to hurt you, lass," he murmured against her flushed cheek.

"I don't remember the pain, only the pleasure. Will it always be so?"

Lying on his side, Rory relaxed and moved gently against her. "No, lass, it will get better. Let me show you."

Already tight and aching from his earlier ministrations,

Alyson responded readily to these new caresses. Dreamily, only half-aware of what he did to her, she moved as Rory's hands taught her. Her breath quickened when she felt him grow hard and strong within her, but he moved more slowly this time, giving her time to adjust until her hips were moving in a rhythm with his, then demanding more.

Catching the rhythm of her need, he moved faster, harder, responding to her thrusts, until Alyson no longer knew where he began or she ended. She only knew he had pulled her strings so taut that there would be no help for what happened as the music reached its height and he drew himself once more back and forth across the threshold.

Something happened within her, something so startling that she could no longer control her own movements, could only allow the feeling to roll over her in wave after wave of pleasure. Rory murmured reassuring words in her ear as she clung to him, and as her hips began to rise and fall against him again, he moved swiftly to carry her further into this new world they had created. Alyson emitted a soft cry of surprise as they came together, and Rory's shudders matched hers, bringing them so close that she knew his mind and body as well as her own.

She fell asleep, physically and emotionally exhausted, before Rory could leave her. He held her tender body close to his as her breathing evened, but he did not find sleep so easily. Guilt already weighed upon his mind, guilt worsened by the knowledge that he had not only taken her innocence but also broken his promise to her in so doing.

In the pleasure and excitement of teaching Alyson passion and claiming her for his own, he had failed to protect her from the results of this act of love. Even now, his bastard could be forming in her.

17

With her eyes still closed, Alyson stretched luxuriously against the slippery sheets until her toes came in contact with a hair-roughened and distinctly masculine leg. Her eyes shot open just as Rory leaned over her. Placing an arm on either side of her head, he grinned down into her sleep-tousled face.

"Good morning to ye, lass. How are you feeling?"

Her eyes closed again as she captured the sensation of his long, hard body leaning over hers. She felt a familiar stirring, and she murmured something that very much sounded like "moon dreams."

But she purred contentedly and stretched against him when he rubbed her cheek with the back of his hand, so Rory did not worry over her turtle act. He merely pressed a kiss to her brow and inquired, "Moon dreams? Are they better than daydreams?"

Alyson smiled lazily as his body came close enough for her to arch against him. She now knew the meaning of that jutting shaft rising against her, and her eyes opened again to regard him with curiosity. It had not all been a moon dream, then.

"Much better." She watched the way his brandy eyes took on a golden gleam as he looked down on her, and she felt the need for him begin to grow again. "Much more dangerous. They're impossible dreams, you see. Wild dreams. My grandmother told me to beware of moon dreams because I would never be happy with what I could not have."

A shadow crossed Rory's face as he realized the truth of her grandmother's warning. He had meant only to satisfy his hunger for the dreamy angel with the beautiful hands. He had not dared think beyond that to the complications that would certainly ensue. Hurting her was

the last thing he had meant to do. Somehow, he would have to make certain that her moon dreams weren't of him.

But not right now. The worst damage had already been done. It would not hurt if they enjoyed themselves just a little bit more. The day of reckoning would soon come, but not today.

"It's daylight now, lass. No moon dreams, just me. Will you still have me?"

His voice rumbled low and caressing against her ear as Rory lowered himself to nibble at the lobe, and Alyson gave a shiver of delight. He had no need to ask. He could feel her body's response without need of words. Her hand slid along the muscled ridges of his ribs down to his hips, pressing him closer. His heat scorched her skin, and she was aware of the aching soreness between her thighs, but she made no effort to push him away.

Rory accepted her gesture as the answer it was, but he did not immediately accept her offer. Instead, he rolled over and stood up, holding out his hand to help Alyson rise from the rumpled bed.

She opened one eye and squinted at him warily. Just the sight of him standing there naked was enough to give her heart severe palpitations. What did he mean to do to her now?

"Come on, lay-abed. We have only this morning and then we must be off. Let me teach you to swim."

Judging from what she could see of him, he did not precisely have swimming in mind, but a bath would be nice. Remembering the lagoon, Alyson turned over to look for her shirt.

Rory grabbed it before she could reach for it. He also grabbed his own shirt and breeches, then jerked away the silk Alyson had managed to wrap over and under her, finally leaving her completely unprotected from his gaze.

His eyes caught the telltale stain against the white as soon as she did, and grinning, he spread the silk wide between his hands, displaying the certain sign of virginity. "I should have a flag made of this. Then I will always have something to remember you by."

Alyson scrambled up to take it away from him. "I have heard that buccaneers prefer flags of gory skulls, but this is carrying things too far. You are an embarrassment, Rory Douglas."

Instead of relinquishing his banner, Rory cheerfully wrapped her in it, then lifted her into his arms. "I know that, lass, but you'll have to bear my poor humor for the nonce. The prisoners of buccaneers have no other choice."

Then, wearing nothing but his birthday clothes, he carried her out into the sultry warmth of the day. Arms wrapped in the silk, Alyson could do no more than squirm in protest. She only fought in earnest when Rory strode straight out into the water without letting her down. She had stayed in the shallows yesterday. She had no desire to learn the depths.

"Rory, don't! Take me back. It's too deep out here!"

He lifted one dark eyebrow as he finally wrung this vocal protest from his usually biddable miss. "Is it so, now? Am I drowning? What will you forfeit if I take you back?"

"Just take me back, Rory, please. I will learn to swim another day."

"If you're to be jumping off ships and tangling with pirates, you'll have to learn how. Hold your breath, dear heart."

He had more compunction than to drop her in, but the stormy look he received from his black-haired goddess made him chuckle as he dropped her legs and let them dangle in the water while he held the rest of her against him. Even soaking wet and glaring daggers at him, she had the power to arouse, and he bent to give her a watery kiss.

Without his grip, the silk began to float free, but Alyson scarcely noticed. With the water lapping around her and Rory's body pressed to hers, she could only concentrate on one thing at a time, and the silk did not come first to mind. Her body responded joyously to his, and the swimming lesson was as quickly forgotten as the silk.

They didn't quite make it back to the beach. Half in and half out of the water, they made love in the sand with the water idly licking at their legs and toes. The pure pleasure of Rory's possession drove out all thought of discomfort. Alyson knew only the heat of the sun and the liquid warmth of the water and the burning ecstasy that rose inside her with his every thrust. Last night could not have been a moon dream, for not only was it possible to achieve last night's pleasure, this exceeded it. Alyson cried out her joy as her body quaked in rhythm with Rory's. This could only be heaven, and she could wish no more.

"Couldn't we stay here forever?" she murmured as Rory rolled over and carried her with him. Alyson sifted a handful of sand across his sun-browned chest as she rested atop him.

Thoroughly satisfied for the moment, Rory lay back against the hot sand and basked in the sensations of soft breasts pressing into his side and long hair entwining between them. Her words echoed his own sentiments, though they both knew them to be impossible.

"Moon dreaming again, my love? We should perish of thirst as soon as the water barrels emptied. Or we would drown in the first storm to come along. Whichever came first. There would not be time to worry about starving, come winter." He answered lazily, without looking at her. He didn't want to have to think just yet.

Alyson sighed. "Always the practical Scot. I offer you warmth and love and pleasure, and you think about hunger and thirst. Men are all alike. I'll never understand you."

The strange thing was, he understood exactly what she meant. His daydreaming angel had no use for wealth or lineage or even the common basics of shelter and food. She lived in a world entirely her own, made up of sensations instead of thoughts. Had there not always been someone there to see her clothed and fed, she would have perished long since. He wasn't entirely certain that she would even find dying unpleasant.

Chuckling at that thought, Rory roused himself. They had only until the tide turned. The men would be irritable and restless if left to themselves too long under these conditions. Alyson might dream as she wished. It was his lot in life to be practical.

"You need not understand my mind, lass. You understand the rest of me well enough. Come, let us enjoy what time we have without worrying about the morrow."

Alyson's heart stopped as Rory rose from the sand and pulled her with him, and she knew that the security of this embrace would not last forever. She circled his waist with her arms and buried her head against his shoulder and fought back the tears. Nothing was forever.

*   *   *

Leaning idly against the railing, waiting for some sign of the island Rory had promised her, Alyson felt as if forever might be a long time in arriving. These last lazy days while the ship sailed smooth waters to a port where Rory could unload his goods had drifted by in long, lovely hours. The sun had smiled upon them, as the golden color of her skin could attest.

She really ought to be ashamed of her behavior, but Alyson could not summon the necessary moral rectitude. Garbed in Rory's and William's discarded shirts and breeches, tanned by the sun, her hair plaited loosely in a single braid down her back, she looked the part of grace-less savage. And she played the part, too, when Rory came to her at night and took her in his arms and taught her things no lady should know.

Alyson looked back over her shoulder to find the broad-shouldered figure on the quarterdeck, giving curt orders to Dougall as he sought the first sign of land with the spyglass. As if he felt the path of her thoughts, Rory set the glass down and glanced in her direction. The look he gave her warmed her all the way through, reminding her of what they had just done only a few hours ago. He grinned and turned back to this task, but Alyson knew his thoughts traveled with hers.

Remembering that first night aboard the ship after their first lovemaking, Alyson smiled to herself. She had actually managed to be embarrassed after dinner when Rory had escorted her back to his cabin from the table they had shared with Jack and Dougall. Knowing his officers were just on the other side of the door, she had stiffened uncomfortably when Rory tried to kiss her.

Rory had looked at her with puzzlement. "Alys? What is wrong?"

She tried to pull from his grasp, but he would not go without explanation. She threw a nervous glance to the closed door. Jack and Dougall were still talking on the other side. She turned pleading eyes back to Rory. "They will know what we're doing," she admonished him.

Rory recovered quickly from his surprise and began unfastening her shirt. "And they will be right this time," he agreed easily.

"This time?" Alyson did not try to stop his hands.

The need for his touch had already begun to spread to her breasts.

"We have been sleeping together here since we left London. They just figure I've finally made an honest woman out of you."

That logic completely escaped her. She stared at him in disbelief. "Honest? Surely they do not think that ceremony made us married."

Rory brushed her cheek with his knuckles and gave a wry smile. "For men who live without benefit of clergy or law, that is as honest a ceremony as we can have. In their eyes, we are as good as married. I have lived outside the law for so long that I have forgotten any other way of life. Perhaps we are not bound legally, but in every other respect, you are my wife. Does that make you uneasy?"

For answer, Alyson had come into his arms gladly, face raised to meet his kiss despite the voices outside the door. He could have found no better words to win her heart. If they were lies, they were lies she wanted to hear.

Made restless by the memory of Rory's arms around her, Alyson pushed herself from the railing. As pleasant as these last days had been, she was eager for land and people and, with any luck, books. Rory had the ship to keep him busy. She had very little to occupy her time.

Catching her movement, Rory stopped what he was doing to watch as she grabbed the ribbons she had found to decorate the hat he had made for her. Even in its fat braid her hair managed to curl and peek out from beneath the brim. When she lifted her arm to hold the hat against the wind, the shirt she wore tightened over the full curve of her breast, and the blood rushed achingly to his loins. He had been a fool to think a brief dalliance would cure him of this hunger. If anything, his need for her had multiplied.

"Port is in sight," he yelled down to her when she turned his way. The sight of her sudden smile at this news made him irrational. "Go put on your frills and furbelows, and I will take you ashore as soon as I can."

Blowing him a kiss, Alyson danced below and out of sight.

Having learned something of ship routine, Alyson knew she had plenty of time in which to dress. Rory would not go anywhere until he had his precious ship safely anchored and his cargo prepared for unloading. He had said nothing to her of the loss he had taken by not completing his load in Charleston, but she had heard Jack and Dougall talking. He had only the barrel staves from New England, and none of the tobacco that was so much in demand here. There was some talk about not daring to enter the French ports while she was on board, which she did not try to follow. France was at war with England. She knew that much. Why Rory would want to enter their ports, she couldn't fathom. She only knew it was costing him money to have her around. She would have to have Mr. Farnley pay him handsomely for this journey to make up for it, but she wasn't at all certain Rory would accept it.

That was one of the major problems looming before them, and Alyson was reluctant to face it just yet. Rory might say he lived outside the law, but his gentlemanly upbringing still ruled his behavior in many ways. If he were truly an outlaw, he would have kidnapped her, forced her into marriage, and gone back to England to live happily ever after on her wealth. But he was too much the gentleman to take what was not his, and too proud to marry for money. Perhaps that was the reason she loved him, but it made it damnably difficult to contemplate any kind of future.

Donning the lovely gown and petticoats Rory had bought for her, Alyson tackled the problem of her hair. It needed washing in something other than salt water, a good thorough brushing, and some of her grandmother's lotion. She would never be able to control it in any reasonable manner until then. Besides, she had not enough pins to keep it in place. Wrinkling her nose up at the sunburned, wild-haired image above the lovely satin gown, Alyson merely tidied her braid and returned to the deck.

They had already docked, and she amused herself by watching the scurrying activity around her while Rory completed his tasks. Perching unladylike on a barrel in the shadow of the bulkhead, she stayed out of the way, but in a position where she could see the sights and sounds below.

She had grown accustomed to seeing Africans in this new world, but on this island there seemed to be more black faces than white. Bright colors abounded, not just in the garb of the island inhabitants, but in the flowers hanging from houses and over walls, in the brilliant color of the sky and waves, and in the variety of fruits and vegetables in the market stalls. So engrossed did she become in this rainbow swirl that she began to grow a little dizzy with it all.

The sights and sounds took on an ethereal quality of distance. The brilliance of the scene before her began to blur along the edges. Alyson made no effort to fight the sensation, but surrendered to it, needing the knowledge that always came of it.

An open carriage rolled boldly onto the dock, evidence of the wealth of its owner. A crowd had gathered to find out the *Witch*'s cargo and bargain for its goods, and they gave the occupant of the carriage irritated looks as they jostled aside to make way for it.

A black slave guided the carriage horse expertly and held it steady while the carriage occupant leaned out to look around. Alyson's vision suddenly focused entirely on this lone figure as she emerged from the vehicle in a swirl of pink and white organdy, satin bows and frilly parasol. Her pink-and-white complexion had aid of few cosmetics, and her golden hair went unadorned by cap or bonnet. Her smile brightened eagerly as she looked up to the *Witch*, and Alyson had to fight back waves of dizziness as the vision took on its own life.

Gone were the pink frills and expensive accoutrements. In their place was a nearly transparent night rail. Blond hair cascaded wantonly over white shoulders and voluptuous curves. The crowds disappeared, replaced by a candlelit bedroom and a single man, a man who held the blond temptress in his bare, sun-bronzed arms, arms that had held Alyson just the night before.

Barely able to choke back a scream, swallowing the nausea rising to her throat, Alyson jerked away from the horrifying vision to reality. Reality was scarcely better as the vision in pink glided up the plank to board the *Witch*, her gaze firmly focused on the handsome captain standing in shirtsleeves on the quarterdeck. He made no effort to have her thrown overboard as Alyson violently wished he would do, and it was then that she knew of a certainty that these two were already lovers.

Why this knowledge should come as such a shock to her was beyond her ability to comprehend. Rory was a man of the world and would have many such *amours*, she was certain. He had never led her to believe otherwise. It was just the shock of realizing that she was only one of many that made her stomach turn upside down and her insides groan and her heart shatter into tiny little shards. She had known better this time, but still she had allowed a man to make a fool of her. An even worse fool than the first time.

Refusing even to look in Rory's direction, not wishing to witness the happy reunion, Alyson climbed down from her barrel. Head high, cheeks pale, she lifted her skirts and swept down the gangplank the pink canary had just ascended.

Unaware that Alyson had come out of the cabin, caught up in the multitude of tasks of anchoring and unloading, and severely irritated by the inopportune appearance of the one other woman who had ever lingered in his life for more than one night, Rory did not immediately notice Alyson's abrupt departure. Not until he lifted his head from his charts to fend off Minerva's embrace did he catch a glimpse of gray-blue disappearing into the crowd. That thick curly braid of ebony could belong to only one person, and to the dismay of the woman clutching his arm, Rory shook her off and began shouting furious orders as his long legs carried him hastily to the main deck.

Men scrambled from the rigging and up from the hold. Dougall, on the dock discussing terms with vendors, glanced up at Rory's bellows in time to see the small figure disappearing into the crowd. Remembering the last time he had been blamed for this happening, he shoved the cargo manifest into his surprised companion's hands and sprinted into the crowd after her.

Rory was not so lucky. As he was about to appropriate Minerva's carriage, two uniformed soldiers of His Royal Majesty's Navy blocked his way, and he was forced back to the ship to present his documents for the customs officer.

The governor of this island had always looked the other way when Rory had landed here before. The trade between the French islands and their nearby neighbors in the Americas had been forbidden by the British Navigation Acts, but the island's needs were too demanding to take such nonsense from halfway around the world seriously, and Barbados benefited as much from this trade as Rory. Why should a ship sail all the way to London with the food and raw goods so desperately needed in the West Indies just so some rich man's pockets could be lined in England? And the French wines and silks that Rory carried to trade for Barbadian molasses and sugar were much clamored for by the island gentry. To interfere would jeopardize the governor's position.

So the insult of being boarded not only for the first time but also on a legal trip, by navy officers as well as the customs man, outraged Rory beyond coherent thought. The ship's manifest had been hurriedly returned by some obliging citizen, and the cargo was thoroughly searched for illegal French goods. The search was such that Rory sarcastically asked if they would like to check his private quarters in case he had packed it with runaway slaves, and he was not surprised when they did, indeed, search the officers' cabins.

After ascertaining that the cargo had been legally purchased in the colonies and glancing askance at Rory's insistence that he was here only to fill his hold with sugar to take back to England, the intruders reluctantly withdrew, but only after posting guards.

Too furious at the hours of delay to be puzzled by this unnecessary routine, unmindful that Minerva had fled in a huff, Rory glared bleakly out at the dock as his men drifted back to the ship empty-handed. When Dougall appeared last of all, he knew Alyson had done it again.

Dougall glanced at his captain's stiff features and looked away. For a few short days Rory has been a young and carefree boy again. Dougall remembered him from when he was a studious, gentle lad in Edinburgh who loved the few minutes he had free from his studies. Rory had been that boy once more with Alyson. Now he had returned to the cold and ruthless seaman who had acquired a fortune by circumventing the law and skillfully plying his trade. That much of the fortune had gone to the aid of debt-stricken and ailing clansmen, only Dougall knew. He had hoped this charitable side of the captain would keep him on an even keel, but the look on Rory's face now was that of a hunted man. There would be no reasoning with him.

"I lost her near Swan's Inn. A horse bolted and overturned a couple of stands, a crowd gathered to grab what fell, and she got out of it before I could. I'm sorry." Dougall lifted his hands in a gesture of resignation. He had searched every building around there for an hour afterward, but the Maclean would know that without being told.

Rory glanced at the sun rapidly setting in the western sky. Alyson would be unaccustomed to the sudden darkness in the tropics. He hoped she had found a safe harbor before then, but if the district Dougall had left her in was any indication, she was about to find more trouble than she could handle.

Wishing he could steel himself against caring what befell her, but fully realizing the impossibility of ever hardening his heart to Alyson, Rory nodded acknowledgment of his friend's report. He wished he knew what made her do these things, what set her into flight, but her reticence on the subject made it difficult to discern. On the surface, she was cheerful and as open as any book. What simmered below that surface could be a full-time occupation for any man to explore.

"I'll start at the Swan, then. Divide the others up into districts. I canna believe the whole damned world is blind to her."

Dougall scuffled his foot and made a coughing sound in his throat that brought Rory's attention abruptly back to him.

"Montrose is here," he murmured, almost as an afterthought. Montrose never brought good news, and Rory's temper after meeting with his father's onetime bailiff always rose to new and glorious heights. Montrose's appearance added to Alyson's disappearance could only portend disastrous consequences. "I knew you'd be heading for the Swan, so I told him to wait there."

Rory scowled up at the heavens as if the sky above were at fault. He hadn't expected to see his bailiff until he returned to London. For Montrose to come this distance meant something urgent had come up. Maybe the simplest thing to do would be to burn the whole damn town down until there was nothing left for Alyson to conceal herself behind. Then he could get on with the business at hand.

Nodding curtly, he strode off in the direction of the inn. He ought to forget the little brat, he really ought to. They were no good for each other. Nothing could come of this madness that had overtaken them. Or perhaps it was just he who had gone temporarily insane. Alyson was capable of anything at any time. Perhaps she only amused herself with him and had left when she saw a more interesting sight. With Alyson, it would not even have to be another man. A bright bird, a pretty horse, a book vendor's stall would suffice. She was quite capable of drifting away and forgetting to return.

His thoughts were savage, though his heart protested their untruth. He wanted to believe in her. He wanted to believe that just this once he would be allowed to hold something lovely and valuable and not have it torn from him. But his mind knew otherwise. He had only one goal to follow, one purpose to achieve, and he must be ruthless in its accomplishment. Such a life necessarily barred the love and peace that Alyson craved.

Scowling at this conflict between heart and head, Rory sent his thoughts in another direction. He had spent weeks here this summer trying to track down Alyson's obscure references to her father. There had been a navy brigantine patrolling these waters about the time he judged her father would have been here. An early hurricane had swept through this island twenty years ago, leaving the residents unprepared, making the date fairly reliable. What had happened to the ship or its crew in the aftermath of the storm was not quite so clear. Perhaps his informants had found more reliable information by now. He had certainly left enough messages in every café and tavern across the Caribbean. Barbados had been the only place where anyone recalled the ship.

Rory entered the Swan and searched for his bailiff. This tavern was little different from any one of a thousand he had been in from seaport to seaport. The room stank of unwashed bodies, cheap candles, burning oil, and rum. If there had once been windows, they had been boarded up long ago. The resultant dark gave an evil glow to the candlelit smoke but didn't disguise the fact that the majority of the occupants were of less-than-gentlemanly appearance. Here and there might be spotted a wealthy planter on a binge, or one of his staff looking for willing females. On the whole, the clientele tended to be seamen just hitting port or looking for a ship out, and the ragtag scavengers who preyed on them.

Montrose looked as out-of-place as one of the frock-coated planters. Even in this heat he had not discarded the wig he considered his badge of office, his claim to authority. Once he had managed the laird's sprawling estates. Since the rebellion, he had lived hand-to-mouth until Rory had come upon him one fortunate day. As a twenty-year-old seaman Rory had not been able to offer the man more than some semblance of pride and hope, but Montrose had been grateful for even that small handout. He had been loyal to a fault ever since.

Still, Rory approached him with growing dismay. He didn't want to know what trouble was brewing back in the Highlands to bring the man here. Tales of bankrupt crofters and ailing cousins could be dealt with by letter and his infrequent trips home. Whatever Montrose wanted now would demand time and money, and he had little enough to spare of both. He wanted to find Alyson before he tackled any other problems.

The bailiff had chosen a table at the very rear of the room, near the kitchen. That probably meant he didn't wish to be overheard, for the man otherwise proudly exhibited his wig and worn frock coat for the tavern occupants to admire. His position was more important to him than the very little money Rory was able to pay him for his services. The fact that he managed only rumors and reports of another man's estate seemed not to trouble him at all.

Rory settled in the chair opposite the bailiff and gestured to the barmaid. He hadn't eaten since breakfast, but a drink was what he needed now. "You came a long way to see me, Montrose. How did you find me?"

"Lady Campbell had your letter from Charleston saying you were headed here, and I took the first ship out. When I arrived, I heard you'd already been and gone, and I despaired of finding you. It's the Lord's will that you returned."

The Lord's will and a fey creature with ebony hair and a face like an angel's, but Rory didn't disillusion the man. He threw a coin to the barmaid and drank deeply of the rum she had delivered to him. The fiery liquid burned all the way down to his empty stomach but did not reach the cold place around his heart.

"So what has my esteemed cousin done this time to send you cavorting halfway around the world to tell me?"

Montrose never launched directly into any story when a substitute route could be found, and Rory imbibed heavily as the tales of woe unfolded and grated his nerves to threadbare ribbons while he waited for the real reason for the man's presence. His monosyllabic replies provided no encouragement, but the bailiff diligently proceeded down his list of wrongs while Rory ordered a second round.

On the other side of the wall, nursing a bruised shin while a kindly landlady pressed her newly mended and cleaned gown, Alyson heard the sound of Rory's curt monotone and shivered.

18

Barbados, August 1760

How could Rory have found her? She was quite certain she had lost Dougall in the near-riot outside, and the landlady had adamantly lied about her whereabouts when he returned later asking questions. Rory couldn't know she was here.

Of course he didn't, or he would be in here now dragging her out by the hair. He knew she was gone, but he didn't care enough to search for her personally. His business was obviously more important.

That thought hurt, even though Alyson had known the truth of it from the very first. Rory had never lied about her importance in the scheme of things. He had shown her that quite clearly when he had hauled her across the ocean rather than risk his ship, and again when he had not returned to Charleston for months after he had promised. It was best that she get away now before she began dreaming impossible dreams again.

She glanced toward the older woman, who chatted amiably about the friends and home left behind in Sussex many years before. She evidently considered Alyson a genteel young lady momentarily injured and separated from her servants in the riot outside, and sought to keep her happily occupied while she awaited rescue. She had been a trifle dubious when Alyson insisted that the man sent to find her was not from her family, but she had mildly offered to repair Alyson's gown after Dougall had been sent away. Now Alyson regretted the delay.

She had to get away before Rory's extraordinary ability to find her discovered her location. She tried not to listen to the conversation on the other side of the wall, but the man doing most of the talking had a very insistent voice.

She listened with growing dismay to tales of some family called Crandall, whose breadwinner had been forced from the land that he had always farmed and who had been killed when he tried to poach salmon to feed his ailing wife. The wife had died and the daughters had slowly slipped into the desperation of the streets, forced to sell themselves for the crumbs needed to eat. Somehow, this tale and the others all had to do with the cousin who had stolen Rory's land and title, but she wasn't certain how. She simply recognized the name Drummond spoken more than once and with bitter scorn.

The tales grew more heartbreaking and Rory's replies even fewer and farther between. She cringed and drew the borrowed blanket more tightly around her when the laird's roar finally broke loose and his heavy fist thudded against the table. She desperately tried to remember the words just previous to that roar—something about the lands and Drummond and the market. She was listening more carefully when the other man spoke again.

"Hamilton has agreed to act as go-between, Maclean. The king's too ill to intervene. He'll make the offer and sign the deeds, then transfer them to you when the money changes hands. But he canna do it without your being there. He's poor as a church mouse and canna raise those kinds of funds on his own."

"And what in hell makes you think I can?" Rory's voice broke with a mixture of fury and despair. "I doubt there's that much money in all the Highlands. My cousin taunts me, you fool. Can you not see that?"

Dismay tinged the answering voice. "But Lady Campbell says you have run off with an heiress. It's all about London. Some say you kidnapped her, others say she ran after ye, but it's the truth you both disappeared at the same time."

Alyson heard those words as if they came to her in a dream. London seemed so distant now. She had rather imagined the inhabitants would have forgotten her as she had forgotten them, but the scandal her departure had caused was as nothing to the other implications of the man's words. Deirdre had obviously thought Rory would marry her and had sent Montrose to bring them back to save the family estate. She couldn't blame Deirdre, she supposed. Rory must have sent her a letter reassuring her that she was safe. It was only to be expected that they would have to marry under the circumstances.

Rory's reply was not particularly coherent, consisting of long strings of invectives between phrases, and Alyson didn't linger to hear more. Her gown was complete, and she hastily slid down from her stool to allow the landlady to help her dress. She wasn't at all certain what she ought to do, or even what she wanted to do. She just knew she could not let Rory find her here.

Her benefactors's frequent references to the "governor" had indicated this town had some type of British authority. That seemed an even more logical place to appeal to than a solicitor. If she used the title Deirdre insisted she had a right to and explained her situation, surely the governor would take her in until Mr. Farnley could be notified and funds sent to her.

Remembering the result of that last plea for help made Alyson a trifle dubious of this plan, but she had little other choice. This time she had left Rory without a farthing to her name. She could not even find employment cleaning kitchen floors, garbed as she was.

"Mrs. Brown, if I could only get to the governor's house, I am certain he could find my father. I would be

quite safe waiting for him there. Could I hire a carriage?" The lie did not come with too much difficulty.
After all, her father had last been seen in these waters,
although unless he were a wizard, the governor would
not be able to find him.

The landlady frowned and regarded Alyson's tousled
loveliness with a hint of doubt. Still, something in those
mist-gray eyes softened her thoughts, and she brightened. "I'll have Jacob and Aloysius escort you. The walk
is none too far, and no man would think to lift a finger to
you with those two about."

Alyson understood her reasoning when presented to
Mrs. Brown's two hulking youngsters. Although still in
their youth, they towered well over six feet and had
shoulders like young oxen. Their bland, pleasant expressions gave no cause for fear, and she accepted their
escort with delight.

Rory was not having it quite so easy. After sending
Montrose back to the ship for a meal and a decent bunk,
he had tried to set about his task of locating Alyson. The
number of rums consumed and the agony tearing at his
breast combined to make concentration somewhat limited, however. He found himself relating some small
portion of his woes to a slim, graying man who appeared
as out-of-place here as himself.

With quiet questions, the man pried out of Rory the
reason he was searching taverns for a black-haired lady in
braids and satin gowns. He nodded understanding at
the parts left unsaid and stared glumly into his own mug.

"I hope you find her, son. I know what it is to lose one
you love from sheer youthful enthusiasm. The cause may
seem worth it today, but take my word for it, lad, you
will regret it when you are older. If the lass loves you,
she will marry you whatever your fortune might be.
Women are like that. They don't see things as we do, and
thank the good Lord for that. If I were you, I'd inquire at
the governor's. He's a hard man, but fair. He'll not want
a young lady to come to harm in these streets. And when
you find her, marry her, lad, marry her proper and legal.
If she were my daughter, I would want that. You look
like a likely young man. Lack of fortune should be no bar
to love and honor."

To Rory's drunken mind, this logic made good sense,

even knowing he possessed very little honor any longer. He left the tavern feeling much as if he had been given a father's blessing. He'd find the wench and wed her, and then she would have no reason for flight. Wives didn't run from their husbands. It would serve his wicked angel right to have her wings clipped.

An even more fortuitous thought crossed Rory's befuddled mind. By damn, if he married her, Cranville couldn't! That would put an end to the notorious earl's pursuit. He would marry Alyson to protect her! Even Alyson could understand that.

Montrose's insinuations that all of London thought her ruined and expected her to have to wed him did not linger long in Rory's reflections. Alyson would give no care to what all of London thought. Besides, they would have to live at sea until he had earned the fortune necessary to pay off his greedy cousin. What London thought was of little concern to him. Finding Alyson and keeping her was what mattered.

He would have the governor send out troops to look for her. That was the least his old friend could do after insulting him by searching his ship and delaying him this day. They would have the wedding here, with the governor in attendance. That should quiet any clacking tongues.

Quite proud of his noble decision, Rory returned to his ship long enough to wash and change into decent clothing. He would play the part of gentleman for Alyson's sake. He could not offer much, but he could offer that.

The memory of how little he had to offer caused a sudden depression, and Rory swigged heavily from his flask to return the golden haze of earlier. The whisky on top of the rum and an otherwise empty stomach did wonders for his well-being, and he left the ship with determination and Dougall in tow.

Dougall did not even try to fathom what mad bent Rory's mind had taken now. He was content to believe that the captain had found some solution to Alyson's disappearing ways, and he followed eagerly.

By the time Rory arrived at the governor's mansion, the evening was well advanced. Light streamed from the windows and music drifted through the open panes. Carriages lined the drive, and couples strolled unhurriedly about the spacious grounds.

Rory glared at this unexpected delay to his plans. The governor would scarcely be available for a private audience while this melee was going on, and Rory still had presence of mind enough to know it would take very serious conversation to have troops sent out to locate one misplaced female.

Stationing Dougall outside as a precaution, Rory entered the festivities without difficulty. His face was known here, the servants had no hesitation in giving him entrance.

Entering the crowded ballroom, Rory tried to locate the short rotund figure of his powerful friend, but the swirl of dancers and onlookers confused his already befuddled brain. Minerva found him before anyone else did.

The pretty widow flounced up to greet him while clinging to the arm of a particularly wealthy planter, and Rory wondered idly what he had ever found attractive in her colorless features. True, she had been willing enough and he desperate enough to try her favors, but to think such coy blandness could distract him from Alyson's fascinating beauty . . . ! He must have been temporarily insane. Or perhaps it had become a permanent condition. His gaze rudely drifted over Minerva's shoulder to search the room, until her chatter finally penetrated his cloudy brain.

"And Lady Alyson is such a delightful creature! Why, she has charmed every man on the island this evening. How quaint of her to come quite unattended. There is some mystery about it all, I'm sure. The governor has welcomed her like a long-lost cousin, and she did seem particularly eager to leave your tender care, Rory dear. That *was* her you were chasing through the crowd this noon, wasn't it?"

Rory ignored Minerva's maliciousness in favor of returning his gaze to the ballroom. Alyson, here! Damn, but he must be drunker than he thought to be chasing her through taverns, when he ought to know by now that she always landed on cat's feet.

Now that his target was Alyson and not the portly governor, he found her soon enough. Some lady's maid had brushed and coiffed her hair into an elegant chignon with only a minimum of pretty curls to escape about her lovely face. The blue satin held up moderately well under the brilliance of the chandeliers, with the addition of a froth of lace about her bare shoulders. Even from this distance he could feel the effect of the daring décolletage he had chosen for his eyes only. The little witch had not worn a fichu in this elegant company.

Rudely stalking away from Minerva, Rory headed directly for the circle of dancers containing his wife-to-be. Laughing gaily as she twirled from one masculine arm to another, she seemed not to see him, and grimly he vowed to put an end to that conceit soon enough. He was the one who had wooed her and won her to his bed, and it was his arm she should be clinging to. He'd had enough of this flighty dalliance.

The circle of dancers welcomed him as the music struck up a lively country tune. Alyson was situated on the far side of the circle, but the steps would lead him to her soon enough. He was eager to see her face when she found herself grabbing his arm in the allemande.

The circle shifted rapidly and Rory had difficulty keeping his straying feet in line. He partnered some plump miss with a simpering smile, then found himself promenading with a gray-haired dowager. Every time he glanced up, Alyson was with some new young beau, and he never seemed to come closer.

The dance grew more frantic as couples skipped through the center to the clapping of the others. Rory grabbed the plump miss's clammy hand and danced her to where he judged Alyson to be, only to discover her circling the ring with some young scholar with a receding hairline. Groaning in frustration, he followed the circle around to where he had been, only to find himself confronting the old lady again.

His urge to throw aside all convention and make a mad dash for the place he had last seen that cap of ebony curls was thwarted when the fiddlers leapt into the fray and sent the dancers spinning off in another direction entirely. Every time Rory looked up, Alyson was elsewhere, and the plump miss smiled at him as if they were already engaged.

By the time the dance ended, Alyson had disappeared.

Breathlessly running down the stone steps of the terrace to the street below, Alyson had to stop and gasp for air. The music still swirled in her head, and the vision of

Rory valiantly trying to dance his way to her pounded through her veins. He had looked so handsome in his silk coat and ruffled shirt that she had almost surrendered without a fight. Almost.

The other vision had saved her, the one of Rory and his blond lover. She could not put that thought from her mind. Not until she had time to learn to deal with that betrayal could she face him again, and that might not be anytime soon.

The governor had been so excited to see her that she had not even considered his turning her immediately into Rory's hands. She had received the distinct impression that he held Rory in particular disfavor for some reason, but then, she had never been very good at understanding other people's motives. She just knew she wasn't safe even here, and she knew nowhere else to run.

So it was with quiet resignation that she stepped into the carriage-lined lane, to come face-to-face with Dougall.

Dougall respectfully lifted his cocked hat and folded it under his arm as he blocked Alyson's escape. She looked a trifle wild-eyed but weary, and he felt only sympathy at her despairing look.

"If ye will, lass, I know of a place ye can get a good night's sleep in a proper bed, in a proper house. Will ye trust me to take you there?"

She had expected to be led unceremoniously back to the ship and locked in the captain's quarters. This reprieve seemed only miraculous. She looked at the bushy-browed mate with suspicion. "What kind of a house? I don't want to be foisted off on strangers again."

" 'Tis an empty house. The owner will have no objection to yer using it, I'm certain. It will be better than running in the streets all night."

Incredulous, Alyson tried to find the catch in this. "Does this house have a key? Can I lock the doors?"

Dougall shrugged with a measure of embarrassment. "It does that, lass, but I'm not makin' ye any promises where the captain is concerned. He's a hard man, sometimes. I just thought to offer ye a chance to be alone. Living on a ship is hard to get used to sometimes."

He wasn't offering a permanent haven but a temporary respite. That was better than any other choice she had at the moment. With a shrug to match Dougall's, she fell into step with him.

Not one to converse idly, Alyson drifted along, lost in her own thoughts, as Dougall led her from the palatial estates of the influential to the more modest residences of the town, their feet crunching the shell-strewn streets. In the faint gleam of the moon she admired the pastel colors and lush foliage and hoped one of these houses would be where they would stay.

They came to a halt before a sadly neglected narrow house that still held considerable charm even though overgown by flowering vines and giant hibiscus. Dougall unlatched the door and gestured for Alyson to enter.

They passed through airy dark rooms, sparsely furnished but scrupulously tidy. Dougall found a candle and lit it to guide their way upstairs, and Alyson had a glimpse of polished dark woods and leather, but little of feminine touches of color and softness. She glanced uncertainly to Dougall's craggy face.

"Are there no servants?"

He gave another of his diffident shrugs. "A maid comes occasionally, I believe. It is too late to fetch her tonight. I'll send her in the morning, if you like."

Somehow, that reassured her. He seemed to know the house and its routines well. Perhaps it was even his own, and he was being modest about it. She felt safe here, and a real bed would be a luxury.

The thought of a bed turned her thoughts swiftly in another direction. As they stopped outside the bedroom door, she turned to study Dougall's honest face. "Are you going to send for Rory now?"

Dougall shoved his hands in his pockets and returned her look carefully. " 'Tis not safe to leave ye alone. He will have to figure it out for himself."

Those terse statements could have several meanings if Alyson considered them with care, but she preferred to accept them at face value. Dougall had no intention of going back to the governor's house to get Rory. She gave him a small smile of gratitude.

"Then I shall trouble you no more this evening, sir. Thank you."

Dougall watched her enter the bedroom and exhaled heavily as the door closed. The captain had found himself a handful with this one, for all that she appeared as sweet and docile as a summer rose. He did not envy either of them when the morning broke and Rory arrived with pounding head to find this fey sprite well-rested and ready for him. The captain would be in a foul mood and ready for a battle, but he'd never had to fight honey before. Dougall had no intention of wagering on the outcome.

Morning came sooner than Dougall anticipated.

Having confronted the governor and spent an hour of wine and argument with him before being given permission even to leave the premises, Rory had gone beyond anything so amiable as a foul mood to the nether regions of dangerous implacability.

He wanted to commit murder, but since no convenient victim was immediately at hand, other drastic action needed to be taken. His earlier drunken plans solidified into determination with the knowledge that Cranville's lies were responsible for half his troubles, and the cause of the other half had evidently escaped with his first mate.

Alyson could be the only reason Dougall had deserted his post. From what information he had dragged from the governor, Rory knew Cranville and the *Neptune* had come in search of them but had sailed this morning to search elsewhere, so there was no danger that the damned earl was responsible for Dougall's rank betrayal. Only Alyson was capable of leading grown men astray so quickly.

Discovering Dougall had not returned to the *Sea Witch*, Rory dumped his sleeping men from their hammocks and sent them scurrying with furious orders. If he wasn't going to get any sleep, neither were they. There was no time to lose, in any case. He had to carry out his plans and make them a *faint accompli* before Cranville had time to return.

Dougall had not made any attempt to sleep, but propped his feet up on the rolled arm of a leather couch downstairs and rested with hands behind his head, waiting for Rory's appearance. He showed no surprise when the captain roared through the door shouting his name, but he did raise an eyebrow at the retinue of half-dressed, hung-over seamen stumbling in his wake.

Rory scowled as the older man slowly unfolded himself to stand. "Where is she?"

Dougall shrugged. "Asleep." Now standing at eye level with his young captain, he regarded him with a trace of doubt. "The lass is weary. Ye have not given her much rest these last days. Wait until morning before ye tear her to shreds."

"You have some promise that she will be there come morning?" Rory asked scornfully. Then, striding to the window, he pushed aside a shutter and indicated the hint of light on the horizon. "It's dawn now. How much longer does she need to make her escape?"

Sending up a silent apology to the lass sleeping peacefully upstairs, Dougall spread his hands in surrender.

Alyson woke from her fretful slumber with the knowledge that someone else was in the room besides herself. Wearing only a short shift and no covers in the room's warmth, she reached immediately for the protection of a sheet.

"Ye needn't fash yerself. I'll not be stayin' long."

Rory's voice slurred out of the cover of darkness, and it took Alyson a minute to focus her gaze on the pale gleam of his ruffled shirt near the door. He was leaning against the panel as if to block her escape, but all she could think about was the strength of those muscled arms crossed over his chest and how much she longed to have them around her again.

"Where are you going?" she murmured foggily, wondering if she were still dreaming. Did he mean to leave her here?

"To find a clergyman. There's bound to be one in this forsaken place somewhere. Dougall's gone to fetch Rosie. She'll find something suitable for you to wear."

He spoke in stilted intonations, trying very hard to enunciate clearly. Alyson paid more attention to his forced speech than his actual words, thus entirely missing his meaning. "Why are you talking like that?" She sat up in the bed, and pulling the sheet more securely around her, watched him with curiosity.

How in the hell could a man vent his justifiable rage when its object sat like a wanton mermaid in the middle of his bed asking inane questions instead of fighting back? How could anybody argue with a misty vapor who defied logic?

Grinding his teeth together, Rory made another attempt. "I am trying very hard to be patient, Alyson. If you wish to explain why you ran away again, I'm prepared to listen, but nothing you can say will change my mind. It has been made very clear to me this night that we have no other choice. As soon as I can find a clergyman, we will be married. There will be time to shop for a trousseau afterward, and then we will return to London."

That penetrated Alyson's understanding, but she continued to stare at him in perplexity. "You are very drunk," she whispered.

"I was, but I'm cold sober now." That came close enough to the truth. As he saw her there in the first rays of dawn, her satin-soft hair streaming in thick cascades over nearly bare shoulders, his mind had nearly stopped functioning altogether. Not even drunken thoughts could intrude through the desire racing through him.

Alyson realized that Rory's shadowy figure was slowly emerging from the gloom as the sun's light began to reach the bedroom window. His unshaven face had a worn look to it, and his long auburn hair was working untidily from his queue to curl around his collar. It was quite possible that she loved him even more like this than when he was sober and in complete charge of himself, but that was a moot point.

"Were you cold sober when you made love to that pink canary?"

Had that question made any sense at all to Rory's befuddled mind, he might have recognized it as the opening for the fight he sought. But Alyson didn't play the game fairly, and he stared at her with incomprehension before regaining control of the conversation.

"I don't see pink canaries when I'm drunk, and I don't think I even want to know what you're talking about. Just be ready when I return." He lifted his shoulders from the door and started to turn away, when Alyson's reply brought him to a halt.

"You can find all the clergymen you like, Rory Douglas, but I'll not marry you."

For Alyson, this speech was quite firm and decisive, and Rory turned to stare at her in disbelief. She was the one who had wanted marriage in the first place. Now what in hell had she got in her mazed brain? He glared at her unreasonably and approached the bed. "You have someone else in mind, perhaps?"

Alyson shrugged. "Not particularly. I do wish you would leave, Rory. You are making me quite uncomfortable."

"I am making you uncomfortable?" He repeated her words with incredulity. "Uncomfortable, is it? Someday let me tell ye how I've spent this night while ye played at yer fancy ball and slept soundly in my bed! It is more than uncomfortable I will make ye, should ye ever lead me such a merry dance again!"

His control was rapidly slipping and Alyson glanced nervously at the door, wondering if Dougall would come to her rescue should he turn violent. She had never seen Rory truly violent, but she remembered quite clearly the day he had ruthlessly challenged Cranville to a duel. The violence had been well-hidden, but it had been there, just the same.

She glanced back to Rory's rigid features and realized what he had just said. His bed. This was Rory's house Dougall had brought her to. He might even have made love to the pink canary in this very bed. With sudden distaste she flung her legs over the side of the bed and stood up, trailing the linen sheet like a Grecian goddess.

"If we make each other so uncomfortable, then it is quite obvious we should not be married. I'll dress and leave you to your bed, if you will but give me a few minutes' privacy."

To touch her would be fatal to what remained of his control, but Rory contemplated grabbing those lovely white shoulders and shaking her until her teeth rattled. "I'll give ye privacy enough for now, but I'll be back with the clergyman before noon. I expect you to be ready when we arrive."

Alyson peered at him uneasily as she clutched her sheet and backed toward the window. Rory had never been quite this unreasonable before. "He cannot marry us against my will. Even I know that much."

It had never truly occurred to him that she would refuse, and Rory had no formulated plan at hand to persuade her otherwise. He only knew that he had made up his mind it was in her best interest, and that she had best agree to it now before anything else happened. Having little expertise in the fine art of persuading maidens, he fell back on his practical business sense.

"Then I would suggest, lass, that you change your mind or find yourself staring at the cold walls of Bridgetown's charming prison."

He had gone stark raving mad—that much was clear to
Alyson as she stared at Rory's disheveled handsomeness
in dismay. Something or someone had driven him quite
over the edge. She tried to gather her wits about her to
combat this new problem. "I have done nothing wrong. I
can't be put in prison for refusing to marry you. The
governor would not allow it."

Rory stonily disregarded this mention of his erstwhile
friend. "Do you remember the voucher you left in my
trunk when you 'borrowed' that gold from me?"

That had been so many months before that Alyson was
left at a loss for a reply. Voucher? Was that what she had
written? It had a faintly ominous ring to it, and she was
almost afraid to nod acknowledgment of the fact.

Rory advanced his case at her barely perceptible nod.
"Are you prepared to repay it?"

Bewildered, Alyson almost lost her grip on the sheet.
Rory seemed some stranger to her, not at all the tender
gentleman of yesterday. Could a person change overnight? "Of course," she responded faintly. "Just as soon
as we return to London."

"That's not what I had in mind, Lady Alyson." Rory
sneered at the title the governor had continually thrown
in his face earlier. "I need the money now. People who
give out vouchers are expected to repay upon demand,
otherwise they go to debtors' prison until they raise the
sum. At least, in there I would know where you are."

Not at all certain this could truly be happening, Alyson
backed against the window seat and sat down abruptly.
She couldn't tear her gaze from the frozen features of
Rory's square-boned face. There was nothing of gentleness in the cloudy darkness of his eyes, and the hawklike
nose suddenly had a fierceness to it that she had not
recognized before. She had been warned, but she had
never believed. She still couldn't believe it.

"You wouldn't do that," she whispered uncertainly,
waiting for him to laugh and tell her he teased.

"Try me. I'll be back with a clergyman and a soldier.
You can choose which one you prefer."

Rory swung on his heel and stalked out, leaving Alyson
cringing in the window seat, crying for the man she had
thought she loved.

19

The bright light of a Caribbean midafternoon caught the golden strands in the tall, distinguished man's otherwise silver locks. Dressed properly for a formal call, he took the slip of paper from the pocket of his beige silk frock coat, looked up to the shabby town house across the street, and back at the paper with a frown. The gold braid edging the turned-back cuffs of his coat sleeves and tails matched the golden elegance of his embroidered vest and the shining buckles of his shoes. The years had been kind to him in some ways, but the lines about his eyes and mouth revealed it had not been without harsh experience.

Returning the paper to his pocket, he regarded the stream of surprisingly well-turned-out sailors and polished soldiers entering the house. He had already noticed the governor, several distinguished gentlemen, and a clergyman enter, and there seemed to be a fluttering of maids and dressmakers and people with flowers running in and out and back and forth every time the door opened. Obviously it was not an auspicious time for a drop-in call. It seemed quite possible that a wedding was in preparation.

Remembering the drunken young sea captain from the night before, the gentleman smiled sadly and started to walk away. He was no stranger to the odd quirks life takes. Perhaps he had been talking to the man he sought just last night and didn't know it. He hoped so. He liked what he had seen of the man, and he hoped he had taken his advice to wed his little heiress. His own daughter had just recently married, and she seemed quite content with her wedded state, although the man brought only his wits and strength and good name to the marriage. Wealth wasn't everything.

He remembered Brianna laughing at what she had

called his "moon dreams." He had thought it was necessary to prove himself to his father, to prove that he was worthy of being his son and heir, and earning the right to choose the woman he loved instead of the one chosen for him. How foolish he had been; what lives he had wasted on those foolish dreams.

In guilty memory of the woman he had finally married and who had borne his children, he had to admit that he had not suffered terribly for his decision. True, he missed the love that had bound him to the home and family of his youth, and the memory of Brianna would always tear at his heart, but he had no reason for complaint. Had it not been for his wife, he would have died and had no life at all. Given that alternative, he could have no regrets.

Yet he continued to finger the flimsy sheet of paper in his pocket. Why would anyone be searching now, after all these years, for a ship and crew long since buried in the deep? His active mind worried at the question, prying at it with curious fingers from all directions.

There surely must have been an official inquiry at the time, although Diana and her father had never mentioned it to him. That was the only thing he held against them. Withholding his past had been cruel, although he certainly understood why they had done it. Old Morris had been a dying man even then. The plantation had been in ruins and was scarcely a promising dowry for a daughter whose kind and generous nature did not overcome the lack of physical beauty with which to attract suitable young men. A healthy young man with no memory must have seemed a gift from heaven at the time. The chance that his memory might come back at sight of his uniform could not be risked. They must have burned it in hopes that his memory would never return.

He sighed and headed for the tavern, where he could submerge his loneliness for a little while longer. Memories were all he had anymore, it seemed. His deceitful Diana had died in the epidemic of yellow fever that had claimed his sons last year. Only his daughter survived, and she was happily wedded and breeding his first grandchild. That gave him something to look forward to, but not enough. His son-in-law managed the plantation well enough on his own. He needed something new to occupy his mind.

That was why his mind kept returning to the scrap of paper in his pocket and the life he had left behind so many years ago. Thinking him dead, Brianna would be happily married by now, with probably a dozen children around her feet. She had always loved children and scolded him for making her wait. She had been right, of course. He should have taken her home right then, and they could have made babies within the secure walls of the old Hall and lived happily ever after. Instead, he had had to live up to his responsibility and prove himself, and so had lost it all.

Well, perhaps the hard lesson he had learned would bring luck to that nice young sea captain. He might even inquire of the man the best ship to take should he decide to finally make that return to England. It had occurred to him to write to see if his father were still alive, but the story was too difficult to put on paper and he feared to disturb again whatever lives he had once shattered.

Diana had never realized his memory had slowly returned. It would have only brought her pain to know he had already been married and that their entire respectable life was a sham. Besides, he had his sons and daughter to think of by that time. It had seemed best not to dredge up the past.

But he could see no obstacle in doing so now. Perhaps he should inquire into family affairs first. If his father were no longer alive, his cousin's son would have inherited. The lad could not possibly recognize him after all these years. Or his father could have remarried and there would be complete strangers in residence now. His return would upset a lot of lives. It would be best to make a few inquiries first.

It gave him something to look forward to, and his step became a little jauntier as he strolled down the hill and out of sight.

From the window of Rory's bedroom Alyson watched the slender, distinguished-looking gentleman disappear from view, and gave a sigh as reality intruded once again. As the clergyman behind her had droned on, she had lost herself in daydreams of the gentleman's identity and why he would stand looking so forlorn outside a house that had seen much better days. She was quite certain he had a fascinating story to tell, but she was equally certain she would never hear it. Had she been free to do so, she would have wandered out of the house and followed him. It seemed like quite a natural thing to do, but she knew Rory and the clergyman would never understand when she explained she wished to follow a stranger simply because he resembled the ghost of her father.

Wearing the lovely silver satin gown adorned with yards of white lace at neck and sleeves that the mantua-maker had produced and hurriedly adjusted to fit, Alyson turned back to face the black-clad vicar. He seemed a kindly man, if somewhat nervous and anxious, and she should not have been so rude to him. She simply had no idea what on earth he was talking about.

"You do understand, then, my lady, the seriousness of the step you take today? It is not a decision to be made in haste. There is your family to consider . . ." He hesitated as Alyson turned her vacant blue-gray stare back to him. The child was quite likely simpleminded after all. It seemed a pity that that adventurer below was the one to take advantage of her, but from the looks of things, it would be wisest to legalize this union hastily.

"Family?" Alyson's mind came back to the present with a sudden mad glee. "Yes, there is my family to consider, of course. Thank you, Reverend. You have been so very helpful. You may reassure the Maclean that I will say my vows as promised."

Since he had spent the better part of an hour trying to persuade her otherwise, the vicar was not in the least reassured by her reply. Still, he had done his duty to the best of his ability. The governor would not be pleased, but the governor was a fair man and would not hold him to blame for the decisions of others. The Maclean, as she styled him, would have no such compunctions. He was much safer this way, he decided with relief.

Alyson watched the vicar go without regret. It was time to get this over with. She had been bathed and perfumed and pinned and sewed together for what seemed like hours. There really was very little choice when it came right down to it. Every man she met would look at her money first and like what he saw through the haze of greed. It seemed a pity that Rory wasn't any different, as she had hoped, but at least he had a good reason for his greed. Once they were married, he could buy back his lands and save his family and tenants from the life of poverty that was destroying them. That was a noble cause.

She had never seen Scotland, but that had been her grandmother's home, and she had heard the tales of the glorious Highlands. She wouldn't mind living there and helping Rory return his estates to production. She could almost imagine some semblance of happiness in that life. It wouldn't be too bad.

And it would put an end to Cranville. That thought again filled her with unholy glee. He would be so furious he would most likely have an apoplexy. 'Twas a pity she couldn't be there to see it when he found out. Marriage to Rory would certainly be better than anything the earl had to offer.

She hoped. Remembering the strange Rory who had come to her room this morning, she prayed she was doing the right thing in making this choice. She didn't seem to be very good at doing things on her own. Since her grandfather's death she had gone from one disaster to another. She could very well be walking into the worst one yet.

She wanted to talk to Rory again. She needed to reassure herself that this was the right thing, that this sense of impending doom was only a matter of last-minute nerves. He had had time to sleep off the drink and make himself presentable again. If she could just see the Rory she knew, and not that ruthless stranger, she would know she had made the right choice.

All the maids and mantua-makers had left, but she knew the house was full of Rory's men. One of them could find him for her. Acting on the wing of inspiration, she flew to the bedroom door. And found it locked.

Alyson shook the latch in disbelief. He had locked her in! She was a prisoner in what was soon to be her marital chamber. She stared at the latch in growing dismay. How could he?

Remembering that first night aboard his ship, and the horror of finding herself locked in, Alyson felt all the doors to freedom clicking closed behind her. She had been Rory's prisoner from the very first. There never had been any escape. He had just given her time to adjust the noose around her own neck and await his pleasure.

Alan had but bent her heart in comparison to what Rory had done. The horror of it washed over her as her hand slipped away from the latch, and she stared at it as if it had just turned into a Gorgon's head. Backing away, she tried to gather her thoughts, but could not. Images of Rory in another woman's arms intermixed with the demon Rory who crushed her beneath him in a mockery of love. It could not be like this. She had to remember the man who had held her with love and taken her with gentleness. She had to remember he had rescued her from kidnappers and saved her from her cousin's masquerade.

Only, the evil thoughts corrupted the good ones. He had seduced her with his gentleness, claimed her in the only way left to him, since he had already stolen her from home. She had only Rory's word for it that Cranville had hired her kidnappers. It had been very convenient that he found her before they returned her to her cousin. Too convenient.

And someone must have told Cranville that she was in Charleston. Mr. Farnley surely wouldn't betray her after what she had said in her letter. Only Rory could have done that, Rory, who had written to his aunt to tell her she was with him, destroying her reputation so she would have no other choice than to marry him. It was all beginning to make some kind of insane sense. Rory had been waiting for her cousin to chase after her so he could come sailing to her rescue, hoping she would fall into his arms in gratitude.

And she had. Oh, my Lord, she had. With all her heart and soul she had fallen into his arms and betrayed herself. She was no better than her mother, never had been. There must be something wrong with her, that she believed the lies of men so eagerly just so she could share the pleasures of their kisses. No lady would do that, she felt certain. She was as wanton as Rory had called her, and now she would pay for it for the rest of her life.

Desperately she glanced out the window to the street below, but she wasn't mad enough to fling herself from such a height. Steps sounded outside her door, and she looked around frantically for somewhere to hide, but there was none. The room didn't contain so much as a curtain or a wardrobe to cower behind.

A weapon would be useful, but the door opened before she could even think coherently of what would constitute a weapon. She stared wildly at a stiffly formal Dougall and stifled her scream of terror.

She looked even more like a cornered wild creature than she had the night before, Dougall thought glumly as he stopped in the doorway. Rory had gone too far in trying to tame this one. She looked ready to break at any minute. Sorrowfully he held out his hand to guide her to what she apparently regarded as her execution. "Come, lass, the company is waiting for ye."

Rory watched Alyson come down the stairs on Dougall's arm and felt his insides contract into tight curls. Her beautiful misty eyes had transformed into glass-hard mirrors that appeared ready to shatter at the slightest sound. Her sun-tinged complexion had gone pale overnight, and her skin seemed drawn tight over the fragile structure of her cheekbones. He should never have done this. He should back out now, send the whole company home, go drown himself in the ocean and be done with it.

He couldn't, of course. The governor stood at his elbow, and his official men-at-arms were interspersed throughout the room. He had vowed that the marriage would be made legal before church and state, and they were all here in plenitude to see that Rory kept that vow and henceforth trod the path of honesty for Alyson's sake.

Rory hadn't quite determined how he was to uphold all the promises he had made in these last hours, but there had scarcely been time to think about it. His head hurt like the seven hammers of hell, and he hadn't had any sleep for nearly two days. His every waking thought since seeing Alyson running down the dock had been fully occupied with getting her back. There had not been time to contemplate what he would do after he caught her.

And now it was too late. He could tell by the brittle lines of her face as she approached that he had already destroyed something rare and precious. He had been given this one chance to share something special, to hold something lovely, and he had destroyed it with his need to possess. Perhaps everything had been taken from him for a reason, and he had yet to learn the lesson.

She stood without touching him as the words of the service were directed at them. Rory's neckcloth felt too tight, and in the warmth of the afternoon and the crowd of people, his long formal vest and frock coat began to melt the linen of his shirt against his back. Lack of food and rest and the aftereffects of too much drink made his head spin, and when Alyson finally turned to look up at him, he lost all thought of what he was supposed to do. Her eyes were like the gray clouds that formed on the hills before a winter storm, and he felt their frozen winds blowing through his heart. If he believed in witches, he would know she had cast an evil spell on him at that moment. The effect would be much the same.

Dougall prodded him, and Rory remembered the ring. Alyson's eyes suddenly went blank as he slipped the band of gold on her finger, and she gazed down at the place where their hands joined, as if in disbelief, as the clergyman continued his ritual chant. The pagan ceremony they had celebrated earlier had much more meaning than this one. These were just words. The love and joy had disappeared. Alyson's fingers were lifeless in Rory's hand.

The token kiss at the end of the ceremony brought a round of rather stifled cheers from the crew. Alyson's breath was warm and sweet against his lips, but it seemed to come in short gasps. Rory glanced at her worriedly, but they were quickly surrounded by well-wishers and there could be no chance of private conversation. He clasped his hand around hers and felt the ring cut into his palm near the healing wound at the base of his thumb, both signs of his possession. But they didn't make him happy.

The governor claimed precedence in striding forward to shake the groom's hand and kiss the bride's cheek. He clasped Alyson's cold fingers between his and studied her blank expression carefully. "Your grandfather was a good man, Lady Alyson. I hope I have done what he would have wanted. 'Tis a pity your cousin could not be here in time to catch the ceremony so you would have some family present, but under the circumstances, your young man was right in insisting on having the service immediately. I'm certain Maclean here will change his ways now

that he has a good woman to stand beside him." He sent
Rory a meaningful look that the captain met with
equanimity.

The mention of her cousin caught Alyson's attention as
little else had done to this point. "Cranville? Is he here?"

Rory felt her sudden tension and hastened to reassure
her. "He will not return for several days. He is searching
for you."

The governor gave Rory an ironic look. "He is looking
for your head, is more like it. Whatever face you might
wish to put upon it, Maclean, abducting his ward was not
one of your better deeds. I suggest you meet him in a
more amiable manner than with cannon next time."

Alyson turned her face up like an inquisitive bird at
this suggestion. Dark-lashed eyes on the governor, she
intruded sweetly, "The next time, I will order Rory to
blow the odious man out of the water, Governor. You
would do well to do the same."

The older man went blank and glanced to the sanity of
Rory's square face for confirmation. Rory lifted his shoulders casually. "Family quarrel. I did not wish to mention
it without Alyson's permission."

"My God." He stared at the handsome young couple
as if they were both quite insane. "Cranville said as
much, but I thought he exaggerated. He could have you
hanged for piracy. You could spend your wedding journey in the brig on the way to Admiralty Court."

"Cranville is the pirate." Alyson fixed the governor's
stare with a wide-eyed look. "That is my ship he has
commandeered. I do hope you can have him restrained so
it can go about its business. This senseless running about
is costing me money."

Rory resisted staring at her with incredulity by allowing his gaze to drift over the crowded parlor. When
Alyson chose to be coherent, she did it with flair. Unfortunately, the governor had no idea that this was Alyson
at her most cogent. He saw only her porcelain prettiness
and vague expression and thought her simpleminded or
half-mad. Earls did not steal ships and young girls did not
own them. Rory intended to stay clear of this fight. The
governor had already threatened to throw him in jail for
smuggling, kidnapping, and suspicion of piracy on the

basis of Cranville's lies. He just wanted to get the hell out of here before anything else could happen.

"Well, well. We'll have to see about that." Uncertainly the governor bowed over Alyson's hand, and with a nod to Rory, beat a hasty retreat.

"Not very well done, dear heart. I'm the rogue around here, not one of His Majesty's nobles. Cranville had him quite convinced I abducted his innocent but simpleminded young ward for nefarious purposes. The governor does not like being made a fool."

"Then he should not consort with fools." After that terse statement, Alyson greeted Dougall with a false smile and endured the rest of the greetings from well-wishers thinking this to be a happy marriage.

As she stood there beside him, Rory could feel her tension build until he was almost certain her brittle facade would crack at any moment. The room was almost entirely filled with men, his friends and business associates and crew, and every one of them had heard some version of their scandalous story by now. On top of everything else, their considering looks at the ruined heiress were enough to put Rory's nerves on end. He didn't even want to contemplate what they were doing to Alyson.

When a fight broke out in the back of the room between some of his crew and some of the younger men in the crowd who had imbibed too much of the brandy Rory had provided for the occasion, he decided it was time to remove Alyson from the scene. Taking her elbow, he began to guide her firmly through the mingling throng.

Alyson offered no resistance. Like a lifeless doll, she allowed him to push her past the happy winks and jests of the crew into the passageway outside the kitchen. A muscle jerked in Rory's cheek as he gazed down at her vacant expression, and he had the sudden jolting realization that she might very well escape him even now. He wanted her mind as well as her body, but she seemed capable of separating the two.

"Go up the back stairs. I'll send Rosie to you and see our guests off. You needn't wait up for me. They're quite likely to make a night of it."

Alyson nodded, and lifting her skirts, trailed slowly up the narrow stairs without a word.

Leaving Rory to wonder what the devil he was going to do now.

When the house was finally cleared of all but his watchful crew, Rory dragged himself up the stairs, much the worse for too many toasts. And the night was not yet over. If he had any reassurance that his wife would welcome him to bed with open arms, he could relax and indulge himself in the pleasures this marriage entitled him to. But he had indulged in those pleasures before the marriage, and he felt certain he was about to pay the price. Everything had a price. He had learned that the hard way long ago.

No candle flickered in the bedroom as he opened the door, but he knew she was in here. There had been men stationed at all the exits, and Rosie had assured him that Alyson was resting quietly and had eaten some of the meal that had been taken up to her. As his eyes adjusted to the dark, he could see that the bedcovers had not been folded back, and his gaze began to search the room.

She was not hard to find. She sat curled in the window seat, shoulders propped against the wall, her wedding gown trailing to the floor below as she gazed out over the street. Weariness overwhelmed him, and he had half a mind to turn around and walk out. Only the knowledge of the wrong he had done her kept him standing there. If they were ever to retrieve any shred of happiness, someone had to be reasonable. He wasn't at all certain that he was capable of it anymore, but he had to try.

Alyson turned to watch without curiosity as Rory's shirt-sleeved figure staggered into the room. He dropped his coat and vest across a nearby chair, then came to an uncertain standstill at the foot of the bed. His queue was still tied, but one recalcitrant strand had escaped and fallen over his cheek. In the darkness she could see little more than that, but she had committed his face to memory. She could see him with her eyes closed.

"You're drunk again," she stated simply, without condemnation.

"Aye, it seemed the thing to do." Rory took another step forward, but Alyson made no attempt to rise and greet him.

"I'll not disturb your sleep tonight. You may go on to

bed without me." Alyson dismissed him politely, turning back to gaze out the window again.

Momentarily dumbfounded, Rory swayed slightly as he stared at her silhouette in the window. She had not even taken her hair down. "I think not, lass," he finally answered. "You are my wife now. I have the right to ask you to share my bed with me."

Her pale face turned toward him again, but he could not see her eyes. "I suppose the law and the church give you the right to force me, also." Her voice remained quiet and without emotion. "That is the only way you may have me."

"I'm too tired to force you to anything. Come to bed and get some sleep and we'll discuss it in the morning."

"No." She turned her back on him again.

That simple word drove him to fury faster than any argument or excuse she could have given. Rory clenched his fists at his sides and tried to keep a rein on his temper as he spoke. "What have ye to gain by refusing me? What is done cannot be undone. We must make the best of what we are given."

"You weren't satisfied when I gave myself, so you are a fine one to preach. Now you have what you want, go find your pink canary to share your bed, and leave me alone. Otherwise I shall talk to Mr. Farnley and see if this mockery of a marriage cannot be undone. I see no reason to take your word for it."

Pain followed the fury, and Rory rocked unsteadily on the brink of disaster. This was no time to have a head full of cotton batting. He was a man accustomed to thinking quickly under fire, but she almost had him to his knees, and his brains refused to function.

"Alyson, I had to do it. Do ye not ken? It was not myself I sought to protect, but you. I could have sailed away and left ye here, and Cranville would have been satisfied, but I dinna think that was what ye wanted." Inspiration came to him, and he offered his final plea. "I thought it was marriage ye sought, to protect any bairn ye might have. If I have misjudged, I am sorry, but I couldna give ye up to Cranville."

His story was a very plausible one with the exception of a few minor facts, such as his other lover and the estate he wished to buy back. But those arguments fled Alyson's mind with the revelation of new betrayal. She glared at him in astonishment and renewed rage. "Bairn? Child? I might have? You said there would be none. You said I would be safe. And that was all a lie too? Had Cranville not come along, would you have let me keep on making a fool of myself until I ended like my mother, with only shame for my child's name?"

Inspiration had certainly failed him this time. He was guilty as charged, with no words to explain. " 'Twas madness, I know now, but I wouldna have left ye." Rory turned away and found a chair to hold his weariness. These last days had become a nightmare that would not end. He leaned his head against the upholstered back and stared at the ceiling. "Take the bed, lass, I'll not be bothering ye."

Rory's admission of guilt left Alyson no target for her rage, and she continued to stare at him even after his eyes closed and his breathing fell into light snores. A child could have come from these weeks of madness they had shared. Her gaze involuntarily drifted to the flat valley between her hipbones, and her hand covered it wonderingly. This all had to be a moon dream, and she would soon wake. She wasn't prepared for a child. She wasn't even certain she wanted a husband. And now she might have both.

Her grandmother had been right. Moon dreams were the most dangerous of all, particularly when they were granted.

20

Rory woke to the soft rustle of satin skirts against taffeta petticoats. Keeping his eyes closed and his pounding head still, he tried to recover some memory of his wedding night. The fact that he sat fully dressed in a chair warned that the memory would not be a pleasant one.

He closed his eyes tighter and stifled a groan as the sum total of his manifest errors came back to him. He might as well have cut his own throat. It would be a good deal simpler than trying to mend the mess he had made. Why he had ever involved himself with a woman was beyond his reasoning, but he deserved whatever happened when that woman was Alyson. She was beyond the reasoning of any mortal man.

Still, there were a few explanations she owed. The fault was not all on his head. With that scarcely reassuring thought, Rory opened his eyes.

The first thing he saw was his new wife rearranging the folds of her blue satin skirt in an attempt to hide a mended patch in one of the creases. That hit a raw nerve that he had not yet learned to shield.

"Don't fash yerself o'er it, lass. We'll order new ones this morn. I may not be a rich man, but I can keep ye well enough. Is Rosie here yet?"

"I've just been waiting for you to wake before calling her." Alyson went to the door and nodded to someone waiting outside. A clatter of footsteps on the stairs signaled breakfast would soon be on the way.

Rory regarded her warily as she turned back into the room. She had found a fichu to hide the rounded rise of her breasts behind the low neckline of her gown, but the transparency of the filmy scarf could not disguise what he already knew by heart. She must know she could not hide from him forever, but he would give her time. Or try. A familiar ache had already begun to build in his loins.

Alyson stared out the window as Rory stood to strip off his shirt and began to wash. It had been easy last night to decide to cut him out of her life. The morning light and his physical presence brought a new reality to the situation. The whole world looked on them as man and wife. They would have to share this room or Rory would become subject to the jeers of his crew, and their marriage would become prone to question, Cranville's questions, at least. Then there was the return journey to London to face. The matter did not seem so simple anymore, and that was without looking into her own feelings. If she looked closely in the windowpane, she could see the reflection of Rory's sunburned shoulders leaning over the washbasin and easily imagine that unruly auburn lock falling over his face that caused him to raise his arm impatiently to brush it away. The feelings just that familiar movement engendered made it clear that her body would not care less about his betrayal.

"I thought I saw my father's ghost again yesterday." She sought distraction in the sound of her own voice.

Rory rubbed the cold water across his eyes, seeking to clear them. He grabbed a towel at her words and turned to stare. "When?"

"Before the wedding. Outside there, on the street. I thought he was a stranger who had lost his way, but now I think on it, he was too much like the man in the portrait, only older. Do ghosts age, do you think?"

When she talked like that, she scared him, and something hollow opened up in the pit of his stomach. This was the Alyson he could not reach, the dreamy angel who drifted off into some world that did not exist for others. The man outside could have been quite real, and her mind had transformed him into something else, something she wanted desperately. Or she could very well have seen a ghost, if such things existed. Or the Sight could have given her a vision she did not yet know how to interpret. He suspected that was much of the reason she would not talk about her gift: it had few practical purposes unless she could also interpret what she was seeing. It could have been anything, and he did not know how to respond.

"I have had men searching this island for someone who knew anything of the wreck of your father's ship." That was something he could relate without fear. Perhaps it would help. "It was last seen near here, and apparently disappeared before it reached any of the other islands. There was a hurricane here then, and a few of the older inhabitants remember it. So far, none remembers the wreck or any survivors."

Alyson turned around as Rory pulled on a clean linen shirt. The small chest of drawers was open beside him, and a single pair of breeches lay inside. He would buy her silks and satins, but for himself, he had little or nothing. Her wealth might as well have some use. She lifted her gaze to his unshaven face.

"May I talk to the men who remember the ship being here?"

"If you wish. I can see no harm in it. Just do not hope too much."

He reached for the buttons of his breeches, and Alyson hastily turned around. She was not yet immune to the sight of Rory's nakedness. She would have to work on that somehow.

Her hastily turned head brought a grin to Rory's lips, the first in several days. Alyson might be angry and confused right now, but she would never be cold. That didn't necessarily mean there was much hope for him—in fact, she could very well be right in wishing to pursue an annulment—but it made him feel better just the same.

That small jolt of well-being did not last through their wedding breakfast. The little maid delivered a selection of delights to their bedroom, where they could dine in privacy. Rosie seemed slightly shocked to find bride and groom already dressed, but she discreetly bowed out without a word. Dougall was the one to demolish their momentary peace.

At his mate's curt knock, Rory scowled. He had been enjoying explaining what the various delicacies on their plates were, and he was in no hurry to confront the myriad problems of the day. His usual store of coins had been sadly depleted when deprived of his profits in Charleston and Bridgetown. He would have to deplete it further to finish filling his hold with sugar to return to London. He didn't know what the hell he would do with the barrel staves he had intended to sell here, now that he had been forbidden the outlet of free trading. Their profit would not be so great in London. And then there was the problem of what he would do with himself when he reached London. In return for the governor's agreement to his hasty wedding, he had vowed to return to honest trade, but one ship would scarcely produce the income needed to keep Alyson in gowns. All that and more lingered outside the bedroom door. He had no desire to let them in.

At Rory's abrupt command, Dougall entered. His gaze immediately traveled to Alyson. She seemed in better command of herself this morning, and, relieved, he turned his gaze to the captain. There was a man who teetered on a dangerous brink. The news he brought could very likely send him over.

"Well?" Impatiently Rory rocked back in his chair and waited for his officer to speak.

Dougall nervously contemplated Alyson's back as she rose to go to the window. Since Rory made no motion to rise or to dismiss his wife, the message would have to be repeated here. "The governor's just had word from one of the planters just in from one of the other islands, and he sent a warning." Again he glanced at Alyson, but Rory didn't take the hint. "Cranville has apparently found the captain of a navy frigate willing to listen to complaints of piracy and kidnapping. They're on their way here now. I don't know how much of a start the messenger had on them."

Rory rocked his chair slowly as he contemplated this latest complication fate had thrown in his path. Why he should think his life would ever be smooth sailing was beyond him. Cranville and the navy. He wouldn't be surprised if Drummond didn't show up soon to make his life even merrier.

At Rory's silence, Dougall offered, "We've got legal cargo. They can't touch us."

Rory's black grin had no reflection in his eyes. "You want to prove that to an officer of His Majesty's finest when he has a bloody earl breathing down his back?"

That brought silence. Innocence would be very hard to prove on any of the charges Cranville presented. There would be any number of witnesses to testify that the *Sea Witch* was a free trader, that she had fired on a British merchant, and that Alyson had been on her. Alyson might testify that the kidnapping charge was false, but it was altogether too close to the truth for comfort. Remembering that night in London and the dead man left behind, Dougall had to shake his head in agreement. The truth was black enough without Cranville's lies.

"Get the men together and sail out tonight. You can get her to Plymouth without me. Don't attempt London. Even with clean papers, I'll not take the chance of losing her. Then sail north and drop one of the men near Glasgow as usual to await my message."

"Aye, Captain." Dougall was too good a sailor to ask questions, but he raised an eyebrow, as if waiting for more.

Knowing Alyson listened without seeming to, Rory responded as much for her sake as his mate's. "With any luck, the navy will get word you've sailed and race off after you. If they find you, let them search, follow orders, and get word to Lady Campbell when you reach London. They'll be mad as hell not to find their prey, but there isn't much they can hold you on."

As Alyson realized Rory sent his own men and ship as bait for her cousin, she turned to stare at him in confusion. She didn't understand why all this was necessary, although she truly had no desire to meet her cousin again. The question remained, how did he intend to get them home? Or did he?

"Margoulis still in port?"

Rory's question caught Dougall by surprise, and he hesitated a moment before nodding. Margoulis had a reputation worse than Rory's, and his run consisted of only this side of the Atlantic. His ramshackle ship would never make it to London.

Rory answered his unspoken questions. "There will be few enough ships out of here before hurricane season. We'll aim for Charleston or Boston and look for a ship from there. We shouldn't be much behind you. We'll be down shortly to see you off."

Dougall touched his hat and departed, leaving Rory to handle his newly acquired wife. The wild look was returning to her eyes despite Rory's attempt to keep his tone casual.

He rose and headed for the door. "I'll be back shortly to take you to the mantua-maker's. We'll see what we can buy on short notice, and find the rest in Charleston."

"Rory." For the first time since Dougall had intruded Alyson spoke. Rory turned to look at her inquiringly, and she wasn't certain what to say. She just didn't like the sound of any of this, and the sense of impending doom grew closer and more suffocating. "Is this necessary? Can we not go with Dougall? What could they do to us?"

Rory's lips tightened into a thin line. "They can clap me in irons and leave Cranville to do as he will with you. Any more questions?"

Her stomach knotted into painful lumps, and she simply shook her head in reply. It had been bad enough contemplating sharing the captain's quarters on the *Sea Witch*. She didn't even want to think about how this new ship would accommodate them.

True to his word, Rory was back within the hour to escort her into town. Only they didn't head directly for the shops, but to the port instead. Alyson sent him a curious look. Despite the heat, Rory wore his formal frock coat and a lacy jabot and gold-braided tricorne. He looked every inch a sea captain, with his sun-darkened skin and athletic physique, but Alyson could see the crease of a grim frown over his nose, and she knew he played some part.

At her inquisitive stare, Rory spoke without looking at her. "We want Cranville to think we went with the *Witch*. Look around you. There's the customs officer watching us, the guard the governor set on us, and half the people who were at our wedding are down here somewhere, all of them waiting to see what we will do."

Holding his arm, Alyson gazed casually about. She recognized several of the faces from the wedding, and she lifted her hand in greeting, smiling vaguely in their direction when they made polite bows. Rory ignored them all, seemingly intent on making his ship before it sailed. She could see the men up in the rigging already. How did he intend to do this?

She wasn't long in finding out. Safe in the privacy of the captain's cabin, she gave Rory a look of disgust when he handed her an old pair of William's breeches. "If I did not know you better, I would say you are determined to keep me in rags to save money." She took the worn breeches from his hands with two fingers.

Observing the soft fullness exposed as Alyson removed her kerchief in preparation for changing into her disguise, Rory had to admit honestly, "I would prefer no clothes at all if money were the object."

Startled by the warm tone of his voice, Alyson glanced at him suspiciously, but Rory had already returned to the trunk for his own change of clothing.

As he slid off his coat and began to pull at his jabot, Alyson realized he fully meant for them to change here, together. Her hand instantly returned to her neckerchief, pulling it closed as he turned her back on him. The action was pure defensive instinct. The sight of Rory with his shirt unfastened and open to the waist brought back memories too explicit to be trusted. She remembered how the bronzed ridges of his chest felt against her palms, the warmth of his skin beneath the sun, the slippery softness in the water. All the traitorous pleasures he had given her had been for the sole purpose of seducing her out of her money, despite his grand display of heroically resisting. He would have done better had he simply asked for it. She would have respected him more.

Standing up to pull off his shirt and unfasten his good breeches, Rory found himself faced with Alyson's taut, straight back. He had no time or patience for wooing her out of her tantrum. With simple expedience he began unlacing the bodice presented to him.

Alyson attempted to jerk away, but one strong hand clamped her shoulder as the other finished its job. When he had found all the tiny hooks of the inside lining and released the bodice to his satisfaction, he pushed it down over her shoulders, revealing the fine silk of the chemise beneath.

"Unless you wish me to finish the job, you had best get changed quickly. I'll turn my back if that will help any."

Choking on humiliation, Alyson threw a hasty glance over her shoulder to find he kept his word. She gave the door to the cabin a wishful look, but she had learned a lesson about running away. The problems didn't go away just because she did. Cranville was still out there, and she still had no means of protecting herself against him. Reluctantly she began to undress.

As she pulled on her overlarge shirt, she heard Rory moving about, and she swung around to watch what he was up to now. He had donned common seaman's garb, the baggy trousers long and tattered from ill use, his shirt gray with age and tied in front for lack of buttons to hold it closed, exposing a rather overwhelming expanse of very masculine chest. Around his distinctive auburn hair he had wrapped a red scarf, enhancing the costume's distinctly piratical flavor.

Alyson glanced down at her own disguise and wrinkled her nose in distaste. There was no means by which Rory could disguise her as a boy The overlarge shirt fell to her knees, hiding some of the curves of her waist and hips, but she had no means of flattening her bosom. She glanced up in time to catch an expression on Rory's face that indicated he had come to the same conclusion.

Tucking the last of his valuables into a sack he strung

at his waist with a stout length of rope, he gazed help-lessly at the stack of ebony curls piled around a face as fragile and lovely as fine porcelain. It wasn't just her womanly curves that gave her away. Nothing she wore would ever disguise the fact that she was totally feminine, from the tiny white shells of her toenails to the delicate wisp of curl upon her forehead. All that lovely femininity belonged to him now, and he groaned inwardly at the task he had assigned himself. Slaying dragons would be easier.

"I've a better idea. Wait here." Striding out without further explanation, Rory left Alyson to stare after him in bewilderment.

He returned shortly carrying what appeared to be a length of bold cotton print. When he held it out, how-ever, Alyson could see it was a skirt of an amazing array of colored stripes. Red and orange and pink mixed with violets and blues in a rainbow of hues she had never seen in one piece before. She glanced at Rory dubiously.

"I will not tell you where it came from. It's clean. Just put it on."

Alyson complied hastily. The skirt stopped short of her ankles, and the sailor's breeches could be seen beneath. She struggled out of them as Rory obligingly turned his back. That left the skimpy cotton to cling indecently to her hips and thighs. Combined with the low neckline of the seaman's shirt she wore, she looked the part of whore or worse.

"I need petticoats," she whispered in dismay. Her own would trail out from beneath the indecent length of this skirt.

Rory turned and caught his breath at the sight of round curves boldly displayed by the thin costume. He had never understood the appeal of the variety of different women's clothes until now. In silks and satins, Alyson was an unattainable goddess meant to be worshiped. In peas-ant's cotton, she was a much more earthy goddess, one meant to carry a man's seed and burgeon forth and be fruitful. Had they time to spare, he would lay her back against the bunk and take advantage of the promise she unconsciously exuded, but time had ever been his downfall.

"No, it's perfect just the way it is. We'll need to braid your hair. There isn't time to find you a bonnet."

Surely he could not mean for her to appear in public like this! Her shirt sleeves had been cut off so she could at least find her hands, but they left her lower arms exceedingly bare, and the sleeves were so loose they fell back to almost nothing when she lifted her arms. She had only her silk chemise beneath the worn cotton, and it served as a reminder of how bare she actually was. Every movement betrayed her body, and she felt strange urgings in her middle as she caught Rory observing the same thing. Her nipples pressed achingly against the thin material as his gaze drifted there, and Alyson had all she could do to maintain her composure. Lifting her arms to unpin her hair would be certain destruction.

Rory abruptly swung her around and began the process himself. His rough fingers burrowed into the silken ebony strands, searching out all the elusive combs holding them in place until they fell in rippling cascades over his hands and arms and down over Alyson's shoulders. Gritting his teeth against the temptation to lift them all and press a hungry kiss to the delicate nape beneath, Rory began jerking the heavy strands into a single braid. For once, Alyson held completely still.

When he had tied the braid off with a scrap of red rag, he hurriedly opened the cabin door and gestured for Alyson to precede him. If he had been forced to stay any longer in this proximity, he could not be responsible for his actions.

Sensing some of this, Alyson obediently scurried out the door. She did not wish to be the one to push Rory over the brink of that dangerous precipice he lived upon.

They left the ship in the company of dockworkers finished with the chore of loading the last barrel of molasses. Dougall stood on the quarterdeck studiously ignoring their departure. William leaned over the side of the ship waving his battered hat silently, unlike some of the crew, who had taken to whistling and catcalling from their places in the rigging. Rory's jaw set angrily, but mimicking the actions of some of the women on the wharf, Alyson threw back her head and grinned upward, jauntily waving in farewell. The cheers multiplied, but the sails were already unfurling and beginning to fill with wind. With a wrenching feeling of final farewell, Alyson followed Rory's tug into the crowd.

No one paid heed to the sight of a sailor and his whore taking a room at a waterfront inn. It was too early in the day for Alyson to be subjected to the lewd stares and comments of drunken men. They had the place almost entirely to themselves as the innkeeper opened the door on a narrow room with only a pallet for a bed.

Alyson nervously clasped her arms in front of her as soon as the door closed and Rory released his hold on her. The room's one wooden chair looked too rickety to support the weight of a child. Before she could drift to the window, Rory usurped the spot, staring out over the harbor as the *Sea Witch* sailed without incident.

He had left the ship often enough before, taking on the more dangerous expeditions himself rather than risk his men. He was no stranger to the sight of the ship sailing off without him, but he had always been alone and responsible only for himself on those occasions. He now had the responsibility of another, and one too tender and innocent to protect herself. He scowled out at the dancing waters. It should never have come to this. He had no experience at gallantly protecting ladies.

"You are wishing me to hell right now, aren't you?"

Far from being accusing, her voice was sweetly melodic as it wreaked havoc with his thoughts. Knowing his need for her too well, Rory shoved his hands in his pockets and morosely continued staring over the harbor. "Not hell. Half a world away would suffice."

Alyson accepted that with a wry curl of her lips. "I know the feeling. So what do we do now?"

"We wait for His Majesty's finest to appear. I rather suspect that is them approaching on the horizon."

Because of the prevailing east winds and currents, most vessels found it necessary to approach the harbor from the east end of the island, sailing in from the south coast and departing from the west. The *Witch* had scarcely been lost from view in one direction when the massive frigate appeared from the other.

"If the captain of the frigate knows what he's doing, he'll head for the Mona Passage as soon as he's heard we've sailed. He'll think he can cut us off near the strait. We're cutting the hurricane season too close to linger in the Caribbean any longer than that, and it's the fastest route back to England."

"And what will Dougall do?" Alyson came up behind him and watched as the massive sails of the navy ship billowed into full view.

"I left it up to him. He knows the winds and the currents as well as I. Normally the Florida channel is safest, but that's a long distance to take. The Windward Passage is between the other two, but it's by far the most dangerous. He would have not only the sea and wind to combat but also most likely privateers and the French. The Caribbean is something of a trap for the unwary. 'Tis a pity Cranville found someone as familiar with it as the navy."

Without thought to what he did, Rory wrapped his arms around Alyson's slender waist as she tried to see out the window he effectively blocked. She stiffened at first, but when he made no other motion but to pull her in front of him where she could see, she relaxed. He held her like that, feeling her soft curves pressed intimately against the length of him, and his need for her swelled to aching proportions.

As the navy ship sailed into the harbor, Alyson could feel Rory's fingers begin to stray up and down the un-bound curve of her side, but her attention focused on the activity outside. She felt strangely vulnerable at the knowledge that they were so close to their enemies, but her vulnerability had other forms too. She ached for the moment when Rory's hands would stray farther to caress her breasts. Unconsciously she leaned into him as the frigate anchored but gave no sign of lowering the mainsails.

She could feel Rory's tension as a gangplank was lowered to the wharf and several dignified figures stalked from the confines of the ship. In their braided regalia, they appeared more like play soldiers than real people, but the one civilian among them made her heart clench with fear. Taller and broader than his companions, Cranville presented a fearful apparition to her eyes, and she shrank back into the safety of Rory's comforting arms. His hand slid up to toy with her breast, but the tension building inside them wasn't entirely sensual.

A small crowd of officials hurriedly gathered to greet the newcomers, and as the men reached the street below, Alyson could better see her cousin's visage. The months at sea had taken away his fashionably pale coloring, and the languid grace of his lazy expression had hardened into something much more grim and dangerous. She gasped as his hard gaze drifted over the windows of the buildings along the street, and Rory pulled her safely back into the darkness of the room.

She turned and buried her face in his shoulder as he continued to watch the confrontation. The angry gesticulations below indicated the earl's opinion of the governor's allowing the *Witch* to sail unimpeded. The heat coming to a boil in Rory's loins was fair warning of another kind of confrontation altogether. The heated words outside paralleled the argument going on inside himself as he felt Alyson's breasts rubbing intimately against his chest. Action of some sort was needed to relieve the mounting tension.

Rory watched the earl and the navy officers jerk away in anger below and head back for the ship. His eyes closed in silent thanksgiving as his theory proved correct. They would chase after the *Sea Witch* now. He and Alyson were safe.

That left only the bundle of fragrance and softness in his arms, and Rory bent his head to plant a gentle kiss on the top of her bent head. Unexpectedly, her face turned up to his, and their lips sought and clung to each other for long, frenzied minutes.

She needed him too desperately to heed the warnings of her mind. Rory's kiss was as hungry as hers, and she parted her lips to greedily partake of the passion he offered. His arms held her so tightly she was lifted from the floor in the strength of his embrace. She wrapped her arms securely about his neck and surrendered to the heady demands of his tongue and lips. As their breaths mingled, Rory groaned with a mixture of need and frustration, and his hand came up between them to find the fastenings of her shirt.

The heat in the tiny room had already reached tropic heights, but it could not match the conflagration of their flesh as Rory's hand forced her bare breast from the untied chemise. Alyson cried out as he returned her feet to the floor and bent his head to sample the fruit swelling beneath his fingers. The tug of his teeth and lips sent burning trails deep inside her, and she wished only to be rid of the cloth hampering his access to the rest of her.

All pride had flown with the need for him to be a part of her again.

Rory's competent hands pushed away shirt and chemise, shoving them over her shoulders and halfway down her arms, then returning to fill his palms with the round heaviness of her breasts while his mouth sought her approval. He found it in the eagerness of her kiss, and his fingers took full possession of his claim, eliciting a tormented sigh from his captive as he bade the tender crests respond to his command.

Filled to bursting, conscious only of the willingness and desirability of the woman in his arms, Rory lifted Alyson to lay her back against the mattress. It was only by chance that he spied the large insect scuttling across the filthy pallet, but that chance returned him to full consciousness of what he was about to do. His depraved existence was about to reduce the lovely innocence of Lady Alyson Hampton to the status of seaman's whore, with legs spread upon any filthy surface that he laid her.

Loathing and disgust for himself reduced raging need to a dim ache that he must learn to live with. Returning Alyson to the floor, Rory ruthlessly squashed the insect with his foot. He turned back to Alyson to find all the expected emotions of dismay and despair sweeping over her face before she had time to hide them.

Curtly he pulled her clothing back in place and began rapidly refastening it before he weakened again. "We need to find you some clothes before we sail," he reminded her.

Alyson nodded numbly. She didn't have time to assimilate all her feelings, so she simply pulled a curtain over them, hiding them from all the world and herself. They would creep out one by one in the days to come, but in this frozen instant she could feel only Rory's hands too closely to her, and she held her breath until he moved away.

21

Financial transactions completed some hours later, Rory carried Alyson's assortment of bundles in his arms as they ventured out into a darkened street. The wind had picked up during the day and now whipped about them, and he struggled to hold the packages and his hat while Alyson clung to her new skirts. She seemed oddly quiet as they walked swiftly toward the wharf, but he needed this time to gather his own thoughts, and so did not inquire into hers.

The crew of the other ship evidently expected them. As they climbed on board, Alyson gazed around her. It was too dark to discern much other than that this ship seemed larger than Rory's and carried more canvas. She felt an uneasiness stir in her as they stepped into the great cabin, but whatever warning she was meant to receive was lost in the effusive welcome of the captain and his officers.

In the lantern light, Alyson could see that the cabin was not so neatly scrubbed and highly polished as Rory's had been. Rory had been adamant that his crew keep all surfaces well scrubbed, calked, repaired, sewn, or polished, depending on whether it was wood, trim, or sail. This captain obviously did not have Rory's appreciation for neatness and order.

The man introduced to her as Captain Margoulis stood half a head shorter and several stone heavier than Rory. He sported a full beard, but the top of his head was nearly bald. He grinned and bowed over Alyson's hand as the introductions were made.

"Lady Alyson, it is a pleasure. I've heard so much about you. I am honored that Maclean trusts me with your safety."

"I don't trust you any farther than my sword can

241

reach, Margoulis," Rory interrupted dryly. "But you're a damn good sailor and we need a swift ship. I'll trust you with my business."

"It is true, the weather grows foul. We should be out of here by now. I am thinking of sailing this night, before the winds have time to increase."

Rory frowned, listening to the wind creaking through the spars above, flapping at loose canvas. Normally he would not leave port in such weather, but if the hurricane season had arrived early, he would prefer to be out of the Caribbean ahead of it. He nodded agreement with the other man's assessment of the situation.

"Good, then we sail tonight. There is only one problem. We are shorthanded. If you would not mind . . . ?" Margoulis posed the question tentatively. The Maclean was a paying passenger and the captain of his own ship. To ask him to take on a sailor's place bordered on insult, but he counted on Rory's desire to get away. He was rewarded by a curt nod.

"Let me see Alyson to our bunk, and I will join you shortly."

Margoulis had made his youngest officer surrender his bunk for the use of the passengers. Alyson looked dubiously on the cramped closet with its one hard bunk and the hammock swung over it for a second bed. She certainly need not worry about Rory forcing her to share his bed under these conditions. The only question was what she would do with herself for days on end staring at these narrow partitions.

There was scarcely room for Rory to close the door behind them. A small trunk of necessary toilet articles had been sent ahead and rested against one wall. Other than that and the bunk, there was no other furniture.

"It is not much, lass, but with this wind, we should not be long about our journey. Margoulis will let you use his cabin for washing. I'll come for you when the water is drawn in the morning. It looks as if there might be a bit of a gale tonight."

They stood so close they were practically in each other's arms. Remembering the rashness of her passion earlier, Alyson tried to look away. If she could not see the smoldering desire in Rory's eyes, she could pretend it was not there. It was a little more difficult to pretend away those square shoulders and narrow hips when they practically pressed against her. She could feel her skirt brushing his leg, and her hand trembled with the struggle to keep it at her side.

"I shall be fine. Do not concern yourself about me."

Her voice was cold and distant, not the melodic softness that so enraptured his ear, and Rory's fingers wrapped painfully about the door latch as he gazed down at her averted face. He had hurt her more than once, and probably would again. They must be the mismatch of the century, but there was nothing to do for it now but try to keep things as painless for her as possible. Obviously his absence would aid in that cause.

"Fasten the latch behind me and do not lift it until you hear my voice. None of this crew is to be trusted, including Margoulis."

Alyson heard the grating of anger in his tone and did not know how to reply to it. She nodded silent agreement.

With nothing better to do, Alyson undressed and lay in her chemise upon the rough bunk, listening to the wind and the shouts of the men above. Perhaps it would be better to be a man and express all this pent-up emotion in the form of action instead of keeping it inside, where it festered and grew out of all proportion. She could not define what she felt for Rory. It had seemed so calm and good and strong, at first. Now it was all chaos, and she didn't have anyone to help her understand.

Up on deck, Rory had little time to diagnose the cold anguish wrenched out of him by Alyson's averted face. Margoulis had understated the situation by calling himself shorthanded. It appeared that one-third of his crew had decided to ride out the hurricane season in port. It was pure madness to attempt to stay ahead of the storm with only one overworked crew to man the sails.

He threw aside shirt and sword and bent his back to the arduous task of keeping the ship afloat and sailing without capsizing in one of the sudden rough gusts of wind. As the night wore on, Rory judged they were making good time, if he could only be certain they weren't being blown farther out to sea in recompense. He had to trust in Margoulis' judgment on that.

By the time the raw dawn broke, the immensity of the clouds behind them became visible, and Rory knew they were fighting a losing battle. Jagged streaks of lightning illuminated the distant sky, sending eerie flashes of yellow across the tired, dirty faces of the crew. If they were not too far from land, they would have to seek port soon.

He knotted off the hawser he had been adjusting and strode aft to locate the captain. Margoulis gave him a black frown as he sought their course, and the reason was ample.

Rory glared at him in astonishment. "You cannot make the Windwards in this storm. We'll be blown to shore, if not to pieces. We'll have to try for Jamaica."

"Its no good, Maclean. She won't make Jamaica in one piece. I've got friends in St. Domingue. We'll shelter there."

"Friends! Those French renegades will slit your throat if they see you're helpless. Friends don't count when it's war and there's a prize to be won. I'll take my chances on the storm."

" 'Tis easy for you to say when it's not your ship. I'm taking her in."

Margoulis could read the mutiny in Rory's eyes, but the Maclean was too loyal a seaman to breech their unspoken contract. Without another word, Rory stalked off to locate his weapons.

He allowed Alyson to sleep undisturbed. There was nothing she could do against weather or pirates. There was very little he could do under the circumstances.

The storm hit with the first sign of land. A breaker half the size of the mainmast crashed against the stern, sweeping thousands of tons of water across the deck, splintering weakened wood, and leaving men clinging to anything nailed down. A gust of wind caught the gaff mainsail before it could be furled, and the vessel lurched dangerously to starboard.

The heavy clouds above seemed prepared to descend and engulf them, and the brief dawn became dark again as the foundering ship limped toward shore. No one dared mount the rigging to right a loosened spar, and with the loss of a lateen, there was little control over direction. The wind sank its teeth into every spare inch of canvas still open and ripped it with a violent jerk.

"Ship ahoy!" came the cry from some poor battered sailor clinging to his roost on the mainmast. Rory glanced sharply in the direction indicated and clenched his fingers tighter around the hilt of his sword that he had returned to his hip. This was where Margoulis would be proved right or wrong. If he did not mistake, the ship idling to leeward of the jutting coast of St. Domingue bore French colors.

There would be little chance to fight. Crippled, short-handed, the crew exhausted by the night's travail, they could offer little in the way of defense. Without giving a second thought to Margoulis and his beleaguered crew, Rory headed for the cabin and Alyson.

She was dressed and waiting for him, her pale face pinched with fear and worry, her dark brows drawn together in almost a single line as she scanned his face. Beneath the heavy fringe of lashes, her eyes were entirely gray without a hint of blue. Rory had learned to be wary of that look. It foretold anger or premonition, and he had no desire to know which. He didn't need the Sight to tell him of the dangers outside.

She showed some sign of relief that he returned unharmed, but it rapidly disappeared as he made no attempt to don his shirt, but only secured his sword and tucked an ivory-hilted dagger into his breeches. She stared at him wordlessly, waiting for him to speak.

Alyson's silences were as evocative as another woman's tirades, Rory decided grimly. He planted himself against the wooden door and watched her face carefully as he spoke. "The ship is foundering off the coat of St. Domingue. There's a French ship out there. Margoulis claims he is welcome here. I'm not too certain of his claim."

"What will they do with us?" Having already sensed the danger waiting for them, Alyson dismissed the notion of safety without a thought. Rory with hair tied back in pirate's kerchief, bare shoulders rippling with tension, weapons at hand, did not create a sense of security. Nervously she ran her tongue over dry lips, not having any notion of how the sight of that small pink tip affected her husband.

Rory felt the pain of hunger drive through him like a stake, and he hid his despair as he drowned in her Scots beauty, for he was certain no part of her English heritage tainted this vision. Hair black as the coal of the hills, eyes the color of a Highland mist, complexion as fair as the mountain snow, she was his home. He would not lose her again.

"Hold us for ransom, I suspect. Steal the cargo, of a certainty. But perhaps I am being a doomsayer. I just don't intend to take chances."

They could hear the bumping and grating as the two ships ran abreast, then the unmistakable rattle of chain as grappling hooks held them in place. The ship seemed to shudder and shake, then sigh with surrender. The shouts above did not sound welcoming.

"You are not a doomsayer," Alyson said quietly, lowering her gaze from Rory's hardened visage. She could see in his eyes what was happening above, and her fears multiplied at a rapid rate. She was no stranger to the horrifying tales whispered on the wind about buccaneers. They were a dying breed, some said, but war brought out the violence in men. Any excuse would do to halt a ship and search for contraband, and in so doing, steal and plunder and kill at will.

A piercing scream from above emphasized the direction her thoughts had taken. Rory muttered a curse, and his jaw tightened as his gaze, too, lifted to the roof over their heads. A man died up there, not many yards from where they stood. Foes, then. Not friends.

Rory did not have time to rail at the fates. Booted feet trampled the corridor outside without any sign of a fight. They were boarded, and the captors had come for the loot. A woman as beautiful as Alyson would be parceled out as a valuable along with what gold and cargo they took. Rory's fingers curled over the hilt of the sword with the certain knowledge of what he should do, but when a hand shoved against the door at his back, he spun the sword in the direction of his attacker, not toward Alyson.

The grinning face of the rapier-wielding Frenchman at the door did not elicit a single scream from the woman at his back, but Rory could feel her tension as her fingers curled in panic against his spine. The pirate's dark eyes assessed the danger of approaching Rory's drawn sword in a narrow space, and he opted for assistance.

When his shouts brought two of his mates, Rory cut through their leering threats with the voice of command. In the French learned as a student many years ago and polished only in the waterfronts of the Atlantic, Rory demanded, "We will see your captain."

They laughed at this, but a swift arc of Rory's sword as they attempted to approach caused them to fall back and regroup. The longest weapon between them was the rapier, and the sword would easily break that in two. Rory knew it was only a matter of time before they sought out firearms, but he hoped to gain some authority before then.

He was grateful that Alyson chose to hide herself at his back. She could not hide her wide skirts, nor her presence, but the men did not yet know whether they dealt with child or dowager, and curiosity kept them entertained. At Rory's repeated command, the rapier-wielding pirate laughed and ordered one of the others to fetch someone by the name of Courvais.

The buccaneer who appeared topped Rory's height and breadth, undoubtedly accounting for his leadership among his smaller crew. The scars of hard living marred one side of his florid face, and the thin line of his lips gave evidence of a cruelty their other tormentors had not exhibited. Rory felt all hope of reasonable compromise flee, but fate had left him little choice. One bullet would put an end to his protection, and the French captain wore a pistol in his belt.

"The lady is an heiress whose fortune lies in my hands. We are worth more to you alive than dead. But understand this: harm one hair of her head, and I will not give the order that would release your ransom. Kill me, and there will be none to sign the order. Do you understand?" His French was poor, but not so poor that the man did not understand. The greed leaping to those filmy eyes was unmistakable.

Rory thanked the heavens that Alyson had no understanding of French as they were led out under the direction of the pirate captain. The lewd noises and whistles were understandable in any language, however, and she clung tightly to his arm as they walked the gauntlet of the main deck to the plank that served as access to the other vessel. Rory wrapped his arm around her and pulled her head against his chest when he saw Margoulis and his officers tied to the mainmast. Undoubtedly the remainder of the crew had decided to side with the pirates. In these waters, it wasn't unusual. The men lived from day to day, hand to mouth, heeding no loyalty. Any leader would do. But the officers would be a subversive quality and thus expendable. There was nothing Rory could do for them, even when he saw the pile of debris being set afire at their feet.

He had relinquished sword and dagger, and in return his captors had allowed his hands to go unbound. That was the best he could expect, and he had to use this limited freedom in Alyson's behalf. She was the injured party here. Margoulis had knowingly taken his chance and lost. He could not expect help from any quarter. Rory greatly expected his own actions now were little better than the same gamble, but he could not have drawn the sword across Alyson's throat any more than he could have placed it to his own. Should he lose as Margoulis had done, he was throwing her life away with his own.

They were led down into the dank, unlit hold and shoved into the narrow confines of a cell, which was luckily unoccupied by the usual drunken or insubordinate sailors. The door slammed behind them with only a minimum of speculation on who would have the lady first. The dividing of spoils was already going on overhead.

Alyson retreated to the far corner of the smelly space and stared at him with wild-eyed fear. For someone who had once been inclined to show no emotion, she had made amazing progress, Rory thought wryly. All thanks to him, he imagined.

"What did they say?" she demanded.

Although terrified, she still turned to him with some semblance of trust, a trust he did not deserve. She could have no idea of what lay ahead of them, and Rory had no words to tell her. The depressing stink rising around them smelled of a prison for condemned men. He belonged here. She didn't.

"They are holding us for ransom," he answered curtly.

Wisely, she did not ask of the others. The smoke of a burning ship would penetrate even these depths before long. The rain was holding off, and the wind would sweep the flames through Margoulis' vessel as quickly as the wave that battered it earlier. With the storm approaching, the pirates would not even attempt to carry the captured vessel to shore. If they had any intelligence at all, they would be sailing for the nearest protected cove immediately.

That the pirates ship was under way, Rory could tell, but the ominous sounds of argument above did not bode well. The stout captain might argue in favor of ransom, but his younger, more hot-blooded crew would have other ideas. Women were few and far between in these parts; ones like Alyson were nearly nonexistent. Only the captain's prowess in commanding order would stand between Alyson and certain rape.

Alyson crossed her arms in front of her and shivered as if she had read his thoughts. Pale eyes turned beseechingly to him, trusting him, pleading to him for reassurance, and something inside Rory snapped. He should have killed her while he had the chance. His guilt had brought her to this, and his indecision would bring her innocence to harsh destruction. The thought of those vulnerable soft curves given up to the repeated debauchery of the filthy swine above broke the few remaining threads of sanity.

When he heard the shots fired above and the sound of footsteps on the ladder, he swung around, and with the force of his body behind the blow, caught Alyson squarely under the chin.

22

Like a wounded dog, Rory crouched beside Alyson's body as he listened to the unexpected noises overhead. They had been anchored offshore for some time, but the footsteps had retreated and none had yet come for them, apparently distracted by the growing violence of their greed. This latest argument had resulted in the sound of shots, and he no longer heard the angry commands of Courvais. If there had been a mutiny, there was no hope left for them. Raw anguish tore through him at his help-lessness. He should have killed her when he had the chance.

The sound of cannon suddenly breaking the brawl into howls of fury caught him by surprise. He had noted cannon mounted on deck, but it did not make sense that they would fire on empty sea or their own ship. Margoulis couldn't possibly have cut himself free and sailed after them. Rory could think of no other mad enough to be out there in this storm.

He heard the rattle of heavy anchor chains being weighed into the hold. Surely the madmen didn't mean to set sail again? The ship was still heaving wildly even in this bay, and the winds were making the timbers shake and squeal. Had they been fired upon from shore? Perhaps Margoulis' friends had come to the rescue.

The cannon roared again, but this time Rory felt the distinct shudder of the ship as a ball veered off some portion of the stern. They were being fired upon! Crossing his arms over his bent knees, Rory pressed his fore-head against them. Sinking would be preferable to the fate that otherwise awaited them, but he still could not help but wish things had turned out differently. He tried to imagine what a life with Alyson would have been like, but he had no experience in his adult life to compare it with, and his imagination failed him. Alyson moaned and stirred restlessly, and Rory bent to take her into his arms. Would she hate him in heaven, or would she un-derstand and forgive? An angel would forgive, but Alyson was a very human angel. If he could not forgive himself for any of his actions since he had spirited her away from home, he could scarcely expect her to ever forgive, even in heaven. He had wanted too much, and as a conse-quence, he had lost all.

The firing above was sporadic as the ships fought each other and the wind. From the shouts he heard, chaos commanded the buccaneers. Every man would be captain if he could, and no man would win. Whoever fired upon them had picked the perfect time to attack. Unfortu-nately, they seemed to be shooting very badly.

Weary in body and soul, Rory no longer cared. He wrapped Alyson in his arms and buried his face against her hair and waited for death, no longer certain if God existed or if it mattered. He had been wrong about everything he had done since he had first met Alyson. Possibly he had been wrong about everything he had ever done in his life. Had he allowed those first incompetent rogues to carry Alyson from the coach, she would be married to Cranville now and safe in Cornwall. He had never been meant to be a white knight to rescue fair maidens. If they did not sink this ship soon, he would take leave of what remained of his senses.

By the time the firing stopped, Rory no longer felt surprise at anything. Fate or God had made him the puppet of a giant joke over which he had no control. His strings were being pulled by some invisible hand, guided by some cruel mind that wished only to see him suffer. When he realized the pirate ship was being boarded by some unknown assailant, he merely waited to see what would happen next.

The sight of the blue and white-braided coats of His Majesty's Royal Navy brought a wry twist to Rory's lips. It seemed only fitting that a navy officer should be the one forcing the lock to their prison.

Calmly he brushed a stray stand of ebony hair from Alyson's forehead, then rose to his feet, holding her draped across his arms. Those strands that had come loose from their combs hung nearly to the floor, but he was aware only of her shallow breathing. He had accomplished nothing but his own destruction. Perhaps that would be best for Alyson in the end.

The officer looked at the defiant stance of the half-naked auburn-haired man clutching the lady in his bare arms and decided not to move too swiftly. There was something mad behind those dark eyes, and just as he would not attempt to remove a bone from a mad dog's grip, he made no gesture to remove the man's frail burden.

"Captain Rory Maclean?" the officer inquired cautiously. At Rory's nod, he added, "I have orders to place you under arrest, sir. If you would come with me . . ." To his relief, the madman followed without protest.

On deck, a man garbed in civilian clothes broke away from the troops securing the ship. The wind howled through the masts overhead, but at the sight of Alyson lying limp in the prisoner's arms, his roar of rage could be heard over the storm, bringing several men scurrying to his side.

"He's killed her! The scoundrel's killed her! I want him hanged! I want his head right here and now!"

Rory merely halted where his guard indicated and awaited the verdict. His gaze moved with disinterest over Cranville's less-than-immaculate appearance. The man appeared to have undergone a dramatic change in the last few months. Gone were the fashionable wig and expensive silk coat, replaced by the earl's thick dark hair and a more practical broadcloth coat with no adornment but a cravat. The lazy, bored expression of a spoiled dandy had hardened into the fury of a tormented man. Overall, Rory rather approved of the difference.

"Call the surgeon! Get her to a bunk. She's still alive." The officer wearing a captain's insignia shouted his commands after ascertaining that Alyson still breathed. He ignored the man holding her until the physician arrived. When Rory relinquished his burden without protest, the captain turned a piercing gaze on his prisoner, yelling over the voice of the approaching storm, "Well, Maclean, it looks like we're well met, wouldn't you agree? You have your lucky stars to thank that we spotted that fire and traced the bastards here."

Torn between staying to see Rory brought to justice and following Alyson, Cranville hesitated. "Don't welcome the bastard," he snarled. "Hang him."

The captain gave the earl a mild look of reproof. "He must be brought up on charges and tried. If he is guilty, he will be hanged with all due process." Turning to Rory, he emphasized, "I'm certain once the lady recovers, she will be willing to testify against him."

Rory met the man's gaze without flinching. "My wife will do as she thinks best, but I believe legally she cannot be made to do any such thing."

"Wife! You scum! If you think you're gong to pass off some heathen ceremony as a marriage . . ."

Rory's passive gaze halted the earl's tirade. When the spluttering stopped, he spoke to the captain and not to Alyson's livid cousin. "The governor sent the marriage papers to London in his official packet. Signed and witnessed copies are aboard the *Sea Witch*. You may verify it directly in Barbados if you intend returning there. The lady is my wife. I will recommend her into your care, Captain, not to this scoundrel's."

Since the prisoner was behaving with more gentlemanly aplomb than the irate nobleman, the captain gave an understanding nod.

As the wind raged and squalled about them and the waves threatened to toss the two ships into the black clouds boiling overhead, Rory's hands were tied behind his back and the small party returned to the navy frigate.

Alyson stirred and groaned as the ache shot through her insides, then spread downward. Her head pounded and her stomach felt queasy and her throat was parched beyond endurance. She moved restlessly; the pain in her jaw ached and she finally settled back against a welcoming softness with a small whimper.

A rustle beside her indicated she was not alone, but she could not wake to any desire to discover the person's identity. A moment later, she heard voices at the door, and then a second presence entered, a much larger presence, but she was too tired to care. She sank once more into a deep, protective sleep.

The ship's surgeon shook his head, and the young cabin boy looked dismayed. Despite all their precautions, the lady didn't seem to want to wake up. An impatient rap at the door caused them both to turn around.

"Well, how is she? Can she talk?" Black eyes swept over the surgeon's shoulder to the discolored pale face lying unconscious against the pillows, and the intruder gave a low groan. "Wake her, Buscombe. I cannot bear it any longer."

The surgeon turned away from the nobleman to lay his hand across a cool brow. "Neither can she, my lord."

Cranville stared at his cousin's pale features and with a twist of anguish turned away. He saw now the result of his unthinking actions, and he didn't like it at all. He didn't like himself very much either. She had been little more than a child when he had all but driven her from her home and into the arms of a scoundrel and fortune-hunter. His poor attempts to right that wrong had failed. For the rest of his life he must learn to live with the torment he had caused her. Somehow, he must find some way of rectifying his mistakes, and he would begin by making the man in the hold pay for what he had done.

The next time Alyson woke, she felt the darkness and the silence all around her. Not a real silence. She could hear the creaking of the rigging, the flapping of canvas, and the other faint sounds of wood against timber, but she heard no voices. Sighing with relief, she opened her eyes.

The dim starlight from the porthole only clarified shadows. She could see nothing of her surroundings. The lurch and sway of a ship at sea told her where she was to some extent, but the cabin did not seem a familiar one.

She lay still, locating and summing up the various aches and pains of her body. None of them equaled the savage pain in her heart.

She had known Rory would bring her pain from the very start, but she had persisted in her fantasy of love. She doubted if love even existed in this world. Surviving seemed to be the main purpose of life. Well, she had survived. What now?

By morning she was aware that someone sat guard outside the cabin door. Desperate for water, she gave a hoarse croak and went silent at the sound. Lifting herself on one elbow, she gazed down at her chemise-clad body. Somebody had removed her skirts, but not her petticoats, and the blanket had been pulled up to her neck. Her captors were obviously modest people, but she would prefer to see if she were still in one piece.

Swinging her legs over the side, she decided on the whole it might be better if she were not in one piece. The parts she discovered ached abominably, and her stomach seemed prepared to heave its meager contents at any moment. A water pitcher sat snugly in a hole carved for it on the wooden table at her side, and she reached for the tin mug dangling beside it.

By the time she managed cup and water and sipped carefully, someone was sleepily questioning her silent guard. At a rap on her door, she pulled the blanket across her lap and up to her chin. She suspected she looked a fright, but she could think of no good reason to worry about it.

With the sound of her soft reply, the door swung open to admit the surgeon. He regarded her sitting position with approval, then took careful note of her pale cheeks and the dilation of her pupils. Deciding she ran no fever, he bowed formally.

"Good morning, Mrs. Maclean. It is a pleasure to see you awake this time. Shall I have them send up some broth and tea?"

The thought of food sounded particularly repulsive, and Alyson focused on the title with which he addressed her. As Rory's wife she was entitled to the status of Lady Maclean, but of course the English would not recognize his Scots title even if they knew of it. On the other hand, as the daughter of an earl, she was Lady Alyson, unless they knew of her bastardy. Since even the governor had used her title, and Rory had no reason to name her bastard, she had to suppose this man knew Cranville. She grimaced.

"Where are we going?" She held her hand to her forehead, trying to remember the circumstances that had brought her here. She could only remember Rory and the nightmare.

Deciding the blow to her head had left her momentarily confused, the surgeon explained her whereabouts and destination. When he mentioned London, she looked at him with a small sign of hope, and he continued cheerfully, "Your cousin is most anxious to see you. He is overjoyed to have you returned at last."

Panic fled across her features, and, wild-eyed, Alyson backed against the wall, "Rory? Where is Rory?"

That wasn't exactly the reply he expected, but Buscombe decided it might be sensible for a wife to be concerned about her husband. That put him in a very awkward position if so, and he did not relish being the one to delve into the various intricacies of the lady's situation. "Your husband is well and on board, be assured. Let me have some food brought to you. You will feel much better with some sustenance in you."

Alyson did not like the way he said that, and her gaze unfocused as she tried to reason out this situation. Cranville was asking after her, but Rory was not. No, there was something wrong here. Even if Rory did not love her, he would be concerned about her wealth. Unless he thought her dead. Would a husband inherit a wife's estate even if she had a will stating otherwise? That would be one horrifying explanation of Rory's behavior, if so.

The physician watched uneasily as the lady's mind seemed to wander off and not come back. She made no attempt to answer his question or even acknowledge his presence. She must still be dazed from the blow. Pursing his lips anxiously, he backed out of the room, leaving the lady to her mental wanderings.

Matters did not improve with time. She sipped at the tea brought to her but ignored everything else on the tray. When handed a brush, she obediently began to stroke her hair, but it was obvious she did it out of habit and without any thought of her appearance. There was no woman aboard to help her dress, but when a gown was laid out from the trunk the earl had brought on board, she stared at it with disinterest and returned to brushing her abundant tresses.

Unable to get more than monosyllabic replies from his patient, the surgeon finally sought out her cousin, hoping a familiar face would jog her interest.

When Cranville entered the cabin, Alyson began to scream before he could even open his mouth to speak. She screamed without terror or feeling of any kind, but the nearer he came, the louder she screamed. When he returned to the passageway and out of sight, she grew quiet and returned to brushing her hair.

The surgeon followed him out and shook his head in sympathy for the young nobleman's plight. "I fear the shock has made her mad, my lord. We cannot know with any honesty what she has undergone these last months. Perhaps rest and quiet will restore her nerves with time."

Cranville's mouth twisted into a bitter line and he regarded the older man sardonically. "You underestimate my cousin, Buscombe. Tell her I've fallen overboard, and she will smile. Bring Maclean here, and we will see the true state of their affairs."

They talked as if she were deaf or witless, and Alyson smiled inwardly as she overheard their words. So her cousin was not entirely the fool, after all. She could not hope that he would ever attain Rory's level of understanding, but some degree of rational discussion might be achieved if he at least had the brains to seek it instead of forcing her physically.

When they brought Rory to her, she wore a robe she had sought for herself in the trunk she remembered from

Charleston. She had made no attempt to pin up her hair, and it streamed over the gray lace of the robe in wild disarray. When Rory entered, her eyes widened slightly at his state, but no one but Rory noticed this change in her expression. To the others, her gaze seemed perfectly blank and devoid of emotion.

She had never seen his hair so matted and dirty. He had made some attempt to keep it pulled at his nape with a string, but with his hands bound except when he ate, it had become a senseless task. Someone had provided him with an ill-fitting shirt that he had tried to tuck into his torn and blackened breeches, but large folds still hung about his narrow hips. The hemp at his wrists had worn the skin raw, and the blood of the scrapes stained his cuffs.

He held his shoulders back and waited for her verdict, but he could not keep his gaze from caressing her face. He winced at the sight of the blackening bruise he had caused. She was much too pale, and the icy gray of her eyes displayed a fear and a wariness he deserved.

The men behind Rory waited for some sign of recognition, some acknowledgment of love or hate or fear. Alyson simply drifted from her seat, past Rory, out the door and past her cousin and the physician, and down the passageway to the center of the great cabin. When she picked up a knife from the table, Cranville hurried to take it away from her. With a smile, she raised it to the vicinity of his manly parts, and he quickly stepped out of her way. The surgeon continued to watch her with professional curiosity, and she ignored him as she swept back down the passage again, her long robe trailing the floor like a royal train, her head held proudly erect.

Rory turned to face her as she reentered the cabin, and Cranville chuckled as Alyson raised the knife to him too. "It would serve you right if she gelded you, Maclean. Buscombe, what say we leave the happy pair together for a while?"

The surgeon sent him an angry look, but Alyson did not seem to hear the jest. Rory's hands were bound in front of him, making him less vulnerable to the pointed tip of her knife than Cranville. As Alyson inserted the knife between his wrists in an apparent attempt to do just what Cranville suggested, the surgeon hastened to stop her.

Rory threw him a cold look. "Leave the lass be, lest you get the dirk in you."

Buscombe hesitated, then watched as Alyson methodically began to saw at Rory's bonds. "Why does she not say anything?"

Rory lifted a brow with an ironic look. "And would you have cut the bonds had she asked?"

"But she says nothing. It is not natural!"

Rory gave a grim chuckle. "It is when you're accustomed to being ignored. Alyson seldom speaks if action suffices. For all I know, she fully intends to emasculate me for your amusement. Lord only knows, she has every right to do so."

He sighed in relief as the rope fell free and she set the knife aside. Alyson gave him a fleeting grin before turning away to search her trunk. When she came up with a jar of lotion to rub into Rory's wrists, Cranville raised a protest. "The man is a dangerous prisoner! You cannot let him go unfettered for the sake of some besotted female."

As he attempted to intervene, Alyson calmly lifted the knife to his midsection again. Cranville's gaze went shrewdly from her pleasant expression to Rory's grim demeanor. His prisoner shrugged.

" 'Tis your life, mon. I cannot know how far ye've pushed her." The mockery of his heavy accent was not lost to Cranville, who scowled.

When Alyson held firm, Cranville backed away and allowed her to finish rubbing Rory's wounds. When she was done, he once more demanded, "Buscombe, have your men escort the scoundrel back to the brig."

Alyson merely returned to her bunk and placed her hands in her lap. Rory looked down at her with a mixture of compassion and resignation. "You're on your own now, lass. Ye know that, don't ye?"

Something flickered behind the pale gray mist of her eyes, but to the surprise of all but Rory, she murmured in perfect musical tones, "Go to hell, Maclean."

23

London, Fall 1760

When they led Rory away in chains, leaving Cranville to walk free, Alyson understood the enormity of the mistake that had been made. Rory did not even turn to glance at her as he strode down the plank to the dock. She had not seen him since the day she had cut his bonds and he had said she was on her own. He had released her from all the vows they made, and she had thought that was what she wanted. She was a free woman now, their marriage a matter of inconvenience that Mr. Farnley would soon put asunder. So why did she feel so devastated when it was Cranville at her side and not Rory when she first set foot in England again?

Rory had trapped her, forced her into marriage, nearly brought her to death in a pirate's hold. He had no love for her, only for her money. She could find no other reason for his actions. He had used the same words of love as Alan, and had meant them just as little. Senseless, then, to regret what had never been.

Cranville tried to take her arm and lead her into the waiting carriage, but she shook him off. He had treated her with the care due to fragile porcelain throughout the journey, but she had been too miserable to notice. She blamed it on the seasickness that had kept her abed. She would get better now.

She turned to the gruff captain who had befriended her. "Would you see me home, please? Lady Campbell will be worried."

Cranville attempted to step in and protest, but she ignored him as she had ignored the man who claimed to be her husband. Pain glittered momentarily behind the hard mask of his face as she wandered off with the navy officer, but, squaring his shoulders, he set off in another direction. He had other responsibilities to meet before his conscience settled to any degree.

Deirdre ran to greet them, but her face grew taut when she found Alyson accompanied only by a stranger. She stared at Alyson in concern. During her previous stay, Alyson had often been quiet and reserved, but her smile had been infectious and her eyes had brimmed with eagerness to see and delight in everything. The woman who stood here now was not that young girl any longer. She was still quiet, but when she spoke, it was with more authority. The dreamy expression Deirdre most remembered had disappeared, replaced by a frigid composure that was not natural to those soft features.

Not daring to inquire into her nephew's whereabouts in the presence of a navy officer, Deirdre merely took Alyson's arm, expressed her gratitude to the man, and led Alyson away.

A few hours later, Mr. Farnley left the Campbell residence shaking his head. Never had he seen such a tangled web, but the glittering gold that spun its sticky treachery was not so much his concern as the innocents caught in it.

It took a week before the solicitor could locate Rory, hire barristers, and have him freed on bond. The bedraggled scarecrow who emerged from the cell in no way resembled the confident man who had once visited his offices, but Farnley was too old to be fooled by appearances. The fire behind the dark eyes of this scarecrow burned more fiercely than he had thought humanly possible.

With no other place to go, Rory made no protest when the solicitor delivered him to his aunt's doorstep. Alyson had had an entire week to slip away into whatever world she sought now. He would linger only long enough to bathe and dress and seek word of the *Witch*. What he would do after that, he could not yet consider. The charges held him bound in London for the nonce. Somehow, after that, he would get to Scotland.

Deirdre welcomed him with open arms and tears and led him to his old room with admonishments about hot baths and good food and lots of sleep. Rory humored her with polite nods, knowing full well he hadn't slept a night in weeks and might never sleep another again. He needed to ask of Alyson, inquire into her health if not her whereabouts, but he could not bring himself to utter the words just yet. Wearily he shut the door after his aunt and stared at the empty candlelit room. He had exchanged one cell for another. As long as he stayed in London, he was in a prison more relentless than any iron bars. He needed the solace of action to amputate the emptiness and pain. He needed to go home to the welcoming heather of the hills and forget the lovely woman who had been his for so short a time. He had never deserved her, and he would never forget her, but he had to let her go. For both their sakes, he had to let her go.

The ivory-handled brush in his hand snapped, and he stared down at it in dull confusion. He didn't remember picking it up. He forced his fists to relax. The brush seemed familiar, but he was in no state to think about a brush. He needed a drink. First, he had to wash.

The servants brought a bath and he tried to soak in it, but restlessness kept him from relaxing. He scrubbed hurriedly and climbed out, drying impatiently and padding about the room in search of old clothes he might have left behind. He was nearly dressed by the time a footman arrived to announce a caller.

Surmising that Dougall had found him before he had time to go looking for the *Witch*, Rory pulled on his coat and hastened down the stairs to the guest salon. The sight that met him struck him with disgust.

The earl had evidently hurried here as soon as he was notified of Rory's release. Garbed in the same simple style he had worn on the ship, his hair bound and unwigged, he appeared more a country gentleman than the elegant dandy who had last visited. He swung around when Rory entered, and his dark eyes raked over his host's gentlemanly attire.

"Going out already, are we? So eager to spend your new fortune that you cannot even bide awhile to see to my cousin's comfort?"

Shoulders straight, fist clenching the sword he had donned earlier, Rory met this insult with coldness. "You are not welcome in this house, Cranville. So long as I remain her husband, this house is Alyson's. If you have any concern for her at all, you will show it by removing yourself before creating the scandal of being physically thrown from her home."

"I'll leave, but not before accepting the challenge you offered once before. I'll be waiting at White's for your seconds." Cranville picked up his hat and cane and waited for Rory to move aside so he might leave.

Rory walked to the decanter on the sideboard and poured a tumbler of the brandy he'd been needing all evening. He would enjoy nothing more than taking out his vengeance and frustration on this arrogant Englishman, but just the thought of the pleasure he would receive from such measures warned that he had not only himself to think of. "The challenge is withdrawn, Cranville. I would have fought you then, when Alyson was no relation to me, but I cannot kill her only relative now that she is my wife."

To Rory's utter shock, the object of their discussion materialized in the doorway, her eyes widening with some emotion he could not discern as they found him. His fingers cracked the fragile snifter in his hand before he set it aside, and his heart suddenly began pounding with a ferocity that made his head ache. She could not be here. Greedily he watched her lovely figure enter the room; then, seeing something in her eyes, his gaze swerved to the intruder and his hand rested on his sword as warning to Cranville. Rory had seen that look on Alyson's face before, and a protective instinct he had never known he possessed came to her defense.

Both men remained silent as Alyson drifted through the room without a word of greeting. She cast neither of them so much as a look as she came to a halt before the long draped windows at the front overlooking the street below. She didn't need to speak; her presence spoke for her. Caught in the turmoil that was her mind, she could not have put a sensible word to her tongue, but she sensed the effect she had on the two men, and so kept silent to wrestle her own private demons.

Cranville sent her an anguished look, but Alyson's blank gaze turned away to search the street outside. Worried, but refusing to let the earl know that, Rory merely waited for his unwelcome guest to leave. Alyson's blank gaze did not bode well at all, and he wanted Cranville out of here immediately.

"Then I will seek satisfaction in the courts, Maclean."
Cranville's grip tightened on his cane as he glared at the
stoic Scotsman. The other man's cold face gave nothing
away, however, and the earl had no choice but to depart
with one last look at Alyson's turned back.

Alyson did not hear him go, nor did she see him as he
climbed into the hackney waiting outside. Rory's unexpected appearance had filled her with a sudden cold, and
now the window had become a winter-white blizzard. She
fought the chilling wind rushing around her, searching for
something or someone she could not see. She clutched
her arms, fighting the vision, but a black rock reared out
of the distance, and she screamed. The sound was whipped
from her breath by the roar of the wind. Horse and rider
rode toward the swirling darkness where the only difference between land and air was the shades of gray behind
the blinding snow. She tried to go after him, to scream
for him to stop, but he was galloping away to certain
death. She felt death all around her, piercing her with its
cold talons, laughing at her in the howl of the wind,
approaching ever closer, but invisible to her blinded eyes.
She fought its hold, crying into the wind, screaming for
mercy, but she was strangely weighted and could not
move. When horse and rider disappeared over the precipice, she crumpled into the welcoming blanket of ice.

Seeing only her stiff back, Rory could detect none of
these struggles. His own shock prevented him from speaking, but the odd tension in her shoulders and the look in
her eyes as she passed worried him. When she began to
sway and make sounds as if something were choking in
her throat, he went white and began to cross the room.
Before he could walk the length of the salon, she crumpled to the faded Persian carpet on the floor.

"Alyson!" Shocked into shouting, Rory raced past the
long table littered with his aunt's collection of Dresden
figurines, lunged over the new Chippendale grouping
before the secretary, and knelt on the carpet to gather
her into his arms.

His yell brought servants running from all corners.
Deirdre's lady's maid took one look at the crumpled
figure in the captain's arms and raced for the smelling
salts and burnt chicken feathers. The others milled around
uncertainly until Rory yelled for a physician. A footman

did as bidden and the housekeeper, regaining her senses, hauled her stout figure up the stairs as quickly as she could go, trailing a contingent of maids to light fires, fetch hot water, and warm the bed.

Terrified by Alyson's stillness as he carried her in his arms, Rory was reluctant to release her to the care of others when he reached the chamber they directed him to. He sat upon the bed and held her close, willing her to open her eyes. He had thought her lost to him before, but not like this. Panicked, he watched her breasts rising and falling—not with lust, but as proof she lived. Gently he smoothed the linen sheets and laid her upon them as the maid entered with her salts.

With Rory's embrace gone, Alyson began to stir restlessly. Her eyes flew open, and Rory could see the shock still in them. The maid began waving smelling salts and burnt feathers beneath her nose, and Alyson coughed at the strong odor. Weakly she pushed to sit upright in an attempt to escape the bed.

"I'm fine. Leave me alone," she muttered, waving away the maid and her odoriferous remedies. She sent Rory an accusing glance. "Tell them to go away."

Rory noted the bruised look of her eyes, then turned a questioning gaze to his aunt, who had followed the servants in. He had some suspicion of the cause of this spell, but he daren't speak it aloud without Alyson's consent. On the other hand, it could be the sign of some illness of which he had no knowledge. For that, his aunt would have to decide.

"A physician has been sent for," Deirdre murmured. "Keep her here until he comes."

Alyson breathed a sigh of relief as Deirdre firmly removed her maid and ushered the crowd out the door, but when Rory's aunt followed close behind, purposely leaving the young couple alone, Alyson averted her head and closed her eyes. The blizzard still lingered there, and, shuddering, she was forced to open them again. She found Rory still sitting on the bed beside her, a thoughtful frown puckering the bridge of his nose.

"What did you see, Alyson? Can you tell me?" He took her pale hand and rubbed the knuckles, feeling the iciness of her fingers, warming them with his own. He couldn't halt the still-frantic beat of his heart, and he fought for some simple explanation to reassure himself that he had not somehow caused her faint, that she was well and all was right with her world.

Alyson shook her head wearily and looked away. Rory's hands were like burning brands of coal, but she welcomed their heat, wishing it could spread across her body. The thought of those strong hands upon her breasts as they once had been brought another kind of heat, and she felt the fire of it ignite the dry tinder of her heart. After all that had happened, she still wanted him to touch her. Just touch, and no more.

Sadly she listened to his pleas, but she could give him no sensible answer. She could not describe the scene, nor the danger. She only knew that it in some way involved Rory, and common sense told her the snowy landscape had to be Scotland. What could she say that would make him understand?

"At least let me know if 'twas the Sight or if you are ill, lass. You canna keep everything to yourself."

The rough concern in his voice brought her wandering gaze back to her husband. She did not know how he came to be here. Over and over she had debated why he had treated her as he had done, but her wealth was all the conclusion she could find. Perhaps he had meant to sell her to the pirates, but she could not believe that of him. She did not understand him or his actions, but there were many things in this world she did not understand. Why he was here was one of them.

She retreated behind a daze of indifference. "I am fine, just a little weary perhaps. I'll rest . . . you go on with whatever you were after."

Rory set his jaw stubbornly. "I'm not a child to be dismissed at a whim, Alys. As much as you may dislike the notion, you are still my wife, I assume, and while I can, I will take care of you. Deirdre has sent for a physician. Perhaps it would be best if he examined you."

"No, Rory. I cannot abide yet one more person poking and prodding at me. Let me be, please."

She spoke in a whisper, and her pale face seemed taut with strain. Rory ached to hold her and promise her everything would be all right, but he could not. He was no magician, and he could not turn back the hands of time.

"Persuade me you are not ill and I will go away and

send the physician home." That was the most he could promise her.

Alyson closed her eyes, but the blizzard was gone. She could feel the heat returning to her bones through the medium of Rory's hand. Her fingers wrapped unconsciously around his as she spoke.

"They are not things I can describe, Rory. Sometimes I might see someone I know walking up the road when I have no access to a window, or I can see the ground crumbling away in a tunnel when I am above, but there are others that I cannot see so clearly. Grandmother said they are windows into another world, a future world, and we cannot see them clearly because they have not happened yet. But I *feel* them. I am there and I experience them, but I do not know what it is I see or do." Alyson gestured at the futility of explaining what she could not explain to herself.

"Can you tell me what it was you felt today?" Rory kept his question soft and simple, fearing she would avoid it, as she so often did. He wanted to understand, but his mind rebelled at the idea of a future that would happen no matter how hard he worked to change it.

Alyson chewed on her bottom lip and tried to put the sensation into words. It was better than trying to disentangle the chaos of her emotions. "In the vision, I feel cold. Very cold. And it is white all around me. There's a man on horseback. I cannot stop him. My throat is hoarse from screaming, and he keeps riding." She hesitated, waiting for Rory to voice his skepticism, but he stayed silent, waiting patiently. "The danger is all around, something I can feel; I don't know why. Then the rider disappears. I think he has gone over a cliff." She drew a deep breath and held his gaze. "I'm certain the rider is you."

The impact of her words sent Rory's head spinning, and he could only stare at her for a full minute before replying. Then logic returned, and he groped for a way to reassure her, though the sudden fear her eerie words had caused held little enough reassurance for himself.

"A storm like you describe would be found only in the northernmost part of the Highlands, lass. I would have no business there. My home is in the hills along the coast, where the winters are mild." Rory shoved his hand through his hair and stared down into dark-lashed eyes, searching for better words of reassurance. Her paleness against the black backdrop of her hair gave her an appearance of almost ethereal frailty, and he knew a sudden fear that she could be taken from him in a manner more final than any other he had yet contemplated. He fought against that thought. "If there is naught we can do to change the future, then there is no use in our worrying over it, is there? Now, get some sleep, and I will send the physician away."

Perhaps he was right. Perhaps she couldn't change the future. But if she had not seen the vision of Rory making love to her, would she have allowed him the liberties that she had? Would she have thought of marriage? Or would he have taken her innocence forcefully, until she had no choice but to consent, to give any result of their coupling a name? Either way, the end was the same, but that was because of another vision entirely.

If she had not seen that vision of Rory with another woman, she would have married him happily and been innocent of his true nature.

Alyson frowned as Rory quietly rose and went out the door. If she had not run away that last time, would he have married her at all?

It made no sense, no sense at all.

24

"I am sorry if I have called at an inconvenient time. There are some important matters that must be discussed, but if you would prefer to come to my office later today . . ."

James Farnley, Esq., narrowed his bespectacled eyes as the young man paced the parlor with every outward sign of irritation. In the week since his release from prison, the captain had evidently spent little time or money on embellishing his wardrobe or acquiring any of the fashionable accoutrements of gentle society. His well-tailored broadcloth coat was impeccably kept and definitely serviceable, but not exactly of the required fashion of rich and colorful silks and satins. Although evidently dressed to go out, he wore no wig, did not powder his hair, carried no decorated walking stick, disdained red heels and clocked stockings, and had no expensive sedan chair waiting outside for him. The oddity of a newly wealthy man acquiring none of the material symbols of his success, combined with the fact that the Maclean had made no attempt to inquire into his new wife's considerable business affairs, made the cynical lawyer more than suspicious.

Rory halted his impatient pacing, and tapping his fingers against the desktop, tried to turn his mind to the solicitor. "I have given your messages to my wife, sir. I do not know why she has chosen not to respond to them. If there is some matter of importance that must be discussed, I will hear of it, but any decisions are Lady Alyson's."

The solicitor raised his eyebrows slightly. "As her husband, you are the one with the legal responsibility of seeing to her business affairs. I recognize that the lady is of exceptional character, but as I have already informed her, your signature is required on all legal documents."

Rory's fist closed around the handle of a letter opener. "You have spoken with Alyson? She did not mention it to me."

Farnley coughed slightly. He did not know the current state of affairs between the young couple, but in Alyson's best interests, he had thoroughly investigated the episode and the young man his wealthiest client had married. He had many reservations about the marriage and the man's character, but none about his business acumen. Since that was Farnley's main concern, he attempted to placate his profitable client.

"Lady Alyson has never shown any interest in her holdings. I have asked her opinion on several matters outstanding, but she always refers the decision to me. I have helped the former earl with his business affairs for a good many years, but I must face the fact that I am growing older and more cautious and have not the will to seek the more aggressive investments that I once did. I had the presumption to inquire into your finances when it came to my attention that you had taken on the responsi-

bility of protecting Lady Alyson." That was as polite a
way as he could state the case of Alyson's abrupt disappearance. The clerk who had intercepted her original
letter and sold it to the earl had never returned to London, but Farnley had learned much from Lady Campbell.

Rory gave the elderly solicitor a look of cynical respect. "And?"

Not in the least intimidated by the captain's cold tone,
Farnley continued, "You have amassed a considerable
fortune from your choice of investments, Captain. You
are very daring. I would not advise risking a large fortune
in such undertakings, but I think you are well aware of
that. I'm quite convinced you are capable of managing
Lady Alyson's wealth without my interference."

Rory's hand clenched the engraved brass letter opener
so tightly that the metal began to cut into his palm. "I
don't believe you quite understand my position, sir. I
believe the barrister you have employed has forwarded
copies of Cranville's charges to your office. There are
also several indictments pending in the Admiralty. Law
has never been my profession, but I understand I could
be hanged or transported for just one of these charges. I
don't believe it is in Lady Alyson's best interests for me
to be involved with any of her affairs. I am surprised that
she has not already requested an annulment."

That shocked the elderly solicitor. He stared at the
young Scotsman in some consternation before recovering
his tongue. "An annulment? I should think not. I would
advise against it, most certainly. The charges are spe-
cious, at best. The lady has suffered enough indignity by
reason of her birth. I knew her father and grandfather
well. They would not approve of such shabby treatment
of one so dear to them. No, whatever the problems are,
they must be overcome. The lady is your wife, Captain—it
is your responsibility to look after her. Shall you come to
my offices later today to take a look at the books?"

Rory set his jaw in a manner Alyson would have recognized instantly. "I am resigned to the fact that I have
been assigned the task of responsibility by some immuta-
ble force, for whatever dubious reasons, but my protection does not extend to include Alyson's fortune. Find
somebody else, Farnley."

Understanding suddenly seized the older gentleman,

and he looked at the reluctant young husband almost with benevolent approval. "It is difficult to find someone competent and trustworthy enough not to be tempted by such vast sums, Captain. Your wife would be left destitute if the wrong person had access to those funds. In the interest of her protection, perhaps I could hire you to manage these investments? They require a goodly amount of time and effort. I am certain a percentage fee would be needed to adequately compensate for your time."

Rory's grip on the letter opener relaxed, and he crossed his arms over his chest as he leaned against the glass-enclosed bonnet of the secretary. "You are a clever man, Mr. Farnley. I begin to understand why you and the former earl must have got on so famously. The only way I can protect Alyson from fortune-hunters is to take on that task also?"

Farnley beamed. "Exactly, Captain. Shall we say two-thirty this afternoon? I will have my clerks gather the necessary papers. A quantity of matters has gone unattended in these last months. I am certain you will be able to dispose of them adequately."

After a day spent grasping the enormity of Alyson's inheritance, Rory staggered home with aching head to discover his wife in their shared dressing room, scantily garbed in what appeared to be silver tissue as Deirdre's maid coiffed her hair in powdered ringlets. He eyed the powder with disfavor and gazed in the long vanity mirror at the image of Alyson revealed. The daring décolletage of her gown left little to the imagination. The full globes of her breasts pressed distractingly against the thin material without need of extravagant jewels to draw the eye. Rory could well imagine every male eye in the town resting on his wife's bosom, and he gritted his teeth in frustration at the thought. He had not imagined spending this time before the trial trapped in his wife's company. For the life of him, he did not know why she stayed. Perhaps she had some foggy notion of being noble and standing by his side until he was proved guilty.

"Have I forgotten some occasion?" he asked warily, wondering why his normally reticent bride had suddenly decked herself out in all her glory.

Alyson puckered up her nose at her image in the

mirror as the maid inserted yet another silver butterfly in the intricate net of her hair. "Nothing of importance," she answered absently. "Lady Hamilton is giving a small soiree, and I told Deirdre I would accompany her." She started to tie a velvet ribbon with another tiny butterfly upon it around her neck. "Do you think this is too much? The modiste recommended it if I did not wear diamonds, but it seems a trifle foolish."

"Alyson, you have enough wealth to buy every diamond in London. It matters not whether you wear butterflies or nothing at all. Am I expected to attend this function?" Wearily Rory shrugged out of his serviceable frock coat and in vest and shirtsleeves waited for some reply.

Alyson turned from the mirror to look at him in surprise. "I did not think you would want to, but I'm certain Lady Hamilton would be delighted if you could come." She tried not to stare too closely at the rugged lines of Rory's face or the breadth of his shoulders straining at the tailored vest. They had grown quite good at avoiding each other, but there were certain intimacies that could not be avoided. Their paths crossing in this small suite of rooms was one of them. She expected him to leave any day, but they never discussed their plans with each other. She had no plans other than to get from one day to the next. Someday the pain would go away, as it had with Alan. Rory's constant proximity did not make it easy.

Rory's initial reaction was relief. He had no desire to waste an evening making polite conversation with the same people who would have seen him hanged for a Jacobite without a second thought not too many months ago. Alyson had been correct in her judgment as far as that went. But as Rory watched the rise and fall of her breasts in that shimmering gown, his next reaction was purely emotional. He'd be damned if he'd let her out of the house like that unless he were close at her side to black the eye of any man daring to look too closely.

"I'll be ready shortly." Curtly he swung out of the room toward the chamber he used as his.

Alyson stared after him with amazement and growing palpitations. To have Rory glowering at her all evening was enough to cause any amount of alarm, but even worse, she could not contain her excitement at knowing he would be at her side. This past week, he had spent the evenings out of the house, and she very much suspected he had found a mistress. At least this night he would be with her and not the other woman, but her happiness at this thought was equal reason for alarm.

Unwilling to sort out such complex emotions, Alyson retreated behind her wall of vagary. When Rory finally returned to claim her, dressed in his sparse finery, he found a mindless butterfly smiling vacantly up at him. He frowned, but there was little he could do to draw her from her shell at this point. He hastened her down to the drawing room to meet Deirdre.

As far as Rory was concerned, the evening was an unmitigated disaster. Despite his attempts to keep Alyson at his side, she was constantly being swept away into the swirl of dancers, with a different fawning beau each time. Rory glared at their effusive compliments as they simpered over his wife's hand, but there was little he could do to stop Alyson from accepting their requests for dances. After spending most of the evening contemplating emasculating half the male populace of London, Rory finally quit the dance floor to bury his frustrations in drink and cards.

Alyson noticed his absence immediately, but she had no right to go chasing after him. Rory had made it abundantly clear that she was on her own now. She sensed his preoccupation, knew his mind was on the upcoming trial and perhaps his lands in Scotland, but they never spoke of either. She was trying to learn how to get along without him, but she didn't seem to be very successful. Perhaps she ought to learn to be the powerful lady she had once told him he needed. Perhaps they would have something to share in common then, and he would at least speak to her.

Unaware of his wife's impractical intentions, Rory occupied his time with a halfhearted game of cards, wondering when he could successfully persuade Alyson to leave. The conversation at a neighboring table kept him amused as some half-drunken young man quoted Macpherson's so-called Highland poetry at the baiting of an equally drunken Samuel Johnson. He didn't know what source Macpherson had translated that nonsense from, but it was nearly as amusing as Johnson's witty criticisms. Unfortunately, neither was sufficient to distract him from a second conversation somewhere behind him.

"Who would believe all that beauty would possess so much wealth? Had I known, I would have been tempted to abduct her myself."

Drunken laughter met this idle jest. "Lud, for all that wealth, I would even endure a fool. Have you noticed how she looks right through you, as if you wasn't there? I almost thought a ghost had appeared over my shoulder. Deuced spooky, if you ask me."

Rory's hands tightened around his cards. He wasn't known in these circles, and he doubted that the speakers would even recognize his name, but they had certainly identified Alyson as clearly as if they had used hers. He clenched his teeth and held his peace.

"You must be losing your touch, Trevor. I knew a time when you wouldn't let a woman like that out of your sight until you had her in bed. Are you telling us a heathen Scot has more to offer than you?"

Raucous laughter filled the air, and Rory carefully folded his cards and laid them on the table. When he glanced up, he found the elder statesman of literature watching him with cynical curiosity. Neither said a word as the table of young rakes behind them continued their drunken conversation. The other card players at the table simply counted Rory out, took on another player, and proceeded with their gambling.

"I'll wager you'll not get any further with her than I!" the first young blade declared hotly. "She's as daft as a Bedlamite. You could call her a blue-eyed mule, and she wouldn't bat an eyelash. I'd like to know how that heathen husband of hers talks her into bed, or if he even bothers. As heavy as his pockets are now, he could buy ten mistresses and not notice the cost."

More laughter greeted this sally, but the second young rake took at least part of these words seriously. "You're on, Trevor. I'll wager I can have Our Lady of the Melting Eyes in my arms within the hour, and in my bed before the week's out."

Rory turned slowly in his chair to observe this self-confident speaker as the wagers were thrown on the table amid much jesting at his braggadocio. Rory's lips curled in disdain at the sight of the overdressed peacock who fancied himself as Alyson's lover. It wouldn't even be amusing to run him through with his skian dubh—his veins would probably bleed water.

As Rory started to rise from his chair, a heavy hand rested on his shoulder, and he turned a skeptical look to the stout old man bracing himself against the table. "Sir?"

"You wouldn't be about to do something rash, now, would you? I understand the Scots are a barbaric race, but you look a gentleman to me."

Rory watched as the young bucks rose en masse to follow their latest leader in pursuit of this new amusement; then he lifted a sardonic eyebrow in the older man's direction. "Dr. Johnson, am I correct?" At the man's nod, Rory began following the others out. "I understand you enjoy a good wager. I'll gamble fifty guineas that young dandy won't get my wife any farther than off the dance floor. Care to join me?"

Chuckling and carefully wielding his walking stick, the man of letters followed him out. "Your wife Scots too?"

"Half, by birth. All, by temperament." Rory placidly stalked his prey, keeping well behind them as they spread out along the far wall, where a row of doors led out onto the terrace and the garden beyond. The young dandy homed in on Alyson immediately. Rory could see her checking her dance card with a puzzled frown, then gazing blankly as the young man quickly persuaded her next partner to give up this dance.

"Lovely, she is. I always had an eye for a pretty face. I understand it's another language entirely in Scotland. I've been wondering if it wouldn't be worth looking into."

"The old language is still spoken in the farther regions of the Highlands. Education is not yet available to us all, the same as in England. I understand the Cornish often speak a dialect not found in your dictionary." The English ignorance of his homeland never failed to amaze Rory, but he was willing to be patient while he waited for this dance to end. The steps of the minuet were harmless enough. He could afford patience, though he would very much like to eliminate the smirk on the face of Alyson's partner as he gazed down at the lovely display of her décolletage.

Their desultory discussion of language ended sometime later, when the music came to a halt. Gauging the direction in which the dandy led Alyson, Rory followed in his wake, not caring if his companion followed or not.

Not far from the couple rested a large jardiniere of ferns on a stately pillar, and Rory stopped there, leaning unobtrusively against it, partially hidden by the heavy velvet draperies over the wall of glass doors. Crossing his arms over his chest, he waited cynically as the bewigged and bejeweled rake led Alyson toward the terrace. She appeared slightly bewildered at whatever nonsense the man was spouting, and Rory's lips lifted in a slow curve as he watched her lovely hands flutter from the impudent man's reach. He could almost mark the moment when Alyson discovered him standing in the shadows of the ferns. The bewilderment disappeared from her eyes and that heart-stopping smile she used for him began to form on her face. It almost crippled Rory with longing, even though she meant nothing by it. What it did to her partner was not worth knowing. Rory simply straightened and waited to see what she would do.

The self-confident smile on the dandy's face slipped away in confusion as the lovely lady on his arm drifted right past the door he opened for her, her beautiful smile now turned toward a statue in the corner rather than on himself. He hurried to redirect her, only to find the statue stepping from the shadows to greet her.

"There you are, Rory. I thought myself completely deserted. Is Deirdre ready to leave?"

Rory heard Johnson chuckling behind him, but his senses were temporarily filled by a cloud of soft perfume and fragile lace and the shine of blue-gray eyes. Soft hands clasped his arm and inquiring eyes lifted to his as the older man presented himself, and Rory had to quickly regain his bearings. The approach of the bemused young dandy served as further impetus.

"Dr. Johnson has an interest in language, lass, if you would speak with him a moment." He gave her hand up to his companion. "My wife, Lady Alyson Maclean." Without further explanation, he stepped away from the pillar to intercept the dandy and his rapidly approaching cohorts.

"Sir, I would have a word with you." Rory's cold tone made it quite clear that his was more than a polite request.

The dandy gazed insolently at Rory's unadorned plain navy coat and breeches and unpowdered queue and sneered. "I'm certain you would, but I have more pressing business."

He moved to pass by, but Rory caught his shoulder, and with a single scarcely noticeable shove pushed the man through the open door to the terrace. "The only business you will need pressed is your clothes when I am done with you."

Fully aware that a number of onlookers had followed them out, most of them partners in the wager, Rory took his time and held his anger in tight rein. "I would take offense at your using my wife as a subject for speculation, but you weren't worth the challenge. But just in case you think I take the matter lightly, I will leave you with one reminder."

Rory had backed the man against the terrace wall by now. Ignoring his sputtering protests, he caught the peacock's elegantly embroidered lapels in both fists and lifted the slender dandy bodily into the air. Before the others could rush to their friend's rescue, Rory neatly tipped him over the wall and into the shrubbery below.

Dusting his hands off and straightening his coat, Rory turned to raise a quizzical brow at the crowd of elegantly garbed Londoners staring at him. Over the cries of the furious dandy below, he announced, "As a heathen Scot, I reserve my claymore for the field of battle, but I would be happy to meet any of you gentlemen there, should you abuse my wife's name any further. Now, if you will excuse me . . ."

He stalked past his audience, leaving them to watch in amazement at the brightly lighted scene just inside the windows. The daft heiress appeared to be in animated conversation with the intellectual Dr. Johnson, and as her husband joined them, the pair broke into delighted laughter, greeted him, and drifted away.

Trevor whistled under his breath and glanced over the wall to his cursing friend below. "That's ten quid, Neville. The lady has a penchant for heathen Scots and dirty old men. You'll not get near her again."

The curses below multiplied with the sounds of laughter above.

Inside, Alyson and Rory sought Deirdre, found her entrancing the navy captain she had been introduced to several weeks before, and, assured she would find her own way home, bade farewell to their hostess and ordered the carriage around.

Alyson sent her silent husband a sidelong glance as he waited stoically for the carriage to appear. She wasn't quite certain what he had said to the obnoxious young man he had taken outside, but she could see no anger in his eyes now. She almost felt as if they had achieved some level of understanding without her knowing how. She simply enjoyed this opportunity to be with her husband and act as if they were a normal married couple.

Once inside the carriage, it was another matter entirely. Deirdre's equipment was narrow and confined, and even though Rory sat across from her, their knees were in constant danger of bumping. Alyson desperately sought some topic of conversation to ease their ride through the darkened city streets.

"Have you known Dr. Johnson long?" she tried tentatively.

"Just this evening. I thought perhaps you might be familiar with some of his works." Rory tried to concentrate on the street outside and on the jarring bumps of the holes in the cobblestone road. This proximity to Alyson was too similar to their first encounter, when he had only desired to see her face and know her name. His desire now was a little more complex than that.

"I fear he is a little above my head, but I would like to see his dictionary. Imagine trying to write down all the words in the language and their meanings. It would take a lifetime."

Rory made no reply to that, and Alyson pursed her lips and stared at the street also. The one carriage lamp did little to define his shadowed features, but she knew his face too well to need light to see it. It was infinitely preferable to stare at the street than to confront her emotions when she looked upon her husband.

"I have not seen Cranville since the day we arrived." Alyson broached a subject she had contemplated uneasily for some time. "Do you think he has returned to Cornwall?"

Rory had wondered when she would finally confront him with this question. He did not know if she would approve or disapprove his answer, but it was too late to change his decision now. While Cranville wandered the streets, Rory could not leave Alyson alone. It had seemed an expeditious decision at the time.

"If he has any sense at all, yes, he ought to be in Cornwall by now."

Alyson turned to scan his face in the darkness. He was watching her, waiting for her to ask the next question. Annoyed that he offered nothing unless she pried it from him first, she contemplated asking nothing, but her curiosity was too strong.

"What did you threaten him with?"

"Debtors' prison. I bought up all his debts, then offered him a quarterly stipend from your grandfather's trust if he would go back to Cornwall. He protested for a while, but I believe Mr. Farnley convinced him I am not quite the blackguard he envisioned, at least where you are concerned."

Alyson tried to sort out this information and the words behind it, but she understood only that Cranville would not bother her again as long as he was well paid. She wrinkled up her nose at the thought. "I think I would rather see him in prison."

"I gathered that." Rory gave her a wry smile. "But it would in all likelihood entail my joining him if he chose to return the charges, and then he could file suit against the will. I didn't think you'd object to the first, but the latter would cost you more in legal fees than you are currently paying the villain."

He had not thought to consult her in this use of her money, but it was his money now, she understood. He could do whatever he liked with it. She could only be grateful that he didn't choose to pension her off as he had Cranville.

"I trust you have collected on my voucher and destroyed it by now. I would hate to have you holding that threat over my head again."

Rory heard the anger and disdain in her voice and acknowledged her right to it, but he still felt a swell of disappointment that she could not forgive what he had chosen to do for her own good. Perhaps his reasons had been all selfish, and she was right to think their marriage wasn't for her good, but there had been a time when she wanted it. Why couldn't they return to that magical time? Because he did not believe in moon dreams.

Quietly he replied, "I gave the voucher to Mr. Farnley. You need not worry more about it."

He made no excuses and no apologies, Alyson noticed. He had just stepped in and taken over her life, and expected her to accept it without question or complaint. And so far, she had. Closing her eyes in an agony of despair, she fought back the tears. All she had wanted was a home and someone to love. How had it come to this?

The carriage wheel hit a particularly large hole, throwing them together with a jolt. Rory braced himself with his feet and caught Alyson by the waist. His hands lingered there as he gently returned her to the cushion. He seemed physically incapable of releasing her while his head was bent so close to the parted surprise of her lips.

The intimate placement of his hands sent a nervous chill down Alyson's spine. She shivered and tore her gaze away from the dark desire heating her husband's eyes. Not again. Never again. She shrank back against the seat as far from him as she could go.

Furiously Rory tore his hands away and shoved them in his pockets. The sooner he got away from here, the better it would be for both of them.

25

The little seamstress frowned as she tried to lace Alyson's gown so the final fitting could be made. "If madam would hold her breath a little more . . ." she suggested tentatively, preparing for the blow such a hint would have brought from many of her employer's customers.

Absently staring toward the window beyond her mirror, Alyson tried to oblige. It was the modiste who stepped forward, enraged, to box the servant's ear.

"Fool! Can you do nothing right? The lady is as slim as a willow wand. All my gowns fit her to perfection. Why you cannot perform so simple a task . . ." Muttering to herself, she pulled the lovely rose silk skirt down more snugly over Alyson's hips, adjusted the stomacher to her satisfaction, then began to pull the stiffly boned bodice tight. The resulting gap was scarcely noticeable, but was nevertheless a gap of disastrous proportions. The modiste stared in disbelief.

"This cannot be! I took the measurements myself. There must be some mistake. Those fools have sewn the seams too tightly." Muttering curses under her breath in an unknown tongue, she hastily began unlacing the bodice once again.

A small frown began to form on Alyson's brow. Bored with the collection of lovely gowns she had accumulated in these last few weeks, she had little concern that this latest would not be ready for the ball tonight. There were certain to be a dozen others she could wear in its place. But she feared the modiste would vent her rage further on the poor cowering seamstress in the corner. She didn't think she would ever accustom herself to the violence in which most of the population of this city lived.

"Perhaps the measurements could be taken again and the seams let out accordingly," she suggested gently. "It is not necessary that I wear this tonight."

Still frowning, but not daring to refuse the request of her best paying customer, the modiste whipped out her measuring tape and waited impatiently as the seamstress hastily removed the gown and petticoats. She knew full well she had used those same measurements last month to create milady's spectacular silver tissue gown, and it had fitted without a flaw. The problem was the worthless help one had to hire nowadays.

With a grudging "harrumph," she pulled the tape around Alyson's high, full bosom, perfectly aware of the splendid proportion that made her a joy to dress. No padding or extra boning was needed here. The silk would lie in gentle folds like a lover's caress . . . She stared in horror at the measurement her tape recorded.

For the first time this day, the older woman gave her young customer an expert perusal. What she saw made her eyes narrow with suspicion, but as a matter of insurance, she spanned Alyson's narrow waist with the tape. The measurement read as she had suspected, slightly larger than the last. Giving the slight outward curve of milady's usually flat midriff a knowing look, she made a slight sniff of disapproval.

"My lady should have informed me she was *enceinte*. The seams could have been made wider to adjust. I will somehow contrive to arrange it, but the gown may not be ready until late."

Alyson felt her cheeks grow warm at the woman's tone, but she was not at all certain she understood her meaning. Not wishing to show her ignorance, she kept silent, and it was with relief that she saw the pair bustling out the door.

When they were gone, she glanced down uncertainly at her figure, outlined in the brief silk chemise. There did seem to be a slight rounding where there never had been one before, but she had been terribly idle and eating a great deal too much of late. She would be getting fat if she were not careful. Even her breasts felt tight and uncomfortable beneath the scanty covering of the loose chemise. She hoped her other gowns would still fit.

In a sudden panic, she flew to the wardrobe to draw out the silver gown this particular modiste had created for her just last month. Her newer gowns had been made by different hands with newer measurements. The old one would prove that she had not grown so large she could not fit into her own gowns.

Hastily she pulled the lovely skirts over her head, not daring to call her maid for assistance. This was something she would have to discover for herself. She pulled the bodice down until it cupped her breasts, and reached behind her to try to tighten the laces. It was an impossible job even if the bodice fitted, which it didn't. Alyson gave up in dismay as she watched her bosom practically spilling from the décolletage.

Trying not to panic, Alyson nervously discarded the gown and put on a new day frock that fitted to perfection. Examining herself in the mirror, she could see none of the telltale signs revealed by the thin chemise. Fewer sweets and a little more exercise, she vowed firmly. But for the sake of reassurance, she went in search of Deirdre.

She found her in the small sitting room Deirdre preferred when not entertaining. Deirdre smiled at her entrance and continued weaving her needle through the cloth. "Is the gown all ready, then? The color should look magnificent on you. I can't wait to see it."

Alyson shrugged and picked up the book she had left lying there before the modiste arrived. "There is some complication that may not be corrected in time. I'm rather tired today. Perhaps I should stay home. Captain Rogers will be coming for you, won't he?"

Deirdre shot her nephew's young wife a quick look. Alyson seemed paler than usual, and her eyes were unnaturally bright. The girl had never backed out of an invitation, once accepted, thinking it discourteous to do so. Something must be wrong.

"The kind man has offered, yes, but we were expecting you to join us. Are you not feeling well? Perhaps just a quick visit from a physician . . ."

Alyson smiled and waved away this suggestion. "I have never needed the services of a physician. I am quite fine. I don't believe Rory plans to attend this function, so I just thought I could beg off." She tried to hide her frustration at not being able to ask the question she had come to ask.

That was a suggestion Deirdre could understand, and she nodded knowingly. "The two of you seldom have much time together. You are quite right. I will give your excuses to our hostess. I would certainly like to know what that young scamp did to bring all your admirers into line, but they have been rather cautious in attending you lately, haven't they?"

That was an understatement, but not one Alyson would argue with. All the eager young men who had crowded around her in those first weeks had depleted to a few bold ones who would squire her on the dance floor but leave her sedately in Deirdre's company afterward. If she'd ever had any idea of learning if men were capable of love, her chances had become visibly dimmer since that last ball Rory had attended. She really didn't mind, though. She had seen no young men who could interest her in the way that Rory did.

Restlessly Alyson started for the door, book in hand. Almost as an afterthought, she turned to ask, "What does *enceinte* mean?" She pronounced the French carefully, hoping to convey the sound correctly.

Deirdre's eyes widened as she looked up from her needlework. "*Enceinte*? Who is *enceinte*?"

"I would tell you if I knew what it meant," Alyson answered with patience. "My governess tried to teach me French, but I never saw the purpose in learning."

"Ah, that will not do. You will never know what people are whispering behind your back if you do not speak French. We will hire a tutor to teach you the phrases you should have. *Enceinte* means someone is with child. Who? You aren't by any chance *enceinte*, are you? I'm rather looking forward to a baby in the house someday."

Alyson avoided the sharp look in Deirdre's eyes and began drifting toward the door again. "Lady Douglas is *enceinte*. Perhaps I could learn just a few phrases." She left the room without answering Deirdre's other question. She didn't want to lie, she just didn't *know*.

With child. Pregnant. That was the word she remembered being whispered in her grandfather's kitchen when the servants thought she didn't hear. The way they had whispered it had made it sound something awful until Cook had scoffed and said that having a baby wasn't nothing no woman hadn't suffered before. She had tried to listen closer then, but their talk of the apparent sinner not having monthly napkins to wash had left her bewildered at the time. The conversation came back much too clearly now.

Alyson shut her bedroom door and stared at the dresser with the neatly folded linen cloths she had not needed since Charleston. She had learned how to fashion makeshift ones from rags on that first voyage, and had worried about doing so again on the second, but her worries had been for naught. Her monthly courses had never come. She had assumed it had something to do with what Rory had done to her, and she had been right. But not in the way she had imagined.

Sinking into the nearest chair, she held her hands to her burning face and tried to puzzle this out. She had suspected what they had done together could make a baby, and Rory had as much confirmed it. Did it happen so easily, then? Just those nights on the ship . . . ? Her cheeks grew hotter as she remembered how many times they had turned to each other in those nights. Their need had seemed insatiable then. And all that time Rory had known he could be planting his child inside her.

She wanted to feel rage. She wanted to summon indignation. She wanted to remember Rory's betrayal and not the feel of his arms around her, his kisses upon her face as he made her body quake with his passion. He had tricked her, seduced her for money, and now neglected her when he had what he wanted. The child would merely be a guarantee against annulment.

But all those cynical thoughts could not change the way she felt. She was going to have a baby. Rory's baby. Her hand covered the small rounding of her abdomen as if to test this change inside her body. She could be wrong. It could be that something else was wrong with her, but she knew it was not. A child was already growing and taking shape inside her, a child to whom Rory had given his name.

Giving a sigh of relief that she did not have to bear her mother's shame, Alyson sat back in the chair and closed her eyes. She didn't know what she was going to do now, but she had never known before, either. Each new day brought a different surprise. She would have to think about this one for a while.

Rory tilted his chair back, took a sip of port, and eyed his table companion with disfavor. "English politics are not for the likes of me. I'm a simple man with simple wants. Sword fighting, I know. Playing the courtier, I don't."

Samuel Johnson pushed his heavy cane against the empty chair between them. "You damned Scots always want to bash heads instead of use them. Think, man! That weak-minded grandson of the king will someday inherit the throne, and Prince Georgie Porgie does nothing without Bute's approval. Bute is a Scot and a lot more likely to support your cause than your English cousin's. It certainly can't hurt to court his favor."

Rory scowled. "Bute is an ass, even if he is a fellow countryman. I don't want to be anywhere around if he comes into power. If I can't buy back my estate, I'll sail for the colonies, where George's long hand can't reach so quickly."

Johnson whacked his stick against the chair. "If your whole damned country is stocked with fools such as you, I'll make certain not to visit it. What of the charges in the

Admiralty, then? What of your wife, sir? How will she fare while you starve in the colonies? And if you think Parliament will not drain every ounce from the colonies that it can, you're a bigger fool than I thought."

Rory sighed and lifted his drink again. Farnley had said much the same thing, but it went against the grain. Once, he had been a student of medicine with the glorious intention of saving the world from disease. He had become a soldier by force, but he had learned to survive. Now the fates would make a courtier of him, when all he wished to do was return home and make a living for himself and his family. But even the return to his home was fraught with politics. And if there were any way of removing Drummond from his estate without physically dragging him, it would be best to consider it. Johnson was right. He did have a wife to consider now, for a while longer than he had expected, it seemed. He wondered how long it would take before Alyson quit being noble and sought the annulment she had threatened him with once before.

26

Rory spent the next days managing the intricacies of Alyson's extensive inheritance and the nights pursuing his own goals. He had never been a stranger to hard work, but for some reason, it seemed increasingly shallow.

Rory pushed himself harder, until even Deirdre began to look at him with reproach. He ignored her comments. He really needed to ride out personally to investigate the complaints of the tenants in Bath and to oversee the loading of the ships in Plymouth, but the ever-present threat of the Admiralty case kept him tied to London.

Alyson became a pale ghost who slipped by him occasionally in the hallway. It tore his heart in two to watch her turn away at his approach, but he felt closer to his

goal than he had in years. Alyson could have no place in
those plans, even had she wanted one, which she obviously did not. She had a life of her own now. He often
saw her out on the street, laughing up at some dandy,
shopping with her new friends, slipping into a bookseller's
for the latest publications. She couldn't have all that
where he was going.

On the twenty-fifth of October, when the bells of every
church in London began to toll and excited crowds
streamed out into the streets in thunderous uproar, Alyson
was at home with Deirdre miserably contemplating Sterne's
Tristram Shandy, finding the whole premise ridiculous.
The commotion outside gradually reached their ears, but
not before the messenger at the door and the wailing of
the servants.

Alyson looked up in astonishment to meet Deirdre's
eyes. Before either could so much as mutter, "What on
earth?" the drawing-room door burst open and the butler
intoned formally, "The king is dead, my lady. Shall I
hang out the bunting?"

When Rory came home, he found both women waiting
for him. He regaled them with the tale circulating the
coffeehouses—that the king had strained so hard over the
pot that his heart had burst, but he successfully hid his
elation. King George II had destroyed the Maclean home
and family. Rory did not regret the fat old man's passing.
He didn't rejoice in the prospect of the foolish young
king either, but he already had promises from the prince's
court that meant freedom. Soon he could return to
Scotland.

The days after that passed in a dismal pallor. With
official mourning descending on the city, there were no
entertainments to fill the empty hours. Alyson diligently
practiced the French the tutor Deirdre had hired taught
her, but though the man was amusing, she found little
interest in his scandalous choice of phrases and seductive
hints. She fared little better with the knitting that Deirdre tried to teach her, but it was at least something she
could take up to her room with her and served some
practical purpose. She rather enjoyed imagining dressing
tiny cherub feet in booties she had knit herself.

So it was that Rory found her the night he came home
with the news that the Admiralty had dropped the charges

against him. So filled with plans was he that he failed to notice the objects Alyson hastily tucked into the knitting bag beside her.

Finding her sitting in the near-dark sobered him somewhat. He had imbibed more than a pint or two in private celebration, but it had the ring of a hollow victory. He could leave England now, but in so doing, he would leave his heart behind.

He had to be fair to Alyson first. He had tricked her into this marriage, made her miserable with the kind of life he led, and hurt her far beyond his abilities to repair. He had desperately hoped there would be some means to minimize the damage, but finding her sitting here in the dark only served to remind him that she belonged in happiness and sunshine. Where he was going had neither at the moment.

"You have news?" Alyson asked quietly when he did not speak first.

Rory had doffed his coat earlier. Now he loosened his jabot while he sought the words he had not planned in advance. She looked so serene and young sitting there with her hair tied back in a ribbon, leaving only a few ebony curls to spring around her pale face. The pearly gray of her satin robe was gathered to fit snugly around her breasts, and the lamplight gleamed on the luminous globes revealed above the lace of her chemise. He remembered how it felt to slip his hand in there, and his loins tightened punishingly.

"Farnley says you have never discussed the possibility of an annulment with him." There was no point in treading delicately all around the subject until he had bewildered and frightened her. He owed her honesty, at least.

"Annulment?" A sinking fear plunged to the depths of Alyson's stomach. Annulment! She had not thought of that since the very first day of their marriage. What made him ask that now?

Rory sank into a dainty padded chair with a heart-shaped back. She did not sound as if she had thought about this, but he had to continue, once started. "I never meant to force you to something you did not wish, lass. I was drunk and hasty, but I thought wedded life was what you wanted. I can see now that I made a mistake, that I cannot make you happy with the kind of life I lead. If you still wish your freedom, I think it can be arranged.''

Stunned, Alyson could only stare at him, her hands clasped in her lap. She tried to sort out the jumble of emotion rioting through her, but the pain of his words was so excruciating she could scarcely breathe. Thinking seemed impossible.

He wanted to end their marriage. That meant he wanted to go away, to leave London. For Scotland or the sea? Or had he found that rich, powerful woman who could give him the favors she could not? The blinding pain this thought created caused her to hastily reject it in favor of others. If the marriage was annulled, that meant he would have no further access to her money, didn't it? Or had he stolen it all already? She could not believe that of Rory, and she looked at him with curiosity. If he did not want her money, why had he married her in the first place?

"Where would you go?"

That was a strange question under the circumstances, but patiently Rory gave his reply. "The charges have been dropped against me, lass. I will go home."

"Your cousin has sold you the estate, then?"

He shook his head. "No. He agrees only to sell the worthless parts, and those for enormous sums. I have saved enough to offer him a fair value, but he will not take it from me or any I appoint in my stead. He steals the money he needs from the tenants, and so far he has not completely exhausted their resources. There was wealth there once. It is nearly gone now. I have to return to help."

That did not sound as if he meant to abscond with her money or that he had found a woman powerful enough to unseat his cousin. So why would he seek an annulment?

"Why can't I go with you?" she asked reasonably.

Rory stared at her in astonishment. "To Scotland? Away from your friends, from all society? I told ye, lass, I have no home. I will live with the crofters. That's no life for the likes of ye."

Alyson began to grow annoyed with these evasions. He threatened her entire existence and gave her platitudes in return. "And that is the reason you ask for an annulment? Is there some Highland lass waiting for you there to keep you warm?"

"Alyson, be fair!" Rory cried, standing up and pacing the room. "If I could keep any woman at all, it would be you, but I cannot ask that of anyone. I only wish to return the freedom I stole from you. Farnley will go over the books with you, show you what I have done. You can hire someone else to manage it when I'm gone. Keep paying Cranville, and he will most likely leave you alone. If not, I'll come back to quiet him. I will not desert you entirely, lass. I just want you to be happy."

"Then you will not ask for an annulment."

Rory stopped his pacing to stare at the woman illuminated in the lamplight. There seemed something different about her, changed, but he could not quite put his finger on it. Those misty eyes still hid behind a black fringe of lashes, keeping her thoughts from him.

"What are you saying, Alys?" Her quiet words had sent his heart into a dive from which it wasn't quite possible to recover swiftly.

"I am saying I don't want an annulment, Rory. Even if I thought it would make you happy, I'm not certain that it can be done now."

Rory wished for another drink to clear the clouds of fog in his brain. In her own oblique way, Alyson was trying to tell him something, but his brain was too numb to accept it. "You have talked to someone besides Farnley about it?"

"I don't think I need to. I understand enough to know there are certain conditions to an annulment. I fear no court in the land would acknowledge that those conditions exist."

He could dismiss her words as naiveté. Judges could be bribed. Physicians would lie. The proof that she was no longer untouched did not have to actually exist. There was only one thing she could be talking about, and he didn't think he could survive that news standing up. He promptly sat down on the edge of the bed nearest her chair.

"Tell me, Alyson, why do those conditions no longer exist?"

His nearness was a torment, but she resisted fleeing. She could reach out her hand and touch the smooth doeskin of his knee breeches covering those long legs braced so near her own. She wished desperately just to hold his hard brown hand. She could do neither.

With a deep breath she replied, "Because I am three months gone with your child."

Rory felt the air rush from his lungs. He lacked the presence of mind to draw it in again. His child! She was going to have his child! He gulped a breath before he passed out, then did hasty mental arithmetic. He didn't need to. He already knew when it had happened—in that very first week of their loving. Thank God he had had the sense to marry her!

He didn't know what to do, what to say. She had just hit him over the head with a brickbat and he was still dazed. The soft sweet sound of her voice repeating his name returned some portion of his senses.

"Alyson, I didn't mean to . . ." But he had meant to, his conscience warned him. With a sigh, Rory acknowledged his guilt in trapping her in this predicament.

Rising slowly, he bent and lifted Alyson from her seat, swinging her frail weight into his arms as he sat down and pulled her into his lap. Small hands fluttered against his shirt, and he captured them against his chest.

"I'm that sorry, lass. There's nowt fair in what I've done to ye, but I'll try to make it right. I'm a wretched excuse for a husband, probably worse as a father, but I'll see to it that neither of you lacks for anything."

Alyson huddled forlornly against his broad chest, hearing his words as a bleak wind dissipating all her dreams. Even telling him of the child wasn't going to hold him back. Tears rimmed her eyes, but she refused to give in to them. Whether he wanted one or not, Rory was going to have a home and a family. She wouldn't settle for anything less. She'd had enough of this living in purgatory. It was her turn now.

"Take me with you." She spoke into the lace frill of his shirt, not lifting her head from the sound of his heartbeat.

Rory sighed and caressed the long spill of hair down her back. "If only I could, dear heart. Someday, maybe."

"Not someday. Now." Alyson pushed herself from the comfort of his arms to glare into his dark features. "You're not leaving me behind, Rory Maclean."

"Alyson, be sensible. I could not take a lass such as yourself even before I knew of the child. There's twice the reason to leave you here now. I can live off the land, sleep on the ground, survive the winter wind off the loch. You canna."

"I will not have to. I found a map in your library. Your home is on Loch Linnhe, isn't it?"

Surprised at this sudden expertise from his dreamy lass, Rory narrowed his eyes and watched the unusual animation on her face. "It is."

"So is my grandmother's home. Can it be so very far from yours? My grandfather kept up the house even after she had gone. It cannot be in too poor a condition."

Rory couldn't quite believe how this conversation had traveled from annulments to homemaking in such a short space of time, but a peculiar feeling much resembling hope began to take root somewhere near his heart. He condemned it to banishment, however. She could not know what she asked.

"What was your mother's family name?" He tried caution, not yet certain how to handle this.

"MacInnes."

Rory leaned his head against the back of the chair and frowned. MacInnes. It had been nearly fifteen long years, but he vaguely remembered the name. Like any lad, he'd had little time for any families without children of his own age, but he remembered seeing the rocky castle and hearing the tales of the witch. The witch. Of course. That would undoubtedly be Alyson's beloved grandmother. She had no idea of what she asked.

"Aye, I know of them, lass. The castle was crumbling to the ground when I was but a lad. There was nowt but the tower left. 'Tis doubtful that even that is habitable now. In the winter, it would be a cold, drafty place to be."

Alyson set her chin stubbornly and shoved from his lap. Setting her hands on her hips, she glared rebelliously at him. "I am going, Rory Maclean. You can come with me, if you like. Or you can freeze your toes off on the moors for all I care. My grandmother had no money to make the tower comfortable, but I do, if you've left me any."

"Left you any! I haven't touched a farthing of your fortune, Alyson. Even the wages Farnley insisted I take, I spent on you. Don't go throwing your bloody blunt in my face!" Rory threw himself from the chair and stalked toward the sitting room. This had gone far beyond what he had ever dreamed. He had known Alyson hid a wild streak behind that placid facade, but this was far and away more than he had anticipated.

"I don't care about the money!" Alyson cried as she saw him trying to escape. "You can have it all, buy back your estate, feed your tenants, just let me come with you. This child needs a father."

Her plea tore at Rory's heart, swinging him around against his better judgment. She stood so small and fragile against the backdrop of the massive bed. The robe swirled around her, transforming her into a ghostly specter in the lamplight. He could feel the silver mist of her eyes pleading with him, drawing him back, and his fingers curled into tight fists against his palms. She was so young, so helpless, like the child she carried. The thought of that burden broke the sweat from his brow.

Sensing his hesitation, Alyson whispered her final argument. "I'll do anything you want, Rory, anything. Just take me with you."

That promise—more than any promise of riches—broke his resolve. For he knew, without any shadow of doubt, what she offered, and how much it cost her to say it.

Rubbing a hand across his brow, he nodded slowly. "Very well, lass. We'll talk of it in the morning. Go to sleep now."

Joy swept through Alyson at his surrender, joy muted with fear. She knew the promise that had changed his mind. How soon would he call on her to make it good?

27

Scotland, November 1760

As the icy deluge began once more, Rory cursed his haste for the hundredth time on this leg of their journey. He could have waited for Dougall to complete his shipment and ordered him back to London so they could travel safely around the coast on the *Witch*. It might have meant a delay of a month or more, but at least Alyson would not have been subjected to the worst of the winter weather as she was now.

As the carriage lurched through a particularly deep mudhole, Rory realized his memory of riding across these unmarked roads at great speed had much to do with youth and a spirited horse and little to do with carriages and pregnant wives. His foolish notion that they could save time by taking the first ship out going north and hiring a carriage to ride the distance from Edinburgh to Loch Linnhe had certainly given Alyson a fine insight into the country he called home.

Glancing over his shoulder to be certain the carriage had pulled out of the hole intact, Rory had to admit Alyson had not voiced a single complaint throughout the abominable journey. Pulling his hat down farther to allow the rain to funnel down the back of his cloak instead of his neck, he sent his mount on ahead to test the condition of the road.

She had agreed to his every command, smiled politely at the other female inhabitants of the ship's cabin she was forced to share, and didn't murmur when their first day on land and every day since had been accompanied by a steady downpour. There had been times she looked a little green, when he found a stopping place for the carriage and helped her down, but if she heaved up the better part of her breakfast after a particularly rough road, she never mentioned it to him.

Her ability to still smile at him at the end of the day multiplied Rory's guilt to proportions well beyond his ability to command. He should never have brought her. Even without the burden of a child to carry, she had no place in these wild, barren lands. If anything should happen to her, he would not survive the loss, let alone the guilt. Just the thought of losing her twisted a knife of pain his heart, and Rory slowed his horse to turn and make certain the carriage still followed steadily.

His reasons for bringing her had been entirely selfish. Despite Alyson's pleas, he could have left her behind. Common sense told him she would be safer and happier in London than in these harsh lands in midwinter. But just as they had from the first, her desires and emotions had twisted his logic until he could no longer think straight. He didn't want to leave her behind for the admiration and benefit of London society. He wanted her with him. He wanted his child to be born in these hills that he loved, and most of all, he wanted Alyson to love his home as he did. Some insane quirk of his mind believed that if they ever had a chance at happiness, it would be here. It was that madness that had brought them to this boggy trail in the midst of barren hills with daylight fading fast and no shelter to be found.

Cursing again, Rory spurred his horse over the next hill. If he had ever imagined bringing a wife home, it would not have been with her fingers turning blue with cold and her trunks turning green with mold as she gazed out upon sheets of rain and the bilious brown of mud and rock. He would have liked to bring her in the spring, with the broom blooming a brilliant yellow over the hillsides and the purple rhododendron and wild foxglove spreading across the valleys, or in August, with the heather turning the hills to celestial colors. Anything would be preferable to this.

A but-and-ben cottage nestled into the next hillside, sending up a thin gray swirl of smoke from the rock chimney, a luxury that indicated the owner had given some care to the building of his home. Inside it would be warm and dry enough, and Rory would have called it a

day and stayed here had it not been for the entourage
following behind. He could not ask Alyson to sleep in a
mud-daub-and-thatched cabin, no matter how cozy it might
be. If he remembered correctly, they were near enough
to some friends of his to pass the night. The friends'
house had been cold and drafty when he was a lad, but at
least it had wooden floors and bedrooms and beds. After
a day like this, a feather mattress would be welcome.

Not wishing to think too hard on the subject of beds
and mattresses, Rory pushed his tired mount to the crest
of the hill overlooking the next valley. He gave a tired
groan as he realized that the trifling burn he remembered
cooling his heels in during the summer had become a
river with the onset of heavy rain. The carriage could
never ford it tonight.

Resolutely he turned back to break the news to those
riding behind. The crofter's cottage would have to serve
as inn for the night.

Alyson set her heavy patten on a rock conveniently
situated near the carriage door. Holding Rory's hand,
she lifted her skirts from the ankle-deep mud and guided
her other foot to the next outcropping of stone. One
wrong move and she would be facefirst in the pebble-
strewn yard, but she feared she would never pull her feet
from the mire should they land in it.

From beneath lowered lashes she studied Rory's stony
expression more than the low hut to which he guided her.
She could see where a land like this would cultivate
stoicism, but she thought his rigid expression hid more
pain than his features acknowledged. Rory had learned
to hide his feelings from the world, but she understood
his emotions more than his thoughts. The tension in the
hand holding hers told more than words.

Once inside, she shed her dripping cloak and muddy
pattens with the aid of a wizened old woman who murmured reassurances in an accent so thick Alyson could
make little sense of it. Her gaze drifted to the smoke-
blackened beams barely giving Rory's height headroom.
The ill-chinked fireplace sent sudden gusts of smoke
into the room, and the heat of it circled in a cloud just above
their heads. The hard-packed dirt floor beneath her feet
was neatly covered in some coarse grass to form a carpet

of sorts against the damp, and the warmth of the tiny
peat fire took the moisture from the air.

She smiled, thanked her hostess, and drifted toward
the fire. Coming in from tending the horses and securing them in a small shed attached to the house, Rory and
their host exchanged glances as they watched her. The
older man's murmurs of appreciation in the old language
brought a tired grin to Rory's face. Answering in kind,
he agreed his lady wife had the face of springtime, then
added she had the patience of a saint.

The old woman hurriedly chopping more vegetables
for the simmering pot looked up at this, then glanced to
Alyson with a gap-toothed smile. Somewhere in her thick
speech Alyson recognized the word "bairn," and she
turned from contemplation of the fire to discover all eyes
on her. She glanced to Rory for explanation.

"She said carrying a child teaches patience. Would you
agree?"

Alyson blushed that the woman had guessed so easily.
She had not thought her condition so readily noticed.
The old man and woman laughed at her sudden color and
went about their activities without expecting any reply,
leaving her to look to Rory. The intensity of his gaze
made her face even hotter, and her gaze faltered before
the sudden desire blazing up in his eyes.

He had not taken advantage of her offer or even showed
any desire to do so since she had made it. She had
thought his desire for her must have died upon gaining
what he wanted, but she could see now that she was
wrong. She did not know the reason he still stayed from
her bed, but his decision to do so saddened as well as
relieved her. It would be difficult to build a marriage
without the loving they had once shared, but she would
be the first to admit that after what had happened, it
could never be the same.

She swallowed a sigh and accepted the offer of the
room's only chair. Rory had tried to explain why he had
done what he had, but she never had been very good at
following logic. She had finally come to realize that that
day had caused him as much pain and anguish as she had
suffered, and she had only recently come to suspect that
he tortured himself with the memory of it. She didn't
know how to ease his pain, any more than she knew how

to ease her fear. The gap between them had seemed almost unbridgeable in London. Perhaps here they could have the time to themselves necessary to conquer it.

The carriage driver and footman came in out of the rain, stomping their filthy boots on the clean floor and cursing as they gazed around the dismal hut. Rory's scowl silenced them, and they settled on a rough bench in the corner out of the way of the kitchen activities. The offering of tin cups of hot cider brought grudging nods.

Alyson sipped at her mug of cider and listened as the old woman chattered and Rory replied in careful English so both she and their hostess could understand. They talked of people and places she did not know, but her desire to know everything about Rory compelled her to listen. When the conversation came around to her own family, Alyson was startled by the old woman suddenly making a rapid sign of the cross as she glanced in her direction.

"What did she say, Rory?" Alyson intruded in the quiet conversation for the first time, drawing the eyes of everyone back to her again. She hid her discomfort at this attention and waited patiently for Rory's reply.

To her surprise, it was their host who answered. "It is an old woman's foolishness." He spat into the fire and glared at his wife before speaking in guttural but careful English. "Your mother was a lovely lass with no harm in her. There are those who still mourn the day she left these lands."

That piece of information brought a smile to Alyson's lips, but the look she threw him warned Rory she was not satisfied with the diversion. Her grandmother might have taught her to love the Highland tales, but she had never taught her of Highland superstition. He hoped his angelic lass learned to live with both sides of his world. It would not be easy for one with her gift.

Almost apologetically the old woman set out bannocks kept warm in the iron oven by the fire and poured bowls of thick soup for their supper. When Alyson exclaimed with delight at this simple offering, the woman looked dazed and turned to Rory for confirmation. She had known Rory since he was a lad, and his simple but richly woven attire was in keeping with the laird's status, and expected. The lady, on the other hand, although dressed in woolens and not silks, managed to convey elegance in touches of lace and hints of ribbon and with every graceful move she made. It seemed incomprehensible that such nobility would exclaim over crofter's fare.

"My wife has simple tastes, Peg," Rory replied to the woman's look. "Else why would she choose me?"

This brought a round of laughter to spice the meal, and the food was devoured with eager hunger despite its simplicity. More than once Alyson glanced at Rory's expression to find the lines about his mouth relaxing into a smile and the creases on his forehead all but disappearing. He was at home here. She would have to learn to be the same.

She had doubts about her ability to adapt sometime later when they were thrust into the narrow back room and given the honor of the cottage's only bed. The others would make do on the floor of the main room. She glanced at the thin, sloping pallet, then back to Rory.

In the light of one frail candle, he caught her look and shrugged. "It is this or the carriage, lass. Would ye hurt their feelings by refusing?"

Practical Rory. Silently Alyson turned her back to him to help with her gown as she had learned to do these last days without a maid. The number of heavy chemises and petticoats she wore beneath the gown prevented anything so intimate as a touch, but her spine still stiffened as his fingers worked their way through the fastenings.

Rory discarded only his coat, cravat, and shoes. With all Alyson's quilted petticoats between them, they had little choice but to lie spoon fashion to fit in the narrow bed. Rory's arm circled her waist as he formed a wedge between Alyson and the floor.

The temptation to move his hand higher to stroke the full curves and twin peaks of her breasts was subdued by Alyson's tension as she lay scarcely breathing against him. His desire for her went undaunted but unnoticed by its object due to the protection of the petticoats. Rory stifled a groan of frustration and tried to remember where they were. They had made love behind thin walls and in narrow beds before, but that was before the black cloud of his guilt had separated them. He had little chance of winning back her good graces like this.

When he woke in the morning, Alyson was still sleeping, more exhausted by the journey than she would admit. Rory smoothed the ebony silk of her hair back from her forehead and pushed himself up on one elbow to study her face. Dark circles stained the skin beneath her eyes, but her cheeks were flushed with healthy color, and her lips parted in moist sweetness, drawing him like a bee to nectar. Just one taste, he promised himself, just one small taste to ease his day . . .

The clatter of an iron pot in the next room brought Alyson's startled eyes open to find Rory hovering over her. The heavy blankets were pulled up about her chin, so she was well-protected from his sight, but she could not help her brief flinch of fear as his hand reached to touch the chin that had once been black with the bruise of his fist.

Rory withdrew his caress immediately and forced a smile to his face. "The sun is shining, lass. If we rise now, we will be home by nightfall."

She nodded and held the blanket as he rose. There was no water with which to wash and no privacy for using the cracked chamber pot under the bed. Still wearing yesterday's shirt and breeches, Rory shrugged on his coat and pulled on his muddy boots.

Alyson watched him with an anxious frown. "Mr. Farnley said he sent someone on ahead to see the tower was ready, didn't he? Should I change into something suitable for our arrival?"

Rory picked up her perfectly suitable traveling gown and gave her a puzzled glance; then, realizing she was worried about how a laird's wife ought to look so as not to shame him, he grinned and shook his head. "You'll be far too grand for those who greet you as it is. We've left London behind, lass. You need no longer worry if your jewels are rich enough or if your silks sport enough lace. There are those who would try it, perhaps, but not for a Maclean. Keep yourself and the child warm and dry, and you will be deemed a good, sensible lass. There is no higher compliment."

Alyson relaxed and smiled in relief. "I think I'm going to like the Macleans. Will the MacInneses be the same?"

"There are not enough of them left to count, love. Now, up with you. It's time to be about."

She had kept track of the times he had called her

"love" and knew how precious few they were. He said it whenever he was particularly pleased with her, however, so she hurried to do his bidding now. She had long ago surrendered any notion that Rory might actually love her, but she couldn't kill all hope. She had been so accustomed to being loved that she had taken it for granted before. Now she knew the value of what she had once possessed, and she was willing to work hard to earn it. She would just have to learn to overcome her panic when Rory came too near. She would never win him with that behavior.

As he left the room in his knee-high boots, his hair neatly clubbed at his nape, and his woolen frock coat fitted snugly to strong shoulders, Alyson felt the frozen fire inside begin to melt. Whatever Rory was, whatever he had done, she could not hide her love for him from herself. She loved him, and somehow she would have to teach him to love her. He had learned to love as a boy. As a man, he needed reminding.

Having ridden all the way from the docks at Plymouth, the man on horseback arrived at his Cornish estate long past nightfall. His heavy caped greatcoat dripped from the cold rain that had followed him across the moors. Only instinct and distant memories had kept him to the road. He sighed in exhaustion and relief at the plain stone mansion rising above the cliffs. Lights flickered somewhere deep within. His journey was almost at an end.

The heavy knocker clattered against the brass plate, echoing through the hallway beyond. He raised it a third and fourth time before he heard the sound of footsteps on the other side of the door. When the door swung open, he stepped hurriedly in out of the rain.

The butler watched with astonishment as the intruder swept off his soaked but richly braided cocked hat with an air of authority, then glanced around the toweringly drafty foyer with a proprietary interest. "Your business, sir?" the butler demanded arrogantly, hiding a twinge of fear. If the estate was entailed, surely the new earl could not gamble it off to strangers?

The man glanced inquisitively at the elderly servant, searching for some sign or clue to his identity. Twenty years had taken their toll, but he found what he sought, and grinning a distressingly youthful grin for one whose silver-streaked hair declared his age, he declared, "Hevers, isn't it? You were growing bald when I left. The wig had me fooled. Is Alexander in?"

At this informal mention of his employer's name, the butler blanched further and searched the stranger's face, not daring to believe what some long-buried instinct told him. All Hallow's Eve had passed. Ghosts could not walk the night. "If you refer to his lordship, he is not at home at present. If you will state your request, I shall be happy to forward the message to his man of business."

The newcomer only grinned at this formal response and swung off his coat, handing it to the reluctant butler. "I'll not be sent back out on a night like this just because you have a poor memory, Hevers. If my cousin's son is not here, where is he?"

Cousin. The butler's teeth began to click and he blanched several shades paler than the specter standing in front of him. "It is never yourself, my lord?" He lapsed into the accents of his youth in the presence of this apparition.

Faded blue eyes saddened and the lines of weariness deepened on the newcomer's brow as the grin disappeared. "Aye, and it is, Hevers. It's been a long time and an even longer story. They say I have a daughter, Hevers. I meant to question Alex, but if he is not here . . . I cannot be proper and wait. Where is she? Do you know?"

The last time Hevers had seen the little miss had been the night she poured the tea down his lordship's leg and packed her bags and left. There had been rumors between the houses—the Tremaines had seen her—but they were all servants' talk. What could he tell a man who was supposed to be dead?

"I cannot say, my lord. Let me call Hettie to make up your room for you. Perhaps the Tremaines can give you that information in the morning."

Everett Hampton, the rightful Earl of Cranville, stared hard at the nervous butler, causing the old man to quake in his shoes. He had not come halfway around the world to be fobbed off by servants. With the governor's story still burning in his ears even after all these weeks, he had too much rage and anguish to be put off by any less than the devil himself.

"Then perhaps you can tell me where my heir is, Hevers."

It was more command than request, and the butler responded with alacrity. "Hunting with friends in Scotland, my lord."

28

Stagshead, November 1760

Enveloped in the evening mist rising off the water, the square stone tower and crumbling ruins of the fortress seemed somehow insubstantial and not quite real as Alyson gazed from the carriage window up to it. There was little more than a sheep path left for the carriage to traverse, and the ruts and stones jostled so severely that she clung to the window frame to keep from being thrown about. She should have insisted on riding, but she was not a skilled horsewoman, and Rory had refused to consider it. With each curve in the road that gave her a glimpse of her new home, she stared as if to hold it there until she arrived.

They were seen long before they gained the summit, and the massive wooden door was thrown open welcomingly when Rory finally handed Alyson down from the carriage. She clung to his fingers to steady herself and for reassurance as she gazed upward at the full height of the fortress her mother and grandmother had called home. Once it must have been an imposing fortification. Now it had the empty feel of abandonment.

Several small figures appeared in the doorway, and it took a moment before Alyson realized it was not the people who were small but the door which was large. Relieved that she would not be greeting the Scots equivalent of leprechauns, she gratefully leaned on Rory's arm as he led her to their new home.

She was too tired to notice more than a beaming smile here and a dour expression there. Her head ached, and the dizziness that occasionally forewarned of one of her spells made her cling harder to Rory's arm. She didn't want to have one of her spells here, in front of these superstitious people who knew nothing of her.

The pressure of Alyson's fingers brought Rory's concerned glance to her pale face. Vacant gray eyes turned somehow pleadingly toward him, and he felt his stomach lurch as he felt her slipping away from him. One minute she was there behind the mist of those lovely eyes, and the next minute she was gone.

Catching Alyson up in his arms, Rory strode quickly through the huge doorway and into the stone and tapestried interior of the tower. "Where is the lady's room? Quickly!"

Alarmed, a capped and aproned gray-haired woman scurried toward the massive stone stairway filling the central hall. Rory strode after her, leaving his driver and footman to oversee the unloading of trunks.

The flight of stairs seemed endless as they passed one landing and raced on to another. Rory could feel Alyson's shudders against his chest, and fear kept him moving without thought. The stairwell went up still another flight, but blessedly the housekeeper turned down a narrow hall at the second landing, throwing open a door to the right.

It was apparent that moldering bed hangings and draperies had been removed before their arrival, leaving the wainscoted room cold and forbidding as they entered. A small fire licked at the grate, but the draft from the uncovered window more than adequately dissipated any heat from the flames.

Rory shivered and strode toward the paneled bed. The high wooden walls of the bed cut off the worst of the draft, and fresh linens and heavy woolens had apparently been found to make it up. Grateful for any small favor, Rory laid Alyson upon the covers and began to unfasten her cloak.

Aware that the old woman watched every move he made, Rory threw over his shoulder, "Fetch some warm water, and if you have some, hot tea or broth. My lady is not well and the journey has exhausted her."

Relieved with sensible explanations and easily under-

stood orders, the woman hurried to do as bidden, leaving
Rory to cope alone with Alyson's retreat behind vague
walls.

"Lass, I canna see what ye are seein'. Help me, lass.
Tell me what to do," he whispered in confusion. She
terrified him when she did this, leaving him reeling in a
world of uncertainty until she was firmly in his hands
again. Desperately, he feared one day she would leave
into that other world and not return.

Alyson heard Rory's plea, and her eyes flickered. Just
the knowledge that he was still at her side made her feel
secure, and her fingers closed tightly around his comforting ones. "I am fine, Rory," she managed to murmur,
giving him the reassurance she knew he needed. She no
longer feared that he wished her dead or disappeared.
He could not hide the concern in his voice or the anguish
in his eyes when she finally gazed up at him. He might
pretend indifference for whatever reason, but her Rory
could never be heartless.

"Alys, you tear the breath from me when you do that.
I think the first thing we need do is find a physician." He
hid his insane fears behind a mask of practicality.

"Even could you find such an unlikely personage out
here, he would merely say, 'Aye, and she's with bairn,
lad. Call me back in five months or so.' "

Rory grinned weakly at her mimicry. "I'll not survive
that long if you persist in doing this. Do you have any
idea how many stairs there are out there?"

Alyson laughed at his aggrieved expression and struggled to sit up just as the housekeeper bustled in with a
tray and a young girl hurried after her with a pitcher of
hot water.

There was no time to explain that she had seen the
snowstorm again, only a little clearer. He might say these
hills did not receive the snow of their northern heights,
but she knew differently. The landscape she had seen in
her vision was only a snow-covered version of the one
she could see outside their window right now.

If she could do naught else, she could prepare their
home for the winter storm. She glanced around her as
the servants bustled importantly about, then tugged on
Rory's hand. "When will you next hear from Dougall?"

He raised a questioning eyebrow but complied with

this reasonable question. "I have not sent him far. We established a method of sending messages through Glasgow long ago. Why?"

"I will need to order a number of things from London or Edinburgh or wherever one can obtain materials and the like here. I suspect we may be sleeping on the only linen in the house." She whispered this last quietly so as not to offend the servants adding peat to the fire and waiting patiently for further orders.

Rory frowned. "I cannot afford to be sending the *Witch* on shopping trips for luxuries, Alyson. You saw last night how the people here must live. We would do better to study the situation and see how best to use our resources."

Alyson stared at him in dawning comprehension. Far from using their marriage to fatten his pocket with her wealth, Rory meant not to use it at all! There could be no other reason for his parsimonious ways. Furious at his stubbornness when so much could be done with that worthless accumulation compounding interest in some London vault, Alyson sat up and tried to get around Rory's broad frame to reach the floor.

"I never saw such a stubborn, pigheaded, mule-minded, intolerably arrogant excuse for a gentleman in all my life! I thought Dougall would be more reliable and sympathetic to my needs, but I'll send my requests to Deirdre and Mr. Farnley and they will see to them for me. You may freeze yourself blue in some garret if your conscience requires, but I'll not see the people in my household suffer needless discomfort for the benefit of your pride. Go away. I wish to change out of these dratted muddy clothes."

The two servants stared in astonishment as the laird rose and made an icily correct bow at the frail lady's sudden explosion. When the hard-featured gentleman stalked out, they weren't sure whether to hurry after him or stay with the lady. Not until they realized tears poured silently down the lady's beautifully sculptured porcelain cheeks did they grasp the first hint of the tragedy between these two disparate people. The laird had all the strength; the lady had only her beauty with which to defend herself.

In the way of the world, the servants divided between

themselves. The housekeeper hurried after the master to see to his needs. The young maid stayed to help the lady from her gown and to see to her comfort. So it was that the remainder of the household divided as the days passed.

Alyson had little experience in running a household, particularly a newly acquired one in which none of the people had worked together before. The butler and the head housekeeper of her grandfather's establishment had essentially kept that household running properly since her grandmother's death, and she wished desperately for their experience now as she contemplated the enormous task set out for her.

The caretaker had seen that the walls remained standing and the roof didn't collapse, but he had not seen to the little things like the mice in the larders, the leaks in the casements, nor the mold in the pantries. The kitchen had only a cavernous fireplace for cooking. The dinnerware was a motley assortment of cracked pottery and pewter. The magnificent Jacobean pieces of furniture with which the house had originally been furnished nearly two centuries before had been cracked and scarred and rotted from neglect. There was scarcely a suitable mattress or pallet left to house the very limited staff of servants which Rory allowed her.

Since they had not been there all summer to stock the larder, they had sufficient provisions only for the steward and his wife. Lists of necessary supplies had to be drawn up with the primitive kitchen in mind as well as the distance they would have to be hauled.

Alyson was almost prepared to surrender at the hopelessness of the task, when the young maid who had become her staunchest ally casually made a comment that revived her determination.

"Me mam used to work for yer gran'ther when he was alive. She said 'twas a fine hoose then, and there were none that went beggin' that came here. It will be good to see those times ag'in."

Sitting at the knife-scarred kitchen table, Alyson looked up from her endless list to study the dark-haired girl who swept at the ashes in the fireplace. "Where is your mother now?"

The girl swept a pile of ashes into the bin. " 'Twas a poor summer year before last, and she was sickly. When the winter turned cruel . . ." She shrugged her shoulders in resignation. "It will be different nae that ye've coom. She always said, even when the laird died, his lady saw none went hungry. Of course, that was before the uprisin' an' a' that. There's few left to look after nae."

Alyson sighed and set about her list-making with new will. It was her neglect that had allowed these lands to lie fallow too long. The earl had known nothing of this place or the tenants' reliance on their landlord during times of hardship. She had known it. Her grandmother had drummed the importance of her responsibilities into her from an early age. She had just never understood the amount of personal responsibility involved. A steward had sounded sufficient to her. She could see now that it was that sort of thinking that had brought the land to rack and ruin.

With so many of the Highland landowners driven from their estates and the lands left to waste in His Majesty's coffers, there were none to personally oversee the tenants and crofters, to give them aid or education as the lairds had in the past. Absentee landowners were little better than King George. Both demanded their rents and raised them to suit their needs without consideration of what the tenants had to do to provide them. And then they complained when the people who had to live here turned to cattle stealing for support. No wonder the honest, ambitious ones found a way to emigrate.

Alyson knew she did not need to preach her newfound lessons to Rory, even had she the opportunity. He was already aware of the problems and was out every day and half the night compiling his own lists. She knew he ranged farther afield than her own small holdings, to be gone so much of the time, but she had expected that. The estates that had once been his were within riding distance. He could not keep away.

She had become so accustomed to his absence in London that she did not really begin to worry here until she caught a chance remark in the stairwell one day.

"They say there's no respectable girl will work there with Lord Drummond home. 'Tis a shame, it is, with the rightful laird livin' in this drafty auld place when he might have a' that."

Alyson stiffened and waited for more, but the voices

drifted off down the stairs, and she dared not follow. Rory had not mentioned that his English cousin was in residence. She had assumed he was just another of the absentee landlords living in London. Rory's threats to one day have it out with Drummond took on new meaning. Had he already been to his cousin to offer for the estate, then?

She wanted to question him, but the day's tasks and her body's new, demanding needs drained her of the ability to stay awake until he came home. When he did arrive in the late hours of the evening, he made his bed in the room across from hers, leaving her to sleep undisturbed until after he was gone in the morning.

Alyson raged inwardly at this callous disregard of her needs, but none could tell through the docile expression she presented as she consulted the servants concerning the various needs of the household. Let Rory right the world on the outside. She would start at home.

Those things that could be found locally began arriving within the week. Alyson watched in satisfaction as the blanket chests began to fill with fine woolens and the linen wardrobes with finely woven sheets. Dried and salted meats, potatoes, and sacks of oatmeal began to fill the empty pantries and cellars. Next year there would be gardens and jams and jellies from the fruits her grandmother had said were to be found. For now, such luxuries would have to come from afar. Alyson signed still another invoice for the latest shipment of plain woolen yard goods and posted it to Mr. Farnley. Let him make what he would of it, along with the other lists of necessities she had sent to him.

Alyson suspected Rory still managed her finances, for the post to him from London was formidable, but if he did not wish to discuss it with her, she had too much pride to inquire. He would just have to discover her purchases from Mr. Farnley. She wasn't about to beg for the use of her own money.

Slowly she began to learn the names of the servants and their various capabilities. They all knew her story, knew her for a sailor's bastard, but they still held a respect for the MacInneses and a wariness of the memory of her grandmother. Often she caught them watching her with suspicion when she drifted through a room without speaking, her mind on other things. But as rumors of her pregnancy made the rounds, they relaxed their guard, and she actually caught an occasional smile on their faces when she exclaimed over some hitherto undiscovered aspect of her new life.

There were no smiles the night the rain turned to wailing winds and sleet, and Alyson discovered a more heartbreaking facet of this life. The howling storm made her shiver even though workmen had begun to line the windows with paneled shutters, and she had hired a seamstress to create heavy draperies to go over both shutters and windows. Fires were kept burning in all the grates, but nothing could keep out the howl of the wind. Terrified for Rory's safety, Alyson walked the floors and listened to the wind and refused to be comforted by the improvements she had made.

The noise outside was such that she almost didn't hear the faint pounding at the great oaken door. Since the castle overlooked a cliff, there was only one entrance to the tower. Rory would not have lingered to knock at his own gate.

The servants had retired to the warmth of the kitchen, leaving Alyson to struggle with the massive door. The wind took care of it once she cracked it open slightly, shoving against the oak in a sudden gust that sent Alyson staggering backward. The heavy door heaved open enough to reveal two forlorn figures on the doorstep, one carrying a tattered woolen shawl in her arms, protecting the tiny form wrapped inside against her breast.

Alyson stared at the scarecrow figures of the two women as she hurriedly ushered them in and pushed the door closed. They wore no cloaks or coats against the icy wind, and their tartans had frozen into shapeless mounds around their shoulders. The ice began to melt and run in rivulets from their garments as they stood in the warmth of the hall, and Alyson gasped in horror as she realized both women wore nothing but rags on their feet. Her eyes flew to the weathered, worn lines of the older woman's face and read the bleakness there.

"They say the Maclean has returned," she managed to say through cracked lips, speaking slowly but in a thick accent that forced Alyson to listen closely. "Is he here?"

"He should be here soon. You must come in and dry

yourselves." Alyson couldn't keep her gaze from wandering to the younger woman clutching the infant. The child hadn't moved or uttered a cry since they entered. She had never tended a baby before, had never had any close contact with one, and her hands itched to touch the tiny bundle, to see the child's face. The young mother's expression had frozen blankly at the first sight of Alyson, but she moved toward the warmth of the fire as Alyson indicated.

As they crossed the planked floor, their tattered rags left a trail of water. The bundle containing the infant was equally saturated, and obeying an urge that had no voice, Alyson took her own shawl off and approached the younger woman. She slipped the warm wool around the bundle and lifted the child from its mother's arms so swiftly that the woman had little time to protest. She stood helplessly, her large eyes dark and staring in an emaciated face, as she watched Alyson cuddle the child in her arms.

It was only when Alyson moved aside the soggy wool covering the infant's face that stark horror found its way into her bones and curdled her stomach. She glanced up past the young mother, whimpering for the return of her child, to the older woman, who met her gaze with unflinching sadness.

"Hush, Mary. The lady will only take Jamie to the kitchen to get warm. Everything's fine now."

Alyson caught the warning in the woman's carefully pronounced words, and grateful for any excuse to flee, practically ran from the room.

Tears were streaming down her cheeks, and she opened her mouth to cry out as she entered the kitchen, but nothing would come out. The servants still sitting around the fire turned to stare at the lady wordlessly holding a bundle of rags wrapped in her fine woven shawl. They had grown accustomed to her vague and often speechless ways, but they had seldom seen her without a smile. Her expression now smote them with an inexplicable helplessness, until the elderly housekeeper finally recovered her feet and shouted to the young maid who served the mistress.

"Meg! Take Lady Alyson upstairs." The housekeeper shifted her aching bones to remove the rags from Alyson's arms, and then exclaimed in Gaelic, causing several of the others to jump to their feet.

"He's dead, isn't he?" Alyson asked softly, her eyes searching the other woman's for verification as she reluctantly surrendered her small burden.

"Aye, lass. Many a bairn born this time o' the year has not the strength to live. Yer own will be born in the spring, and a fine time that will be. He'll be a big strapping lad, ye will see. Dinna fash yerself o'er it nae. Yer man willna be likin' to see ye so."

The girl Meg tried to lead Alyson away, but the emptiness in her arms where the infant had been would not let her leave. Unaware of the tears still streaming down her cheeks, she turned and silently returned to the waiting women, scarcely aware that Meg still followed.

When she returned to the front room without the infant, the mother began a wail in a language Alyson did not need the words to understand. Lifting her head, she met the older woman's gaze with a sorrow that ate right through her heart. The woman nodded in understanding and proceeded to reassure the young mother in an incomprehensible dialect.

As Alyson turned to give Meg orders for warm clothing and blankets, the front door flew open and Rory entered the front hall with a burst of wind and rain. As he slammed the door closed, the high keening wails from the neglected front room drew him in that direction. The rage and weariness on his face only deepened when he took in the scene before him.

"What the devil is this about?" he roared as the keening gave no evidence of quieting. He threw his soaked cloak over a massive carved mahogany chair with utter disregard for its antiquity. The young maid instantly stepped in front of her mistress as if to protect her from his fury, and Rory's frustration reached new intensity, until his gaze met Alyson's.

He was a man of practicality, a man who used logic and action to attain his goals. He had buried emotion with his brother and father and had no notion how to deal with it. But the sight of Alyson standing there with her soul in her eyes ripped open something raw inside that demanded release. He struggled to regain control, but he had married a woman who communicated only in emotions, and his response had to be in the same language to reach her.

He could not do it. He could not release the anguish and love and fear bound up inside him for all to see. Turning from the silent plea in Alyson's eyes, he spoke sharply in Gaelic to the two women by the fire.

As if knowing the lady could not understand their words, the older woman looked at Alyson with compassion and spoke to her as well as Rory, using her halting English.

"The child was forced on her by one of Drummond's men. When she grew too big to work, they threw her out of the house. I took her in, but the bairn was born sickly, and she had no milk for it. The roof leaked and the mold got in the oats. I had nothing to give them. When we heard the Maclean had returned, I told her he would help, he would remember Gregor. So we came here."

This last came on a note of defiance, as if daring them to have forgotten the man Gregor or to think that she begged. Alyson understood at once and glanced fearfully to Rory, praying that he knew of whom she spoke. She should not have doubted.

"Gregor! How could I forget the man who gave me my first claymore and showed me how to use it? He had a lass that was only knee-high when last I saw her. And this is Mary, then?"

Perhaps compassion could not be heard in the tone of his voice, but it was in his words, and Alyson sighed with relief. Rory would make things right. If she gave it thought, she would realize that this Mary was much the same age as herself, and had fate decreed differently, Rory might never have left the Highlands but stayed in his family home and married this daughter of his old friend. She could not allow her thoughts to follow those lines, but concentrated on what must be done now.

The conversation had gone on without her, but Alyson understood enough to realize Rory offered the women a home and positions in the household and looked now to her for assistance. With a nod of her head, Alyson sent Meg on the errands she had ordered earlier. Then she turned to the sobbing woman.

"I know you would wish to live near where your little boy will be buried. You have a home here, as he will.

When you are strong again, we can talk of what you can do. I don't suppose either of you knows aught of weaving?"

Rory looked surprised at this change of topic, but the older woman immediately looked relieved. "If you have looms, my lady, I know the trade, and Mary is very quick."

Alyson smiled absently and nodded. "Good. There are no sheep now, but there will be. It is too costly to rely on others for what we can provide ourselves." Without changing the tone of her voice, she greeted the maid who entered with warm blankets. "Meg, can you find Mary and her friend a bed and some hot porridge? They will be staying."

Seeing the newcomers led off, Alyson began to drift off after them, but Rory stepped in her way, blocking her passage from the room. She gazed up at him without surprise, with none of the pain-filled sorrow he had seen there earlier.

"What is this talk of a child to be buried?" His voice was gruff, but the hands coming to rest on her shoulders were gentle.

"Her baby died. They are tending it now in the kitchen."

He could still see the streaks of tears on her fair face, but she had concealed her feelings behind that damned vague look she acquired to protect herself. Dimly he began to realize she was protecting herself against him as well, and that raw ache inside began to throb painfully.

Rory knew what he should do. He should take her in his arms and kiss the tears from her cheeks and hold her until she let go of the pain and cried out her fears for their own child. But he also knew that to do that would release this painful need of his own, and he had forfeited the right to do that.

There was only one other offer he could make, the only certain way he knew to protect Alyson and the child from the cruelty of this world as he knew it. Sadly he brushed a strand of silky ebony from her face.

"Dougall will be arriving soon with the *Witch*. He can take you back to London safely by sea. You and the child will be warm and safe, and there will be physicians aplenty if they are needed. Our child will be fine, lass, you will see."

He understood as much as the housekeeper, but no

more. Alyson smiled faintly at the uncertainty in his voice, ignoring the reassurances of his words. "No, Maclean, you will not rid yourself of me that easily. All my life I've lived in a cocoon, sheltered from the world. I cannot complain, because I never knew any other way to live, and I was not necessary to anyone, anywhere, then. But I know differently now, and I cannot go on hiding from the way things are anymore. Did you think I could go forever watching people starve and babies die and do nothing? If you do not mean to use my inheritance to help, then someone must. Good night, Rory."

She walked out and up the stairs to the bed she no longer shared, leaving Rory staring after her with an aching longing so deep that he knew he would never recover.

The beautiful child he had carried away and shown the world had become a woman at last, but a woman who no longer needed him.

He, on the other hand, was back where he had started, admiring a lovely object he could never have, fearful that his jaded touch would destroy her.

29

"He's not evil. The devil is evil. Drummond is just greedy, like most English lords."

"He's a devil! You have not seen him as I have! A cross should be driven through his black heart and he should be burned at the stake!"

"Perhaps Lady Maclean could put a curse on him," a third voice snickered.

Alyson chose that moment to wander into the kitchen. The senseless argument instantly quieted as the servants returned to preparing dinner. Alyson glanced toward Mary, surprised to find the girl already out of her sickbed. She was wearing one of the serviceable woolen gowns Alyson had ordered made from the yard goods purchased for the staff, but at the time it had not occurred to her to order materials for shoes. She made a mental note of that lack as she observed the odd bundle wrapped about Mary's feet to keep them warm on the cold stone floors.

The girl didn't look her way as she entered, but Alyson knew she had been the one leading the argument. After a thorough bath and a few days' rest, she could be seen as attractive in a rather harsh, high-boned manner. She was still much too thin, and the spots of pink on her cheeks warned that a fever still lingered, but she was working diligently at kneading a large bowl of dough without any sign of weakness.

Alyson did not attempt to discover which one of the staff had made the comment about the curse. Her gaze lingered thoughtfully on a young girl scrubbing a pot near the fire, and the child blushed, but spying on the servants had not been her intention.

"We will need extra for dinner tonight, enough for another twenty men, I would say. Can we do it?"

Unlike her grandfather's trained English staff, these people were inclined to question orders and offer opinions without being asked. All in all, Alyson found it much simpler to consider their opinions than impose her own. Her experience was too limited to be trusted.

"Twenty men?" The cook and established ruler of the kitchen looked to her in surprise. A stocky, hearty woman in her forties, but with dark hair already graying, she had worked in these kitchens before Alyson was born. She remembered Alyson's mother and grandmother well, but it was the grandmother the new lady of the house most resembled. Those gray eyes could see through souls they had said back then. Cook wasn't at all certain that the same might not be said about this one. "Has there been a messenger, then?"

That was one of the problems with living in such isolation. Nothing went on without everyone knowing it. They knew there had been no messenger this day.

"Rory is expecting his ship to arrive. If it is not today, then we will have to preserve what we can for the morrow. I am certain there are mouths enough to eat what we cannot save."

That was an unarguable statement, and, satisfied, the

cook agreed they could provide the meal. Even though she had given them what she considered adequate explanation, Alyson could hear a voice pipe up as soon as she left the room.

"She has the gift, I tell you. The laird's been expecting that ship for days. I heard him say so. And did you see the way she looked right at me? She knew!"

"Mackle-mouth, anyone would know your whining! Get that pot scrubbed and start on the potatoes."

Alyson took a deep breath and sailed down the hall. She had told Rory she no longer wanted the cotton batting of protection that had surrounded her all her life, but there were times when she wondered if she hadn't been just a little hasty in her declaration of independence.

Climbing to the second floor to see what progress had been made in refurbishing their private apartments, Alyson was surprised to discover Rory still at his desk. When he had appropriated this room for his study, she had ordered draperies made for it as soon as the bedrooms were done. A fire was kept burning in the grate to keep his books and papers from becoming damp and to keep the temperature reasonable whenever he chose to use the room. Alyson wasn't at all certain that he noticed the improvements, much less appreciated them, and she raised her eyebrows delicately when he rose at her appearance and made a courtly bow before speaking directly to her thoughts.

"I had not realized the difference a little wool and a fire can make until I tried to work downstairs in the hall. I have spent too much time in the West Indies these last years to be comfortable in the cold for long, I fear."

Rory made no motion toward Alyson, but drank in the heavenly scent of heather as she drifted further into his room. He had few opportunities to be alone with her anymore, a circumstance he had devised for his own protection, and for good reason. Just her presence here now sent his head swimming, and his gaze hungrily devoured the sight of her translucent face turned inquiringly to him, dark-fringed eyes holding him captivated with their mirrored gaze. With her lovely figure bundled in high-necked woolens and shawls, he could not readily see the signs of the child growing within her, but he did not doubt her word. He wanted just the touch of her soft hand to ease his day, a small kiss to make the sun shine again, a chance to hold her in his arms to make the whole world lighter, but he dared not. He had forced his way into her life, shattered her trust, and now reaped the consequences. She shied from his touch, his look, his very presence. He hid his disappointment as she walked past him to contemplate the newly hung draperies.

"This place was built by men of war with no thought other than to protect themselves. I wonder that they felt such a life worth protecting." Alyson pushed aside the heavy gold fabric to gaze down upon the harbor below. "Men died down there, fighting over this land. Are material things worth dying over?"

Rory knew what she asked, but not why. It had nothing to do with the men who died down there and much to do with his fight with his cousin, but he had no way of knowing how much she knew or guessed.

"Life is worth nothing if it cannot be lived as a free man. Those who lose their land often lose their freedom. It is not the land so much as the idea that men fight for."

Dropping that argument, Alyson turned and gazed at the stack of bills piled on Rory's desk. "What keeps you here today?"

Rory gave a ragged sigh, and shoving a loosened strand of hair behind his ear, lifted the stack of invoices for her to examine. "There was no need to have these sent to Mr. Farnley, Alyson. He only returns them to me for approval. I did not imagine the improvements around here appeared by magic."

He had wrestled with these accounts and his conscience all the morning. Had he come to Scotland alone, he could have lived on bread and water, with no need for servants and draperies and fires in all the rooms. His income could be diverted almost entirely to feeding and clothing his clansmen and the tenants of what had once been his estates. He did not look on it as charity, but as a means of gaining their support when it came time to drive Drummond out of his holdings. But Alyson had changed that simple plan into something much more complex and, likewise, expensive.

He had to admit he enjoyed the warmth of the fires, the comfort of clean, unmended linen, the nicety of food waiting on the table for him, but the cost of such would eat into the capital needed to buy back his estate. Alyson meant for him to use her wealth for these things she ordered, but that meant he could not even provide for himself or his wife. That thought angered him.

"If you do not wish to be troubled with my extravagances, you need only tell Mr. Farnley to pay whatever I send to him. Surely I cannot have spent everything we own."

"At this rate, you could not spend everything if you live to be a thousand. That is not my concern." Rory set the bills back on the desk when Alyson gave him only a blank stare. He felt like an ogre, and he shoved his hands into the deep pockets of his coat as he gazed on her still-slender figure hovering there. "Hovering" was the word for it. She flitted like a butterfly from place to place, everywhere at once, never lighting anywhere. She appeared on the verge of flight right now. Her unexpected reply staggered him.

"Your concern is only for your conceited pride," Alyson answered calmly. "When will you learn there are more important things in this world than pride and money?"

She gave him no chance for reply. Without a second look, she left the room, gently closing the door between them. On the other side, where Rory's eyes couldn't find her, Alyson's cool expression crumpled into wrenching torment, and she hurried up the stairs to the privacy of her own chamber.

She would have fared better had her grandfather left her penniless. Rory would never forgive her greater wealth. Throwing herself across the bed, she remembered the dull look of pain in Rory's eyes as he looked on her. He had looked so handsome standing there, the firelight sending flickering copper through the thick strands of neatly clubbed auburn hair and accenting shadows across his broad cheekbones. He had worn both coat and vest against the chill, but neither could disguise the strength of his wide shoulders or the restless energy of those powerful muscles. She had wanted him to understand, had wanted him to accept her as she was. But he was blind. He could not see beyond the stack of bills to the person behind them, the one who so badly needed his love that she had followed him here and offered everything she possessed, including herself. He was so blind

that he could not see that offer for what it was, and his
rejection hurt more than anything else she could imagine.

She had never understood people. She didn't know
why she continued to try. If Rory didn't want her or her
wealth, why had he married her? Guilt? Was guilt the
only reason he had forced her into this marriage? Did
that make sense? He hadn't felt guilty the day he had
taken her virginity. Had something happened on Barbados to change his feelings?

Remembering the pink canary, Alyson closed her eyes
and shuddered. There was nothing to be done about it
now. The child made their choices irrevocable. Her one
goal now was to keep Rory alive so the child would know
his father as she had never known hers. That was a task
that could engage every parcel of her energy.

She didn't think Rory would ride into battle with his
cousin, as his Highland ancestors might have, but he was
quite capable of robbing his cousin blind to draw the man
out. The result would be the same. There would be
words and bloodshed, and neither would be the winner.

If only she knew more about this mysterious cousin
and how he would react when he discovered Rory was
systematically undermining his tenants, encouraging rebellion, and endangering the rents he needed to live,
then she might better prepare her defenses.

But Alyson's gifts could not see into the magnificently
paneled dining hall with its gleaming chandelier and polished mahogany table with places for twenty-four, where
George Drummond sat drinking his morning coffee. His
frowning gaze did not appreciate the exquisite workman-
ship of the carved lintels or the ornate plaster design
winding around the distant ceiling. He was accustomed to
such luxury, even though it was highly unusual to find it
in these hills. The Maclean family had always been an
educated, sophisticated lot who had brought in the finest
art and workmen wherever they found them. Drummond
had made no effort to improve upon their accomplish-
ments. He simply accepted the result as his due.

He leaned back in his chair and gazed with contempt
on the other casually dressed members of his small party.
They were dressed for the country, in loose tweeds and
woolens and leather breeches, instead of in their usual

fine silks and satins, but they exuded wealth in just the
way they wore their expensively tailored clothes, in the
accents they favored as they laconically played at words
while idling over their meal. He enjoyed this company,
although to feed them for a week cost him the entire
year's rent of one tenant.

There was one exception to this idle, elegant company,
and his gaze fell thoughtfully on the powerfully built man
just entering the room. Since coming into his title, Cranville
had become a changed man, and Drummond wasn't sure
yet if he approved the changes. Once, Cranville had
fitted into this company without notice, his pale features
and languid airs blending well with his expensive silks
and laces. Only his cutting cynicism had marked him as
one of a slightly better intelligence than the others.

Drummond contemplated the changes and their source.
He knew the man had not gained the inheritance he had
expected to pay for the debt incurred while living the life
his breeding required. That went a long way toward
explaining the less ornate coats and waistcoats and the
abandonment of all personal servants but the one valet.
He also knew the earl had spent considerable time chasing after the elusive heiress who would have made his
fortune. The time spent in the tropics would explain his
unusually healthy color. Perhaps life on board ship was
also responsible for the energy that seemed to generate
from him as he entered the room. His controlled restlessness was certainly out of place in this idle group. He had
actually bagged half the grouse shot yesterday—a disgust-
ing performance, considering the amount of good whisky imbibed during the hunt. Drummond had rather
hoped one of his inebriated guests might bag another of
the company before the day ended, but Cranville had
kept them fascinated with his skills, and the party had
ended without mishap.

Yes, there could very well be reasons for the changes
in the new earl. Drummond could only hope they worked
in his favor. It was time he sounded him out about the
presence of the charming heiress on the neighboring estate. He wondered if Cranville realized his elusive cousin
was so close. He certainly couldn't know how much trouble her infuriating husband was causing, but Drummond
wagered the earl would have his own tales of woe con-

cerning one Rory Douglas Maclean. Yes, they might very well deal nicely together.

Maclean must think him a fool if he thought he didn't realize what was going on. Sheep didn't escape stone walls without help. The pitiful peasants who could not raise a crop good enough to both eat and pay the rent did not suddenly inherit enough to eat well. He had hoped to starve them out, since he could make more money raising sheep than they could pay him in rent. Their surprising ability to struggle on in the face of economic reality had other sources beyond God's will. The mysterious losses he had taken in various other investments over the years began to take on new meaning. If Maclean wanted a fight, he would get one, but it wouldn't be on the battlefield of his choice.

Being ruthless had its advantages, and Drummond's lack of conscience had never troubled him. He considered Cranville's bored expression with a feeling of triumph. He knew how to destroy Maclean without lifting much more than a finger.

Blissfully unaware of the nearness of her cousin or of her neighbor's dangerous arrogance, Alyson watched the *Sea Witch* anchoring in the loch with pleasure. She still loved to watch the sails, and she felt a longing to have the deck rolling beneath her feet again.

She sent Rory a surreptitious look as he stood with hands in pockets, gazing at the harbor too. Did he miss the ship and the life he had led then? Could part of their problem be that he wasn't ready to be tied down to home and family? She ached to know, but his expression gave away nothing.

Alyson was the one to run and joyfully greet the men as they entered. Dougall's beaming face rated a hug, but as he lifted her exuberantly from the floor, Alyson's gaze fell on a startled female face behind him.

"Dougall! What on earth . . . ? Put me down and introduce me." She struggled to right herself as he gently returned her to the floor and stepped aside to bring forward the woman sandwiched in between the mingling horde of sailors.

Even Rory watched with mild astonishment as his burly officer grew crimson and his gaze gentled as he took the hand of the woman beside him. Cloaked in heavy wet wool, little could be seen of her other than large luminous eyes, a head of luxuriant hair, and a serene smile.

"Well, lass, it seemed if the Maclean here could go and get himself shackled and give up the good life, then it was time I did the same." Embarrassed, he attempted a formal introduction. "Lady Maclean, my wife, Myra."

As Alyson reached out to make the new bride welcome, Rory gave a joyous exclamation and pounded his friend on the back. The celebration began then and lasted well into the evening as the supplies of rum and brandy the men carried in were opened and sampled.

Weariness required that Alyson retire well before the celebration was near its end. Delighted as she was to see familiar faces again, she knew the men preferred their own company. Giving a few orders as to the arrangements for beds, Alyson slipped from the hall.

Rory watched her go with a longing he could not conceal from himself. Dougall and his new wife were holding hands and looking at each other as he and Alyson had once done. Was there no way to go back to those days? Was there no way to erase the time in between and go back to the time when Alyson had looked at him with trust and affection and had come into his arms eagerly?

When it became apparent that Dougall meant to take his bride from the rough company to their bed, Rory got to his feet with decision. Perhaps he was making another mistake. Where Alyson was concerned, he seemed to do that frequently, but he could not sit and watch their lives wither and die. He gestured to Dougall and led the couple toward the stairs.

Only two bedchambers had been refurbished since their arrival, Alyson's and his own. Rory knew that a guest room had hastily been ordered opened and a clean pallet laid on the floor for Dougall and his wife, while the others would make their beds in the great hall, but that cold, unadorned guest room was a poor excuse for a bridal chamber. Smiling grimly to himself, he led the pair past the first landing to the second.

With a gallant gesture, Rory surrendered the comfort of his own newly decorated bedchamber, gambling away all his chances on the throw of one die. Not realizing the sacrifice offered, Dougall and Myra extended their gratitude and their good-nights and closed the door. Rory turned and stared at the solid oak panel separating him from his wife and her bed.

He could choose to enter those forbidden chambers or he could drink himself into a stupor below with his men. Given the possibility of heaven over the certainty of hell, Rory did not linger long over the decision. He reached out to grasp the latch.

30

Alyson had stripped to the soft, clinging flannel of her winter shift so she might hurriedly wash while the water in the bowl remained warm. The bedchamber in this master suite was excessively large and the heat from the peat fire did not reach all four corners of the room. She was eager to find the comfort between the walls of her unfashionable bed, where the maid had laid hot bricks to warm the sheets.

She had given little thought to anything but warmth in furnishing this room. There was too little reason to linger in its hollow vastness to require beauty. The wooden panels of the bed cut off drafts on three sides, and she had filled the open side, where the door once had been, with heavy pale blue hangings. The same velvet had been hung on the narrow windows, and recently there had been time to add silver braid and tassels to the draperies to make them a little more elegant. The only decent carpet she had found in the tower she had put in Rory's room. She wished to order one for the cold wooden planks in here, but Rory's lecture on bills made her hesitate at purchasing such luxury.

Perhaps if she employed local weavers to make the carpet, he would approve of the extravagance. It made sense to spend money where it was needed instead of sending it to rich London merchants who would never miss it.

Satisfied with this compromise, Alyson reached for a hair ribbon to tie her hair from her face. In the act of fastening the bow, she was startled to hear the latch on her door turn.

Rory entered and pushed the door closed behind him. Silhouetted by the fire, Alyson's slight figure in the thin white gown was accentuated by the flickering light. With her arms above her head to fasten the ribbon, every curve could be seen clearly, and Rory took a deep breath as his gaze focused on the changes he found there.

Her high, full breasts were rounder and heavier. Without thick skirts and petticoats to disguise it, the beginnings of a pear-shaped curve extended the once-flat plane of her abdomen. She was so beautiful, he could feel his chest constrict with the strain of holding his breath and his words. The pain was too great, searing his lungs with all that needed to be said. He couldn't hold it in any longer.

"Don't tie it." His first words came as a harsh whisper as he crossed the room toward her.

Alyson let her hands drop, and the cascade of ebony curls fell about her shoulders and over her breasts. The intensity of Rory's gaze frightened her, but she held her ground. She did not understand how the same Rory who gently taught her the acts of love could also hurt her so cruelly, and she had no means of telling which man stood before her now, but she could not move away. Her heart pounded like that of a frightened rabbit, but she offered up a prayer and sought his eyes with tentative hope.

Holding her gaze, Rory gently placed his large hand over the curve of her stomach. "Do you have any idea how beautiful you are like this?"

Black lashes flew upward, startled at this tack he had taken. She had never thought of herself as beautiful. In truth, she seldom thought of her looks at all, but now that she grew fat and unshapely, she could not imagine beauty there. She searched his face for some sign of his real reason for saying this.

"You prefer me plump?" she asked with genuine curiosity. The pink canary had been considerably larger than herself. Perhaps that was what Rory liked.

Rory had to smile at the tangent Alyson's irrepressible mind took. Any other woman would have been satisfied with the compliment. Alyson had to know its reason. "I prefer you, period. No exceptions, no exclusions, without qualification. It could be I'm biased, but I think you are the most beautiful woman on this earth. And selfish, conceited male that I am, I like seeing my child growing within you."

Alyson's smile at these blandishments could have blinded the sun. Rory's hand resting on the small protrusion of her stomach was protective, not harmful, and she did not shrink from his other arm when it circled her back, providing support for her. This was almost as it had been before between them. Wondering at the change, she tilted her head back to study the square line of his jaw and the slight bristle of his beard grown since morning. Her fingers came up to touch the sensual curve of his underlip, and she smiled again at the wariness in his eyes.

"Are you drunk, my lord?"

Rory carefully considered that question. "No, I think not. But I gave Dougall and his bride my room. If you wish me to go away, I'll have no alternative but to go down and join my crew in their revels."

A slightly worried frown creased Alyson's brow, and Rory instantly dropped his arms to his sides, giving her room to escape if need be. "I'll not force you to anything, lass. If ye wish me to go, ye have only to say."

Without his arms to warm her, Alyson felt the chill of the room. She wished desperately to be in his arms again, but she no longer trusted her instincts or Rory. What could he want from her now that he did not already have?

"I thought you didn't like me anymore," she whispered in confusion, more to herself than to him. "Is it just the bed you wish to share? There is room enough for two."

Rory stared at his moonstruck angel in a daze of disbelief that bordered on the laughable. Gently lifting her chin with the side of his hand, he gazed into the shifting mists of her eyes, willing the clouds to part so he could see into her heart.

"Lass, I wish your gift would give you understanding

and not pictures of nightmares. Why would you think I did not like you anymore?"

"What else should I think? You had to get drunk to marry me. You made love to your pink canary, but not to me. You hurt me terribly, then tell me I'm on my own. You avoid me constantly. You didn't even want to bring me here. I try very hard to understand, Rory, but what else should I think?"

"Devil take it, Alys, is that how it seems to you? What a pair we make." Despairing at the gulf separating them, Rory wasn't certain where or how to bridge it. Seeing her shiver in her bare toes and thin shift, he recovered enough of his senses to remedy this error.

Swinging her up in his arms, he deposited her on the bed, pulling back the heavy covers so she could slip beneath their warmth. Gingerly he sat down upon the bed's edge and tried to gather his scattered wits.

"Will you tell me what this is of a pink canary? You have mentioned such before, but I think I would remember anything so ludicrous as pecking at a bird."

Alyson slid her toes down in the bed until they rested against the warm brick wrapped in towels and pulled the blankets up over her knees as she sat there watching Rory in the firelight. "She's not really a bird. You know who I mean. All that blond hair and pink ribbons and frilly lace. Don't tell me you never made love to her, Rory Douglas. I saw her, and you didn't act as if she were a stranger."

Minerva. Rory stretched his legs and sighed as he stared at his knee-high boots. "Alyson, I don't expect you to believe me, but until you came along, I couldn't remember the name of a single woman I'd ever gone to bed with. They were few and far between and I'm not at all certain that I ever knew their names. I know I seldom spent more than a few hours in their company. Then, there you were, all wide-eyed and innocent and more tempting than any woman has a right to be. I knew I couldn't have you, so I looked for someone else. Your pink canary served the purpose of distracting me for a few nights when you were not near. She ceased to exist the moment I set eyes on you again."

Alyson digested that information slowly, wanting to believe him but still not willing to trust in Rory or her instincts again. It would be lovely to believe she was truly the only woman who ever mattered to him, but there still remained the matter of his change in attitude after the pink canary arrived in their lives.

She gazed distractedly at the powerful masculine legs balancing at the side of her bed. She knew the danger of those legs, but she could not send Rory back to the liquor below. She did not think the drink was good for him.

"You had best take off your boots if you wish to get in here," she admonished him.

Hope flared suddenly in Rory's heart, and then, as he turned to look into her carefully blank expression, he almost had to laugh at his blind eagerness. She had traded his boots for her pink canary. That was a long way from where he wanted to be, but much closer than he had been in months.

Pulling off one boot and resting his stockinged foot against the floor to pry at the other, he noticed the cold coming up from the bare planks, and he glanced down at the uncovered wood with perplexity. "Lass, what have you done with your carpet? You'll freeze your toes on these cold boards."

"I thought to have one woven," she offered tentatively. "I know there is wool aplenty hereabouts. I need only locate looms and weavers. It would not cost so much to have one made, would it? And it would keep the money here, where it is needed."

Her soft, careful words shot an arrow straight through Rory's heart, unmasking his vulnerability. He jerked with the pain of the knowledge that she tried to please him, but there was an odd pleasure to it too. Dropping the second boot to the floor, he leaned back on one hand to better see her face in the shadows.

"Alys, I did not expect to feed my people at your expense. It will be years before there are looms and weavers enough to produce a carpet such as you need. The thought was a good one, but I'll not have you take cold because of it. Order a carpet and have mine brought in here until it arrives."

"*Our* people," Alyson replied indignantly, if not to the point. "These are my lands as well as yours. My mother grew up here too. I have responsibilites as well as you."

She feared to let down her defenses at the gentleness of his words. What he said tonight in tender tones might not be the same in the morning, but she could not prevent a feeling of warmth at the thought behind them.

Rory had always known she was intelligent, but each day brought a new surprise at the number of things she grasped and accepted without being told or reminded or coaxed into. Not easy things, but hard ideas that most women would balk at and most men argue over. She was the granddaughter of an English earl, raised in luxury. What could she know of the responsibilites of the harsh environs of his home?

"Aye, you have responsibilities, lass, and that child you carry is one of them. I'll have the carpet moved in the morning." Rory knew better than to allow her to distract the path of his thoughts. It was the only way he could feel he held some semblance of control; otherwise, things could get amazingly out of hand when Alyson was around.

Incapable of argument when he looked at her as he was doing now, Alyson found another escape route. Eyeing the pressed tailoring of his good velvet coat with the fancy brass buttons on the turned-back cuffs, she changed the subject. "I don't think you should wrinkle your good coat and vest by sleeping in them."

The twinkle leaping to Rory's eye had more confidence than his demeanor of earlier as he gazed upon the tumble of his wife's silken curls and read the challenge in her eyes. One wrong move might easily land him shivering to sleep on the cold, hard floor, but he had ever enjoyed a challenge. The prize to be won if he played this game fairly was well worth the effort of minding the rules.

Alyson dropped her blanket and helped pull the coat from Rory's broad shoulders as he shrugged out of it. He stood and hung it neatly over a chair, then slid off the long vest beneath it. Folding that over the coat, he returned to the bed in shirt and breeches, not daring so much as to loosen his jabot or remove his stockings for fear of unsettling the balance between them.

Freed from the cumbersome coat, he lay back against the pillow, propping his hands behind his head as he gazed up into Alyson's fathomless eyes. She appeared puzzled as to what to do next, but if he went slowly, he would have a lifetime in which to teach her. He let his gaze drift over the fullness of her bosom, concealed beneath the modest shift, to the thickening of her waist, where their child grew.

"Dougall tells me Myra is an experienced midwife. I had it in mind to ask them to stay awhile." Rory took the reins of the conversation, leading it in the direction he wanted.

Alyson glanced down to where the heat of his gaze burned, and her cheeks grew warm as she saw what his eyes must. Sliding hurriedly to conceal herself fully beneath the covers, she found herself lying beside his long length. It had been a long time since she had been this close to him, but the sensations this proximity engendered had not dimmed with time. If anything, they had grown stronger.

"I think I would like that," she responded uncertainly. "But who would sail the *Witch*?"

"Do not concern yourself over those matters, lass. I want to hear of the child. Does he rest well? Does he give you trouble? I know you did not want this burden. I would make the time easier for you if I could."

Tears formed in her eyes as these gentle words touched all the fears and desires Alyson had kept bottled inside her for so long. She had wanted desperately to talk of these things, had not known how much she wanted it until now, here in the darkness with her husband beside her once more.

"It just feels so very strange," she murmured, turning on her side so she could see the outline of Rory's face against the firelight. He had not drawn the curtain, and for this she was grateful. "I sleep too much, and the oddest things make me cry. And he grows so quickly, I fear soon I will not fit in a single gown."

It took every ounce of his strength not to reach out and pull her to him. Rory squeezed his eyes shut and concentrated on the subtle fragrance that was Alyson's own, on the warmth of her slight body next to his. Nothing could alleviate the growing pressure in his loins, but he knew Alyson's thoughts were not yet turned in that direction. He feared they might never be again, but he wouldn't give up trying.

"I will buy you new gowns every month, it you wish,

dear heart. You will be beautiful in all of them. I just don't want you to hate me for what I did out of foolishness."

Perhaps "foolishness" was the word for what they had done, for if it had been love, they would have done it with the promises of a lifetime together. Sadly Alyson caressed the small bulge, then lifted her hand to loosen Rory's awkwardly tight jabot. She knew now that it was love that bade her sleep by him now. But she hadn't known it then. And she would not put Rory off with such notions now. He suffered enough guilt without knowing the full extent of her foolishness.

"I was angry with you, but I don't hate you. I could never hate you. Perhaps I'll never understand what you expect from me, but I'm not unhappy. I'm even growing used to the idea of a baby, if I just wasn't so frightened by it. I've never even held a baby before."

As her hand loosened the ties of his shirt, leaving his throat bare, Rory caught her fingers and pressed them to his lips. Her every word tore at his flesh, baring his soul to any ammunition she wished to pierce him with. For fifteen years he had worked to build a protective armor against the world, and her soft words were ripping it into shreds as if it were made of the rottenest of fabric.

"Alyson, my love, I would give all I own and am to have done this differently or to make it easier for you. I am as terrified as you. I've never been responsible for taking care of a life as precious as yours. To add to that the needs of a wee bairn . . . It scares me witless sometimes. But then I think of all the others who have done it through the ages, and I know the two of us can do it, even in our ignorance, if we learn to help each other."

Her fingers burned where he had kissed them, and it seemed only natural to hold the warmth a little longer by burying them beneath his shirt when he returned her hand to his chest. Without conscious thought, Alyson began toying with the soft feathering of curls there.

She had thought Rory fearless. His admission of terror at the thought of a child brought a smile to her lips. It seemed odd to think of such a large, strong man fearing a tiny, defenseless babe, but she heard the emotion behind his words and knew their truth. "You will be a good father, I think, if you can only learn to stay home a little.

Will you ever do that, or will you always be restless to be off elsewhere?"

Astounded at this train of thought, Rory wrenched his mind back to the conversation and away from the pleasant sensations of her bare hand against his flesh. "Lass, if I had my choice, I'd never set foot from my own ground again. I've had enough of traveling homeless. I want to sit by my own fire with my wife at my side and my children at my feet. That is my dream, though I'll be the first to admit it is far from being accomplished. Perhaps it is but a moon dream."

Alyson pushed up on one arm to lean over him and gaze down into the dark wells of his eyes. Her long hair fell across his chest and shoulders, and Rory caught strands of it between his fingers as she spoke.

"For a man who wishes never to leave home, you certainly spend little of it there. I scarcely see you except to pass you in the hall upon occasion. Your children will think you a stranger if that is all they know of you."

Your children. He liked the sound of that. He liked even better the way she leaned over him so he could see the full orbs of her breasts behind the loose neck of her shift. The hard urgings of his loins made it exceedingly difficult to think of anything else, but he had made too much progress to throw aside all restraint now.

Knowing full well he made impossible promises when all his dreams were of a home owned by another man and not this drafty ruin they lived in, Rory spoke as if dreams could come true. "Lass, if you had any idea what you are doing to me now, you would know why I cannot stay in the same room with you for more than the space of a minute. And since no other woman but you suits my needs, I must keep busy elsewhere to keep my hands as well as my mind off you. Should the time come when you no longer fear my touch, you would not be rid of me so easily."

There was pain behind his calm words, the pain she had sensed and not understood before. Suddenly aware of what she was doing and the stiff tension of his body beneath her, Alyson retreated. Rory's hand rose as if to keep her from going, but then he determinedly returned it behind his head.

"You stay away because of me?" she asked in puzzlement. "Why? Did I not tell you I was willing to be your wife?"

Rory tried to control his breathing. She had not moved far. He could still reach out his arm and press her against his side. He just had to learn to control his natural instincts.

"Alyson, I have seen how you flinch when I reach out to touch you, how you avoid coming near to me when we are in the same room. I have no intention of ever harming you again, but I do not know how to make you understand that. I do not want a victim for my lust, but a warm and willing woman who shares my needs and desires."

He had never been so blunt before, and Alyson regarded him with curiosity. "I thought you resented having to marry me. The pink canary is much more beautiful than I. How can you still desire me even when I am fat and garbed in ugly woolens all the time?"

Rory gave a rueful laugh. "Alyson, dear heart, you need only use your lovely eyes to see how much I desire you. I am near to bursting with need for my fat, ugly wife. It has been this way with me since I first set eyes on you. If I remember correctly, you were wrapped in a hideous cloak that smelled of the stables that day, but I would have gladly taken you to my bed even then. I did not have to marry you. I forced you to marry me because I did not think I could live without you. I knew better than to cage a wild thing, but I possessed so little and wanted so much, I could not resist the temptation."

As he spoke, Alyson's gaze traveled wonderingly to the long bulge pushing at the tight cloth of his breeches. She knew what waited behind that flap of cloth, and her cheeks flamed crimson as she remembered how she knew. She could not forget the harm he caused her, but the times before that took precedence in her thoughts now. Memories of warm summer nights when they had lain naked together in a narrow bunk, learning the pleasures of their bodies, came back unbidden. Her hand drifted of its own accord to rest on that hard bulge, and the response she felt there stirred a deep excitement inside her, an excitement she remembered embarrassingly well.

She lifted her eyes to Rory's as her hand tested the promise of his words. She stroked harder as he gave an involuntary shudder and the smoldering intensity of his gaze became a blaze that lit wildfires everywhere it touched. He wanted her, but he would not make a move to take her, even though her touch made him shudder with need. She had never realized the power she held over him, and the knowledge that she had any power at all was startling to an extreme. Stunned, she did not move away, but neither had she the knowledge to go further.

Rory spoke softly, giving her time to think. "Wreak your vengeance as you will, lass, but remember I have suffered for my error too. I berated myself at the time for not killing you quickly to prevent your suffering. My only consolation since has been that in my cowardice, I did not, because selfishly, I wanted to know you were still in my world."

She scarcely heeded this confession, hearing only the torment behind it. Vaguely she understood he had thought to protect her with what he had done, but she would worry over the intricacies of his mind some other time. The need to hold him was much stronger, although fear could not be completely eradicated. She experimented by rising to meet Rory's lips with her own.

He tasted slightly of whisky, but the heat of his response prevented savoring all the flavors she found there. His lips were like fire, searing her with their brand, and she could not tear away. Her hands flew to his shoulders for support as the probing touch of his tongue drew her downward, closer into the rings of flame. He lifted no hand to pressure her, but his passionate response to her touch burned away her resistance.

She surrendered to the need for more of this hunger, parting her lips until their breaths mixed and he was caressing her deep inside, arousing a need she had denied for too long. The need grew wilder beneath the heat of his kiss, but still he did not touch her. Alyson slid her hands over his shoulders, stroked the straining muscles of his neck as he held her mouth captive, ran her fingers through his hair, but he made no move to caress her as she needed to be caressed. She wanted his hands on her breasts, against her flesh, telling her what she needed to know, but she did not know how to tell him.

Daringly, as their kiss deepened and Rory groaned

against her mouth, she ran her hand downward, finding the length of him, spreading her fingers to stroke him there. He jerked spasmodically to her touch, pressing into her palm, but still he did not move to take her in his arms. His kiss grew greedier, more demanding, until she felt he would steal her breath away, but he would not force her in any way. With fumbling fingers, Alyson began to unfasten the buttons that would release him.

Rory tried not to tremble as she inexpertly worked to free him. He feared to hurry her, but he was not a man of iron restraint, and he had waited a long time for this release. As her cool fingers brushed his burning flesh, he smothered a groan of relief. He choked back a laugh at her startlement at the eager response of his uncovered parts.

"Perhaps you should bind me hand and foot so I cannot do anything you do not wish me to do."

There was laughter in his voice, and, relieved, Alyson gazed thoughtfully to where he gallantly kept his hands held behind his head. Shyly she admitted, "I am not at all certain what I would do with myself then." He had given her complete power over him, but she had no idea yet how to wield it.

Rory had a desperate need to pull her down over him and show her just what she could do, but fear still inhibited her, and he would be rid of that fear first. Softly he said, "Then think of what you would do with me. Strike me, if you like. I certainly deserve that and more, but I have no intention of giving you other ideas than that, lass. I'll take whatever you mete out, but I prefer pleasure to pain."

"So do I. Show me how." Alyson touched him carefully, exploring with her fingers, feeling his body tense beneath hers. In the short time they had been intimate before, she had never been so brave, but she was filled with curiosity now.

Rory closed his eyes and fought the waves of desire demanding action. Through thickened lips he murmured, "Unless you wish me to remain bound, we'll have to do something about the breeches, lass. They're damned confining like this."

Alyson eagerly applied herself to the task of peeling off his breeches, rolling them over his narrow hips when he lifted them from the bed, then carefully rolling down his stockings so she could find the knee buttons and unfasten them. She could feel the male part of him rubbing against her breasts as she pulled the fabric downward, and that produced inexplicable urges she found hard to resist. When she hesitated, Rory sat up to assist her with the remainder.

Suddenly desirous to see him naked, Alyson knelt beside him and began to unfasten his long shirt. She fumbled at the tiny buttons over his broad chest until Rory caught her hand, pressing it against his chest, then raising it to his lips to draw gently on her fingertips.

When her gaze fled uncertainly to his, he suggested, "I'll take it off if you will remove yours."

The low rumble of his voice sent shivers down her spine, and she responded without question. As he swiftly finished the workings of his lace-cuffed shirt, she slid her shift over her head.

For a moment they just looked at each other through the deep shadows thrown by the dying fire. Rory found the patience he needed in the sight of her shy smile of pleasure. Gently he lifted her heavy breast in his palm. When she did not flinch from his touch, he slid his arm around her waist and drew her closer, touching, exploring this lovely body he had been given to cherish and hold. His rough hand caressed her satin-soft skin until she quivered against him; then, gently, carefully, he leaned back against the pillows and pulled her down with him.

Alyson snaked her bare legs over Rory's rough ones, pressed her breasts against his wide chest, and gave a sigh of delight as his hand cupped her bottom and settled her against his hip. She did not have to do anything yet but enjoy the sensation of Rory's body against hers. She needed time to reacquaint herself with the feeling of the strength rippling beneath her hands with his every move. She knew that strength could hold her powerless, but he was using it now to keep himself in check. That knowledge stirred much more primitive urges than fear.

She kissed the stubbled plane of his cheek; then, avoiding Rory's attempt to capture her mouth, she traveled to his ear and from thence down his neck. She felt as well as heard the growl in his throat as she pressed her lips at the base, and his arm tightened deliciously around her waist as he fought the urge to conquer her. To Alyson's delight, he allowed her to continue unmolested as she explored the male body that had so neatly trapped her own.

When she came to the masculine part of him straining for release, she hesitated. Modesty had prevented exploration here in the first days of their lovemaking, but her rounding belly was reason enough to shed modesty. He had planted his babe inside her, and she had a need to know more about this miracle. The first tentative touches of her fingers elicited a moan from her victim as Rory buried his hands in her hair, and the need to exercise her new power gave Alyson confidence to carry her kisses to the limit.

Rory trembled at the delicate, searching touch of her tongue, and, grasping her hair tighter, he pulled her away. "Lass, I am but a man, and if you keep that up, you'll learn more than you wish of a man's ways. Come here, and let me pleasure you."

With the taste and smell of him filling her senses, Alyson went willingly into his arms, her body sprawling along his as his fingers danced and played along her skin, lighting fires everywhere they touched, until she squirmed against him for relief. His fingers teased her breasts to aching points, driving her to a new madness. She couldn't get enough of him. She needed more, and urgently she began to move against him.

Unable to hold back any longer, Rory lifted her hips and guided them to his own.

Alyson cried out the sweet bliss of this joining, sinking deeper until he filled and stretched her with excruciating pleasure. All patience fled, they moved quickly together, seeking that release they had found before, needing the reaffirmation of this physical bond. With cries of joy, they discovered new heights, and clinging to each other, they fell from the cliffs with dizzying delight.

All too aware of Alyson's new fragility, Rory reined in his hungry impatience for more, satisfying his greed with lingering kisses as he pulled her back to him. Fearing to let her go, he held her securely in his arms as he rolled over to let her find the more comfortable surface of the bed. He held her next to him, not wanting this magic moment to escape as all his dreams always had.

Alyson burrowed against his shoulder, kissing the saltiness of his flesh where her lips touched. She liked it better this way, when she didn't have to think about right or wrong or any of the other worries and fears that the world engendered. It was good to rely on instincts again, to seek shelter in Rory's arms until she felt the strength to come out and meet the world. She wanted it always like this.

Feeling the telltale signs of his arousal rising against her belly, Alyson giggled.

Pressing a kiss to her forehead before pinching her delightfully soft bottom, Rory growled, "You laugh? Is that what you think of me?"

Alyson raised her arms to circle his neck. "You would think us the newlyweds instead of Dougall and his bride. Shouldn't an old married couple suppress their ardor?" She moved suggestively against him, indicating her awareness of his state.

"You're enjoying this, aren't you? Are you going to make me regret my confession of weakness?" Rory's hand surrendered to the twin temptations pressed against him, circling first one erect tip and then the other, until she squirmed with delight. "Or are you going to realize it works both ways?" he whispered against her ear before sending a shiver down her back with the judicious use of his tongue.

"I already know that it works both ways," Alyson murmured as she moved to take him between her thighs. "I just want to know what you're going to do when I'm too large to mount."

"Wait until the brat comes out to join us, and contemplate planting another, of course. But there's time enough to worry about that when it comes. All I want now is to know that I'll be welcome here every night for the rest of our lives." His hand slid across the sensitive juncture of her legs, making his meaning plain as he waited for her permission to make this haven his permanent home. He had little enough to offer her but the pleasure of their bodies. For now, that was all they needed.

"Was there ever any doubt, my lord? Perhaps for you it is different, but I can give myself only once. You will find it difficult to be rid of me now."

Rory caressed her hair and bent to burn her lips with his kiss before easing himself into her a second time. As

Alyson closed tightly around him, drawing him inside, he laid her gently back against the bed and sank deeper into her welcoming body.

"Aye, lass, you may regret your choice, but there will be no separating us now. You're a Maclean now, and a Maclean never gives up his own."

Alyson heard his words with her heart, not her head, and her body responded joyously to his possession. Now wasn't the time to contemplate the differences between lust and love. He wouldn't leave her, and that was all she needed to know.

31

December 1760

Alyson looked out over the snow on the hillsides and the valley below and held her hand to the growing mound where the child lay. Uneasiness made her restless, and she could settle down to no task of any duration. She drifted from window to window as she went about her work, looking out over the loch when she brought her knitting to the kitchen, checking the sloping hillside when she remembered a needle left in the hall.

The *Sea Witch* had left the loch weeks ago, sailing for warmer ports, leaving Dougall and his wife behind. Myra had become a welcome part of the household, her serenity providing the balance Alyson needed when the dark clouds were upon her, as they were today.

Perhaps it was just the snow. The snow haunted her dreams, and she could not escape the recurrent nightmares. Rory and Dougall were out there now, as they were every day. It was going to be a harsh winter, and few were prepared for it. Rory had scoffed at her vision, but he was not scoffing now. He was laying in provisions and helping repair cottages as quickly as man and beast would allow. She just wished he didn't have to oversee these activities personally.

There was something wrong, something out of kilter, but she could not put her finger to it. It made her nervous when she could not define the problem. If it were not the snow or her dream, it must be something else, but what?

Myra watched Alyson's nervous pacing with concern. It could not be good for the child to be subjected to such constant turmoil. As she quietly sewed tiny stitches in an infant's gown, she reflected on ways and means of occupying the lady who was rapidly becoming her closest friend. Her quiet observance over these last weeks had led her to believe there was much more to this smiling butterfly the Maclean had married than could readily be seen. Dougall had called her simple and innocent, but it was more than that. Despite her occasionally childlike manner of dealing with people, Lady Maclean knew at a glance or a whisper what was going on around her at all times. She had an uncanny knack for being in the kitchen when Mary began one of her tirades about the evils of their neighbor, or in the top of the tower to observe a crofter's cottage when it caught fire. Mary's frightening tirades somehow came to a halt in Alyson's presence, and the cottage or any of a dozen other emergencies were tended to with lightning speed. Myra had the feeling that Alyson's restlessness now did not bode well for some unfortunate creature.

True, it was not always danger that Alyson sensed. The servants had told Myra of how the lady had known when the *Witch* would arrive. She had also been all smiles and running from window to window just before the shipment had arrived from London. Half those packages were still stored in some secret hiding place waiting for Christmas; the others had been spread generously throughout the household: shoes and shawls and yard goods and a new loom to replace the broken one upstairs, among other things. It wasn't that Alyson just sensed danger, it was that there seemed more danger than pleasure these days.

That was why Myra watched Alyson's pacing with such caution. Danger to just one could easily be danger to all.

Dougall had explained the feud between the Maclean and his cousin. She knew men didn't ride out to battle anymore as they once had, but she was beginning to think it might be simpler if they would. From the tales she heard in the kitchen, there wasn't a man in the countryside who would rise to arms at Drummond's call. Maclean would emerge victorious from a clean-cut battle. These underhanded undertakings now were of a different nature.

She felt certain Rory had not told his pregnant wife that he was helping the tenants slaughter Drummond's sheep so that they might eat and keep warm this winter. Nor would he have told her how someone had taken to shooting at him whenever he strayed too far alone. There were other things, too, legal documents that he and Dougall pored over, letters going back and forth between here and London and Edinburgh, but Myra didn't know their contents beyond Dougall's worried frowns. All of that was enough to keep the oversensitive Lady Maclean walking the floors night and day. That she did not, made it seem as if this pacing now represented something even more dangerous.

"If I brought you a hot toddy, could you lie down and sleep awhile?"

"No. No, I think I'll go out. The snow has stopped, and the wind seems to have died. A little fresh air would be nice. I wish there was more greenery to decorate the house." Murmuring her thoughts to the air, Alyson drifted from the room in search of warm wraps.

Half an hour later she was traipsing up the side of the hill with more exuberance than she had felt in days. She enjoyed being outside, feeling the brisk wind on her face, crunching through the crystalline snow. It made her feel alive as Rory made her feel alive when he touched her. All her senses prickled and danced and brightened with the brilliance of the sun glinting off the snow-wrapped hills.

The shot, when it came, echoed and bounced in her ears long after it rang out and she fell to the ground.

Behind a rock on a nearby rise, one man knocked wildly at the rifle in his companion's hand, sending the charge echoing off into the atmosphere. Furiously he spun the gun holder around.

"Are you mad? What are you trying to do? That looks like Alyson out there."

Drummond dusted the snow from his shoulder where the anxious earl had knocked him against the boulder. With a shrug, he lifted the rifle to load it again. "I would only have winged her enough to give excuse to carry her home. She so seldom comes out, it seemed an auspicious occasion."

Cranville gave his friend a look that should have burned through his soul, if he'd had one. "You would shoot her to save her? I scarcely think she would appreciate the thought."

"Faith, sir, I can't see that you have come up with a better idea. When the prey is Maclean, I enjoy stalking him more than anyone, but I grow bored with the waiting." Drummond glanced over his shoulder to see his ruffled bird rise and shake the snow from her cloak. He could take aim again, but already voices were traveling from the direction of the tower. Better to try later. He hurried toward the horses.

"You would have me invite her to tea, perhaps? Other than the fact that Maclean practically holds her prisoner and no message would reach her, she isn't likely to race off to my welcoming arms. She hates me more than she ever did that rogue of a husband of hers." Cranville grudgingly mounted his own horse. Instinct told him to ride to see how Alyson fared, but common sense sent him after his host.

Drummond scowled. That was the whole problem with his plan. Cranville was virtually useless in luring the heiress away, and seemed uninterested in using any other method to carry her off. As always, he would have to do everything himself. Maclean had grown so confident lately, it might not be necessary to abduct his wife to get at him. Time would tell.

Perhaps he could console the wealthy widow afterward. That would be entertaining.

Shooting Cranville's thunderous expression an amused glance, Drummond spurred his horse to the safety of his own grounds.

Rory grabbed Alyson's shoulders and shoved her behind a protective outcropping of rock before racing his hands over her bundled figure in search of damage. Finding none, he gathered her in his arms and vented a stream of curses.

Even with his greatcoat wrapped around her, Alyson shivered, and gratefully she slid her arms around his back and rested her head against his shoulder. She had not known for certain that it was a gunshot she heard until Rory and the others had come running. She knew the men were now surrounding the rocks that provided the only hiding place, but she also knew the danger had escaped.

"Why the deuce were you out here alone, Alys? Have you taken leave of your senses?" Rory's voice shook with fury. Seeing Alyson falling to the ground after that shot rang out had taken him to hell and back in seconds.

"I like to walk alone. Nobody told me it was a crime. What is happening, Rory? Couldn't it have just been someone hunting?"

Relieved that she had given him an easy explanation, Rory caressed her back and pressed a kiss to her forehead. "Of course, but seeing you fall like that terrified me. Are you sure you're all right? Shall I carry you home?"

He lied. Alyson felt the lie, and her arms tightened around him, fearing to let go. "I'm fine. Just hold me. I don't want to go back alone. Come with me."

Rory gazed out on the gray, forbidding sky and the hilly snow-covered terrain. He could see Dougall and one of his tenants circling the far hill, and he wanted to be with them. He wanted to find the tracks of the men who had hidden there, and follow them to their lair and tear them limb from limb. But the reason for his violence was safely in his arms, and he could not risk leaving her alone again.

"We'll go back to the house and get you some dry clothes. You shouldn't be walking out alone. Think of the child, lass. You're no longer responsible for just yourself."

Alyson pulled away to read Rory's expression. She saw the pain there, and understood the torment well enough. Sadly she lifted her heavy skirts above her boots and started down the path toward the house. He was merely reminding himself when he scolded her about responsibil-

ity. That was all she was to him. Once again, she was but
a nuisance in the path of his plans.

"You will not tell me what is happening?" she asked
quietly as Rory caught her elbow to help her over the
rocky path. The snow was just deep enough to be treacherous for the footing.

Rory pulled Alyson's hood farther over her face as a
gust of wind hit them broadside. Silently offering up a
prayer for forgiveness, he offered her the only protection
he knew. " 'Tis nothin', lass. Dinna fash yerself."

Alyson's lashes grew wet with tears at the soft burr of
his voice. She loved the way he spoke, and she wanted
her child to know his voice as well as she. What chance
was there of that if Rory persisted in this feud?

"Drummond will not sell?"

Rory sent her a quick glance, but her face betrayed
nothing. "It is no matter. There is much to do here. Are
they cooking Christmas dinner yet?"

He would tell her nothing. Did he still think her so
empty-headed that she thought only of dinners and children? If that was what he required of a wife, she would
try it to please him, but she could not be happy about it.

"The puddings are made long since. The goose and the
cow have been slaughtered, although where you found
them is a mystery to me. We'll have enough for all the
tenants."

"And enough for me, I trust. An expectant father
needs to keep his strength up."

His grin warmed a smile from her, and the lovely
blue-gray of Alyson's eyes at last lifted to caress him with
gentleness. Finding all he needed in that tender look,
Rory bent a kiss to ruby lips before leading her back into
the safety of their stone fortress.

That night the fire crackled in the vast fireplace of the
old keep, taking away some of the damp as Alyson
worked nervously with a piece of cloth and thread. The
gifts to be exchanged the next day were piled high on a
table in the room's center and adorned with what greenery could be found. Earlier, the room had been filled
with music and merriment as the entire household had
congregated for prayers, followed by much eating and
drinking as they added their bundles to the growing stack.
The hall was a public room for the use of all, and Rory

had kept the custom, enjoying the camaraderie as much as any.

Alyson gifted her husband with a quick look as he sat beside the fire shuffling through a stack of papers that had arrived by courier earlier. The rich glow of his auburn hair framed the molded contours of his square, stern face. His lace and linen were snowy white against the weathered skin of his throat and hands and the dark broadcloth of his coat and vest. He looked severe as he studied the papers, but Alyson knew that when he looked up to her his expression would soften and his dark eyes would take on a heady gleam that would make her want to throw herself into his arms. She wished to see a smile upon his lips more often, but she would have to be content that it was there when he looked on her.

The uneasiness of earlier had not entirely subsided, and she still had the urge to inspect the narrow windows for some sight outside in the darkness, but she resisted. Myra and Dougall had just retired with warnings that she must do so soon, but Alyson felt no weariness. She waited expectantly.

Not realizing his wife still anticipated an uncertain ending to this day, Rory glanced up to catch her stare. She had discarded apron and shawl for this festive evening and looked very much the lady of the manor in her blue-green velvet. Nearly five months pregnant, she gave little evidence of it except in the occasional shadows of her eyes and her riper figure. Giving the full curve of her bosom an appreciative look, Rory set his papers aside for another day. Married life had certain definite advantages if looked at from the proper perspective.

Before he could rise, Alyson threw a nervous look toward the window. Built as a fortress, the tower had been graced only with narrow leaded panes in later years. They provided small glimpse of the outside on a night like this, even though they remained undraped as yet. But Rory caught the same sound that had alerted Alyson.

A horse. Some madman was out in the dark and blowing snow riding the unmarked roads of these hills leading to the tower. The gale winds blew in from the sea, freezing the snow to treacherous ice. No sane person would be out on such a night.

Rory stood and reached for the musket. The hall had a

rambling display of swords and rapiers, hatchets and knives that had never been confiscated after the '45, probably because the place appeared abandoned and its owner was an Englishman. The musket was the most modern weapon among them, and Rory had kept it cleaned and oiled and primed from their first night here. He ignored the way Alyson's face paled as he lifted it from its hooks.

"Go on upstairs, Alyson. Call Dougall if it will make you feel better, but I daresay it is no more than some drunken fool with a complaint to make."

There was no time for her to defy him. The horse had come to a halt just outside, and the sound of footsteps muffled in the trampled snow came quite clearly through the silence of the empty hall.

The household was full of female servants. The few men left tended the land and slept in their own beds and not the hall. Besides Rory, only Dougall and a few old men too crippled to work their plows stayed within the tower walls. The sound of a horse coming up the road had aroused the occupants of several chambers, and curious faces beneath a variety of mobcaps peered from the kitchen or abovestairs, but the only man to step forward was the steward who had kept watch over the keep all these years. Nearly eighty and bent with rheumatism, he still managed to wield a broadsword as he lumbered from the direction of the kitchen.

The huge door knocker pounded furiously, startling Alyson from a stupor of amazement. Closer to the door than either Rory or the steward, she lifted her skirts and swept in that direction. No man should have to stand in that inhospitable wind on her doorstep.

With a swiftness startling even himself, Rory caught up with her and held her back, nodding for the steward to answer the demand for entrance. Drawing Alyson back into the room with the fire, he waited for the door in the tapestried foyer to open.

Content to wait for the old man to proudly uphold his position, Alyson leaned against Rory's hard frame and basked in the reassurance of his strong arm around her. He still held the musket barrel, resting the handle against the floor, but one horse signaled no army. He was tense and ready to shove Alyson behind the protection of the massive stone-and-plaster walls if need be, but he, too, expected no trouble on Christmas Eve.

So they stood when the doors flew open to reveal the tall, travel-weary stranger in his snow-covered hat and cloak. Without waiting for welcome, the furious nobleman strode in.

Cold blue eyes glared at the laird protectively holding his lady wife. Gloved hands swept off cocked hat and cloak, handing them to the steward with a practiced gesture that gave evidence of his aristocratic heritage. A sword hung at his side, and as he removed his gloves, one hand came to rest on its hilt. His gaze left Rory's imperturbable features to focus on the shining brilliance of black-fringed eyes and satin skin accented by thick waves of ebony curls.

Before his gaze could so much as soften or his lips speak a word, Alyson flew from Rory's protective embrace with a cry of unadulterated delight. "Father!"

All knowing her history, the entire household stared at her as if she were demented, but the nobleman's lined face grew less rigid, his frozen eyes melted, and his arms opened to lift Alyson in his embrace.

Stunned, Rory could only watch this scene with growing comprehension and disbelief. Not even in his worst nightmares had he imagined that his wife's noble father would return to life to claim her. An earl, a naval officer, and a furious father all rolled into one dreadful apparition to haunt his guiltiest thoughts—not even Rory's conscience could have conjured up such a fate. With lessening hope he waited for the stranger to set Alyson aside and disavow her mad claim.

Instead, the pair seemed to be content in exploring the miracle of reunion, making senseless exclamations as they searched each other's faces. With a gesture, Rory sent the servants back to their beds, commanding only one kitchen maid to fetch some hot drink. He had no idea where they would house an earl unless they threw Dougall and Myra from their bed, and he felt disinclined to think on it. He would much rather the apparition disappeared into the night from whence it came.

The scurrying of the servants was sufficient warning to remind the earl of his position. Keeping his hand on Alyson's shoulders, he coldly met the stare of the man who had abducted and ruined her. It came as a shock to recognize the drunken young sea captain from the Swan, but he recovered himself admirably as it became apparent the captain did not recognize him.

"I have come for my daughter." He had wasted a lifetime. There was no point in dallying over trivialities at this late date.

"She is my wife now." Still holding the musket barrel, Rory stood firm. If this man was as Alyson claimed, he represented all that Rory was not—aristocratic, wealthy, powerful, and presumably honorable. But still Rory could not yield his most precious possession.

Alyson blithely ignored this test of wills. Tugging her father's hand, she led him past Rory's obstinate stance to a place by the fire. The earl refused to be seated, however, and shrugging her shoulders at this foolishness, she floated back to Rory's side. Removing the gun and setting it aside, she led him back to the fire too.

With a polite curtsy, she made the introductions. "Father, this is the Maclean, Rory Douglas, my husband. Rory, my father, Everett Hampton, Earl of Cranville." She sent a mischievous look to the stern nobleman. "I did get that right, didn't I? I've never raised an earl from the dead before, and so I'm not sure of the proper courtesy."

The stunned look was now on her father's face and not Rory's. Rory would almost have managed a smile at Alyson's conceit had he not been more concerned with getting his hands on her and holding her until this challenger to his possession had disappeared.

Deliberately not extending his hand, the earl spoke first after this introduction. "Under the circumstances, I cannot say it is a pleasure to meet you, Maclean. You will forgive me if I overlook the pleasantries." He turned his watchful gaze to Alyson. "As much as I wish to spend this time with you, my dear, I have to come to terms with your husband first. I would not subject you to our discussion. Perhaps if you could just show us to a private room . . ."

Despite a deep-seated feeling of distress, Rory couldn't help a small grin from appearing as Alyson gazed pleasantly at her father, ignored his words, and hastened to help the kitchen maid with the tray. Without any sign that she had heard a single word, she set the tray on a

table near her father's hand, poured a steaming tankard
of rum punch, and handed it to him.

"I saw you outside my window the day Rory and I
were married. Of course, I thought you were a ghost.
You aren't, are you?" she asked anxiously.

The distinguished gentleman gazed at his lovely, fey
daughter in confusion. Very well aware of that feeling
himself, Rory seized the moment to establish the upper
hand. "Alyson, take a seat so your father need not stand
all night. Lord Cranville, I apologize for my cold reception. You must admit I had some reason for surprise." If
Alyson accepted this stranger as parent, he could do no
less, although he continued to harbor definite reservations.

As Alyson settled herself comfortably in a small chair
next to the one she had assigned him, Rory took her
hand and waited for his guest to be seated. Given no
other choice, the earl reluctantly lowered himself to the
massive Jacobean armchair across from them. He watched
warily as the plainspoken laird took his chair next to his
lady.

"I would prefer Alyson be kept out of our differences,
Maclean." The older man frowned as he sipped his drink,
his hooded gaze carefully studying the couple before him.
"You do yourself no favors by hiding behind her skirts."

Rory accepted the insult without rancor. "Alyson is
free to do as she wishes. I would protect her from harm if
I could, but I have already learned the hard way that she
will make her own choices." Turning his head to confront
Alyson's too-bright gaze, he asked, "Lass, I am quite
capable of dealing with this gentleman's accusations alone.
Wouldn't it be easier if you went upstairs now and let me
handle this? All will be settled by the time you come
down in the morning, I promise."

Alyson favored him with a look of annoyance at this
formal speech. "I'm certain it will, but then I would have
missed all the entertainment, wouldn't I?"

The earl began to unbend slightly as he observed this
byplay between the young couple. After hearing the scandalous rumors of how Alyson had been abducted from
London, ravished, and hastily wedded by a notorious
fortune-hunter, he had been prepared to have the villain's head on a pike. Instead, he was beginning to de-

velop some inkling that the villain hadn't had everything his own way, after all.

"I remember her mother as being much more even-tempered. I suspect Alyson takes after her grandmother," the earl mused out loud, apropos of nothing at all.

Alyson's eager look tore at Rory's heartstrings, and he surrendered the battle without a fight. "Perhaps that's so, but to my mind, Alyson is one of a kind. I would have her no other way."

Alyson sent her husband a surprised look. He used loving words when they were alone and he wished to woo her, but never had Rory said such a thing in public. Could he truly mean it? She had been a nuisance and an obstacle to his goals since they met. Perhaps he referred only to their physical relationship.

Not understanding, but keeping a quiet eye on the interplay between the couple, the earl continued to test the waters. "How did you know me, Alyson? You look enough like your mother that I could recognize you anywhere, but you have no such advantage."

Trapped by a familiar face but a stranger's understanding, Alyson smiled absently and dismissed the subject with a wave of her hand. "You are very much like your portrait, sir. How do you come here? Where have you been? Will you tell us your story?"

It would be easy to be pleasantly distracted by her polite questions, but the steady gaze of the man at her side challenged him to beware. Knowing the stories of her mother's family, the earl stirred uneasily, not wanting to delve too deeply in muddy waters, but he could not ignore the challenge.

Quietly he tried again. "If I remember rightly, that portrait was done when I was little more than a boy. I wore one of those deuced wigs that made the head scratch infernally, and I proudly sported a ridiculous hat with enough gold braid to match the king's crown. Do I still look so foolish, then?"

Alyson had never had difficulty getting out of these situations before, but this was her father and she could not dismiss him lightly. Rory understood, but he always had, trusting without question and accepting her oddities for what they were. She had no desire to alienate her father by speaking of ghosts and visions he would not understand, but she had no ability to lie.

Distraught but revealing none of it, she smiled dreamily and rose to take away the empty tankard. "I loved that portrait, sir, and memorized every line of it. Let me refill your drink."

Her father stopped her hand, holding it in his own. "You said you saw me at your wedding. How was it that you did not make yourself known?"

Alyson threw Rory an anxious plea for aid, but his imperturbable gaze was focused on her father. Their battle of wills had found a new target, and she was it. Throwing up her hands in disgust at this discovery, Alyson returned to her seat, picking up her embroidery as she did so.

"Perhaps Rory would care to explain about our wedding, Father. And then you might explain why you were alive and in Barbados all these years we thought you dead."

Rory gave a silent cheer, grinned, and lifted his tankard in toast to this neat delivery of the hot potato to proper hands. Alyson gave him a wicked scowl in return, but he was not fooled by her sudden tantrum. She had been momentarily thwarted, but she had emerged victorious and knew it.

The earl lifted a languid brow in Rory's direction. "Yes, I think I would like to hear about the wedding. As I understand the tale, my heir scoured the islands after your head. You smuggled in your ill-gotten goods behind his back, were forced into making an honest woman of my daughter, and fled in a pirate ship before my heir could return. Would you care to elaborate?"

"It will be my word against your heir's, sir. I removed Alyson from an intolerable situation, only to embroil her in a worse one, admittedly, but I will not allow it to be claimed that I was forced to marry her." Rory hesitated, unwilling to reveal that Alyson had been the reluctant one. That would not shed a good light on either of them. He sent her glossy curls a quick glance and received a misty smile in return. Taking a deep breath, he proceeded, "There was some misunderstanding of my intentions, but they have ever been honorable toward Alyson. Now that you have returned, perhaps the misunderstanding can be remedied. I want Alyson, not her wealth. If you can prove your claim to the estate and the title, then you are entitled to your father's inheritance also." Rory met the earl's eyes squarely. "Just leave me Alyson."

Remembering something of the drunken sea captain's story those many weeks ago, the earl knew there was a great deal more to the tale than this. He had believed the young captain, but now that he realized it was his own daughter of whom he had spoken, he needed a good deal more reassurance than these half-truths. Without blinking an eyelash, he replied, "Well said, Maclean, but not convincing. I don't need my father's wealth. He meant Alyson to have it. What I want is what is best for my daughter. I cannot believe an impoverished, fortune-hunting Jacobite is the solution."

Seeing Rory's hands clench in frustration, Alyson smiled sweetly. "Being declared a bastard in front of the whole world probably wasn't very good for me, either, but I survived." Laying aside her embroidery, she looked comfortably to Rory. "Your son is growing restless, my dear, and I find I am overtired, after all. This discussion would be better held after a good night's rest, would it not? Let us show my father to his chamber, and we can all talk again on the morrow."

The earl's lined face paled at this mention of a child, and when he and Rory rose politely with her, his glance instantly went to what he had not noticed before. Alyson's full skirts hid a decided thickness that could be explained in only one way, and she swayed noticeably as she reached for her husband's arm. His furious gaze flew to the Scotsman's impassive face.

"You wasted no time, did you?"

Still holding Rory's arm, Alyson reached up to kiss her father lightly on the cheek. "If you had wasted any time, I would not be here today. Good night, Father. I'll have the steward show you to your chamber."

She felt the irate exchange of looks over her head, but Alyson smiled contentedly. Neither man might love her as boundlessly as her grandparents had, but she loved them, and for now, that was enough.

The future might be a different story.

32

They were at it hammer and tongs over breakfast before Alyson even came down. A bemused Dougall and Myra sat at one end of the table, staying out of the line of fire, as Rory and the stranger politely—and sometimes not so politely—stabbed at each other with words. The resultant silence as Alyson swept into the room was greeted with smiles of relief from the spectators and wariness by the combatants.

She kissed both men on the cheek and sat down at the place beside Rory, where the maid hastily laid a bowl of oatmeal. Smiling innocently, she inquired, "Have you figured out yet how to buy back Rory's estate to put an end to this feud?"

Dougall choked on a laugh and hastily covered his mouth with a napkin at the sight of two battling lions laid low by a lamb. This was worth whatever he would eventually have to pay for it.

"I have decided it would be preferable if you returned to Cornwall with me, Alyson." The earl threw his host an indignant look. "I will need to track down my cousin's son and come to terms with him, I suppose, but the estate is entailed with the title. There is little he can do to stop me from returning. I meant to bring your mother there. It is your home now."

"I believe you will find our cousin with Rory's, not far from here, Father. Shall you go to see him before you return to Cornwall?"

Rory stared at his ingenuous wife in shock. How long had she known that? Was there any use in trying to keep anything from her? Before he could voice his concerns, the earl's face lit with a mixture of anticipation and anger.

"Alex is here? They told me he was hunting in Scotland, but this is rather late in the season, is it not? I certainly shall go to see him. I do not at all approve of the way he is ignoring the management of his estate." He set aside his napkin with a finality that indicated immediate departure.

Rory caught the other man's arm as he raised from his chair, ignoring his noble in-law's indignant expression. "Were it just myself, I would let you leap blindly into the fire, but for Alyson's sake, I give you warning. My cousin has taken the lives and the lands of my family and mistreated the innocent ever since he had the power to do so. That your heir is in the company of such as he does not bode well for me or mine. He has already attempted Alyson's rape and abduction. Just the other day, someone shot at her. If you wish to visit that nest of vipers, it is upon your head. I will not come to your rescue."

Stunned by the vehemence of Rory's words, the earl returned to his seat and searched his face for truth. He read the bitterness there and knew it warped a man's thinking, but he also saw the fear and concern that forced the words into the open. Slowly he turned his gaze to his daughter. She hid her thoughts behind an impenetrable mask, but her hands clutched convulsively at the linen she placed in her lap. He directed his questions to her.

"Is this so, Alyson? I heard no such tale from any other."

"Because there is only my word to speak it, Father. How many besides Rory would take my word over the Earl of Cranville's?"

The earl drew in a sharp breath at the cruelty of that truth. For the first time, he began to understand the life he had left to his unknown child. His fingers dug into the lion's-paw arms of the ancient dining-hall chair. "You might not bear the title, but you had my name and my father's protection. Why should you not be heard?"

Alyson lifted her delicate eyebrow with a whimsical look. "Your name? Had it been so, perhaps some would have listened with righteous indignation. As it was, all society would have thought your heir did me a favor by making me his mistress. A bastard has no rights, Father."

An ashen pallor began to replace the earl's normal healthy color. Rory watched him with interest. The earl was his enemy in all things, but he almost felt sorry for the man. Alyson sometimes had that effect on people.

"You are no bastard, child. Your mother and I were legally and truly wedded, although I swore her to secrecy until I had time to tell my father. Why did she not tell you this?"

"She died when I was just a babe, but I do not think my grandparents would have hidden the truth. I asked once, and they said my mother believed she was married, but as she had no papers or witnesses, they thought her confused. I can see now that they most likely thought you had led her astray with promises. Apparently your reputation was not of the highest." Alyson delivered this speech with remarkable candor and no condemnation while she laced her oatmeal with milk and broke off a piece of brown sugar to sweeten it. Rory nearly choked on his own meal as he watched her father's incredulous expression.

"Bigawd, the deuce they did! Astray! Of all the . . ." His words muttered into incomprehensible phrases as he realized their impropriety at a lady's table. Gathering his ruffled dignity, he glared at his choking son-in-law. "I wedded her on board ship, with all the officers as witness. If you know anything of your own laws, you know no other license or church was needed. I carried the papers with me to present to my father when I returned. She is no bastard, but my daughter. She belongs in society, not in this desolate ruin. I am taking her back with me to Cornwall."

Alyson calmly buttered her bannock. "How interesting. Are you planning to abduct me too?" She lifted laughing eyes of blue to the company, her joy at knowing she was not born in shame making her lighthearted.

Rory chewed thoughtfully at his bread as he considered the consequences. Unlike Alyson, he knew the earl was serious and had every right to be concerned. Under any other circumstances, he would never have been allowed close enough to a lady like Alyson to touch the hem of her gown. Despite his aunt's attempts to pass him off as a gentleman, any proper father would have known him for the rogue he was and forbidden him the door. But he came from a lineage older and more aristocratic than the English earl's, even if good King George had tried to strip him of it. He finished the bread and met his father-in-law's defiant gaze with equanimity.

"We're married under English law and in the eyes of the church. That is my child she carries. I would have every right to kill you if you tried to take her away. The choice to leave is Alyson's. I have never held her against her will."

Alyson smiled approvingly at this less-than-truthful reply and offered her father more tea with a gesture of the pot. "I can see that it is most important that someone return to Cornwall, but it won't be me. I have too much to do here. Rory, my love, you are going to spill that cup all over the table if you don't watch what you're doing."

Beginning to adjust to Alyson's casual dismissal of momentous subjects, her father ignored this silliness to address her more intelligent husband. "You've already admitted that this feud has someone shooting at her. How can you in all conscience keep her here?"

That struck a raw nerve, and a muscle in Rory's jaw jumped as he clenched his teeth together. He could not imagine what anyone would hope to gain by shooting at Alyson, but Drummond's hatred had many outlets. He would be low enough to get at Rory through Alyson if necessary. A rage of conflicts warred within him.

When Rory did not reply immediately, Alyson sent him an anxious look. It had never occurred to her that he would wish to send her away, but that was because she was so blindly in love that she could not see the nose on her face. But the veil had briefly lifted, and she saw him clearly for a moment. Rory had never claimed to love her. He had married her for expediency and seemed content with the arrangement while it suited him. But she had ever been a nuisance to him. She had forced him to bring her, and only that with promises of her body. Now that her body was growing unwieldy and unsuitable for his play, he might find reason to send her away. She didn't think she could bear it, but none of her thoughts were revealed as she withdrew behind the curtains of her eyes.

"Myra tells me the child will most likely come in April. I could not possibly travel before then, so you have plenty of time to argue." Alyson set aside her uneaten bannock and lifted a casual gaze to her father. "When are you going to tell us where you have been all these years? I'm certain it will make a fascinating story on a day like this, when no one wishes to brave the winds."

Just stepping out-of-doors would put the truth to Alyson's casual remarks. The journey out of these distant hills was a difficult one at the best of times. In the middle of winter and with Alyson five months pregnant, the journey would be an impossible one by land, a difficult one by sea. Rory could not hide his relief at this prosaic knowledge, and he generously allowed his good feelings to overflow in his father-in-law's direction.

"It is Christmas Day, lass. Give your father some peace and let us open our gifts. I, for one, cannot wait to see what is in that wicked assortment of packages Mary was smuggling into the hall this morning. And there is one in there that must weigh two stone, at least. I have been waiting for days to find out what is in that one."

Alyson flashed him a mischievous grin. "You have been shaking those packages all week! You're worse than any child. Next year I will know to fill them with sticks and stones so you'll not guess."

"Do that and see what you get in return," Rory murmured against her ear as he pulled her chair back from the table.

His breath blew intimately against her cheek, sending shivers of pleasure through Alyson as she accepted his arm to rise. Next year. That did not sound as if he planned to send her away, but she knew better than to let her hopes run away with her. She would be content with the moment.

Not only the entire household but also tenants close enough to brave the weather gathered in the towering hall in time-honored fashion for this festive day. The small kirk had no minister, but several of the men took turns reading from the Bible, and Rory led the final prayer, offering fervent thanksgiving for what they shared this day. Alyson had tears in her eyes when his gaze sought hers after he finished. She had felt his passion all the way to her soul.

The merriment began after that. Rory's ship had carried many of the items Alyson had requested on that last voyage without Rory's knowledge. There were sweets for the children, bundles of coffee and tea for the adults, bolts of warm wool for clothing for everyone, and enough leather to build brogues for every man, woman, and child on the estate. None of the gifts was lavish enough to cause guilt that there was little to give in return, but all appealed to both the practical and the pleasurable.

Alyson had no gift prepared for her father, but in the early-morning hours she had thought of one thing she possessed that he might enjoy. In the trunks she had taken from Cornwall and left with Deirdre and then carefully transported to Scotland had been one precious memento that she had never thought to part with. But on this day she would gladly trade an image of what had been for the reality of what was now. She carefully wrapped the locket with her mother's portrait into a silk handkerchief and saved it for the proper moment.

While Rory triumphantly discovered the heavy box addressed to him among the riot of packages, Alyson pulled the tiny silk bundle from her pocket and gave it to her father.

"It is not much, but it is all I had until you arrived. Merry Christmas, Father."

The nobleman looked down upon the slight figure of this daughter he had only met and felt himself transported back in time. It had been in this crumbling ruin that he had first met Brianna, and she had looked at him with those same large, lovely eyes. Her skin had been as fair and fine, her hair the same dark riot of curls, and he had fallen madly, wondrously in love. He felt that tug of emotion now, although he had already begun to discover that Alyson wasn't quite the same sweet, complacent young maid her mother had been. Just the way the innocent blue of her eyes faded to gray when she was stirred warned that there was more of her indomitable grandmother in her than could readily be seen in a glance. He carefully opened the small bundle she had presented to him.

As he opened the locket, tears sprang to his eyes, and he was forced to turn away. Fortunately, at that moment, Rory decimated the wrapping of his package to discover the contents, and his roar captured the attention of everyone in the room.

"By all that is holy, lass, how did ye know?" His joyous cry rattled the rafters, and Alyson turned to smile at the way he rapturously stroked the elegant leather bindings of the books. With trembling fingers he lifted the covers to examine the freshly printed pages and beautifully drawn illustrations. Alyson felt her heart being wrung dry at his rapt expression. There was the boy he had once been, and she dropped to the floor at his feet, leaning her head against his knee to examine the gift with him.

"Deirdre told me you were studying medicine and that you had to leave your books behind when you left Scotland. I didn't know what books they were, but a friend of Deirdre's told her what ones were most important to have. I didn't know if you would still want them, but I could think of nothing else."

Rory's broad hand caressed her cheek and rested on her soft curls as his other gently turned the pages. The emotion choking in his throat made it impossible to look at her and speak at the same time. He chose speech and touch instead.

"You could have found no better gift had you read my mind, lass. I know I am truly home now." He set the books aside then and lifted her into his arms, cradling her against his shoulder as he absorbed the love she offered. There was little enough fairness in this world, but this one moment of joy equaled many years of torment. He buried his face against her hair to hide his tears.

To cover this private moment, Dougall and Myra began a game of chase with the children, with oranges as a prize. The screams and yells of excitement returned the chatter to the room, awakening the laird and his lady to their public positions. Without embarrassment, Alyson smiled up into Rory's weathered face and tugged at his neatly tied auburn queue. "Myra can teach you to be a midwife," she informed him wickedly.

"Ach, and I thought all there was to do was lift up a cabbage leaf." Rory kissed her nose and glanced to their aristocratic guest, who had retired to a relatively quiet corner, where he clutched something in his hand while staring vacantly out over the noisy room. "What spell have you cast over our noble visitor? He seems strangely absorbed in our small gathering."

Reluctant to leave Rory's arms, Alyson turned to see what he spoke of. Her father's expression left no doubt as to where his mind traveled. "It is the past he is seeing, not us. He would not lie about marrying my mother, would he?" This last she asked anxiously. Too long had she accepted another truth to believe this one readily.

Rory hugged her, enjoying the fresh fragrance of Alyson's hair and the welcoming softness of her body against him, wishing they were alone so he could say the things he felt, things that he had kept buried too long to release easily. Instead, his words only prattled nonsense meant to please, even while they spoke the truth. "If your mother was anything like yourself, lass, he would need be a Bedlamite not to marry her. Does he look a Bedlamite to you?"

Alyson laughed, kissed his cheek, and went to return her father to the present. Rory watched her go with a hunger so deep and gnawing he could almost cry out with the pain of it. Never before had he seen the crude rawness of his life until it had been invaded by her gentle beauty, an innocence too rare to belong anywhere but in a jewel box surrounded by the best life had to offer. This cold stone fortress surrounded by bare hills and icy blasts of wind was not the setting she deserved. Ruefully Rory wondered if he should have kept her in Barbados.

Refusing to allow his terrifying doubts to mar this day, he went in search of the packages addressed to Alyson. The silly wench had found so much enjoyment in gifting others, it had not occurred to her that any might wish to return the favor. Perhaps few enough had in the past, but Rory knew that was one mistake he could rectify.

Alyson looked up in surprise as Rory approached with an armful of bundles, followed by a procession of children carrying a varied assortment of oddly disguised packages. Someone had struck up a tune on a fiddle, and here and there other instruments materialized to add the first tentative notes to a merry song. Color leapt to her cheek as she realized she was the focus of everyone's attention.

With a gallant, if somewhat overburdened bow, Rory laid his gifts at her feet. Then, propping his arm against the massive timber over the fireplace, he waited for her reaction.

Sitting beside her father, Alyson could feel her parent's curiosity and amusement as she looked from the tall auburn-haired figure draped over the mantel to the stack of gifts at her feet, and then to the crowd of small expectant faces all around her. Grubby little hands clutched an assortment of oddities, all generously created by loving hands for just this occasion. Never in her life had she been the recipient of so much love and attention by so many. She felt it surrounding her, washing over her, and filling her with a rare happiness that she could never have envisioned. She burst into tears.

Her father broke into gales of laughter as Rory's face fell at this unanticipated reaction. As Rory hastily came to his knees beside Alyson's chair to gather her into his arms, the earl's good humor expanded.

"Just like her mother in that, she is. Never saw such a woman for tears as Brianna. Even on our wedding night . . ." He chuckled. "Enough said on that. She's just happy, lad. What is it you Scots say? Don't 'fash' yourself?"

The children giggled at the English aristocrat's attempt at a Scots dialect, and Alyson sent them all a wavery smile as she wiped the tears from her eyes. Her fingers wrapped shakily in Rory's hair, loosening long strands from its knot, but neither noticed as their eyes met.

The contents of the packages mattered little in comparison to the overwhelming love with which they were given. Alyson exclaimed and laughed and admired as Rory sat on the colorful wool rug on the hearth at her feet and handed her each one to open. The knowledge that he had taken time from his busy days and coins from his meager purse and the thought to purchase what he hoped she would enjoy far exceeded the actual value of the gifts. She cried over an exquisite lace christening gown and laughed over an outrageous rag-stuffed baby doll. She kissed the top of his head over a lovely sapphire necklace that matched the gown he had once bought for her, and then laughed with delight to discover he had had another gown made of the same lovely satin.

The children's gifts called for a kiss on each shining brow and expectant face, and somehow pockets went away filled with chewy candied fruits and a ha'pence or two. The music grew livelier, and chattering voices and laughter filled the once-empty hall as tray after tray of food was laid upon the long table where the gifts had once been.

To Rory's surprise, a final large package was spirited

out of some hiding place and laughingly dumped in his lap by Myra and Dougall. From the conspiratorial looks exchanged, he gathered well enough that his irrepressible wife was somehow involved, and he lifted a crooked eyebrow in her direction.

"Should the laird be only giver and not receiver, my lord?" Alyson questioned archly. "It seems I can remember being told not to look a gift horse in the mouth, or some such faradiddle. Open it."

Skeptically Rory tore open the strings, only to find a dozen smaller packages inside. Beginning to grin at this extravagance, joining in the spirit of this first Christmas celebrated since he was a child, he opened the bulkiest package first.

Out fell a long frock coat of rich navy velvet, beautifully embroidered in gold braid and thread on the narrow buff cuffs and along the stiffened edges beneath the brass buttons and narrow, short tails. It was a gentleman's coat of the latest mode, fashionably simple for ease in riding but carefully tailored for elegance. A gift from Deirdre in London, it was a style to suit Rory's taste and needs as well as the fashions.

Like a child, he shed his threadbare coat and quickly donned the new one, testing the accuracy of the tailoring by shifting his wide shoulders and standing to hover over his seated wife. "Do I look the part of laird now?" he asked, striking a pose with hand over heart and head flung back.

Alyson giggled as an auburn lock fell across his broad cheek. "If you should try on all your gifts as you open them, you will provide a great deal of entertainment. Perhaps we ought to retire upstairs before you open the next." She lifted a smaller package and handed it to him.

Their audience laughed as Rory broke the string to discover a matching pair of breeches. These he held up and announced a perfect fit without need to try them on. This announcement brought a roar of disappointment. To appease the crowd, Alyson produced an awkwardly wrapped bundle which, when opened, revealed a black cocked hat trimmed in gold, complete with gold pin to hold one side in place. Rory instantly donned his new chapeau and chose the next gift himself.

A bundle of hand-stitched soft linen shirts tumbled

out. Every woman in the household and the estates had worked at the cutting and stitching of the fine fabric Alyson had purchased. When this news was imparted through a small whisper in his ear, Rory gallantly strode into the crowd to buss every woman he encountered and swing her in a circle in time to the music. By the time he made a wide swath through the room, there were red cheeks everywhere and the dancing had begun in earnest.

The festivities lasted all day and into the night, many of the guests choosing to sleep on makeshift pallets in the hall rather than to leave in darkness. Alyson surrendered her position as hostess to retire early, leaving her father and Rory to entertain the crowd. She was not surprised when the door opened shortly after she climbed into the feathery softness of her bed.

Without any self-consciousness, Rory still wore parts and pieces of his new raiment mixed with the old. Over it all he had flung the illegal clan tartan woven and given by the tenants of his former estate. Along with bagpipes and weapons, the plaids had been forbidden after the '45 as being an incitement to war. Rory had defiantly worn this gift since it was opened.

Alyson smiled as he sat on the side of the bed. She reached up to slide her fingers over his bare neck above his neckcloth, loosening his queue until his unruly hair fell loose over shirt and tartan. Against his dark face, the strands of auburn and the bold plaid created the image of his warrior ancestors.

"I always wondered what it would be like married to a Highland laird," she murmured, gently drawing him toward her.

Needing no further invitation, Rory braced his arms on either side of her and brushed a kiss across her welcoming lips. "Very demanding, I should say," he whispered against her ear. "Have you tired of the dream yet?"

"Give me another hundred years to think about it." Wrapping her arms about Rory's neck as he lowered himself over her, Alyson stretched luxuriously against his hard frame. He was her husband now. Whatever happened in the future could never change that.

Joyously she returned his kiss and surrendered to the bliss just his touch could produce.

*   *   *

A few miles distant, the merrymaking was of a less innocent sort. George Drummond stretched his long booted legs before the fire, swigged deeply of his brandy, flung the empty glass against the wall, then plunged his long-fingered hand down the bodice of the plump wench on his lap. He ignored her grimace as she winced at the sharpness of his pinch. Idly contemplating whether he ought to take her here without the necessity of staggering from his chair or carry her off to bed so he could sleep comfortably afterward, he glanced across the hearth to his drinking companion.

"Isn't my gift a winsome wench? I thought her rather handsome. I considered trying her myself, but I'm a generous man. Drink up, Cranville. Think of the happy new year around the corner."

The brooding man near the hearth gave no sign that he heard these self-praises. The skinny child in his arms shivered every time he so much as laid a hand at her waist. He found little pleasure in her revulsion, and he had spent the evening diligently drinking himself into a stupor.

He had succeeded only in summoning morose thoughts and unwelcome images of a certain black-haired female with eyes that haunted his worst nightmares. He could see her glaring at him with impatience as she poured scalding water down his leg. He saw the terror turning those huge eyes to gray oceans as she leapt from the bridge of her own ship. He saw her tiny, awkward figure drop in the snow after a shot rang out.

She was pregnant. The bastard Scots adventurer had bedded her and filled her with child and carried her off to these desolate hills so he could continue his war on English aristocracy. Or so Drummond's story went. It seemed true enough from the evidence Cranville had seen around him. The tenants had turned increasingly rebellious and insolent since the Maclean had returned. The house was nearly devoid of servants now. Just obtaining a meal had become a daily ritual of torture and humiliation. He ought to leave, but he could not tear himself away from the thought of that hapless female in the Maclean's grasp. It was his fault that she had fallen into the adventurer's trap, and to his horror, he had discovered he possessed a conscience.

Of course, his own empty home and bare coffers and Drummond's promises held an equal grip on him. There was nothing in Cornwall for him but work, and he had never worked a day in his life. He scarcely knew how to go about it. Drummond's hatred of the Maclean practically ensured the adventurer's death at some future date. Drummond was too clever to fail. He only sought the right opportunity to prevent any implication of himself in the death. Cranville had only to wait to rescue the heiress and carry her off with him.

Only the tone of Drummond's drunken promises had changed of late. Through the haze of liquor, Cranville watched as his host lifted the skirts of his reluctant playmate. As he toyed with the girl's intimate parts, Drummond spoke as if she weren't there at all. Cranville tried to concentrate on the actual words, but they kept fading in and out, to the rhythm of the action opening before his eyes.

He found himself squeezing the scarcely ripe breast of the child in his arms as Drummond unbuttoned his pants and brought his wench on top of his ready member. Through the blur of liquor and growing lust, Cranville heard his host's chuckling promises.

"I wonder how that heiress of yours will feel when we get her. Have you ever taken a pregnant woman before? Or shall we wait until she pops the brat?"

Cranville shuddered and stumbled from the chair, carrying his "gift" with him. He intended to be violently sick and go to bed.

Behind him, the crying of the servant girl mixed with Drummond's ringing laughter.

33

Stagshead, February 1761

"My cousin and I went to school together. My uncle died young and James was left to run wild, and so he did. At the time, I rather admired his escapades, and admittedly, I imitated a few too many, but as heir to the title, I had this rigid sense of duty beaten into me, so I admired from afar, as it were."

Everett Hampton, Earl of Cranville, put his elegant buckled shoes upon the needlepoint cushion and sipped at the fine claret in his goblet. Although his chamber had been hastily prepared from remnants found in other rooms and attics and repaired with what was available, he felt quite at home here. The weather had grown increasingly worse since Christmas, and he saw no profit in leaving the snug warmth of this apartment his daughter and son-in-law had provided. Besides, he wished to know more of them before making any decisions. He studied his host's rough-hewn face with interest. The Maclean was restless, but shackled by wife and family, he could not risk the perils of foul weather just to be out and about. Cranville gave him a sympathetic smile and continued his tale.

"James's escapades went too far, too fast, when he dishonored a lady of quality. He had a choice of dueling with one of the finest swordsmen in the country or marrying the girl. Alex was the only issue of that marriage. My cousin broke his neck racing his stallion cross-country on a wager that he could reach Yorkminster before several other young fools bound for the same wedding." The earl shrugged. "I had just joined the navy then and knew little of my cousin's wife or child. I assumed my father kept them on an allowance. I doubt seriously that my uncle or cousin had much to leave them. What surprises me is that my father never brought Alex to the estate when he thought me dead. The boy had a right to learn of his heritage."

Rory sipped at his whisky and stared out the narrow mullioned window to the raging snowstorm outside. "Farnley told me a little when I signed over an allowance to him to run the estate. Apparently the mother had some wealth and thought poorly of the Hamptons in general. After what she went through with your cousin, that might be understandable. She refused to let your father have anything to do with her only child. She was determined her son would be raised a gentleman, not a Hampton."

Cranville laughed at his distinction. "The title isn't ancient, I agree. We more or less bribed and bought it like everyone else in the last century. There always seemed to be one Hampton in every generation good at buying and bribing. The rest were scoundrels, no doubt. The line seems to be dying out, though. If Alex can't make the estate work, we'll become nonentities like so many others. It scarcely seems important anymore. I remember there was a time after I recovered my memory when I spent long, frustrating hours debating whether I should return to Brianna and father a legitimate heir to the title, but with wife and children already, can you imagine the devastation I might have wreaked?"

Despite the rapidly growing darkness, Rory continued staring out the window. If he had known of estate and family in England, he would have done things differently than the earl, but it didn't pay to judge another until you'd walked in his shoes. He acknowledged the question with a polite nod. "Fate leads us down strange paths, I know. I wish you would reconsider your decision about Alyson's inheritance. I feel as if I came by it under false pretenses. It sits upon my shoulder like some great malevolent raven that I will never shake."

The earl chuckled again, thoroughly pleased by the Scotsman's dilemma. All that money sitting there waiting to be planted and tended and harvested, and all of it to be had from an English aristocrat. He clucked his amused sympathy.

"You shall just have to hand it over to Alyson, then. She seems perfectly capable of spending every cent without a qualm. I doubt that my father ever denied her anything."

Rory shuddered and shoved his hands deep in his coat pockets. About to turn back toward the room, he caught a small movement on the hill that held his idle interest. He watched for it again as he spoke. "That is the problem. I would prefer we live within my means, but I cannot bring myself to deny her the things she takes for granted. I am not a poor man, but my income must stretch to include my clan as well as this estate. That leaves very little for the comforts Alyson is accustomed to. So she learns to write to Farnley for what she wants, and scorns my meager offerings."

Cranville understood that he had just been given a very private glimpse of the normally closemouthed Scotsman his daughter had taken as husband. Very few men of his acquaintance would be troubled by a wife's overlarge dowry. He suspected there might be a little more to the story of this marriage than the unequal balances of wealth, but he could wait for the rest to unfold at its own pace.

"If Alyson's wealth is the only concern you have, count yourself a lucky man," he replied dryly, reaching for the decanter.

Rory's back stiffened as he found the movement along the dark hill again. It was no more than one blackness moving against a thicker blackness, but it was distinguishable enough to be discerned moving down the hill toward the house.

"Is there someone out there?" The Maclean's silence and rigid stance warned the earl of some change in the world outside.

"It's a bloody blizzard out there. The man must be mad."

Recollecting his own arrival more than a month ago, the earl could not in all conscience comment on this remark. Madness was come by easily in this environment.

Cursing as he realized the madman was leading a lamed horse straight toward the hidden dangers of the half-frozen burn, Rory strode from the room without noticing the earl's lack of reply.

Cranville contemplated the inviting decanter of claret sparkling in the firelight, then reluctantly followed the sight of Rory's broad back hastening out the door. It seemed a damned shame to waste all this warmth and comfort for an icy blast of snow and wind, but on the other hand, there was little enough to keep a man occupied around here. He rose from the comfortable chair to follow Rory through the hallway.

They came upon Alyson already struggling into boots and a fur-lined cloak, to the anxious protests of Myra. At sight of the two men, Myra flung up her hands in relief.

"Talk some sense into her. She swears there is someone out there, and it won't do but she go out to find him herself. As if anybody in his right mind would be out there. He would be frozen to a block of ice."

Rory snatched the bonnet from Alyson's hands and flung it to Myra. "Keep her here. I'll go."

Myra's eyes widened at this insane statement, but Alyson only looked at him calmly, giving him the information he could not possibly know. "It's my cousin. I can't tell if he's hurt, but there's something wrong. I don't want you to kill him."

Myra drew in a sharp breath and the earl looked exceedingly bewildered, but Rory only scowled at this seemingly impossible knowledge. "You don't even know how far away he is or where he is, and you would go out after him? Is his welfare more important than yours?"

Alyson had given the matter very little thought. She had simply seen the vision and reacted accordingly. Neither Myra nor her father would believe that she knew Alex was out there, but Rory didn't even question her. Already he was pulling on his greatcoat and gloves. She should have gone to him in the first place.

"Take someone with you, Rory." She ignored his harsh words in favor of this more important message.

"I'll go." Not understanding the hidden communication going on between husband and wife, the earl signaled for his outer garments nevertheless. How Alyson could possibly know that his heir was out in this blizzard, he could not fathom, but if Rory was going out after him, he would have to follow. The animosity between the two had become all too apparent over these last weeks.

Well-wrapped against the bitter wind, the two men

stepped out into the dying light of midafternoon. Alyson watched them go with fear, then hurried to seek a window where she could follow their progress. She still had nightmares of snowstorms and dark hills and Rory disappearing on horseback over the edge of that wicked cliff out there, but she had no premonition that this was the snowstorm to be feared. Rory would never take his animals out in weather like this. It would be quite foolhardy.

She found their dark figures staggering against the wind, the lanterns in their gloved hands blinking crazily as they swung between the flapping lengths of caped coats. She did not know how Rory knew which direction to take until she spied the man and horse limping down the snow-covered hillside. She held her breath as the trio of figures espied each other.

She could see the musket in Rory's hand. He must have taken it from the stable before heading up the hill. She shivered as her cousin reached for something on the horse's saddle. She wanted to scream at their foolishness, but screams would be futile in stopping the silent tableau out there. She could only pray that one of them would recover his senses sufficiently to stay his hand.

Outside, the earl caught the Maclean's arm, keeping him from lifting the weapon. The howl of the wind made conversation impossible, but he shouted a furious command as Rory shook off his hold and lifted the firearm. Rory dodged the earl's blow as the older man tried to knock aside his aim. The musket fired, spewing the smell of sulfur, shattering the snow-deadened silence with its explosion.

The man on the far hill stepped backward, shaken, until it became apparent the shot was not aimed at him. Water rushed from the hole in the ice only yards down the path he had set himself on. The layers of snow and thin ice would never have held the weight of both man and horse. Weakly he leaned against his animal and waited for the lantern bearers to show him the safest route.

Minutes later, forced by the wind and exertion into silence, the men traveled down the dangerous rock-strewn path of the hillside to the safety of the stone tower near the cliff's edge. None mentioned the beacon of light in the upper-story window where a lone figure stood waiting patiently for their return. Each man was aware of Alyson's presence in his own separate manner.

By the time they reached the front door, the hall fire had been fed to blazing and warm blankets and hot toddies were waiting. As servants scurried to remove soaked coats and boots, the three men regarded each other warily and in continuing silence. Alyson's entrance focused their attention in a different direction.

Garbed in a loose, rich maroon wool that trailed behind her in a ripple of stiff petticoats that disguised the extent of her pregnancy, Alyson appeared as some royal princess amid the threadbare tapestries and tarnished halberds of the towering keep. Her thick black curls untamed by pomatum and barely restrained by the combs used to keep it in place, she appeared a throwback in time, a Highland princess more than an English one. Only the calm, undisturbed smoothness of her porcelain features revealed the lack of royal hauteur. She welcomed them as if they had strolled in from an afternoon's walk.

Waiting until warm slippers had been found for Rory's feet, she took his arm and steered him toward the roaring warmth of the fire. Chairs and tables had already been arranged for their comfort near enough to be warm and not roasted. Remembering his role as host, Rory gestured for his guest to precede him.

No introductions had yet been made, and although immediately suspicious of the elegant older man, the new arrival bowed respectfully and allowed him to pass first. This display of good manners brought a condescending smile. Everett, the third Earl of Cranville, preceded Alex, his heir, into the soaring great hall of the old keep.

Alyson smiled at the incongruous sight of her father's old-fashioned elegance in long buckram-stiffened silks and red heels and her cousin's stylish velvets, stiff cravat, and plain stockings against the backdrop of the medieval hall. Only Rory in his open shirt and old worsted loose coat appeared at home here, and that was probably because in her mind she saw him with the tartan over his shoulder that he had worn at Christmas. Out of deference to the earl, he had not worn it since, but he walked as if he wore this insignia of his title and position. Ignoring the steaming mugs of punch, he poured himself a dram of whisky before making the introductions.

Alyson settled her skirts on a settee out of the firelight as Rory curtly spoke the words introducing the newly titled Earl of Cranville to the rightful claimant to the title.

After the words were said, Alex Hampton made a mocking bow to the graying older man now seated before him. "Very well done, I must say. It had not occurred to me that Maclean would also wish to usurp the few beggarly things remaining to me by retaining an impostor. Very clever, indeed. Shall I return to Cornwall to find myself locked out of my own house?"

"Damned insolent pup, if you were there where you belonged, you would know, wouldn't you? Damme if I don't believe Maclean is right. My heir is not only a fool, but a damned impertinent one at that."

Everett Hampton crossed his arms and watched the curl of scorn on his heir's face. He remembered that expression well. The boy's father had employed it with great effect when issuing challenges or setting down any rabble happening across his path. Arrogant, obstinate, opinionated to a fault—a man of his time, beyond a doubt.

Rory took a seat with his back to the fire. His curiosity demanded to know what had brought his nemesis here in a blinding storm, but he could wait while the two men took each other's measure. Watching the two Englishmen go for each other's throats might make an interesting spectator sport.

"Out of respect for your age and my hostess, sir, I'll not call you out for those insults. I have come with a message for my cousin and her husband, not to duel with an old fool."

The earl grew livid with rage, and setting aside his mug, began to rise. A gentle hand touched his shoulder, holding him back. None had noticed her rise, but now Alyson's presence filled their senses. The faint scent of spring drifted around them, and her musical voice filled their ears, although not with songs of peace.

"Alex, for once be sensible instead of hasty. Rory and I have no need of your estates and would not go to such lengths as to hire an impostor. This is my father, returned from Barbados apparently by the vicious rumors you planted all over the island about me. Had you held your tongue, he might never have returned and none would be the wiser that you are not the rightful earl. As it is, you would do well to listen before you spoil your chances of ever seeing Cornwall again. Can you not see the resemblance to the portrait in the main drawing room?"

Alex stared at her in mockery and incredulity. "I thought you had some modicum of sense, little cousin, but if you believe this faradiddle, you are as great a fool as you look. You would take some faint resemblance to an ancient portrait as proof positive that this man is your father? Isn't it odd that he does not happen along until you are worth a king's ransom?" He turned to Rory with equal scorn. "Surely you have sense enough to see the convenience of his disguise? I can only believe you play along with him for nefarious purposes."

The earl patted Alyson's hand reassuringly when it tightened in anger upon his shoulder. "I can see why you did not take a liking to him on first sight, dear. I've not seen such arrogance since his father announced he could drink every man in White's under the table and did. Drinking was certainly a poor talent to cultivate, but he did it exceedingly well, while he lasted. I suppose you have cultivated equally useless talents?" He directed this last to his handsome heir. The man definitely had the dark good looks of the more favored Hampton side of the family. It must have irritated that petite blond mother of his to find he so resembled his rakehell father.

Alex fingered the hilt of his sword. "I am accounted a fair swordsman, sir. Would you care to try me?"

"As to that, I'll let the Maclean settle those differences. I daresay he is quite proficient with that broadsword of his, and he seems to have good reason for taking arms against you. I myself prefer fencing with words. Do you remember aught of your father?"

Alex scowled and took a large drink from his mug. "I was but a child when he died. I doubt if his visits to the nursery were frequent."

"No, they wouldn't be. So I cannot convince you with a word picture of his mien and manner. It seems we have little in common, then. You will have to accept Farnley's witness that I am the man who left these shores twenty years ago. My signature has not changed much, and I should think old acquaintances might recognize me still, despite the graying hairs. In the meantime, you will simply have to take my word for it."

Alex slammed his mug down and rose to glare at Rory. "I don't have to take this. I came here because I had some foolish notion that I still owed Alyson my protection. Now that I can see she has found a home with villains, I can only assume she can take care of herself. I bid you good day, then."

As he turned to march out, his path was intercepted by a soft round figure in jewel colors who could have stepped from one of the tapestries adorning the paneled walls. The gray mist of her eyes hid her thoughts, but her beauty held him in place. Why had he never seen the ethereal quality of her loveliness before?

Rory instantly materialized behind her, making his protection evident. Alex gave him a scornful glance. "Unlike you, I do not take advantage of a woman's weakness. She will come to no harm by me. That was why I came."

"I can give evidence of a different sort, but that is an old argument." Alyson spoke softly but with great emphasis. "You are my cousin and my father's heir. I cannot send you out into the storm. Sit, both of you." This command applied to the man at her back as well as the devil before her.

Their gazes met briefly over her head. Neither man being completely free of guilt, they acquiesced to this small request. The hostility between them was a tangible thing that electrified the air around them, but Alyson's presence acted as buffer, absorbing the currents without radiating them.

She gazed with curiosity at Alex, the man she had pictured as the monster who had driven her from her home and bedeviled her life ever since. No longer alone, but safe in the security of father and husband, she could see he was naught but a man. True, he was a large man, one of powerful breadth and muscular grace that were frightening to one such as herself, but she did not find evil in his dark eyes. Licentiousness, perhaps, overindulgence, certainly, but not evil. She frowned as he met her perusal with arrogant amusement.

"Your wickedness will bring you to the same end as

your father if you do not change your ways, cousin," she
answered his look curtly. "You are bold and fearless in
the eyes of the world, but inside, you are alone and
terrified of it. Now, tell me your message, and I will have
a room prepared for you. We will be eating shortly. You
may join us or not, as you wish."

Rory watched this confrontation between the cousins
with interest. Alyson had once been so terrified of this
young giant that she had literally grown speechless in his
presence. She had run from him in terror for months,
accepting his own dubious company rather than return to
Hampton. Now she stood up to him as if she had never
suffered a moment's fear. He was not at all certain that
was wise, but he kept his countenance.

"At least you are listening instead of screaming, for a
change. I think I'll take advantage of the silence to offer
the apologies I have tried to give often enough before.
There is no excuse for my behavior, and I will give none.
If you will accept that I was a desperate man who acted
ignobly but never meant you any harm, I will beg your
forgiveness and ask for a truce, however temporary."

Alex ignored Rory and the earl, speaking only to Alyson.
He wasn't certain he could trust her more than the other
two, but if he were to make things right, he had to start
somewhere. No one could believe less than innocence
from a face like that.

Alyson sat in the chair between her father and Rory.
"I have forgiven worse, I suppose, for what it is worth.
You are the one who must forgive himself. However, the
truce will be temporary unless there is trust. I tell you
this is my father, and Drummond is my enemy. If you
cannot believe these things, we will never hear each
other."

Alex sighed, sent her a puzzled look, and met Rory's
stoic expression. How did the man suffer this woman's
wayward thinking all the time? Still, with wealth and
beauty to balance out, it might be endurable. Barely. He
noticed a slightly sardonic smirk beginning to curl the
Scotsman's lip when he made no immediate reply, and,
curious, he returned his gaze to his fey cousin.

"I'll believe Drummond is your enemy. That is why
I'm here. As much as I despise your husband's tactics,
they do not seem to include harming women and chil-

dren. Drummond may have a right to protect what is his, but when he threatens your welfare, I cannot support him." He threw Rory a grudging look. "And since you have at least made an honest woman of her and magnanimously paid my debts, I owe you a debt I can repay with this warning. Drummond intends to draw you out with some atrocity that will bring you and your men running. I cannot know his exact plans, for he has the cunning of a madman, but it is certain he means to kill you and take Alyson hostage against any reprisals. You may know more of his habits than I, but I have come to believe his drinking has pushed him over some edge between protecting his own and destroying what belongs to others. He has not a gentle way with women."

The aristocratic gentleman across from him spoke before Rory could put his thoughts to words. "Alyson is a lady of quality. No English gentleman would harm her. I think it is likely that it is your own drinking that has muddled the problem here."

Alex lifted his mug in a mocking gesture and drained the contents. "Care to join me, old man? I take after my father in that. I can drink you under the table and still remember everything you said and did. It's a curse, actually. I would prefer to disclaim many things I have done as the result of drunkenness or forget that I had done them the next day. You are a trifle out of touch with the times, sir. English gentlemen hurt ladies all the time, but so as to offend your sensibilities roundly, I will tell you Drummond does not consider Alyson a lady. She is married to his notorious cousin, after all."

That would not be the only reason she was not considered a lady, but Alex did not need to mention that in her presence. Her father had already learned it the hard way. He glared at his heir. "Then perhaps it is time I speak with this mad friend of yours. There seems to be some misapprehension about the circumstances of Alyson's birth. She is quite legitimate, you know. Had she been fortunate enough to be male, she would be my heir, not you."

Alex choked in outrage at this extraordinary announcement, and Rory allowed himself the semblance of a grin as he reached for Alyson's hand.

"Personally, I feel quite fortunate she was not born male. Mayhap neither of you has been around long enough to appreciate that fact." He shifted his gaze to Hampton. "I thank you for your warning. It would be better discussed at another time, however. Alyson has enough strange notions without our playing upon them."

Alyson sent him an irritated glance. "You cannot keep these things from me, Rory. You know you can't. It only scares me more when I don't know what to expect, or when to expect it. I'd rather be prepared."

Rory stood and firmly pulled her from the chair. "You are prepared. You are safe within a stone fortress that Drummond cannot breach, and you have a husband who is wise to his ways. He cannot harm us, lass. Now, go lie down awhile before we eat. There is no sense in getting yourself upset over nothing."

His hands were warm upon hers, his gaze reassuring, and Alyson did not fight his judgment. She knew Rory was strong and capable. Perhaps her vision was meaningless. She had misinterpreted visions before. But she knew the men beside her did not have her confidence in her husband's abilities, and they would need that confidence were they ever to work together.

She smiled and reached to kiss his bristly cheek. "Just promise not to take up sword against my father and cousin while I am gone. Three generals and no army can cause confusion."

For her trust he would like to take her in his arms and cover her with kisses, but in the company of her family, Rory did not feel the freedom to do so. He still felt the need to prove himself to her father. This he would do better without Alyson near to reveal his one weakness. He watched her go, unaware his expression clearly gave away what he would hide. He turned to find his father-in-law regarding him thoughtfully, and Hampton with amusement.

Scowling, he threw himself back in the chair. With his thick brows drawn down over his nose, Rory's square-boned face turned from one English aristocrat to the other. Generals, indeed. These men knew nothing of the animosity and dangers bred in these hills. Were it not for Alyson, he would be better off sending them away.

Before either earl or heir could speak, Rory lifted his glass of whisky and asked, "Can either of you wield a broadsword?"

34

In the weeks that followed, an uneasy truce developed among the three men in Alyson's life. All three were men of independence, highly opinionated, and accustomed to giving orders and not taking them. At times Alyson thought it might be easier to invite Drummond to join them to put an end to the tension. The old walls seemed to strain with the intensity of the tempers building up inside. Only the fact that the weather cleared, allowing daily escape, prevented the explosion that seemed inevitable.

Holding her hand to the heavy weight of the burden that stretched her endurance further with each passing day, Alyson carefully took one step after another down the narrow stone stairs. Soon it would be April. She did not know what the month of spring brought to these cold hills, but she knew of one burgeoning forth that would come of it. It could not come too soon for her wishes. Rory's child was as restless as the man who bred him.

Passing in the hall below, Dougall looked up to see her easing down the stairs, and he frowned before hurrying to help her. "I thought you were told to stay upstairs and out of trouble, my lady. Myra will have my head if she finds I've aided your escape."

The dreamy look he remembered well from the ship passed across Alyson's face. It was there more often than not these days as she waited for the child's arrival. She gave him that heart-stopping smile and continued down the stairs.

"The sun shines, Dougall. I would feel it for myself. Where is everyone?"

By "everyone," he knew whom she meant, and he grinned despite himself. "The earl and his heir have been persuaded from a target shoot to join the Maclean in a fishing expedition. I believe he thought the targets might otherwise become each other or himself.''

Alyson laughed, a melodic sound that drew the attention of all within hearing. The tempers of those trapped within the confinement of these crumbling walls by the weather for so long would have flared long ago, without the need of the explosive friction among the three men. Only Alyson's laugh and gentle ways had soothed ragged nerves and straining emotions. She never seemed to bear any direct influence on anyone or anything, but just the sight of her floating by, giving a smile of pleasure at some particularly well-done job, speaking cheerful words to those she passed, or laughing as she did now, brought smiles to those around her. It was difficult to fuss and fight when everyone was smiling, and none could frown for long in her presence.

They were more accepting of her fey ways than the suspicious Cornish servants in her father's home, and Alyson responded to this easier atmosphere by opening up more and drifting away less. Even now, when all her attention was centered on this living being she carried, she still managed to comment with pleasure on how Mary's new gown made her cheeks pinker, and compliment the steward on the job done of cleaning the tapestries. If she occasionally walked by people without seeing them, they were careful to make certain she came to no harm, and otherwise stayed out of her way until she noticed them again.

Reaching the hall on Dougall's arm, Alyson espied the starched figure of Rory's newly arrived bailiff hurrying toward the back of the house. Montrose had arrived one particularly brisk day with his wig askew from the wind and his formal black coat rumpled from the ride but his dignity unruffled. He and Rory had immediately retired to the study to converse, and the man had been busy ever since. Well aware that this was the man whose tales had sent Rory into a drunken rage, precipitating his marriage, Alyson regarded him with some awe.

"Someday, someone must tell me what a bailiff does," she mused aloud.

Knowing full well that this particular bailiff spent his time manipulating an estate not belonging to his employer, Dougall made no reply. Drummond was a lazy manager and too tight with his limited funds to hire any kind of overseer. He employed a few rough rogues to collect the rents, but they cared little for the condition of the property. Drummond's tenants found it increasingly easy to turn to a familiar face when Montrose rode up. Come next fall, they would pay their rents to the man who repaired their houses. By that time Rory would have enough men and resources to prevent Drummond's men from collecting a farthing. Dougall only prayed that this patient plan would force Drummond to sell peacefully. He rather expected the opposite.

"The sun is bright, but it is still cold. You will need something warm on if you mean to go outside." Dougall halted near the cloakroom off the hall.

"Will it ever be warm again?" Alyson sighed as he helped her don her fur-lined cloak.

"Aye, lass, soon enough. This is a bad winter you're seeing this year. There should be good weather to follow. It is not always thus."

"Good. Is there someone hereabouts who can tell me what flowers we might order for planting? It is all very well to prepare kitchen gardens and fields, but I should like a little beauty along with the practicality, if I could."

"I know naught of such things, my lady, but Mary seems to know most of your tenants. Shall I send her to you?"

"Would you, Dougall? I would appreciate that. I'll be just outside." Relieved not to have to carry her bulk the length of the keep to the kitchen and back, Alyson adjusted her hood around her face and stepped out the door Dougall opened for her.

She was unaccustomed to constant confinement. It seemed exceedingly tedious to always be sitting behind four walls. She wanted to run and jump and sit in the grass and watch the clouds overhead. But the child who had once done that was long gone. Briefly, remembering another sunny day, she wondered how Alan Tremaine fared. How silly she had been to think what she felt for him was love! It hadn't even been lust. More likely boredom, she supposed. Thank heaven Rory had come along to show her how it could be between men and women. Gazing down at the awkward stomach preceding her, Alyson had to laugh at her thoughts. Rory had

taught her all manner of wondrous things. She wouldn't
trade a minute of their nights together for the ability to
run and jump like a child again. She had discovered a
woman's pleasures.

Mary came hastening out of the house, her wool cloak
flapping in the wind as she hurried down the path to her
employer's side. Alyson watched her with curiosity. The
distraught woman who had arrived months ago had not
totally lost the haunted look behind her eyes, but her
gaunt flesh was beginning to fill out, and although her
manner was often harsh and bitter, Alyson sensed it hid a
kind heart. She smiled as the other woman reached her
side.

"On days like this, my thoughts turn to flowers. Do
yours?"

Mary and Alyson were much the same age, but of
widely different experience. Mary gazed jealously at her
employer's burgeoning figure and shook her head. "My
thoughts are of wool bonnets and thick stockings. You
should be resting before the fire, making those pretty
lace things for the babe."

'I'll do that when the skies grow gray again. Show me
to someone who knows of flowers."

They walked down the rocky path together, heedless
of the clouds hidden behind the crest of the hill.

As the wind changed and the cold blew down from the
mountain, bringing with it the heavy clouds portending
worse weather to follow, Rory signaled an end to their
fishing. So hungry was he that he could almost taste the
delicate flesh seeped in butter and wine as he flung the
day's catch into a basket. He could eat half the catch
himself, and ought to, for all the others had done to help
him bring it in.

He grinned as his noble guests struggled wearily up the
hill after him. Had they spent less of their time arguing
and more mending their nets, they might have caught
more. Not until they had reached some amicable resolu-
tion after almost overturning the dinghy had they settled
down to catch anything at all. How Alex could not see
his kinship with the opinionated earl was beyond Rory's
ken. He had never doubted the relationship between
father and daughter since that first night, and the one

between the two men was even stronger. It wasn't just the structure of their bones, but the structure of their minds—inflexible to a harrowing degree.

Entering the keep, Rory surrendered his basket and gear to a waiting servant and glanced around eagerly as his guests discarded their outer coats. Alyson usually materialized whenever he arrived, and he could not help but feel disappointment that she did not do so now, when he was feeling so triumphant. Of course, she was supposed to be resting, and Myra had forbidden the use of the stairs, but that had not stopped her before.

Rather than embarrass himself by asking after his wife in front of his guests, Rory made some excuse to go to his study. He bounded up the stairs two at a time, eager just to have a moment's word with her before tackling the challenge of the long evening with his argumentative guests. He could wish they would go elsewhere to settle their differences, but they didn't seem inclined to believe he could adequately protect Alyson. There were times he felt a prisoner of their scrutiny, but Alyson relieved all that. He smiled as he threw open the bedchamber door.

The smile disappeared in puzzlement when he found the chamber empty. If she hadn't come downstairs to greet him and she wasn't sleeping, where the hell was she? Rory caught himself as he was about to rage down the stairs in search of her. He didn't own Alyson. She had every right to go her own way without waiting on him hand and foot. It had been his possessiveness that had caused the first disaster of their marriage. Alyson was an intelligent, mature woman who had a way of taking care of things herself. She didn't need him to follow her around.

Repeating these things over and over to himself, he calmly returned to the hall to join his guests in a brandy. Alyson would appear in her own sweet time.

Instead, Myra came to the door a while later as the first flickers of snow began to drift past the window. By this time Dougall and Montrose had joined them, and all five men glanced up at her unexpected appearance.

Nervously, she first sought her husband's gaze, but seeing only his perplexity, she looked to Rory. "I need to ask Lady Maclean about something. I thought perhaps she had joined you. I apologize for intruding."

Rory's anxieties immediately leapt to the forefront again, and he came to his feet at once. "I thought she was with you. Has she not returned to her room to dress for dinner?"

Myra shook her head. "I was just there. I thought her sleeping, but the bed has not been touched."

Dougall paled and set aside his glass. "She went out earlier with Mary to visit one of the tenants, something about flowers, I believe. I thought she'd returned by now. She couldn't have gone far."

Rory was already striding across the massive hall. "Which tenant?"

Dougall hurried after him, followed with some reluctance by the others. "I don't know. One who knows about flowers, they said."

Rory cursed and grabbed the coat Myra hastened to bring to him. "Who knows about flowers?" This question he shot at Myra, who regarded him blankly.

"I'll ask in the kitchen," she hurriedly replied when his scowl grew blacker.

"What is the meaning of this, Maclean?" Alex asked laconically, still idly swinging his glass in one hand. "Is Alyson kept prisoner here, and not allowed out without special permission?"

Dougall caught Rory's shoulder and held him back before his fear and anger could fly out in the fist now clenched at his side. With contempt, Rory turned away from Alyson's cousin to pull on the boots he had just discarded minutes before. Dougall was the one to offer explanations as well as he could.

"There's a storm moving in, and it will be dark before the half-hour is out. Alyson does not know her way around yet, and it is easy even for those familiar with the land to be lost when dark falls. Mary knows better than to allow her to stay this late."

This last stated the case as clearly as he dared. If Alyson had refused to leave when told, Mary should have come back here to warn them. Mary knew the dangers of these hills even if Alyson did not; that was why Dougall had sent her. If neither woman returned, there was a good possibility something beyond tardiness was at hand.

Quietly the earl observed the troubled expressions on

the faces of the two men born and bred here and came to his own conclusions. "Is there anything we can do, Maclean? I've found the road in the dark before; I can do it again."

Rory nodded. "Take that way, then. There are only two cottages between here and the river. She could not have gone farther than that. Come back here when you are done." He looked up as Myra hurried toward them, leading one of the kitchen scrub maids.

"Peg says there is someone by the name of Crandall living up one of the hollows, who grows flowers and herbs." Myra held the nervous child by the shoulder as Rory's dark gaze fell on her.

"Crandall?" He turned to Montrose. "One of our Crandalls? I thought you told me . . ."

The older man nodded hastily. " 'Tis the younger. The cottage was empty and in poor repair, but Drummond knows nothing of it, since it is across the boundary. She's been hiding there since late last summer. Her sister went on to Glasgow, it is said. I don't know how she survives."

"You know where it is, then?" Rory stood and reached for his hat, ready to be off.

"Not far." Montrose hesitated, searching the laird's frozen face. The bailiff took a deep breath and continued. "You know where this boundary meets Drummond's along the cliff's edge?" He saw Rory's weathered face go pale beneath the darkened skin. "There is a hollow, barely more than a crevasse there. Do ye not remember it? That ancient but-and-ben built into the hill?"

Gaining a grip on his rioting emotions, Rory jerked on his hat and swung for the door. "You and Dougall send men out to the nearest cottages to make certain they did not stop elsewhere. Everyone report back here when you're done."

"Wait a minute, Maclean, what about me?" Alex set his glass aside and grabbed a coat held out by one of the servants.

Rory turned and gave him a look of disdain. "You can go visit Drummond and make certain she's not found her way there."

That put the fear in every heart that had already found its way into Rory's. Without looking for his boots, Alex hurried out the door after his host.

*   *   *

Mary muffled a scream as the dark horseman appeared out of the cloud, his cape blowing wildly in the icy wind rushing off the mountains. They had waited late to leave, and their progress had been slow because of Alyson's weary pace. There would have been light enough had the cloud not descended, obscuring the path and all familiar landmarks. Even now, she could find her way in the dark if she must, were it not for this obstacle rising up out of the mist. Mary knew that silhouette too well—and had reason to fear it.

Stepping in front of Alyson, she whispered hurriedly, "Go back, milady. Hide in the broom until he is gone. He won't see you in this mist."

Already the snow was falling, tiny pellets that cut like razors against unprotected flesh. Alyson hugged her cloak closer against the whistling wind and gazed at the apparition forming out of the snow and cold. She had learned better than to run when fate arrived. This time, she had not strength left for running. The wordless terror she felt as the apparition took on the form of a man nearly exceeded the ache shooting through her spine and legs.

"What have we here? Fair maidens lost in the storm?" The voice was filled with good humor as the man led his horse closer.

"Not lost, nearly home," Mary spat out between clenched teeth, keeping herself between the laird's lady and the devil.

"I think not," the man mused, coming closer to better observe the two figures huddled against the background of boulders. "This is a long way from any habitation on a night like this. I think I better escort you. It is a good thing for you I am late returning from my ride."

Alyson scarcely heard his words. She had no need to. She could feel them, and they felt like evil. They felt like the terror of her vision. She backed closer to the rocks, wishing she could somehow disappear into their grayness.

"There's someone coming for us. We don't need you." Mary let her cloak blow like wings away from her, concealing her ladyship from wicked eyes. She knew those eyes would find herself, but she could fight. The lady couldn't.

The man's gaze sought the full length of the woman's

curves, recognizing something in their frozen defiance. She was still little more than a bundle of bones, but he had always admired her graceful height. His grin appeared in his reply. "I beg to differ with you. If I remember rightly, I have a score to settle with you. I can think of a pleasant way of making it even. Bring your friend along. We'll be warm, and the night outside promises to be an unpleasant one."

As he reached for her, Mary grasped the hilt of the skian dubh hidden in her waistband beneath her apron. "Go *now*, milady," she whispered fiercely as the dagger's silver point glistened briefly.

The man dodged as Mary threw herself at him, but his scream of rage was sufficient to send Alyson fleeing down the hillside in search of Rory. She had no weapon and no strength. Only her fleetness of foot and words could save Mary.

She had known she never had a chance, but she could not have done otherwise. Just as she knew the child was coming, and she could not stop it, so did she have to run, even though she knew she could gain only a few steps.

She heard the sound of Mary's cry as the man slammed his fist into her. She did not turn to see Mary crumple to the ground. She could hear his footsteps close behind, and then her toe hit upon a rock and she slid in the already deepening snow. As she fell, a hard arm came around her, and the evil in his laughter filled her senses as the pain washed over and under her and blackness descended.

The cold woke Alyson sometime later. Her toes were nearly numb with cold, sending icy prickles up her leg to meet the fiery pains shooting down them. She groaned and tried to lean back to ease the ache in her middle, but a hard obstacle prevented movement. The obstacle shifted slightly, and she realized the binding beneath her breasts was an arm. Fear gradually filtered in to accompany her discomfort as she realized her wrists were bound in front of her.

As she tried to move away from the padded shoulder behind her head, the arm tightened and an impatient voice spoke. "One move, and I'll fling you over the cliff. My side hurts like hell, and I'm in no humor to consider your delicate condition."

She didn't know the voice, but she knew to whom it had to belong. Few men out here owned horses as immense as the one they were seated on. Even Rory favored a sturdy pony on these hills to a fragile-boned thoroughbred. And no other man would have attacked Mary and then held the laird's wife in this blizzard, waiting for someone or something.

With amazing clarity, Alyson realized whom he was waiting for and why. Shivering, she tried to speak. "He doesn't know I'm here. Take me home, and my father will see that you are rewarded handsomely."

That drew a muffled laugh. "Save that for your knight-errant coming up the path. I'm no fool." Drawing something from an inner pocket with his free hand, he pushed it against her lips. "Open up like a good girl. I don't need any screams distracting his attention too soon."

Alyson resisted the soft folds of the handkerchief, clamping her teeth shut and struggling against her captor's iron hold. She tried to scream through clenched teeth, tried to warn whoever was approaching, but the sound came out too muffled to be heard through the wind. When he finally pried her lips open, she bit his hand and hung on with a death grip, but the cloth went down her throat and she gagged.

His curses quickly silenced at the sound of hoofbeats coming closer, and his hand left her mouth to reach for a rifle hung beside his saddle. Alyson screamed in earnest then, attempting to bring her bound hands to her mouth to remove the cloth. Drummond's arm held hers in place and she couldn't lift them, couldn't scream loud enough or long enough to reach the ears of the rider below.

In terror she watched as a horseman rounded the curve at a mad pace and the rifle bore raised to take casual aim. Surely he couldn't aim with any accuracy like that, she told herself wildly, struggling to overset his grip. But as she realized their position and the direction of the road, she knew he didn't have to aim closely. The rocky ledge beyond would take care of whatever the rifle missed. Hysterically, she screamed again and again as the rider appeared out of the snow, just as in her nightmare.

35

The shot echoed through the howling wind, nearly un-heard against the forces of nature. The recoil from the explosion jerked Alyson back against her captor, but her eyes sought only the lone figure riding along the path. Through the blinding snow she could see the horse rear in eerie silence. The rider pitched forward, and the pair swiftly disappeared over the edge of the cliff. Her screams died in her throat.

Without another sound, she gave herself over to the pain and numbness creeping over her unwieldy body. As the man behind her triumphantly sent his mount into a canter, the pain became her only knowledge that she still lived. Her soul had gone over the cliff with Rory.

Alex reined in his horse in a rare moment of indeci-sion. He had no doubt that it was Drummond's weapon that had fired the shot, but he could not see the man from this angle. What he could see was the laird flying over a cliff and disappearing into the blizzard. Whether Alyson was with him or Drummond or still lost, he could not say with any degree of certainty.

Reluctantly he halted his horse instead of chasing after the sound of retreating hoofbeats. If there were any chance the Maclean could be saved, he must take it. He always knew where to find Drummond later.

Cautiously he approached the rocky edge where the horse had gone over. The hillside swept down to the coast below, but unlike his home, it was covered in ragged bunches of stiff gorse sprouting from between sloping layers of rock below the jutting boulder of the cliff's edge. Man or animal caught off-balance would tumble and crash and be dead of injuries before reaching the bottom. The snow blowing in Alex's eyes made it difficult to see, but daylight had not entirely faded, and the hill blocked the worst of the wind. If his eyes were not completely deceived, the horse was standing upright, if anything could be said to stand upright in these damned hills. That did not mean the rider had survived the fall.

Before he could attempt to find a way over the edge, a strange specter rose out of the blowing snow and staggered toward him. Not one given to superstitious fears, Hampton still had to think twice before realizing the ghostly black wings were the flaps of an old cloak. Then, as he remembered that Alyson had been with the tall maid, his heart lodged in his throat. Never before had he cared enough about anyone to worry. He was paying for that lack tenfold now.

"Milord, he's got her, he's got the lady. Help her, please, help her."

The gaunt woman caught at his arm for support, and he could see that she was injured. Fear tightened around the small remaining space of his heart. "Drummond?" he inquired, as if he needed to be told.

"Aye, milord. I tried to stop him. The dirk went in, but he's a devil and willna die. I've tried to tell them, but they willna listen. You need stakes and fires for that one. Save her, milord. Angels know nothing of such."

Oddly, Alex felt no surprise as the horse he had just seen go over the cliff now appeared behind the spectral maid, led by a man he'd felt certain must be dead or gravely injured. In this damned Highland landscape, anything seemed possible. When the apparition spoke, his words made as much sense as anything else that had happened.

"Devils can't touch angels, Mary. We'll have her back, you'll see. Now, come along. We'll be back to the keep now."

The soft burr of Rory's lilting voice calmed the hysterical woman, and she silently accepted his assistance into the saddle. Hampton stared at his host as if he were the one crazed.

"You're going back? That bastard has just ridden off with your wife, and you're going back to the comforts of home? I never liked you, Maclean, but I never thought you a coward." He swung onto his horse and turned it in the direction Drummond had taken.

"Suit yourself." Rory shrugged. "Just don't get in the

way when my men arrive. They'll not know you from your friend."

Spitting expletives at this implied threat, Alex reared his horse around and followed the damned laird back to his keep. His men, indeed! He had been told the Highlands clung to primitive customs, but he felt as if he had just been flung back into feudal times, when lords called their tenants to war. He wished he had a suit of armor.

The scene in the great hall a little later was as medieval as anything Alex could desire. Men poured silently out of the blinding blizzard to enter the open hall doors, summoned by some mysterious call he had yet to discern. Torches were passed around and brandished like clubs. Outlawed swords and halberds and hatchets were removed from the walls, where they had been preserved through the actions of their English owner. Here and there a man could be seen wrapped in his tattered tartan from better days. Even Rory, once his injuries had been seen to, came out sporting the plaid of war he had been given instead of a frock coat, and Alex shuddered at the ferocity firing his dark face.

Murder was written on the face of every man in the hall as the tale of the lady's kidnapping was passed from mouth to ear. Knives bristled from boot tops and belts. To Alex's amazement, he watched as the idle old man who claimed the title of Cranville fastened on a broadsword beneath his English-tailored redingote. Never had he seen a more incongruous sight, but his own blood boiled for the combat to come as he read the fury in the eyes of these courageous mountain dwellers. Fury, he could understand, and he willingly joined them.

They marched or rode according to their means, spreading out across the hills with torches flaring. As they walked, others came to join them, signaled by the flaring lamps in the watchtower. Alex turned to gaze over his shoulder at the strategic location of the keep upon a hill at the cliff's edge. Even through the blinding snow those lanterns could be seen beaming through the darkness, a feudal call to arms. The response to Rory's signal was overwhelming.

The laird led his ragtag army calmly, oblivious of the impossibility of his task. Men couldn't ride out of the hills to storm castles anymore. His Majesty had forbidden wars and weapons, and his wrath would be great.

But Rory sat his horse like a medieval warrior, a wool hat pulled down over his forehead to protect his face, the vivid tartan acting as a flag at the head of the throng, and not a sign of worry or fear on his square, stern face, although his stiff stance revealed some hint of the extent of his injuries. Alex glanced at the savage men pouring around him like a flood and decided he was glad he had changed sides. He didn't want to be with Drummond when this mob knocked at the front door.

Not that anybody intended to knock. With the tenants of two estates up in arms, the servants at Stagshead swiftly disappeared into the darkness, many to join the army marching over the once manicured lawns. Men took up pitchforks and hoes, and women grabbed kitchen knives and pokers. The rent collectors Drummond had hired found it convenient to disappear into the woodwork when faced with the threatening faces of the people they had ridden roughshod over these last years. For centuries the Macleans had followed their laird at his call. They did not fail him now.

Inside the mansion, Drummond heard the deepening silence and began to grow restless. His shouts for a maid had gone unheard, and he had bound the wound in his side by himself. The servants had been increasingly lax of late, but not to the extent of totally ignoring him. He kicked at the peat in the dying fire and irritably considered going to look for someone to build it up again. His side ached abominably, and he didn't have the desire to do it himself. After Cranville left, he really should have returned to London. But he hated to leave unfinished business, and London was so devilish expensive. Now that the Maclean was dead, tremendous possibilities opened, and he felt safe to leave this desolate ruin for civilization.

In the silence of the empty rooms, he could hear a muffled whimper from above, and he scowled. He should have left her gagged. It had seemed amusing to take her hostage to prevent any kind of reprisal. He was even considering marrying her now that she was a wealthy widow. Wouldn't that infuriate Cranville? He chuckled at the thought of the earl's face when he had mentioned these plans for the heiress just before Cranville left. She was comely enough and her fortune wasn't to be laughed at. All he had to do was wait for her to rid herself of the babe and carry her off to London. She'd learn to come around soon enough. She wouldn't have any choice.

He fidgeted as the sound abovestairs grew louder. It seemed the babe might appear at any time. He knew nothing of women giving birth, but she had looked pretty pale when he placed her on the bed. He didn't have to worry about her trying to escape anytime soon, at least. Maybe he ought to unbind her wrists. If he could find one of the wretched maids, maybe he should send one up to her. Or mayhap she was just mad and making those sounds for naught. Who could tell?

Visibly annoyed now, Drummond threw his empty bottle at the blackened fireplace and set out to find the servants. If he whipped a few of them, they wouldn't dare desert him like this again.

He stalked down the spacious marble-tiled hall, past the gilded drawing room, the chandeliered dining hall, the book-lined study, and the paneled game room. The Maclean mansion was of recent vintage, built after the end of the border wars, and still unfinished in many places. The rebellion had interrupted the construction, and only Drummond's intervention had prevented it from being destroyed, as the homes of so many Jacobites had been. He'd never had the wealth to complete the work, but it suited his purposes as it was.

Only now he could see the practical function of the fortress of stone that had once served the Macleans as castle and home. He wished they had provided something of that protection here. Although the fire still burned in the kitchen grate, not a servant was in sight. The bedrooms and servants' hall behind the kitchen were equally deserted. His footsteps echoed hollow against the wooden floors as he retraced his path to the front of the house. On instinct, he pulled back the heavy draperies concealing the wide bank of windows overlooking what once would have been the park. What he saw made him wish for the narrow barred windows of a keep.

Torches illuminated the shadows of men streaming up the hillside. Some were already coming around the house from the direction of the stables. Others approached along the carriage drive. It did not take long to discern the shapes of pitchforks and muskets, and he could imagine what the others carried. For the first time in his life, Drummond felt true, gut-wrenching fear.

He had not imagined this kind of organized retaliation to the Maclean's death. He didn't know how they could even know of it yet. He had made it look like an accident. No court of law could prove anything else, particularly not back here, where they were accustomed to making their own laws.

Drummond blanched at that thought. The fools didn't intend to go through proper courts to exact their retribution. For centuries, the lairds had been judge and jury. But he had killed the laird, hadn't he? All of them. The old man and his favored son and now the younger. *He* was the laird now. His mother had been a Maclean. The old woman had thrown her out when she married an Englishman, and not even a noble one, but there was precedence for the title to pass through the female line. He was laird now. They couldn't march against his orders.

The large public chambers on the first floor with their wide windows would provide no protection at all. The moans from above reminded him of his best source of safety. Grabbing rifle and rapier from the game room, Drummond ran for the gracious curve of stairs to the upper chambers.

He had dueling pistols and his dress sword in his bedroom, but that was at the back of the house. He had dumped Maclean's wife in the first guest room at the top of the stairs. The windows there would provide better observation than his own. There wasn't time to go farther, in any case.

Alyson heard the door slam. Coming out of the haze of pain, she could see her captor forcing a small sofa in front of the door. That seemed an extraordinarily odd thing for a man to do, but when he looked up, she could see the wild-eyed fear in his eyes, and she ceased to think in terms of logic and reason.

She struggled back against the pillows as Drummond strode toward the draperies at the far end of the room. She had never met Rory's cousin, but she had no doubt as to his identity. His hair was fair and not Rory's rich auburn. He was of much the same height as Rory, but he was slender where Rory was sturdy. She already knew he was not a weak man, but in this faint light she could tell that Rory's broad-shouldered strength would be the greater. Despite these differences, she could still find the resemblance in the squareness of his face and the hollowed planes of his cheeks.

She had been thinking of Rory as alive, fighting back the logic that said he could not have survived both gunshot and fall over the cliff. She couldn't accept that thought yet. She felt Rory as surely as she felt this man's fear. Something was terribly wrong out there, but she could do nothing to prevent it. She groaned as the pain came again.

Drummond scarcely gave her pale face a second look. The bloody barbarians were surrounding the house. Did they mean to burn it down around him? There would be no escaping, if so. Surely they must know the woman was here? They wouldn't burn her too.

Alyson dug her fingers into the folds of her gown as she tried to stifle the cries building in her throat. Moisture broke out on her forehead as the pain rolled up and through her and never seemed to end. Rory's son had obviously decided he wished to join the battle. She was almost relieved at the thought. A son like Rory would be a mother's joy. She smiled as the pain eased.

In the flicker of the room's one candle, Drummond caught that smile and felt his stomach lurch uneasily. What could she have to smile about? Did she know something he didn't?

"Are you expecting visitors, sir?" Alyson inquired, indicating with a nod his anxious placement by the window.

Demented, obviously demented. Cranville had said she was a trifle odd, but that was scarcely the word for it. Instead of railing and screaming at him, calling for midwives or maids, she was talking to him as if they were downstairs in the drawing room. He turned back to watch the activity below, seeking the leaders.

They weren't hard to find. Three men on horses had taken strategic positions near the entrances to the house. He could see their coats blowing in the wind and could tell by their bearing that they weren't common laborers. One of the fools even wore a tartan. He would have them all hanged for treason. Even as he watched, they gestured in unison, sending their mob storming toward the house.

It was now or never. Drummond threw open the casement just as the sweat broke out on Alyson's brow again.
Her stifled moans weren't enough to catch anyone's attention. He crossed the room and grabbed her shoulder,
dragging her upward. Alyson fought against this position
as the pain ripped through her insides, but his grip was
relentless, forcing her to her feet. She screamed as he
shoved her toward the window, and Drummond grinned
against the darkness.

She collapsed against him, breathing heavily, and he
half-carried, half-dragged her to the window. He hated to
waste his ammunition firing a warning shot. He waited
until his prisoner could stand again; then, grabbing her
hair, he shoved her halfway through the open window.

Alyson gazed in astonishment at the sight below. Far
from being terrified, she was exultant. The wrongs of all
these years would be avenged, and just that thought sent
her spirits soaring. Without sense or logic, she scanned
the milling crowd, finding what she sought almost at
once. Whether this was vision or reality, she was content.
Rory was with her. His pale shirt provided a ghostly
backdrop for the belted plaid, and his face was white
against the snow as he stared up at her. Perhaps he had
died after all, and this was his specter returned to haunt
his enemy, but Alyson cared only that he was with her to
see his son born.

"If you ever want to see her alive again, you will all go
home and to your beds," Drummond shouted against her
ear, reminding her of her predicament.

Alyson felt the pain building inside her again as the
mob hesitated uncertainly, pointing to where Drummond's
voice came from. Bent partially out of the window like
this, she felt as if the babe must fall from her at any
minute, pushed by her awkward position, and she fought
back the urge to scream in pain. She didn't want Rory to
do anything foolish.

She sought his shadow again. The blizzard had les-
sened to a heavy, wet snow, and he held himself stiffly as
he fought to see through the haze. He was hurt, then, not
dead. She refused to feel fear. He was alive.

When she wouldn't scream to his satisfaction, Drummond twisted her hair in his grip, forcing her to face him
as he drew his rapier and held it across her throat.

Alyson knew nothing of the difference between rapiers and swords, but she felt no pain but the one in her abdomen. Calmly she spat in his face.

Below, Rory watched this tableau with a rage and anguish he had no intention of controlling much longer. His men had secured the house against any escape. He had only to get at Alyson before her wayward behavior enraged Drummond to the breaking point. If his cousin had expected a docile and weeping prisoner, he had chosen the wrong woman. Alyson would simply aggravate him until he pushed her out of the window.

With that as his only alternative, Rory drew his sword to catch his cousin's eye. Here was the enemy who had destroyed his family. He had wanted to come face-to-face with him for years. But little of that had any place in his mind now. Blind fury whipped through him at the sight of Alyson's fragile body in Drummond's cruel hands. The wind had halted, and his voice could be heard plainly. "Come down and we will fight this man-to-man, Drummond. If you win, you walk away. That is the only choice I give you."

Above, the fair-haired man laughed. "I'll not duel with phantoms. You're dead, Maclean. The house and this woman are mine, and there is nothing you can do about it. Go away, and I let her live. Stay, and she will die."

Boldly Alyson grasped the window ledge with her fingers and called out in her usual melodic tones, "I do believe he's wet his breeches, Rory. When you come up, bring Myra with you, would you, love?"

He couldn't help it. Tears of rage and laughter poured down Rory's cheeks as he reared his horse and rode straight for the garden door below. No one would keep him from Alyson. It was madness—he could read it on the faces of her father and cousin as he rushed by—but he was going to her now. For once, logic failed him and passion ruled.

Someone had already broken in the wide French doors, and they shoved them open as he raced forward. Exultantly Rory galloped his sturdy horse across and through the open doors, the rebel cry of *"Tha tighinn fodher eiridh!"* escaping his lips with triumph as he came home again. The cry was repeated in wild yells behind him as the mob surged forward to reclaim what had been lost, but Rory was heedless of what was behind him. Only what lay ahead mattered.

As the mob rushed the house behind the reckless horse-man, Drummond drew back quickly from the window, slamming it shut. Already he could see men running from the stables with ladders. Fools! Couldn't they see he held a hostage here?

Shoving his worthless prisoner back toward the bed, he sought other escape. Fire! That would delay them awhile. Even if Rory cared little about his bastard wife, he would never stand and watch his precious home burn.

Drummond felt the pain in his side as the wound reopened when he reached to pull down the bed curtains. Blood began to seep through the bandages, but he ignored this minor weakness as his mind ruthlessly worked on another plan. He had not come this far to be defeated by a phantom. He had the heiress; he didn't need this house any longer. He had grown bored with the isolation, and the rents weren't sufficient to keep him in style in London any longer. No, the heiress was a much better solution. He would get out with her and leave the rest to burn themselves to cinders.

Alyson struggled to regain her feet as Drummond opened the bedroom door. His chuckles raised the hair on the back of her neck, and her fear grew proportionately as he piled the heavy curtains in the hallway and found an unlit lamp. She wanted her son to live. She had to get out of here alive.

Drummond momentarily ignored her as he emptied the oil from the lamp on the pyre, but she didn't have time to regain her feet before he returned for the candle. In horror she watched as he flung the flame to the explosive oil.

Magnificent! He could hear Rory's heavy boots running up the stairs, but the flames were spreading too quickly for him to get through. Drummond turned back to drag his prisoner from the bed. Her hair had begun to tumble in thick black ringlets about her shoulders, and her face appeared paler than humanly possible, but he had no time to consider her well-being. Even as she began to groan and bend with cramps of pain, he jerked her upright and pulled her toward the dressing-room door. They would go out the servants' stairs.

Thick black smoke had already begun to choke the

corridor as they headed for the back way. Alyson was a deadweight in his arms, scarcely able to stay on her feet, but he needed her. Keeping his arm around her, he dragged her choking and coughing toward the haven of escape.

It wasn't until Drummond realized the back stairs were filled with pitchforks and hatchets that he dimly began to realize his luck had failed him. Turning slowly, he found Rory waiting for him at the end of the hall, claymore in hand, the fire blazing impossibly high behind him and glinting off his soaked hair until he appeared as one of the demons in hell.

Drummond dropped Alyson where they stood. Momentarily encouraged by Rory's distraction at his wife's groan of pain, he grabbed his rapier and leapt forward in a move that would have made his fencing master proud.

The wound in Rory's shoulder made it nearly impossible to wield the heavy sword, but he took little consideration of such inconveniences with the sight of Alyson groaning in pain filling his mind. He could have lobbed the heads off a herd of stampeding cattle in this state. Drummond's meager weapon presented no obstacle.

The rapier went spinning with one swing of the sword. Brandy eyes simmered with murder as Rory advanced toward the coward who had deprived him of family and home and threatened the same again. One more swing of the sword and Drummond would breathe his last.

Finally faced with the living, breathing result of his actions, Drummond turned and fled—straight toward the arms of the tenants he had cheated these last fifteen years.

With the fire still burning behind him and the screams of the mob as they chased their prey in front of him, Rory dropped his sword and bent in terrified despair to Alyson's fallen figure. She moaned softly in his arms as he lifted her, and he cursed at the way her hands had been bound in front of her. He fought the anguish and panic rising in him at the sight of her pale, strained face, and remembering her call for Myra, he knew dire uncertainty. He had to get her out of here. Or he had to get help in.

Alex's tall black-haired figure shoved its way through the triumphant crowd cornering Drummond in the linen cupboard. He listened to the Englishman's cries for mercy with disdain, then gazed past the crowd to the distraught Maclean holding his unconscious wife in his arms. Past the Maclean, he could see men rushing to douse the fire under the earl's command. There was something to be said about carpetless floors, he supposed, as the earl's orders carried the burning draperies away. Hampton's shoulders sagged briefly as he realized he had just admitted the old man's title to himself. He had not even that left now.

But at least he wasn't the man in the cupboard. With a sardonic grin, he gestured for Rory to follow him.

Between them, they made a path through the excited crowd. Silence followed them as the mob turned into individuals once again, people who had worked for and respected and claimed kinship to the Macleans for decades. They watched the laird's expressionless face as he carried his pregnant wife toward the chamber that should have been his, and their blood lust died. Somewhere, a woman began to keen.

The sound grated on Rory's nerves. Knowing Alex had no control over these people, he sought the crowd for a face he could trust. Finding Dougall, he allowed himself a small, a very small measure of hope as he spoke. "Send everybody home and go fetch Myra. I don't think my son intends to wait any longer."

The confidence of his voice brought a cheer from those around him. Alex lifted a cynical eyebrow at this lordly assumption that the child would be a son, but he played the part of bodyguard without question. He held the door open so Rory could pass through, then shut out the crowd of eager well-wishers.

Alyson stirred as Rory laid her upon the wide bed, and her eyes flickered briefly before her gaze came to rest on Rory's square jaw. A smile slowly reached her lips as he removed the cloth binding her wrists, and her hand reached out to touch him.

"Real, and not a vision?" she asked softly.

"A moon dream, remember? I am not really here. We're out on the *Witch*, sailing beneath a Caribbean sun. The island's just ahead. Shall we throw out the anchor?"

Her laughter filled the room with music that lasted long after she began to twitch and moan with pain. Rory threw a look of frustration over his shoulder to the be-mused man at the door. "Devil take it, Hampton, do something. Find hot water and linens and someone who knows what the hell to do with them."

Alyson clutched his hand as the pain rolled past, then gasped, "Your son will be fine. Just stay with me. Tell me how you escaped that cliff."

"A fortune-teller told me it was coming, and I was prepared. I've ridden my horse over it dozens of times. Snow makes it a little tricky, but he's a good horse. I think I'll have his shoes bronzed. And worship the fortune-teller forevermore. Can you foretell when my son will arrive?"

Alyson gripped Rory's hand in understanding, but, unable to restrain his confusion anymore, Alex strode to the fire grate and began groping in the dark for kindling and flints. "You're both Bedlamites, I see that now. How can you be so damned certain it is a son? That's all I've heard talk about. What if the poor thing is a girl? Do you give her away and start another one?"

Rory forced a grin to his lips as he watched Alyson's face go taut with pain. "I'd like nowt better than a wee lass to lighten my days, but my wife says it is to be a braw boy, and I'll not argue the matter."

As the fire finally kindled, Alyson's eyes flew open again, and she saw her cousin silhouetted against the flames. He looked like the devil that Drummond was supposed to be, but her fear of him had gone.

"Alex, you must go now. Find my father and tell him I am fine. Perhaps there is someone below who could help Rory. I don't think the babe will wait for Myra."

Her fingers tore at Rory's hands as the pain came much faster now, pressing at her middle until she could think of little else. She knew her petticoats and skirts were soaked already, but she could not mention that in front of her formidable cousin.

Rory's look was bleak as this last ally began to desert him. "You'd better see to securing Drummond. I'll not have his death upon my hands if it can be avoided."

Glancing from husband to wife, both bravely facing the unknown in this icy habitat, Hampton growled, "I don't mind having it on mine." Leaving them with that grisly thought, he stalked out.

"Your cousin is a rash man. I'd better stop him before he does something foolish." Rory made no immediate move to rise from the bed.

Alyson plucked at a charred hole in his tartan. She wondered what he had sacrificed to the fire to extinguish it. "You'll never have a decent wardrobe, Maclean," she murmured before the pain came back to take her speech away.

He held her against the pain, breathing with her as if they had become one in this moment of trial. He ached to take the pain away, but he was helpless in this.

A woman finally bustled in carrying a pitcher of water and fresh linens. Under her direction, Alyson was stripped of soiled gown and petticoats, washed gently and garbed in a clean nightshirt from the wardrobe, and placed between clean sheets. The tasks were done slowly to accommodate the pains as best as possible, and Rory felt as if he had done royal battle by the time they were done.

"Thank you." Alyson's smile lifted from the pillow to caress Rory's anxious face. "Send for more warm water and good strong soap. You will feel better when you are clean, and the babe will need to be washed."

"I'm supposed to be the one in charge here," Rory remonstrated, only to turn and order the maid to do as she instructed.

"No, God is. Hold my hand, Rory. I don't think I can wait much longer."

"Scream then, lass. Let it go. Let them know our son is coming into the world fighting."

As her cries tore through the air, Rory wished to scream with her, but she needed his strength and not his fears. When the maid returned, he hastily rolled up his shirtsleeves to wash, continuing to murmur senseless phrases so she would know he was still here.

"Good lass, very good. Your grandmother would be proud of you. That's a good Scots cry. Try it harder. Teach our son how to make himself heard."

Lines etched his brow and creased the sides of his face as he sat down beside her again. He wet a cloth and smoothed her brow with it. "I'm proud of you, lass. I don't know what I would do without you. You're all I want, Alys, you and the child. We can sail foreign seas or go find that London house of yours or stay in Cornwall, whatever you wish when this is over."

The bedroom door flew open and Myra rushed in, bringing the cold scents of outdoors as she flung off her cloak and gloves and nodded approvingly at the hot water waiting. The couple on the bed never acknowledged her presence.

Alyson panted breathlessly and Rory's voice continued to soothe her as the pain began to build again. "Push, Alyson. Let him come. Let me see him. A bairn born with so much love should be big and strong, shouldn't he? Remember the night on the island when our blood flowed together so strongly? Do you think he was conceived on that night, lass? Ach, but I loved you so that I thought my heart would break of it. Lass, let me love you again. Hold on and push, *push*, Alys! Now, love, now!"

As the pain subsided once again, Myra whispered, "Almost. He's almost here." She adjusted the sheets more comfortably over her patient while Rory continued sitting at Alyson's side, pleading with her in soothing tones, although she seemed beyond knowing what he was saying.

"Ach, my bonny jo, 'tis bad I've been for you, but never again, my lovely lass. All the home I need is you. I'd see grass beneath your feet and flowers in your hair and our bairn running at your side. I'll make ye love me as I've loved ye since that first day I set eyes on you, all heather and mist wrapped in a stableman's coat. Alyson, for the love of God, now!"

He screamed this last as he held her, while the terrible pain made her weep and cry and cling to him with fear. It went on and on, longer than any before, and Rory felt his life draining away before his eyes, until the violent shudders finally stopped and a thin cry rippled through the air.

"It's a boy, my lord." Myra held the kicking infant in the air while the maid rushed up with warm linens.

Rory could feel the grin pushing foolishly across his face as he gazed upon the perfectly formed infant with a thick thatch of black hair, then back to his wife's lovely black tresses. He brushed the curls back from her forehead, and Alyson's eyes flickered open for just a moment.

"I've always loved you, Maclean. Whatever made you think elsewise?"

Rory's whoop of sheer joy could be heard throughout the house as the last of the burned debris was carried away, servants hurried to light fires in the grates, and the men gathered in the rooms below to discuss their prisoner's fate. The sound lifted heads and brought tears to the eyes of all who listened.

"Alyson's fine and it's a boy!" Rory yelled over the banister as he recognized the expectant faces waiting below. A cheer raced around the room, and from somewhere the defiant sound of a bagpipe began to wail.

Rory looked vaguely startled; then in his excitement, he raced down the stairs to accept the tumbler of whisky Alex held out to him. He drained it at an exceedingly immoral rate, then gestured for a refill for everyone. The crowd cheered again, and the illegal bagpipe grew bolder, filling the long stale air of Stagshead with the wild, haunting strains of the mountains.

Without a word, Dougall grabbed two swords held out by men in the crowd and threw them down on the marble floors. The house had never been properly christened. Never would there be a better time.

Rory glanced to the crossed swords, up to the piper, and around at the expectant faces of friends and family with a growing grin of reckless exhilaration. With the whisky and his joy winging through him, he set his hands on his hips, and in shirtsleeves and breeches, with his tartan flying around him, he flung himself into the wild dance of celebration that his ancestors had known for centuries.

Laughter and yells of triumph combined with streaming tears of happiness on the faces of the crowd as the laird proclaimed his proud possession in this dance of victory. Perhaps the days of Highland warriors were over, but never their courage. The pipes wailed louder, and voices began to lift in old familiar songs.

Rory surrendered the floor to others, throwing an eager glance overhead to where his wife and child rested. He needed to be back with them, but he recognized the needs of others. Panting from his exertion, he gladly clasped his father-in-law's back and shook his hand as the older man came up to congratulate him.

"I never thought I'd see the day when I'd be happy to

have my daughter married to a barbarian, but that day has just come. She needs you, son. Take care of her."

Rory couldn't wipe the grin from his face. He had spent half his life on the grim edge of circumstances, painstakingly plodding his way toward his goals. Of a sudden, none of that mattered. He knew Stagshead still didn't belong to him, might never belong to him. He knew trouble lay ahead when it came to dealing with his cousin. He knew he had broken enough laws to land him in jail the rest of his life. And there was still the small matter of all that money that rightfully belonged to these two men beside him. But none of that mattered any longer. He had told Alyson the truth, a truth he had long denied and felt better to have said. All he really needed was her. Everything else would follow. It seemed so easy, now that he recognized it. His grin broadened as he watched Hampton's skeptical face at the earl's announcement of his approval.

"Aye, we both need keepers, and have chosen well," Rory chuckled, taking another glass that someone offered. He lifted it in toast to Alyson's cousin. "But then, I think there's a wee dram of madness in Hampton blood too. What have you done with my cousin, Alex?"

Hampton shrugged his broad shoulders and continued to look bored as he lifted his glass to his lips. "He's keeping cool. You needn't concern yourself yet. There's another bottle of this gullet lye somewhere around. Care to join me?"

The earl lifted a disapproving brow at his heir's ill manners, but Rory only laughed. "I will, and we will see who is the true Highlander here. But first, I want to see how Alyson fares."

Bowing briefly, he sprinted back up the stairs, carried by wings of happiness, unaware of the aches and pains of his injured shoulder. He had everything now, and everything waited for him at the top of the stairs.

Myra let him in the room, handing him the sleeping infant. With a few whispered words of caution, she slipped out. Rory awkwardly held the tiny bundle in his arms, smoothing a petal-soft cheek and touching infinitely tiny, perfect fingers. Wanting to share this joy, he sat down upon the bed and stared lovingly at the beautiful woman lying upon the pillows.

At first, he thought she slept, and an odd loneliness tugged at his heart. Perhaps he had just dreamed her words. He wanted them so much to be true that he could have just imagined them in the happiness of the moment. It didn't seem possible that a lovely, gentle woman like Alyson could love a cold, hard ruffian like himself, not after what he had done to her. But he would make it up over time, she would see. Then, maybe, he could hope one day to hear those words in truth. He had never realized how much he needed to hear those words, to hear that reassurance again. For too long he had been without home and family, and at heart he had always been a family man. He hugged his son close and smoothed a straying lock from Alyson's brow, his heart filling with the love he had so long denied.

Black lashes lifted, revealing the misty gray of her glorious eyes, and Alyson's lips lifted in a smile as she found father and son at her bedside. "Rory, I thought you were but a moon dream sitting there."

"And so I am, dear heart." He bent to kiss her cheek and hold the infant where she could see. "See what comes of moon dreams? Dangerous, they are."

"Oh, no, lovely, lovelier than any other dream. Let me hold him, Rory." Alyson took the bundle in her arms and lifted the blanket to explore the small creature they had brought into this world. Sighing with pleasure, she smiled up to her weary husband. "He's going to be just like you. I'll have two of you to love."

As her words spoke her meaning clear, Rory felt them burn straight to his heart and knew he would never be entirely parted from her again. He didn't own her, but they were a part of each other, as it should be. He slid his arm around her shoulders and bent to whisper kisses along her cheek. "Aye, and I'll love ye until there's a whole lot more than that, lass, but there's a lifetime for a' that. For the noo, I'll show you how much I love ye. Sleep, and have sweet moon dreams, my bonny jo. I'll be here when ye wake."

Smiling sleepily at the lilting burr of his voice, Alyson closed her eyes and dreamed of a gallant warrior with copper hair and a babe in his arms.

Epilogue

Stagshead, June 1761

Laughing at the cooing sounds and dancing hands of the infant in the cradle, Alyson abruptly lifted her head and tilted it as if hearing something beyond the room. Myra looked up too, and listened, but there was nothing to be heard beyond these walls. So it was with surprise that she watched a lovely, soft smile cross the lady's face as her eyes took on a faraway expression. Without a word, Alyson stood and drifted from the nursery.

Not taking time to arrange her hair or change her gown, she floated down the graceful staircase, past the startled housekeeper, and toward the carved front doors. A footman hurried to fetch a light cloak and place it around her shoulders or she would have stepped out into the breezy sunlight without one. Both servants exchanged glances over her head, smiled, and ran off to inform the others.

A copse of trees planted twenty years before lined the drive and filled the narrow valley at the bottom of the hill. The few carefully planted rhododendrons had spread wantonly along the forest's edge, and new shoots of heather and foxglove sprang up beneath their protective cover. In a few weeks the hills would be a burst of color, but the thick rich greens after the winter's white were sufficient for Alyson. She pulled up her hood and waded into the shadows of the trees.

She could hear the horse coming now, and she smiled at its wild pace. The poor beast would be exhausted if its rider had ridden that way all day. She waited in the dappled pattern of sunlight along the side of the road.

Horse and rider came flying around the bend, the

capes of the rider's redingote flapping in the breeze, his cocked hat balanced precariously over gleams of dark red, polished knee boots clinging tightly to the horse's side now that Stagshead was nearly in sight. At the sight of the nymph waiting in the forest, the horse shied, and the rider swiftly pulled up on the reins, dancing his mount to a halt.

Within moments Rory was off the horse and lifting the laughing nymph in the air. Her eyes were like bluebells this morning, and he filled his arms with the lovely fragrance of heather and the soft curves of a willing woman. His long-denied body responded frantically to this sensual barrage, and he bent to bury her face in kisses.

"Ach, lass, if ye knew how much I needed this, ye'd run and hide," he murmured as his lips found the moist corners of her eyes and traveled down flushed cheeks to at long last settle on her quivering lips.

Alyson drank heavily of the glorious wine of his kisses, breathing in the masculine scents she had missed so much as her arms circled his waist and clung to the muscular line of his back. Her hands curved up to his shoulders as Rory pulled her closer, and their lips parted and melted and intertwined in loving embrace.

Silently cursing the nuisance of cloaks and coats and gloves, Rory reluctantly lifted his head to smile down into Alyson's welcoming face. "Ye know how to make a man feel wanted, lass, but I fear I'll not make it back to the house if we dally here longer."

Alyson laughed and lifted her fingers to the fastening of his coat. "They will all be waiting for you, and I'll not see you again until midnight. It's been months, Rory. Would you make me wait any longer?"

With a wild grin, Rory threw off his gloves and braided his fingers into her hair, leading her off the path into the quiet protection of the trees. "I'll not wait a moment longer than I have to. How quickly does that gown come off?"

Coat and cloak were flung upon the ground, and as the horse idly sampled tufts of grass, Rory laid his wife upon their makeshift bed and joined her.

After the months he had spent in London, they were almost shy with each other, but that lasted only long enough for their lips to meet again. Closing his eyes to better inhale this heady potion, Rory allowed his hand to roam freely, drawing gasps from Alyson as he quickly found the concealed hooks at the front of her bodice and released them, sliding his fingers into the warmth beneath.

"I like this gown. You need a dozen more like it," he murmured as his fingers pushed aside the ribbons and lace of her chemise to explore the firm curves of flesh he needed to touch.

Alyson cried out her eagerness at the play of his fingers upon the aching peaks rising to his touch. When he bent to touch his tongue there, she was lost. Her hands laced through his hair and she rose against him, urging him on, and Rory had no need to be begged. Within minutes their clothes were in disarray, but they were together again.

As she took him inside her, sliding her hands beneath his shirt to mold her fingers against the rippling muscles of his back, he groaned with delight. Their bodies melded together as if it had been yesterday that they had done this last. With exquisite patience Rory brought her to the heights he had reached so easily, moving slowly, then quickly as Alyson caught up with him. Her eyes flew open at the sudden wild leap of their bodies. Overhead, in a break between the towering trees, she found the moon floating in the sun's light and she cried out her ecstasy as Rory's life flowed into hers. Her eyes closed again in joy as her body responded with the electricity she remembered so well. Joyfully she felt his heavy weight pressed into her, and she held him close.

"Lass, we're an old married couple now. We're not supposed to behave like this," Rory chuckled some while later as he gently shifted his weight to one side and pulled her with him. He wasn't ready yet to lose her warmth, and his eyes sparkled darkly as he observed the way her breasts spilled from the open bodice and chemise. They were fuller than he remembered, and he lifted his hand to press the puckered crests against his palm. The erotic sensation brought a tightening in his loins.

"We can be an old married couple when we go back to the house. For now, we will be lovers on an afternoon tryst. We cannot linger long. My husband is expected any moment."

Rory laughed, and Alyson's heart swelled at the sight. He looked so much younger than when first they met. She had worried every day that he was away, but whatever had been decided in London hadn't taken away his hard-won pleasure in life. It had only been returned to him a few short months ago. She had feared the grim privateer might return out of habit if things went wrong, but he was still as he ought to be. She touched the wondering fingers to his sensual lower lip, scarcely believing that it was love she saw warming his gaze.

"I doubt that your husband would be an understanding man. We'd better dress hastily." He made no move to do so, but continued to regard her fair skin and dancing eyes while their legs remained entangled in the lengths of her skirts.

"There is time. Tell me what happened in London. I have not had a letter in weeks. Don't make me wait until you tell the others at dinner."

"And where would you like me to begin? With all the wicked ladies waiting for me behind every door I entered?"

"I'll slay them with a wave of my hand. Tell me of Stagshead, Rory. That's what you truly wanted. Did you get it? Did Lord Bute help you as you hoped?"

He grew serious and pressed a kiss to the worried frown between her eyes. "I told you that it no longer matters. But at your insistence, I am now a pauper. Lord Bute was very helpful, your father was quite persuasive, and His Majesty was naturally receptive to the idea of filling his coffers a second time for the same land. It is ours now, lass, for better or worse."

The frown didn't go away completely. She studied Rory's square face, lined with the weariness of playing the part of courtier, now that the first few minutes of laughter had passed. These had not been easy months for him. She had known they would not be when it was decided he must go, but they had been necessary. He needed to know where he stood, and she had been in no condition to help him. Now she was healed and he was home and they could go on with whatever awaited them.

"And your cousin, then? Does this mean the king took the land away from Drummond? What will happen to him?"

Rory grimaced and lay back against the rough capes of

his coat, pulling Alyson with him. "Your cousin Alex is more ruthless than I'll ever be, lass. He took care of that matter for me. He found a physician who certified George as insane and found an institution which agreed to keep him locked away in comfort for the rest of his life. Don't look so alarmed, Alys." He touched a gentle hand to her cheek. "It is no Bedlam. It is a private home with skilled workers. He is quite mad, lass. It became more obvious as we traveled. He still thinks he killed me. I never said the Macleans were perfect. His mother had the same madness. It happens from time to time. There's naught we can do about it."

His halting phrases didn't reassure. Alyson could tell he still fought with himself over the outcome of that tragic night. He would have dealt better with it had Drummond died at his hand in an equal fight, but these things couldn't be changed. He was right in that. She moved her hips suggestively along his, bringing him back to the pleasures of the present.

"Shall our son be a penniless laird, then, my lord? Have you managed to give away all that troublesome money?"

Rory grinned at the mischievous expression in her eyes. He knew her father wouldn't have let her go these months without a letter or two. She had more than an inkling of where matters stood in that quarter.

"Not quite all. You have been handsomely dowered. There is a nice trust set aside for our children when they come of age. And the rest, your father and Alex intend to help me oversee. Alex has taken a fancy to the shipping line, so I need not travel to Plymouth and London to keep an eye on that. Your father is quite content to open the town house and travel occasionally to oversee the other investments, and I am to sit here and make my wife happy while deciding what to buy and sell. We shall all be paid handsomely for our services, never fear."

"Praise the Lord," Alyson agreed fervently. "Now all we need do is find a nice Scots wife for Alex and hope my father doesn't take a fancy to a younger woman. It would be dreadful if Alex were bypassed again for that silly title."

Rory laughed and kissed her and loved her all the more for this concern she showed a man who had caused her naught but anguish for nearly a year. He could feel the softness of her thighs rubbing against his, and he decided he could wait a few minutes longer to see his son. Turning Alyson on her back, he leaned over her, drinking in the beauty of her laughing features as she rose hungrily against him.

"For your information, dear heart, your father is currently dangling after my aunt. She tells me she always wanted to be a countess, and that you would make a much more satisfactory daughter than I have a nephew. Is there anything else you would like to know before I ravish you thoroughly?"

Alyson lifted her arms to bring Rory's head down to hers, and pressing her kiss against his lips, she murmured, "When do we begin?"

About the Author

PATRICIA RICE was born in Newburgh, New York, and attended the University of Kentucky. She now lives in Mayfield, Kentucky, with her husband and her two children, Corinna and Derek, in a rambling Tudor house. Ms. Rice has a degree in accounting and her hobbies include history, travel and antique collecting.

There's an epidemic with 27 million victims. And no visible symptoms.

It's an epidemic of people who can't read.

Believe it or not, 27 million Americans are functionally illiterate, about one adult in five.

The solution to this problem is you... when you join the fight against illiteracy. So call the Coalition for Literacy at toll-free **1-800-228-8813** and volunteer.

Volunteer Against Illiteracy. The only degree you need is a degree of caring.